More Than Friends

More Than Friends

Barbara Delinsky

PIATKUS

430272

Copyright © 1992 by Barbara Delinsky

This edition first published in
Great Britain in 1993 by
Judy Piatkus (Publishers) Ltd of
5 Windmill Street, London W1

**The moral right of the author
as been asserted**

*A catalogue record for this book is available
from the British Library*

ISBN 0-7499-0181-0

Printed and bound in Great Britain by
Bookcraft Ltd , Avon

For inspiration, encouragement, patience, and love forever thanks to the men in my life.

prologue

Michael Maxwell raised the camcorder to his eye and, bracing his body against the porch railing, let the tape roll. He panned the oceanscape appreciatively, then eased his lens up the rocky beach path to the house.

Pushing his thirteen-year-old voice an octave lower than normal, he began, "Labor Day 1992. Sutters Island, Maine. With me on the front porch of the Popewell summer place are the Popes and Maxwells themselves, gathered on this momentous afternoon for their tenth annual end-of-the-season cookout."

"Tenth," came an astonished echo from the porch swing behind him. "Can you believe it?"

"Hard to," came another voice, a male one this time, and then a second, preceded by a grunt.

"I can believe it. I just saw estimates for a new roof, a new water heater, and a new septic tank. The place is falling apart."

"But we love it," Annie Pope declared. "Right, Teke?"

"Right," Teke said with a wink for Michael as his camera's eye joined the group.

Focusing on the large wooden swing, Michael

resumed his deep-voiced narrative. "Here are the Popewell parents. Left to right, there's J. D. Maxwell, with an arm stretched behind his best friend, Sam Pope. Sam's wife, Annie, is on Sam's lap with her arms around her knees and her bare feet tucked against her best friend, Teke. They are wearing an assortment of T-shirts and shorts, and look preppie, in an older kind of way."

"Hey," Teke protested.

"We are older," J.D. stated. When Sam shot him a look, he added, "I don't see you jumping up to dry-dock the Whaler."

"Jon said he'd do it."

"Because you're beat."

"That was a cord of wood we chopped this morning!"

"Ten years ago we'd have chopped the wood and kept on going."

"Ten years ago we didn't have five teenagers to help do the rest."

Teke sighed. "Ten years ago we were thirty. Face it, Sam, we're aging."

"Not me," Sam said. With the twitch of his mustache, he wrapped his arms around Annie. "I'm just entering the prime of my life. Right, sunshine?" He opened his mouth on the lobe of her ear and sucked it in.

"*Sweet* move, Sam," Michael remarked. He wondered what Kari Stevens would do if he tried that. Probably call him a pervert. But what did Kari Stevens know about tongues?

"He sees everything," J.D. warned Sam. "If he turns into a Geraldo with women, I'm blaming you."

"*Geraldo,*" came an amused cry from the corner of the porch. Michael swung the camcorder that way and caught his sister Jana laughing. "*He*'ll never be another Geraldo."

"Why not?" Michael asked, vaguely hurt. True, he was more a cinematographer than an investigative reporter, but he had every intention of making it big.

Zoe Pope, who was huddled in the corner with Jana, said, "Because you're too nice."

"Oh, I can be mean." Zooming in for a tight shot, he crept toward the girls. "I can tell the world that Jana Maxwell skipped out on three driver's ed classes after she signed in."

"Michael!"

"Did you do that, Jana?" Teke called over.

But Michael had more and better. "I can tell Josh Vacarro that the reason the phone line is busy all night isn't because Jana's talking with Zoe, but because she's talking with Danny Stocklan and Doug Smith."

"You wouldn't," Jana warned.

"Of course he wouldn't," Zoe assured her. She was a calming force for Jana, as Annie was for Teke. She looked like her mother, too, had Annie's delicate look and the same short, blond, wavy hair, while Jana was dark-haired and as exotic-looking as Teke.

Sam snapped his fingers. "Get over here, Michael." Michael drew in the zoom and swung smoothly to the parents. "Snitching on sisters is right up there with swearing at the ump. Real men don't do it. Got that?"

"Got it," Michael said because Sam was too good a friend to argue with. It wasn't every kid who had a Sam in his life. He was like a father without the edge. Besides, he was an awesome athlete. Michael wouldn't be half the basketball player he was without Sam as his coach.

But basketball was for fall and the mainland, not for Labor Day on Sutters Island. "When are we play-

3

ing volleyball?" he asked Sam from behind the camcorder.

"When I recoup some energy."

J.D. checked his watch. "By the time you do that, it'll be time to leave. I arranged for the barge to pick us up at five. Before that, we have to cook and clean—"

"The chicken!" Annie gasped. "I forgot! It's marinating—if I don't precook it—" She started to get up, only to be stopped both by Sam, who tightened his hold of her, and by Teke, who put a hand on her arm and rose from the swing.

"I'll take care of it. You stay with Sam."

"Sam, let me go. I swore to myself I'd help. Teke has spent the better part of the week cooking, and that's not fair. It's her vacation, too."

But Sam's arms weren't opening, and Teke wore a confident smile. "This is what I do best," she said. The screen door squeaked open and slapped shut.

Michael held the shot of the doorway until Teke disappeared from view. He liked filming his mother. She was unusual; her T-shirt and shorts were neon green, her hair was caught at the top of her head with a purple ribbon that matched the funky zigzags dangling from her ears. Of all his friends' mothers, she was the best, and it wasn't just that she was around. Or that she was a great cook. She was also fun.

He went baritone again. "And there you have it, Theodora Maxwell taking charge. Feeding the hungry, nursing the sick, rushing to the ends of the earth for poster board, zit cream, and black spandex shorts. Tell me, Annie," he asked because it was a question Annie always tossed out herself, "what would we have done without her all these years?"

Annie gave the videocam a guileless smile. "I would never have become a tenured professor, and you would never have been born."

Sam looked at J.D. "How's that for a tribute to your wife?"

"Not bad," J.D. said, rising from the swing. He went to the porch railing and looked down the gentle slope toward the dock. "Hey, you guys! You have to help us close up!"

Joining him, Michael trained the camcorder on Jonathan and Leigh, who were at the far end of the dock. Leigh was stretched out on the weathered planks in a bikini, catching the last of the rays. Jon was tight by her hip, with his back to the house. Zooming in, Michael captured the movement of a hand.

In his deep-voiced drawl he said, "This is quite a day for the Pope men, what with Sam's tongue in Annie's ear and Jon's hand in Leigh's bra. It's a good thing there aren't any kids around. They'd be shocked."

"Good *God*, Jon," J.D. hollered toward the dock, "that's *my daughter* you're touching! Use some discretion!"

Jana's laugh came from the corner. "They're *using* discretion."

J.D. shot a look at Sam. "What's your son doing out there?"

Sam had stretched out with Annie on the swing. "Relax, J.D. They're okay."

"Have you talked with him lately?"

"He's not doing anything you weren't doing at his age."

"I did nothing at his age."

Michael stopped filming. "Nothing? At seventeen?"

"I kissed girls," J.D. informed him.

"That's it?"

"That's it."

"Oh."

"What does 'oh' mean?"

It meant that Michael couldn't imagine spending the next four years just kissing. Not that he planned on losing his virginity immediately. But he was beginning to wonder what it would be like to touch a girl, and not on the hand.

"What does 'oh' mean?" J.D. repeated.

"Nothing." Michael raised the camcorder to his eye, pressed the record button, and told the tape, "Jonathan Pope has reformed. His hands are now on the dock in clear sight." His voice jumped. "Oh wow, look at that boat, Dad." He centered the viewfinder on a schooner that had entered his line of vision. "It's a four-master. *Wow.*"

"Not bad."

"It's *awesome.*"

"It won't be so awesome if the seas whip up. It'll be pretty unpleasant. We, on the other hand, will be safe and comfortable."

"But we can't go places like they can."

"The Whaler goes places."

"Not like a schooner would."

"The Whaler is more reliable."

"It's pathetic," Michael informed him. "You can't go *anywhere* good in a Whaler. I want to *travel.*" Cinematographers couldn't make names for themselves limiting their filming to Sutters Island, or Constance-on-the-Rise, where the Popewells lived, or Boston, where J.D. and Sam worked. They couldn't make names for themselves filming family events, or school plays, or—and he didn't care if he *had* won an award for it—documentaries on a day in the life of a dime. Michael wanted to do important stuff. He planned to circle the globe before he was twenty.

"So look into international law," J.D. advised. "It's a growing field. You'll be able to travel while you work."

"I'm not going into law," Michael said.

"Why not?" J.D. demanded.

Michael kept filming the schooner, which was one of the *most* awesome he'd seen. "I'd be bored."

"I'm not bored."

"You're not me."

"Is Sam bored?"

"Sam's not me." Michael had to admit that Sam's work—litigation, to J.D.'s corporate and estate law—was more exciting. Still, Michael couldn't see himself in an office from eight in the morning until eight at night.

"Your grandfather is counting on having three generations of Maxwells in the firm," J.D. said.

"Fine. Let Jana be a lawyer. She was born to be one."

J.D. was silent. In time Michael felt his gaze. There was puzzlement in his voice when he asked, "What do you see out there?"

"Sky. Sea. A boat." Michael paused. "New things. *Different* things. Our lives are too predictable."

"That's your age talking. You're too young to know the value of stability."

"I want adventure."

"Definitely your age talking."

Michael said nothing. If there was one thing he knew about his father, it was that J.D. wasn't changing his mind, which was okay, because Michael had Teke on his side. Teke would stand behind whatever he wanted to do. She was cool. She was his pal. Given what he'd seen of his friends' mothers, he thanked his lucky stars he had her.

one

FLIPPING THE LAST PAGE OF THE DECISION HE had been reading, Sam Pope rose from his chair, took a deep, satisfied breath, and let it out in a sigh of intense pleasure. He twitched his mustache en route to a smile. The smile broadened. He straightened his shoulders, felt his chest fill with excitement. Unable to contain himself, he growled an exuberant, "Way to go, Sam," and strode out the door.

"We did it, Joy," he said without breaking stride.

His secretary's eyes lit. "That explains the media." Even as she held out pink slips for the phone calls Sam had refused to take while he was reading the decision, her phone buzzed again.

But Sam was off, heading down the hall. There was a spring in his step. He felt on top of the world. He passed office after office but didn't slow until he reached the one at the very end. He wanted J.D. to be the first of his partners to hear the news. John David Maxwell was his oldest and closest friend.

The office was empty.

"He's at Continental Life in Springfield for the day," his secretary called from her station.

Sam felt a moment's disappointment, but it was gone in a flash. He was too elated to be weighed down for long. "When he calls in, tell him we won *Dunn v. Hanover.*"

The secretary grinned. "He'll be thrilled. What a victory."

"Yeah," Sam said, and tossed his chin toward yet another corridor. At its far end was a large corner office with generous views of the State House, the Boston Common, and the Public Garden. It was the office of the founder of the firm, the senior Maxwell. "Is John Stewart around?"

"He's in New York for board meetings. But he'll be impressed."

As he should be, Sam thought. Twelve years before, John Steward hadn't wanted a litigation department in the firm. If money was the bottom line, as J.S. seemed to think, this justified it. No one could sneeze at a contingency fee of a cool six million.

Striding back down the hall, he knew he looked smug, but he didn't care. He stopped at the office two short doors from his own and rapped a hand on the jamb.

Vicki Cornell was the associate who, over four years' time, had worked most closely with him taking *Dunn v. Hanover* from the superior court to the appellate court to the Supreme Court. One look at Sam's face and she grew wide-eyed. "Yes?"

He grinned and nodded.

She let out a whoop. It had barely left her mouth when she was on her feet and at the door, extending a hand in congratulations. Sam threw political correctness to the winds and gave her a hug.

She didn't seem to mind. Stepping back, she looked as excited about the victory as he was. "We did it. Wow! Have you seen a copy of the decision?"

He nodded. "It's on my desk."

"Does Marilyn Dunn know?"

"And the others. They're coming in at three for a press conference. Do me a favor and call Sybil Howard? Channel Five has given us good coverage along the way. I want Sybil to have first dibs on questions. And call Locke-Ober's. Let's book a private room." He turned to leave. "Have your husband join us. And Tom and Alex, and the significant others we kept them from while they were working on this case." On his way out the door he said, "We've earned a celebration. It isn't every day that precedent-setting cases are won." To Joy, in passing, he said, "See you in a couple of hours."

"Where will you be?"

"At home. Or at the college. Wherever I find my wife." He had no intention of telling Annie the news on the phone. Not the way he was feeling. Winning *Dunn* v. *Hanover* was a coup. He had to see her face to face, had to hold her. No celebration would be complete without that.

Constance-on-the-Rise lay eighteen miles northwest of Boston. It was an intimate, affluent community whose luxury imports normally made the commute to the city in forty minutes. Sam did it in ten better than that. Granted, it was eleven in the morning, rather than the rush hour. But he breezed past road repair crews without braking once. He was on a roll.

All his life he had dreamed of doing something important, scoring points for the little guy, making a difference. As an assistant district attorney he had prosecuted some heavy murder and drug cases, but none could hold a candle to *Dunn* v. *Hanover.*

Annie knew that. Annie understood.

He was *really* on a roll, because it just so happened that Tuesday was her work-at-home day. She would be all alone—no offspring, no friends. She would be reading journals, or correcting papers, or dictating reports—until she heard his news. Then she would be beside herself with excitement. She always was when there was good news to share.

He recalled other good news times. When his law school acceptance had come in the mail, he had scoured the library, finally finding her in a remote carrel, squirreling her into a nearby storage room, and making love to her with his back to the door. On the evening he'd won his law school moot court competition, they had done it in his car. When he'd learned he had passed the bar, they had run to the inn adjacent to the college where Annie was taking graduate courses. Their room had been charming, all two hours' worth. Nine months later Jonathan had been born.

He drove with a smile on his face and an ache in his groin, both of which burgeoned when he pulled up the circular drive to the front door of the brick Tudor. Flushed with anticipation, he swung out of the car, strode up the short path, and threw open the door.

"Annie? Good news, sunshine!"

He took the steps two at a time to the second floor, then her third-floor office. This time of day the sun would be spilling through the skylights and across her desk. He had visions of making love there.

"Annie?"

She wasn't in her office, though her briefcase was open and the desk covered with papers. He searched the second floor, then the first, calling her name repeatedly. When he checked the garage, he saw that her car was gone.

Undaunted, he picked up the kitchen phone and dialed her office at school. He could be there in ten minutes.

But she wasn't there.

He checked the kitchen calendar. It was blank for the day. She might have gone shopping for food or clothes for the kids, in which case, given her limited patience in stores, she would be back soon. Then again, she might be meeting a friend for lunch. That would take longer.

Frustrated, even vaguely annoyed, certainly feeling he might explode from excitement if he didn't share it soon, he went out the back door and set off through the woods. The trees were newly gold and rust and smelling of autumn. He crossed the brook in a single long stride, passed beneath the tree-house that he and J.D. had built for the kids so long ago—that Annie and he had used *not* so long ago for very adult purposes—and snaked his way along the path and between shrubs into the Maxwells' back-yard.

After crossing the flagstone patio, he went through the back door into the kitchen. "Teke?"

The coffeemaker was on, a good sign. The thought that Annie might be with her raised his arousal another notch. Teke would understand if he dragged Annie back through the woods. Teke understood him nearly as well as Annie did. She was as close to a sister as he'd ever had.

Knowing the Maxwells' house nearly as well as he knew his own, he checked the den off the kitchen. Teke wasn't there. Nor could he see Annie's car in the driveway, though she might easily be parked in front.

"Teke?" he called again, then louder, *"Teke?"*

* * *

Teke stirred at the sound of Sam's voice. She was in the living room, tucked in a corner of the sofa, nursing a cup of coffee that had long since gone cold. She was wearing the silk wrap J.D. had given her the Christmas before. It was too conservative for her taste, not her usual upbeat style, but she needed all the help she could get to remind herself who she was. She was feeling unhinged. Grady Piper's letter had done that to her.

Grady had been her childhood sweetheart, the light of her young life, the source of her fire. She had grown up in his arms, both literally and figuratively. Twenty-two years had passed since she had seen or heard from him, but not for lack of trying on her part. She had begged him. She had sent letters. She had tried to call. But he had turned a deaf ear to her pleas, had returned her letters unopened and refused to take her calls. He had rebuffed her at every turn. In the end he had actually said he didn't want her.

Heartbroken and defeated, finally believing he was out of her life, she had gone off to college, met Annie and Sam, met and married J. D. Maxwell, given birth to three children, found a whole new life.

Now Grady was back—or his letter was, at least—at a time when her marriage was floundering. It was a subtle floundering, a quiet frustration, an impatience that hadn't been there before, and it wasn't only on Teke's part. J.D. felt it. She could tell by the way he talked to her, the way he looked at her. Whatever excitement had been in their relationship was gone. They had fallen into a rut. Grady's letter couldn't have come at a worse time.

She had been shocked when it had first arrived, had held it in her hand and stared at it while a shaking had taken root inside. Since then she had read it enough times to know the words by heart.

He had been thinking of her, he said. He had been

wondering how she was. He thought he might drive down and say hello. For old times' sake.

The casualness of it had cut her to the quick. Nothing between Grady and her had ever been casual. Twenty-two years might have passed, but she didn't think she could look him in the eye and feel anything remotely casual. As it always had then, so now the thought of him sparked things intimate and intense.

It also sparked anger. He had discarded her once, had said he didn't want her, and, though it had nearly killed her, she had succeeded in pushing him from mind. She had her own life now. He had no right barging in. His reappearance could come to no good, no good at all.

She was infinitely grateful Sam had come. She needed him to take her mind off Grady.

"In the living room!" she called.

He was there in an instant, looking ready to burst with excitement. "We won the Dunn case!"

She tried to place it. "The Dunn case?"

"It's a precedent-setting ruling in cases of sexual abuse," he explained, no less excited for her lack of recall. "Up until now the statute of limitations was just three years, but women who've been abused often don't know they were abused until long after that. It took Marilyn Dunn seventeen years to realize why she had been living in hell. *Seventeen years* later she was able to sue her abuser and win. Do you know what this means to the scores of violated women in this state?"

Teke did remember his having mentioned the case before. She felt a glimmer of his excitement. "You won it?"

He grinned. "Twenty million dollars' worth."

She came off the sofa to give him a hug. "That's great, Sam."

Ebullient, he swung her around. "It's precedent-setting. A victory, finally, for people who need it."

"That's so *good,*" she said, basking in the close-ness. Sam was her best male friend. He was solid and sound, not J.D., not Grady, but a force in and of himself.

"Ahhhh, it feels good, Teke. We've worked so hard for this."

She made a satisfied sound and slid her arms under his suit jacket and around his waist. Sam was a toucher, just as she was. He wouldn't mind this. And she needed it. The fullness of him filled the emptiness that had been swallowing her up.

"I've always wanted a case like this," he said against the tumble of her hair. His voice was thick with satisfaction. "They come along once in a life-time."

She closed her eyes in the echo of that thick voice. It was a strong sound, a masculine sound. "You sweat-ed it," she hummed. "You earned the win."

"My clients earned the win."

"You earned it for them." She sucked in a breath. His body suddenly felt too good against hers, but she couldn't step back. He reminded her in odd ways of Grady. In the wake of the hollowness she had felt, his holding her was a relief and a pleasure. She didn't see that it would do any harm. "Have you told Annie?"

"She wasn't home," he said with a moan, and, when he might have let her go, held her tighter. "I thought she might be here."

"No," Teke managed to whisper, but a slow burn was taking root in her belly. It was Grady, damn him, Grady merging past and present.

"Jesus, Teke."

She whispered his name, at least she thought it was his name, though it was little more than a sigh. Her body was fitting itself to his in an attempt to quench the burn, and he was growing to accommodate it.

"*Jesus,*" he breathed.

She knew just what he meant. She could feel the pumping of his blood—or hers—and the resistance that seemed to fizzle in the rising heat. She told herself to pull away, but her body wouldn't obey. She was a teenager back in Gullen, driven by a need long suppressed and overpowering.

He was touching her. She smoked and smoldered and burst into flame. She felt a dire need for more.

Somehow his trousers opened. She was helpless to keep her hands from slipping into his shorts, and once she touched him she couldn't think of stopping. He was fully erect, needing release, and she was was so desperate for the fulfillment of a dream that she opened her robe.

They were both lost then. He tumbled her to the sofa, and while she tore at his shirt buttons and opened her mouth on his bare chest, he thrust into her again and again, with rising fervor, until, with a long, guttural cry, he came. She was on the verge of following him when a clap of noise broke into her pleasure. It was several seconds before an identification worked its way into her consciousness.

"Oh, God," she cried, scrambling out from under him. She tugged on her robe and ran toward the door. "It was Michael! It was Michael! He saw!" She had barely reached the front steps when the harrowing squeal of brakes and skidding tires came from the street.

"*Michael!*" she screamed as she ran, her heart thudding not in passion now, but alarm. She raced down the front walk, afraid to think. A miniforest of pines and rhododendron blocked her view of the street. It was only when she reached the sidewalk that she saw the dirty blue pickup that had skidded to a sideways stop. She darted around it and fell to her knees. Michael was on his stomach, a leg and an arm bent at odd angles. His eyes were closed. Blood seeped from beneath his head.

Her heart hammered against her ribs. She put a terrified hand to his face but didn't quite touch, moved her hand to the back of his head, then his neck, afraid to land at those spots, too. "Michael?" Her voice shook. "Can you hear me, Michael?"

He didn't respond. Fearfully she touched his head.

Sam hunkered down on the boy's other side. "Don't move him. We have to get help."

"I didn't see him," came a deep male voice from somewhere beside and behind. "He ran out of the trees. I tried to stop."

Teke's pulse lurched. It was the voice, the voice she remembered. But it couldn't be. She had to be imagining it. No God in His right mind would do *that* to her. She was feeling horror, fear, and guilt enough without it.

"We need an ambulance," Sam yelled toward the voice. "Go to the Clingers—"

"I've already phoned the ambulance," called Virginia Clinger, who was jogging across her front lawn in a crinkly pink running suit and a cloud of Obsession. "It's on its way. What *happened?*" She bent her blond head over Michael's. "Is he alive?"

"Yes!" Teke cried, desperate to believe it. She had a hand on Michael's back to monitor the shallow rise and fall of his breathing. "What can I do?" she whimpered, frantic with helplessness. "What can I do?"

"Hold his hand," Sam urged softly. "Let him know you're here." Lightly he stroked the boy's shiny brown hair.

"Michael?" Teke tried again, leaning even closer.

"Can you hear me? It's Mommy, baby. Open your eyes."

"He's unconscious," Virginia announced.

"We told him not to leave school," came a new, frightened voice. "We told him not to. But he was sure he'd get home and back before lunch period ended."

Teke glanced up into the ashen faces of Michael's friends, the twins, Terry and Alex Baker. While Alex gaped at Michael's inert form, Terry babbled, "We found out there were still some tickets left for Club MTV next week at Great Woods. Josh's dad agreed to go get them tonight, but only if we all paid up before. Michael figured he'd get his mom's permission and the money at the same time."

"He was coming out of the house," Virginia announced.

Teke's eye flew to hers, then, following her gaze, to Sam. His shirt was open and his belt unbuckled. He fixed the belt, but that was all before he returned his hand to Michael's hair. "Where's the goddamned ambulance," he muttered.

Sam, oh, Sam, what have we done? Teke cried silently, but even in the silence her voice was strange, not its robust self, but a flimsy facade reflecting an absolute horror of thoughts. She hadn't felt such despair since she had been a Peasely, dirt poor and living in the squalor of a fisherman's shack on the northernmost coast of Maine. Grady had been her savior then. Not even he could save her now.

"You'll be fine, Mikey," she managed aloud. "The doctors will know what to do." For her own sake she added a shaky, "Stay calm. Stay calm."

"Why did he leave the house that way?" Virginia asked. "Why didn't he look before he ran into the street?"

"He just ran in and ran out," Terry cried. "We were watching from the Carters' hill. He wasn't in there more'n half a minute."

"Did he ask you about the concert?" Virginia asked Teke.

She couldn't answer. She couldn't think beyond Michael at that moment in time. She held his hand, rubbed the arm that appeared uninjured, felt herself go weak, and swayed.

Sam reached out to steady her. "He'll be okay, Teke."

She gave a spasmodic nod, praying it with all her might.

"Kids are strong. They rebound."

The distant wail of the ambulance pierced the air. It was as unreal as the rest of the world was seeming. Teke couldn't identify with any of it. Nor could she escape it.

The siren grew louder, stilling abruptly the minute the ambulance turned onto the street. It was followed by a police car. Both pulled up close before disgorging their occupants.

Teke was aware of other neighbors appearing in her periphery, but she kept her touch and her focus on Michael. When Sam bodily lifted her out of the way to make room for the paramedics, she resisted.

But he held firm. "They're professionals. They can help him."

"He's my baby, Sam," she whispered, struggling to see Michael around the uniformed backs. "If anything happens to him, I'll die."

"He'll be okay."

"It's my fault."

"No."

"Did you folks see what happened?" one of the police officers asked.

Before either of them could speak, the driver of

the pickup said, "The truck's mine. I tried to stop, but it was too late."

Teke looked at the man before she could catch herself, and her silent voice screamed in anguish. *Grady. No, no, not Grady. Anyone else, please God, oh, please.* But twenty-two years had barely changed his features. Then again, he might have worn a mask, and she would have known him from his eyes. They were deep, dark eyes to drown in, always filled with emotion for her, and they were no different now.

She began to shake in earnest.

Sam tightened his hold. "It's okay, Teke. He'll be fine. He's a strong, healthy kid."

Teke watched the policeman lead Grady out of earshot, then switched her eyes to the paramedics, who were securing Michael on a stretcher.

"She should get dressed, don't you think?" Virginia asked Sam, who tried to turn Teke toward the house.

But she refused. "I can't leave him." She was sure he would die if she did.

"A sweater and leggings would be best," he coaxed. "We may be at the hospital a while."

"I can't *leave* him."

To Virginia Sam said, "Run inside and get her some clothes. She'll change when we get there."

Virginia jogged off.

One of the paramedics looked up from his work. "We have broken bones here, maybe internal bleeding, but the head injury is the main cause for concern. Is Mass. General okay?"

Teke supposed it was. She didn't know for sure. She didn't know what the options were. She didn't know *anything,* and her baby's life was on the line.

"It's fine," Sam said to the paramedic, then to Teke, "It's the best. We can't go wrong there."

Michael was eased into the ambulance. Teke

crowded close behind, linked by an emotional umbilical cord.

"You ride with him," Sam agreed. "I'll follow in my car. I can phone from there. Annie will round up the kids. We'll meet at the hospital."

Teke had a sudden, terrifying thought. "J.D." He had to be called, had to be told, had to come.

"I'll get him," Sam assured her. His eyes held the same unspoken terror she felt.

"Here you go," Virginia said, handing Teke a bulging bag. "I threw in underwear, too."

Teke had just enough time to catch the look Virginia slid Sam, before Sam was helping her into the ambulance. Then she turned her attention to Michael. Her eyes never left his face during the ride to the hospital, and once there she remained by his side, holding his hand, willing him to open his eyes and grin his adorable grin.

But his eyes remained shut, and his mouth was soon taped around a breathing tube. She left the emergency room cubicle only when the doctors insisted that they needed the small space she took up. Borrowing an empty room nearby, she changed into her clothes, then resumed the wait in the hall, hunched against the wall with her eyes glued to the door of the room where the doctors worked on Michael.

Sam joined her. "Any news yet?"

With that little bit of time and distance between them now, she couldn't look him in the eye after what she'd done. So she simply shook her head.

"Teke—"

She interrupted him with a hand. She didn't want to *think* of what had happened, much less speak of it.

But he insisted. "It was my fault."

She put shaky fingers to her forehead and tried to concentrate on Michael, on what the doctors were doing and whether or not he was responding.

Sam said, "Michael must have been traumatized by what he saw."

"Please," she begged. Her mind was clogged with staggering thoughts. She couldn't take another. "Not now."

"It won't be any easier later."

"If Michael survives, it will. *Anything* will, if he survives."

"He'll survive," Sam said with a confidence that lured her, she was so desperate for encouragement. Shifting her hand, she met his gaze, and the confidence was there, in his deep brown eyes, the strong line of his cheek, the firm set of his mouth beneath its mustache. "He will, Teke."

She nodded and tried to focus on Michael again, but other images intruded. She saw Sam's broad chest, felt his erection, heard his climactic cry, then the slam of the door, the squeal of brakes, the sound of a siren. She saw the flashing lights of the ambulance, the blood under Michael's head, the dirty blue pickup sitting askew in the street, the stunned, achingly familiar face of its owner.

Grady. Oh, Grady. Damn it, Grady.

An anguished cry escaped her. Sam reached out to help, but she quickly slipped free. "I'm all right." She took a half breath and forced Grady from her mind. Michael was the only one who mattered. "He broke his leg. He won't be pleased. Basketball starts in a month."

"It's okay," Sam said. "He'll sit on the bench and help Coach until he's up to playing."

"He'll be heartbroken if he has to miss even one game."

"So will the team. He's their star."

"What if he has to miss the whole season?"

"Then he'll train next summer and do twice as well next year."

"What if he can't play then?"

"He'll play then."

"What if he can't *ever* play?" It was the unthinkable that she couldn't help thinking about.

There was a silence from Sam, then a gut-wrenching sound from deep in his throat. Incredibly, given the enormity of her own fear, her heart went out to him. "Not much of a celebration for winning your case, is it?" she asked sadly.

"Fuck my case," he snapped. "I canceled the press conference, canceled the dinner. I can't think about any of that, much less celebrate." He ran a hand through his hair. "Strange, how life is. Three hours ago I was the greatest. Now I'm shit."

"Did you talk with Annie?" Teke asked, feeling a painful twist inside. That was *another* horror to consider.

"Only about Michael. She wanted to come in and be with you. I told her we needed her to get the kids from school."

Teke rested her cheek against the wall. "Annie's so good," she whispered. "She'd never have done what I did."

"It wasn't your fault."

"I practically attacked you." She was appalled by the thought, then bewildered. "I don't know what happened. I've never thought of being with you like that, but when you showed up, my mind was off somewhere else, and I needed—I needed—" She had needed Grady, it was as simple as that. Her marriage was stagnant. She had needed the emotion Grady had always evoked, the depth of feeling, the anticipation, the soul-deep satisfaction that came from being with him—none of which she had allowed herself to think of for years, but all of which had surged back with the receipt of his letter. After reading that letter countless times, she had been desperate for his fire.

Dismay, self-disgust, regret—feeling them all, she turned more fully into the wall. Then the door opened, and she whirled around. While she held her breath, one of the doctors separated himself from the rest.

"We're taking him to intensive care. We'll be doing tests, but I want to be able to monitor his functions more closely."

Teke swallowed. "Has he woken up at all?"

"Not yet."

"Will he?"

"We hope so."

"When?"

"We don't know that."

"Can you guess?"

The doctor gave her a sad smile. "Not now. Maybe later, when we have more of an idea of the extent of the injury. You can come up with us, if you'd like. There's a comfortable room there."

A short time later Teke found herself in the fifth-floor waiting room, trying to relax over the tea Sam had brought, but it was an impossible task. She thought of Sam and his pain, of J.D. and the anger that was sure to be. Mostly she thought of Grady and the shock of recognition she had felt.

Then Annie arrived. Jana and Zoe were with her, both close to tears and needing a comfort that Teke couldn't give. Her heart was too heavy, her worry too great. What she felt, though, when Annie wrapped her arms around her, was a crushing guilt.

Sweet, compassionate, understanding Annie, who understood nothing at all this time around.

Teke remembered the day, in September of 1970, when they'd first met. She had been a frightened freshman praying for confidence as she carted her duffel bags down the dormitory hall. Those duffel bags held the whole of her worldly possessions, none of which suddenly seemed right at all. And the worry increased with each room she passed. With each diligent mother hanging curtains, each sweetly dressed freshman unpacking new clothes, she felt more inadequate. Then she arrived at her assigned room and found, sitting alone on the window seat writing in a worn journal, a girl who looked as frightened as she.

"Theodora?" Annie asked in a timid voice.

"Teke," Teke corrected artlessly. "Theodora's too long."

Annie sighed into a smile. "Thank goodness. I've been *dying*, wondering what I'd ever have to say to someone named Theodora. Teke is perfect. And I love your earrings. What are they made of?"

The earrings were of the fisherman's twine that Teke had picked up from the supply store floor and were knotted into large, ivory flowers that dangled against her neck. Annie had thought them wonderful. Likewise the jeans Teke had inherited from the parson's son and embroidered. And the oversize vests she had taken from her father's trunk before selling the rest.

They had become fast friends. Annie was the writer, Teke the mathematician, Annie the thinker, Teke the technician. They had worked as a team through four years of college, had married men who were best friends, and continued the teamwork through one Ph.D., one apartment and two houses each, countless school fund-raisers, holidays, and vacations, and five kids.

Now, suddenly, things had changed. Teke had sabotaged the relationship. And Annie didn't even know it yet.

"He'll be all right," Annie said softly.

Feeling like a snake, Teke slipped from her arms. "I pray."

"The doctors here are the best. Is J.D. on his way?"

Teke nodded. Needing to move and somehow

dull the agony she felt, she went down the hall to Michael's room. She didn't go inside, simply stood at the window, watching. Annie and the girls joined her there.

"What are they doing?" Zoe asked.

"Tests," Teke answered.

Jana leaned against her. "Is he aware of it?"

Teke swallowed. "No. He's still unconscious."

"Then he's not in pain?"

"I don't think so."

"When can we see him?"

"When they're done."

"Will he be okay?"

"I hope so."

Jana looked at her—no longer up, they were nearly the same height, though at that moment Teke felt lowly as hell—and said, "Annie told us they caught the guy."

With a twist in her heart, Teke saw Grady's face again. So many years had passed since she had seen it last. Then, too, it had looked ravaged.

He shouldn't have come, she cried silently. *Her life was no business of his,* he had told her once. *Why couldn't he leave well enough alone?*

She wanted to weep. Instead she took a breath and said in a carefully controlled voice, "They didn't have to catch him. He never left the scene."

"Did they arrest him?"

"I don't know."

"Was he speeding?"

"I didn't see."

"Why didn't Michael hear him? Or see him?"

Teke didn't know. She could guess, though, and the guessing gave no comfort. Nor did the thought that Jana's questions were nothing compared with the ones J.D. would have when he arrived.

two

O N HIS WAY IN FROM SPRINGFIELD, J.D. WAS stopped for speeding. The cop said he was going eighty-five, and in other circumstances he would have argued. He was a lawyer. He knew the score. Radar guns were unreliable as hell. If he could talk the cop down to seventy-five, an appeal of the ticket would do the rest.

This time, though, he simply passed over his license and registration and said, "I was in the middle of negotiations when I got a call that my son was hit by a car. They say he's unconscious, but that's all I know. He's thirteen."

"Thirteen?" The officer frowned. "That's rough."

"My wife and best friend are at the hospital. I've been trying to reach them, but they're somewhere between the emergency room and intensive care. I can't even get a doctor on the line. They won't take my calls."

"Be grateful, if they're working on your son."

"But I can't get any news," J.D. complained. "It's the not knowing that's so bad. I'm imagining the worst. I'm sorry. I wasn't thinking about driving."

The officer handed back his license and registration. "You have a better excuse than most. I won't hold you up giving you a ticket, but watch it, will you? Especially if you're using that phone. It won't do your son any good if you kill yourself on the turnpike."

J.D. kept his speed down to seventy-five the rest of the way. When he wasn't badgering the hospital to put him through to someone in the know, he was talking with his secretary, with Vicki Cornell about Sam's case, with the public relations person he often used. *Dunn* v. *Hanover* was a milestone. The publicity would be great for the firm.

His father would be eating crow, and what satisfaction there was in *that.* John Stewart had fought against taking Sam into the firm. He had thought Sam lacked the connections, and the social standing, to have much of a practice. But J.D. had been willing to take the chance. For one thing, Sam had distinguished himself in the district attorney's office. For another, he had the drive to succeed. For still another, he was married to Annie, who was Teke's best friend. Mostly, though, J.D. had wanted Sam in the firm because they were best friends themselves. Sam kept him human, social, and loose.

J.D. was grateful that Sam was at the hospital with Teke. He trusted his judgment. If there were decisions to be made, Sam would guide Teke to the best one. And she would need guiding. Her wits were probably scattered all over the place by now. She didn't have the poise in a pinch that J.D. did. She didn't have the breeding for that. She was strictly small-town, backwoods that way.

It wouldn't *occur* to her to call him in his car with news to ease his worry.

As it happened, there was precious little news to ease anyone's worry. J.D. arrived at the hospital to find that Michael's outer injuries had been treated, that he was hooked up to a respirator, that the doctors were doing tests, but that the results were inconclusive. No one knew much of anything, which bothered J.D. no end.

"No prognosis?" he asked Teke, who was standing alone at Michael's window, looking shaken and meek.

"It's too early."

"Doctors always have prognoses," he argued.

"Not with head injuries."

"Is there brain damage?"

"They don't know yet."

"Why not?"

"I don't *know.* They just say they don't."

He knew she was upset, but hell, so was he. Michael was his son, too. She should have been on top of the doctors. But Teke wasn't forceful that way. She was a good cook, a good housekeeper, a good shopper. She presented herself well and staged impressive dinner parties. She made unusual Halloween costumes, could tutor the kids, coach Little League, run school auctions that raised thousands of dollars for arts programs. At times of personal crisis, though, she fell apart.

Annie was good for her at those times. Annie steadied her, set her back on track.

Intent on sending Annie to her now, J.D. strode down the hall to the waiting room. But Annie was occupied with Jonathan and Leigh. So J.D. gestured Sam into the hall. "What do we know about the man who hit him?"

Sam was subdued. "I just talked with the police. He's a carpenter. He's from out of state and currently unemployed, but his license and registration are in order. He's not being charged."

J.D. was incredulous. "But he hit my son."

"Actually," Sam corrected, "Michael hit him."

J.D. didn't buy it for a minute. "The guy must have been going too fast."

"Twenty-five, according to the expert who saw the skid marks."

"Then his brakes were faulty."

Sam shook his head. "Not from what the police say."

"What do the local guys know," J.D. muttered. "Their specialty is citing drivers for parking too far from the curb. I'll hire an independent investigator. Your man Mundy. He'll find evidence against an unemployed carpenter."

"Not if there isn't any." Sam looked pained. "Look, J.D., I know you want to find someone to blame. It's the most natural thing in the world. But that guy wasn't it. He was driving within the speed limit. Michael came out of nowhere, hit the front panel of the truck, flew into the air, and bounced off the hood onto the street, and all that time, the guy was slamming on his brakes. He wasn't drunk. He wasn't stoned. He was just *there* when Michael ran out."

"Are you suggesting it was *Michael's* fault?"

Sam pushed a hand through his hair and frowned at the floor. With a sigh he faced J.D. again. "All I'm saying is that going after the driver is a waste of energy. The accident happened. There may be dozens of reasons why, but they don't matter. What matters is making sure that Michael has the best possible care. I got Bill Gardner to head the case. He's chief of the department."

"But is he here?" J.D. demanded. "Department chiefs are sometimes too involved in the seminar circuit to give their patients adequate time."

Sam tossed his chin toward Michael's room. A doctor was just emerging. "That's Bill."

J.D. made straight for him, introduced himself, and launched into his questions. Unfortunately he didn't learn much more than Teke had. Bill Gardner was a nice enough man, but he could offer little of a concrete nature. As he listened, J.D. took a date book from his jacket's inner pocket to note what Gardner did say, including the names of the doctors on his team. Then he looked in at Michael, who was still surrounded by medical personnel. "How often can we see him?"

"Whenever you want. I've signed a no limit order. It may help for him to hear familiar voices."

"Then he does hear?"

"Possibly. We don't know for sure."

The vagueness irked J.D. He wanted *answers*. "When does consciousness most often return in cases like this?"

"Any time."

"Or no time. Is he in a coma?"

Bill Gardner didn't blink. "Technically, yes. I hesitate to use that word around your wife, though. She's frightened enough already."

That was Teke's problem. J.D. didn't have the time for hand holding, much less the inclination. Annie would help her. "What can be done to bring Michael around?"

"Not much right now. We have him stabilized. He's breathing. He's getting fluids. We've minimized any pain he might feel. Now we wait."

"For complications?" J.D. asked.

"Or improvement."

"What complications might there be?"

The doctor didn't hesitate. "Pressure on the brain from bleeding. Fluid buildup in the lungs. A blood clot traveling through the system. One of the reasons we're monitoring him so closely is to detect any of those."

"Do you detect brain activity?"

"He's definitely with us, if that's what you're wondering. As for how *much* of him is, we won't know that for a while." He looked past J.D. and nodded. "I have a phone call. Will you excuse me?" He was gone before J.D. could ask what "a while" meant, and how long the doctor would be at the hospital, and, when he left, where he could be reached.

Then the rest of the medical personnel filed out of Michael's room, and J.D. felt a swift chill. "Is he all right?"

"He's holding his own," was the answer.

J.D. stared at the pale figure on the bed. He entered the room, feeling unsure and, in that, more unsettled than ever. He and Michael didn't always agree on things, but they had a sound relationship. He normally knew how to act.

The problem was that the Michael lying on the bed didn't seem like his Michael at all. This one was unmoving as his Michael seldom was. This one was colorless, save for a purpling bruise on the side of his face. This one was *quiet.*

Teke came up on the far side of the bed. Grasping the rail for support, she looked down at Michael.

J.D. felt a stab of anger. Teke was in charge of the kids. She was supposed to keep them from harm. "How did this happen?" he asked in a harsh whisper.

She raised one shoulder and shook her head.

"What was he doing home in the middle of the day?"

Her voice wobbled. "He wanted money for a concert."

"So you gave it to him, then let him run into a truck?"

She waved a shaky hand.

J.D. wasn't sure what that meant. "You didn't give it to him? He raced back out because you said no and he was angry?"

"I never spoke with him."

"Why not?"

She rubbed Michael's arm.

"He came into the house, Teke. Why didn't you speak to him?"

"He ran back out before I ever saw him."

"Did he change his mind about asking?"

She touched Michael's face. Her voice was higher than normal, and shaky. "Hi, baby. Can you hear me? Can you hear me, Michael? It's Mommy."

J.D. was furious. Someone had to take responsibility for his son being hurt. "They shouldn't have let him leave school."

"They didn't know," Teke said softly. "He stole out with the twins."

"What does our tax money go for, if not to have the schools look out for our children?"

"It was lunchtime."

"Is that supposed to excuse it?"

"The kids mill around during lunch. It's impossible to keep tabs on them all."

"Someone must have seen him run off."

She sighed. "It's not a prison, J.D. There aren't guards posted in watchtowers."

"Of course there aren't," he said, resentful of her sarcasm, "but this is a clear-cut case of negligence. That school was responsible for our child during the time we left him there."

"*He* broke the *rules*," she cried. In the next breath she lowered her voice and stroked Michael's cheek. "He's a good boy. If he left school, it was because he felt it was important."

"So now he lies in a hospital bed breathing through a machine."

"Shhhh."

"Doesn't it make *you* angry?" J.D. asked in frustration.

"I just want Michael to get better," she whispered tearfully. "I think we should concentrate on that."

J.D. studied Michael's face. He wanted the boy to get better, too, but he couldn't be as passive as Teke. Or as forgiving. Accidents didn't happen for no reason. He wanted the driver of the truck punished. And the school.

"J.D.?" Teke prompted in a guarded tone. He glanced up to see her looking past him and turned to find his parents on the far side of the window.

The sight of them made his stomach jump. It had been doing that for forty-one years and was one of those givens, like heartburn from pizza. Forgetting his anger, he joined them in the hall. "I thought you were in New York," he said to his father.

"I took an earlier flight home," John Stewart informed him. "My secretary had the good sense to call. You should have."

"I just got here myself."

"How is he?" Lucy asked. She was impeccably composed and groomed, remarkable given the circumstances—then again not remarkable at all. Her morning activity, seven days a week, was putting herself together for her afternoon and evening activities. By the time she left the house at noon, whether to lunch with a friend, attend meetings of the ladies' committee, or fetch her husband from the airport for a trip to the hospital, she was eminently presentable.

J.D. related what the doctor had said.

"Bill Gardner?" John Stewart asked. He was an inch taller than J.D. and ten pounds heavier, imposing even before one heard his robust voice. "He's not the best man. The best man is Henry Finch. He's at the Mayo Clinic."

J.D. dared state the obvious, albeit in a conversational tone. "Michael's here, not in Minnesota."

"Fly Finch in."

"That may alienate Gardner."

"But he doesn't know anything. You just said that."

"It's too early to know much."

"Call Henry Finch." It was an order. "Talk with him. His presence as a consultant will keep Gardner on his toes."

Lacking the will to argue, J.D. took out his date book and jotted down the name. He had barely returned it to his pocket when his father said, "Any lawsuits here?"

"Too early, Dad."

"It's never too early to make sure evidence isn't destroyed. Sam ought to know that. I understand he was there when it happened. Why wasn't he at the office?"

"He had driven home to tell Annie about winning the Dunn case. Did you hear?"

"I heard."

"Not bad, huh?" J.D. asked, allowing himself a small smile.

"Not bad."

J.D. would have liked more enthusiasm. Victories over his father were few and far between. But John Stewart wasn't the humble type. He was stern, efficient, and intimidating. That was another reason J.D. liked having Sam in the firm. Sam was a buffer. He could stand up to John Stewart as J.D. couldn't. He could play devil's advocate without worrying that he had insulted John Stewart or let him down or, worse, embarrassed him.

The senior Maxwell glanced from his watch to the nurse's station to Michael. "Why is Theodora the only one in there?"

Theodora. John Stewart and Lucy always called her that. It sounded more proper. More upper-crust. It was ironic, J.D. mused, given the spineless way she was acting now.

"The others are in the waiting room," he said.

"Where is Michael's nurse?"

"She's at the central station. The machines monitor his vital functions and relay the information there. That's the whole purpose of intensive care."

"You need a private nurse."

"Not in intensive care, Dad." J.D. felt the distinct urge to flee. It, too, was a familiar feeling where his parents were concerned. "I have to call the office. You go on in and see Michael. I'll be back soon." He left before his father could order him to rent a portable phone.

By the time he returned, his parents were gone. Feeling instantly stronger, he went to the foot of Michael's bed. From what he could see, the boy hadn't moved. Nor had Teke. Leigh and Jon were there, Leigh talking softly to Michael.

"I can't believe you're sleeping through this, Michael. Everyone wants to see you. Mrs. Baker drove the twins in with Josh, Tommy, and Nat, but the nurses are making them stay in the waiting room. Same with half the football team. They're all rooting for you." Her voice cracked. "Wake up, damn it."

Jon took her hand. "We'll be back, Mike," he said. He looked nearly as upset as Leigh. "Can we bring you more tea, Teke?"

Teke managed a weak smile but shook her head.

J.D. watched Jon and Leigh leave, then slipped his hands into his pockets and looked around. Everything in sight was either stark white or metal, neat as a pin, cold, and sterile. He hated it, which was interesting. Michael's room at home was colorfully loud and forever messy, and J.D. hated that, too. Or so he had always thought. In comparison with this, the image wasn't so bad.

"Did my parents say anything?" he asked Teke.

"Hello and good-bye," she said quietly.

"They don't handle illness well." He scanned the bank of machines at the head of the bed. "Has Gardner been back?"

She shook her head.

"There's a doctor at the Mayo Clinic named Henry Finch. He's the best in the country for head injuries. I'm bringing him in."

Teke looked up. "Don't you trust Bill Gardner?"

"Trust has nothing to do with it. It's common sense. Two heads are better than one. Besides, Gardner isn't brimming with ideas."

Sam wandered in. "How's he doing?"

"The same," J.D. said, then brightened. "I just talked with the office. The media wants you."

"They'll hold."

"Too long and they'll cool off. The story's hot now."

"No matter." Sam looked at Teke. "Are you okay?"

She nodded. He wandered back out.

J.D. was beginning to sense something surreal about the scene. Sam's lack of spirit, Teke's inactivity, Michael's unconsciousness—all were out of character. The accident itself was out of character. The Maxwell children were healthy and well cared for. They weren't hit by trucks and left lying unconscious in the street.

"This doesn't make sense," he muttered. "Why did he run into the house, then run right back out? Where were you?"

Teke swallowed. "The living room."

"Right there when he came in the front door." It didn't make sense. "How could he not see you?"

"He may have," she said, sounding desperate. "I just don't know, J.D. I don't know what he saw."

You should know, he thought. You're his mother. He took a tempering breath and released it slowly. "It's getting dark. Are you hungry?"

She shook her head. Her eyes were on Michael.

J.D. hadn't eaten lunch. "The kids must be hungry," he said.

"You take them to dinner. I'll stay here in case there's any change."

"Maybe I should, too. The kids can go out and bring something back."

"No. You go with them. They'll feel better if you do."

It struck him that he would, too. He was no help to Michael here. He had to *do* something. "Where should I take them?"

She shrugged. "I don't know."

"Well, neither do I," he barked. Meals were Teke's responsibility, not his. She cooked dinner, or she made reservations at a restaurant. She knew he hated making domestic decisions. "Where's there to eat around here?"

She gave him a bewildered look. "You would know that more than I. You work here."

"I work on the other side of town," he snapped. "What do the kids like?"

"Whatever you want."

"I'll let Sam and Annie decide. They have to eat, too. We'll be back after dinner."

"Not for too long. The kids need sleep. Take them home with you. I'm staying here."

"I'll stay, too."

"They need you at home. They're upset."

J.D. wasn't sure he could do anything about that. The girls were apt to talk out their fears with Teke, Annie, or Sam before they did it with him. He wasn't good at discussing feelings. What he was good at was negotiating mergers, executing estates, and writing contracts, not at holding hands, drying tears, and trying to explain things that had no explanation.

He had a quick, horrible image of dirty laundry,

unmade beds, and breakfast dishes in the sink—not Teke's style, but he didn't know how much she had done before Michael had been hurt. "Is there much to do at home?"

"Everything's done," she said. He was feeling momentarily relieved when she made a small, wrenching sound. "All done this morning. So long ago. Oh, God, if only I had—" She broke off.

"If only you had what?" J.D. asked.

She shook her head.

"If only you had what?" he repeated. He didn't like being put off. It was bad enough when the doctors did it. He didn't need it from his wife.

"If only I had been able to grab him," she said brokenly. "If only I had *talked* with him."

She looked ready to cry. He didn't think he could bear that. In an effort to shore her up, he said, "It wasn't your fault."

"I should have been at the door."

"It might not have made any difference."

"It would have."

He didn't argue further. Mothering, like meal making, was her thing. She defined herself in terms of it, set standards for herself that few other mothers did, and she usually met every one.

But she was right. She should have been at the door.

Early the next morning, Annie set down the phone, shifted her feet to the floor, and cushioned her hands in the folds of her nightgown. She had barely gathered her thoughts when Zoe and Jana appeared at the door. Though their faces were fresh from sleep, their eyes were alert.

"He's the same," Annie said before they could ask. She wished she could be more positive, but the girls were fifteen, too old to deceive. "I just spoke with the nurse."

"Is he still unconscious?" Jana asked.

"Uh-huh."

"Is Mom still there?"

Annie nodded. "And your dad. He couldn't sleep, so he got dressed and went back in. It's good you and Leigh slept here. He wouldn't have wanted to leave you alone."

"He still thinks we're little."

"No. He knows you're growing up. It's just that he's never quite sure what's right and what isn't." Where parenthood was concerned, J.D. had two left hands. His heart was in the right place, but his gestures were often mistimed. "That's why he has Teke," she said with a smile. "Is Leigh up?"

"I don't know," Jana said.

"Where's Dad?" Zoe asked.

Annie nodded toward the bathroom. "Shaving."

"Was he the one taking showers all night?"

He had only taken two, but the sound of water pouring through pipes in the still of the night was distinct. "He was restless. He's upset about Michael."

"Are we going back to the hospital after breakfast?" Jana asked.

With a gentle smile Annie shook her head. "After school."

"But today's my easiest day. I won't miss much."

"Your mother wants you in school. She wants things as close to normal as possible."

"Yeah," Jana said. "And Mike'll be running in here any minute."

Annie rose from the bed and went to the door. Putting an arm around both girls, she started them down the hall. "It's hard."

"He's my brother."

"The doctors will be doing more tests this morning, so it's not as though you can be with him."

"I could be with Mom."

"Your dad's with her."

"For now. Watch. He'll be in the office before long—"

"For the same reason that you should be in school. Let the doctors work with Michael this morning. You'll be thinking of him, which is the most important thing. By afternoon, you can go in there and talk."

After separating herself from Jana and Zoe, Annie knocked lightly on Jonathan's door, then opened it. "Leigh? Are you awake?"

The drapes were still drawn. It was a minute before Annie's eyes adjusted to the darkness, and then she moaned. She shooed the other two girls off, slipped into the room, and closed the door.

"Oh, Jon ..." She sighed in disappointment. "You promised you'd sleep in the den."

Jon's voice was sleepy. "Leigh was upset. She's worried about Michael."

"So now we worry about her."

"Nothing happened."

"Leigh?"

"Nothing happened," Leigh said. To her credit, she was wearing a nightshirt. Jon's chest was bare, but that meant nothing. He slept in boxers, like his dad.

Annie sighed. She crossed to the drapes and drew them open, then perched on the end of the double bed that she and Sam had bought—cleverly, they had thought at the time—to accommodate Jon's imminent length. "Nothing may have happened this time, but you're playing with fire, guys."

"I love Leigh, and she loves me. We're getting married."

"Not yet. You're only seventeen."

"How's Michael?" Leigh asked.

"The same."

Leigh moved closer to Jon, who opened an arm to her. It was a gentle gesture, a protective one. It was also a grown-up one and gave Annie nearly as much pause as the fact of their being in bed together.

She remembered when they were babies, then toddlers, then schoolkids, then preteens. They had been best friends all that time, and though everyone assumed they would one day branch out and go their own ways, that had never happened. Like saplings taken root side by side, they had grown taller and more shapely with their boughs intertwined. Annie guessed the future would be more of the same.

What worried her was the possibility of their spawning a sprout. So she said, "You know how your mom feels about this, Leigh."

"Not really. She doesn't talk much about sex. I don't think she likes it."

"Of course she likes it," Annie argued. Teke had never complained about sex to her, and they'd been the best of friends for years. "I think she's afraid of giving you guys ideas."

The two in the bed exchanged a look.

"What?" Annie prodded.

Jon said, "We already have ideas. Hell, Mom, half our friends are doing it. And these walls aren't made of stone. We hear you and Dad."

Annie blushed. "You do not. We're very careful." The words were barely out of her mouth when the phone rang. The color drained from her face.

Jon picked up before she could reach it. After infinitely long seconds, during which her fear for Michael went wild, he said, "It's for Dad. The *Globe*."

"Oh, God," she breathed in relief, then added, "Poor Dad. Such an incredible milestone in his career." Wishing nothing more for Sam at that moment than that he could bask in the glory he deserved, she returned to her own bedroom.

Sam was emerging from yet another shower. He knotted a towel around his waist and picked up the phone.

Sinking down against the headboard, Annie pulled the quilt to her waist. Watching him was a pleasurable activity. She had been doing it for more than twenty years and hadn't tired of it once. He had aged well. His body was more defined—shoulders broader, hips more lean, chest hairier. Years of smiles had etched joy lines by his eyes. His hair was thick, cocoa-colored, and well styled, as was the mustache that had matured along with him.

His face was drawn now, though. He was heartsick about Michael.

"They wanted a statement," he told her as he hung up.

Pushing aside the quilt, she rose to her knees and wound her arms around his neck. His skin was damp and clean-smelling. She rubbed her cheek against his jaw. "I'm so proud of you, Sam. This case was an incredible one to win."

"The time was right," he said quietly.

"Not the time. You. Another lawyer wouldn't have done what you did. From the start the case promised to be a killer, yet you took it on with no promise of pay."

"Yeah," he said, the voice of self-derision, "and now I'm cashing in."

She took his face in her hands. "You worked hard. You deserve your percentage." But that wasn't the main point. "You went out on a limb for a cause. It takes a sensitive, dedicated man to do that. I just wish the timing had been different. I wish you could be ecstatic."

"Yeah. Well."

She looped her arms around his neck. "I wish *we* could. I'm sorry I missed you yesterday. I took my TAs to lunch. I haven't had much of a chance to get to know them. I couldn't have missed you by more than half an hour."

He stared unhappily at the window.

"Michael will be fine, Sam."

He made a pained sound and looked down at her. His eyes moved over her face with a mix of sadness and hunger. His arms went around her and, for a minute, held her so tightly that they shook.

"He'll be fine," she whispered.

"I love you."

"Oh, Sam."

He gave her a deep, desperate kiss—but broke it off when his body began to harden. Annie might have wished it differently, but she understood. He had to get dressed and head into town. She had to get the kids fed, dress herself, and get to school.

Fortunately, getting the kids fed was a snap in her house. Whereas Teke would have put out a spread of fresh-squeezed orange juice, scrambled eggs, and homemade waffles, breakfast at Annie's was simpler. She brewed coffee and drank a cup while the kids poured themselves juice, helped themselves to cereal, made toast, or, in the case of the girls, spooned up low-fat yogurt.

Sam's case had made the front page. That occupied them for a time. When the papers were put aside and the silence went on, Annie knew they were thinking about Michael. She didn't push them to talk. It was enough that they knew she was there.

They were on their way out the door when Sam came downstairs. He was wearing a gray pin-striped suit, blue shirt, and rep tie. It was one of his more conservative outfits and clearly went with his mood. He helped himself to coffee and drank it while he skimmed the paper.

"Don't want anything to eat?" Annie asked.

"Nah. My stomach's in knots." He put the empty cup in the sink. "I'll stop at the hospital on the way in. Want me to call you from there?"

She nodded and raised her face for his kiss.

Five minutes later she was in the shower. Thirty minutes after that she was diffused dry, lightly made up, and dressed for work. She called the hospital again, only to receive a repeat of the earlier report. She wished she could talk with Teke, but for that, Teke would have to call her. Annie was surprised that she hadn't. She usually did when she was upset.

Sam called to say that Michael was the same, that J.D. had gone to the office, that Teke was tired but holding up.

"I should be there," Annie said. "I think I'll cancel my classes. Teke should have someone with her."

"No. Go to school. J.D. said he'd be back in an hour. I'll stay until then."

"J.D. isn't good with illness. Teke needs someone to lean on."

But Sam was insistent. "I asked her. She said you should go to class. She'll feel worse if you're here."

"Worse?"

"Guilty taking you away from school. Wait, Annie. Come in after class. Maybe there'll be some improvement by then."

Annie prayed it would be so. She didn't need a medical degree to know that the longer Michael remained unconscious, the more ominous it was. Heavy of heart, she packed her briefcase with the papers she had abandoned the afternoon before and was in the process of ferreting her car keys from the kitchen basket when there was a knock at the back door.

It was Virginia Clinger. She was dressed in a lavender warm-up suit, had her blond hair arranged with artful negligence around a lavender sweatband, wore lavender shadow above perfectly applied liner over neatly mascaraed eyes, and reeked of Obsession.

Annie Pope wasn't the catty sort. She believed that the beauty of life lay in diversity, which was why she welcomed exposure to, and appreciated the strengths of, a wide variety of people. There were very few whom she disliked.

Virginia was one of those few. She was thrice divorced and had three difficult children—which would have evoked Annie's sympathy if Virginia had been at all devoted to those children, but she wasn't. Her major goal in life was self-beautification. She was sculpted in a way that Annie called "Styrofoam chic." Moreover she was a gossip and a busybody.

Annie produced a polite smile. "Hi, Virginia. I was just getting ready to leave."

"There's no answer at the Maxwells'," Virginia said without apology. "Are they all at the hospital?"

"Teke and J.D. are. The girls will be there later."

"How is Michael?"

"The same."

Virginia clicked her tongue. "Such a tragedy."

"Not yet." Annie hurried to ward off a flurry of negative talk. "With a little luck, he'll wake up and be just fine." She returned to the table for her briefcase.

Virginia stepped into the kitchen. She tipped her head in a pretty little pose of curiosity that Annie suspected was well practiced. "What happened, do you think?"

"What do you mean?"

"What made him run into the street that way?"

"He was in a rush to get back to school. The pick-up was going slowly. He may not have heard it."

"Had he been talking with Sam and Teke?"

"Not to my knowledge."

"That's funny. I could have sworn I saw him running from the house. What was Sam doing there?"

Annie picked up her keys. "He came home looking for me."

"Because of his case?"

"Uh-huh."

"That was quite some win," Virginia remarked. "He must have been wild with excitement. I wasn't sure *what* to think at first. When he and Teke rushed out after Michael, she was wearing nothing but a bathrobe, and his shirt was undone, and his belt. A stranger would have thought something was going on between them, but I know how close your families are. He was probably about to change his clothes when he decided to run over and tell Teke the news."

"You're right," Annie said dryly. "You know how close our families are." What Virginia didn't know—and what Annie wasn't about to disclose—was Sam's taste in celebrations. Annie could just picture him loping into the house and starting to undress as he climbed the stairs to her office. Her heart broke that she hadn't been there. It was a thought she wanted to be alone with.

She touched her watch. "I have to be going." She took Virginia by the arm and gently guided her to the door. "Thanks for stopping by. I'll tell Teke you were here."

"Definitely," Virginia said, and jogged off with a wave.

Within minutes Annie had started her car and pulled out of the garage.

The phone rang four times before the answering machine clicked on. Disappointed, Sam hung up. He had wanted to catch Annie again before she left home. He had to talk with her about what he had done.

After leaving the phone booth, he started down the hospital corridor, berating himself with every step. He should have told her right away, should have taken her aside the minute she had arrived at the hospital the day before. But she had been with the girls, who were terrified for Michael. He hadn't wanted to make things worse.

So he had remained silent. And he could stay that way, he supposed, and save Annie the hurt. What had happened with Teke was an isolated event that would never, ever be repeated. He had never been unfaithful before and hadn't intended to be unfaithful then. In the sense that Annie had been the one on his mind, he hadn't been unfaithful at all. But that was a crude rationalization. The blunt facts were that he had screwed Teke. And that Michael knew. And that Virginia knew. And that even if being caught and exposed weren't an issue, his conscience wouldn't let him be still—because he and Annie talked about everything. There was something between them— Annie called it a soul wire—that ensured communication. It had been there from the first, had been one of the things that had drawn him to her twenty-plus years before, and in the ensuing years he had never met another woman with whom he felt as free. He couldn't hide anything from her. If he tried, their relationship would be sabotaged by the silence, just as surely as it might be by the truth.

He headed on foot up Cambridge Street in the direction of the office. Halfway there he changed his mind and climbed Beacon Hill. By the time he reached the top and the public phones opposite the State House, he figured Annie was at school.

He tried her office number. The department secretary told him she had stopped in for a minute,
then gone straight to class.

He hung up the phone and walked on, not toward
the office but in the opposite direction. The day was
hazy, warm for October, but the warmth was only
partly to blame for the growing dampness of his
skin. Nervousness made him sweat. So did fear.

Crossing the Boston Common, he entered the
Public Garden, walked up the main path to the highest point of the bridge over the pond, and propped
his elbows on the rail. The swan boats had retired
for the season. So had the best of the flowers. True,
the trees were still lush, but shortly they, too, would
fade, turn color, and shrivel. He hated fall.

"Hey, Sam!"

He straightened at the call. Seconds later his
hand was being pumped by Brian Hennessey, with
whom he'd worked in the DA's office years before.
As a lawyer Brian was a hack. But he was a nice
enough guy.

"Good goin', Sam! That was some decision!"

Sam barely remembered reading the decision.

"You're the talk of the town. Got great coverage
in both papers and mentions on the evening news.
You'll go down in history, pal."

"I don't know about that. Cases come and go."

"Not this one. Decide to run for office tomorrow,
and you'll get the vote of every goddamn woman in
the commonwealth. You went to bat for the abused.
You're the man with a heart to match his drive—isn't
that what channel seven said? You're their hero."

Sam managed a weak smile, weathered a final
slap on his back, and, feeling worse by the minute,
watched Brian walk on.

three

TEKE JERKED AWAKE, TREMBLING AND DISORI-
ented. It was a minute before she got her bearings,
but then she came up from the waiting room chair
and rushed down the hall. Michael was just as she
had left him, a motionless figure shackled to the
stark white sheets by tubes connected to a bank of
bleeping machines.

"You look exhausted, Mrs. Maxwell. Weren't you
able to sleep?"

"Not for long," she told the nurse who came up
beside her. "Has there been any change at all?"

The woman shook her head.

Teke had been praying for improvement, dreaming of it. With a sigh she ran tired hands over her
face. "I should be grateful, I guess. He could be
worse."

As the nurse left and she took her place by
Michael's side, she imagined that her feet slipped back
into practiced grooves in the floor. "Hi, sweetheart."
She finger-combed his hair around the inch-long line of
stitches in an attempt to make him look more human.
"I caught a little sleep. Feeling any better?"

She watched his eyes for the tiniest flicker, but there was none.

"Daddy's gone out, but he'll be back soon. Leigh and Jana will stop by after school, and Annie, Zoe, and Jon. And Sam," she tacked on for good measure, though she tripped slightly on the name. It was hard to know what to say and what not to. She didn't know whether Michael was aware of his surroundings and, if so, how much he remembered of what had happened the day before.

She was haunted by the thought that he was lying there in his silent shell, brooding about what he had seen. She was haunted by the thought that he hated her and by the knowledge that his condition was all her fault.

"I'm sorry," she whispered, "so sorry. I didn't mean for it to happen, Michael." She took his hand between her two, trying to rub life into it. "It was madness. I was sitting there feeling so alone, and he was excited when he came in, and before I knew it, you were slamming the door." Michael made no show of having heard, but she whispered on. "I wasn't thinking. I barely knew what was happening. It meant nothing. Nothing. It was a stupid thing, and it was wrong. If I could turn back the clock, I would. I'd do *anything* to turn back the clock, but I can't. All I can do is hope you'll forgive me."

J.D. would have to forgive her, too. And Annie. She had betrayed them both.

"It was the letter," she blurted out in self-defense. "He never should have written it. He was gone, out of my life. I let him go, just like he told me. Then he sent the letter. Damn it, why did he *do* that?"

Her question hung in the air, like the breath in her throat, while Michael's machines beeped steadily. If he heard what she was saying, he didn't let on.

She released the breath in a tired sigh. "It was a

bad time for you to see what you did. You're no longer a little boy, but not yet a man. You didn't know what to make of what we were doing—well, you knew what was happening, but you didn't know why. You didn't know why Sam was there. You didn't know why it wasn't your father. But I swear," she whispered more urgently, "it never happened before. Since I met your father, I've never been with another man. This was the very first time, the one and *only* time I ever came *close* to being with someone else."

She wondered if Michael heard any of what she was saying. It suddenly became imperative that he did. Clutching his hand more tightly, she begged, "Don't be mad at me, Michael, please? Don't stay this way because of what I've done. If you hate me, okay. I deserve it. I won't tell you you're wrong. I'll even go away if you want. All you have to do is to wake up and tell me, but please wake up. Please? We all love you. We want you with us. Please don't punish us this way. If you don't want to wake up for me, do it for your father. Or for Jana and Leigh. You're their little brother. They adore you."

Closely, so closely, she watched Michael's face, one minute fancying that she had seen movement, the next minute deciding that she hadn't. "Come on, Mikey," she pleaded, "come on."

The nurse arrived with a fresh bottle of intravenous solution.

It was a minute before Teke gathered her composure. Then she asked, "Have you been on this floor long?"

"Two years," the woman said in a kindly way that coaxed Teke on. She had so many questions, so many fears.

"Do you see patterns between cases?"

"Some things are similar, some involuntary movements."

"Would you say that either a patient wakes within the first forty-eight hours or not for a very long time?"

The woman gave her a sympathetic smile. "It's impossible to make generalizations. I've had patients wake up three days after an accident, four days, five, eight, twelve days after. I've had patients wake up two months after, feeling nothing worse than groggy."

"That would be nice," Teke mused, then said in a commanding voice, "Do you hear that, Michael? Sleep, if you want, and wake up feeling nothing worse than groggy. We'll love you for it."

The nurse slipped out. Teke held on to the hope she'd been given until it, too, slipped away. She was so tired. So scared.

She was wondering when J.D. would be by when a movement in the window caught her eye. At first she thought it was him, simply because whoever it was wasn't wearing hospital whites. Then she realized that the height was wrong, as were the coloring, the build, the features, the stance.

All were familiar, though. She had seen them just the day before. Sucking in a breath, she put a hand to her chest and in a flash was thirty years and hundreds of miles in the past. The window was suddenly wavy with old glass and marked the local doctor's storefront office. She was ten, hurting from a dog bite and scared to death of what was in store for her when her father found out. He had a temper, Homer Peasely did, and he had warned her to steer clear of the Tuckers' dogs. But she loved animals, and they usually loved her. She hadn't thought to be bitten.

She had known who Grady Piper was. Everyone in town knew who Grady Piper was. He was two years older than her and nearly as poor, which was why he worked with his father. Between them they kept the town docks and the boats moored there in working order. Grady was as tough of body and coarse of tongue at twelve as many a man three times his age.

The county authorities weren't impressed by that. They wanted him in school. Time and again they visited the docks, led Grady off, then found him truant a week later. They threatened to take his father to court and send Grady to a school for delinquents, but so far it hadn't happened.

On that day, Grady stood in the street and stared at her. Teke didn't know what else to do but stare back. Finally he opened the door and came in.

"What's wrong with her?" he asked the nurse.

"Got dog bit."

He studied the bandage on her leg. "Why's she standing here?"

"She's waitin' for her father."

"Homer Peasely?"

The nurse nodded.

"Does he know to get her?"

"No, but he'll pass by on his way to the shack."

The shack was as close as the tiny town of Gullen came to having a general store. Its shabby front room was crammed with necessities. Its middle room was the post office, its rear room the bar. Homer Peasley didn't give a fig about food or mail, but he was a bear until he downed his second shot of whiskey, and he rarely stopped there.

Grady Piper knew that. Without another word he took Teke by the arm and led her out the door. When he got her home he sat her on the chair by the crumbling hearth, built up a fire, and said, "Rest awhile. Do whatever you do normal for him, then get in bed. If he don't see the bandage till morning, you'll be fine."

"But I got to pay the doctor," she whispered.

"Doctor'll wait," Grady said, and left.

She made supper, as usual, then got in bed. Homer was drunk enough when he came home not to notice her, and come morning she hid the bandage under overalls. Homer never found out about the dog bite, the doctor never came around for money, and Teke became Grady Piper's shadow. In time she became far more than that. The memory brought equal parts joy and pain.

With a blink she returned to the present, and at first her vision was so blurred that she thought he had gone. Then she saw that he stood there still, and something akin to panic seized her.

Go! her mind cried as it had once before. He couldn't stay. J.D. didn't know. He would be livid. He wouldn't understand. And she—she couldn't cope with Grady again. Not after so much, so long. Not with Michael at death's door and—*my God—his* truck having been the culprit. *Go!* she screamed silently. *Go!*

That long-ago time, he hadn't listened. He had come into her home and changed their lives forever. He must have learned his lesson, though, because now he stared at her for a last, agonized minute, then turned and walked down the hall.

Sam didn't get through to Annie, though he tried half a dozen times. In guilt-ridden moments he wondered if she knew the truth and was avoiding him. But the secretary's claim that she was running from class to meeting to class was plausible. She would be trying to get ahead on things so that she could spend more time with Teke.

He feared for that relationship when Annie found out the truth. Even more, he feared for his marriage.

He was thinking that he didn't deserve her love,

but that it made his life work and that he couldn't live without it, when J.D. burst into his office looking smug as could be. "I knew they'd find dirt if they looked," he crowed. When Sam eyed him blankly, he announced, "The driver of that pickup isn't so innocent after all. I called our illustrious police chief this morning. I told him there had to be something on the man and that he'd better look for it if he wanted his contract renewed." He made a face. "Hell, wasn't he wondering what the guy was doing there? They said he wasn't speeding. They said he was going slow. Well, *why* was he going slow? He sure wasn't looking to buy a house, not in *our* neighborhood. Was he meeting someone about a job? Or was he staking out the area with a break-in in mind?"

"What did they find?" Sam asked.

J.D. slipped his hands into his pockets and rocked back on his heels. "He's an ex-con named Grady Piper. He served eight years of a twenty-year sentence for—are you ready?—murder."

Sam came forward on his seat. "Murder?"

"Murder. How's *that* for finding something fishy."

Sam sat back again. He could feel the defense attorney in him coming to life. "Just because the man spent time for murder doesn't mean he's guilty of anything here." His phone buzzed.

"Come on, Sam. A thug's a thug. You know that. You work with these people all the time."

Sam pressed the intercom button. "Yes, Joy?"

"A writer for *Lawyers Weekly* is on the phone."

"Take a number. I'll call back." He released the button and returned to J.D. "What else has the guy done?"

"Isn't murder enough?"

"That's it? Just murder? How long has he been on the streets?"

"A while, but—"

"How long?"

"Fourteen years."

"After serving eight of twenty. Is he still on parole?"

"No, but—"

"You don't have a case, J.D. You can't condemn the man because he committed a crime twenty-three years ago. He paid the price. He did his time. Unless someone can prove that he's done something else, or that he broke a law when he drove down your street, forget it."

"I won't forget it," J.D. said with an indignation that struck Sam as pure J.S. "If a little looking turned up a murder conviction, just think of what a little *more* looking will turn up."

Gently, because he knew how often it happened and how much it bothered J.D., Sam asked, "Is John Stewart on your back?"

"I don't need John Stewart to tell me how to look out for my son," J.D. snapped. "I want to know what that man was doing on my street."

"It's a public street."

"And he's an ex-con from nowhere."

"He may have been lost, or sight-seeing."

"He hurt my son, damn it!"

Sam wanted to remind him that Michael had run into the man's truck, not the other way around, but he knew that wasn't what J.D. wanted to hear. In a quiet voice he said, "You're barking up the wrong tree, J.D."

"Where's your *imagination*, Sam? You're the expert on criminal prosecution. You're the courtroom genius. They can get him on something. All we have to do is figure out what."

Sam accepted then that J.D. couldn't hear what he was saying, and he understood. It was J.D.'s son lying comatose, not his. J.D. was upset. He was frustrated. He wanted to do something, anything, to avenge Michael.

Sam tried to imagine what J.D. would do when he found out what Michael had seen. And he would find out—though not from Sam. Sam had done enough harm already. No, Teke was J.D.'s wife. She would have to be the one to tell him. Or Michael, when he woke up.

"Did you reach the Mayo Clinic?" he asked.

J.D. looked away in disgust. He put his hands on his hips. "Yeah. No help there. Henry Finch is delivering seminars in Paris for the next two weeks. I spoke with his second in command and told him about Michael. He said that Gardner's team is first class and that from what I told him, he wouldn't do anything different from what's being done. Which is nothing," he added sourly.

Sam rose and rounded the desk to put an encouraging hand on his shoulder. "They're doing all they can."

"Which is nothing," J.D. repeated, pulling away. He went to the door. "I'm suing the school for negligence. I want you to handle the case."

Sam doubted the Maxwells had a case, but he could go through the preliminary motions as well as any other lawyer. He would do it out of loyalty—and guilt. With a little luck Michael would wake up and be well, in which case J.D. would rethink bringing suit.

"And the police," J.D. added. "Stay on their backs. They'll listen to you before they'll listen to me. You were a prosecutor. And you're not as emotionally involved as I am."

He disappeared, leaving Sam wishing it were so.

The minute Annie pulled up at the high school, the three girls clambered into the car, slammed the doors, and began talking all at once.

"Finally—"

"We thought you'd *never* get here—"

"It's so embarrassing—"

"You won't believe what that twerp said—"

"He's telling *everyone*—"

"*All* over school—"

"Quiet!" Annie cried. She was sitting sideways, looking from one disturbed face to the next. In a soft, calm voice she said, "You're the oldest, Leigh. Please tell me what you're so upset about."

Leigh's cheeks were flushed, a deviation from her usual patrician pallor. She was J.D. in looks, Teke in femininity. "He started a rumor—"

"*Who* started a rumor?"

"Will Clinger. What a *loser!* He can't get people to pay attention to him because he's a dork, so he spreads rumors."

"What rumor is he spreading?" Annie asked.

"It's garbage!" Jana cried.

Zoe chimed in, "He's a troublemaker!"

"What rumor?" Annie repeated, still facing Leigh.

Leigh's nostrils flared. "He's running all over school saying that Sam and Mom were messing around when Michael was hurt yesterday."

"Messing around." Annie conjured an immediate, absurd picture of Sam and Teke digging up dirt in the garden as they planted fall bulbs.

"Sex, Mom," Zoe said from behind.

Annie swiveled to stare at her. *"What?"*

"He is *so stupid.*"

"It's his mother," Jana said, folding her arms. "She doesn't like us because we are who we are. We're successful and we're normal, everything they are *not.* She's a bitch."

"Please," Annie begged, "let's not have that language."

"But she is," Jana insisted. "She was the one who

started the rumor. She said she saw Mom and Sam run out of the house after Michael, and that they were barely dressed. She said Sam had to *fasten his pants* right there in the middle of the street! Can you believe that? What a *bitch* she is."

Annie took a breath. "I still don't like that word, but if Virginia is indeed saying that"—and it was consistent with the visit she'd had that morning—"it may fit."

"And a liar," Leigh added.

"Why would she *say* it?" Zoe asked.

"I told you why," Jana answered. "She's jealous. The Clinger fortune isn't a fortune anymore. Her alimony is going down the tubes right along with the rest of the real estate in town. She didn't get a new car this year. We did. So she's pissed."

"Don't like that word, either," Annie mumbled, but Jana went on.

"He's blabbing all over school, trying to score points, at *our* expense. It's not fair!"

Zoe scrunched up her face. "It's so embarrassing."

"It's so *untrue*," Jana informed her archly. "My mother wouldn't cheat on my father!"

"Any more than *my* father would cheat on *my* mother!"

"Jon was livid," Leigh interrupted. "He would have punched Will if I hadn't held him back. That would have been awful. He'd have been put on detention for fighting in school, and missed practice and maybe the game Saturday, and Will would have felt important." She made a sputtering sound and muttered, "Loser," under her breath.

When Annie started the car, Zoe leaned over her shoulder. "Aren't you furious?"

Annie felt the warmth of her breath and reached back to touch her cheek. Zoe was a cuddler. Annie swore she had been a cuddler in the womb, so content there that she had refused to be born until three weeks after she was due. From the start she had been sweet and gentle. Annie loved that in her, even if it made her vulnerable to things that others could shrug off.

"I'm annoyed," Annie told her now. "Virginia should have known better than to say things like that to her children."

"She does it all the time," Jana said. "That's why the Clinger kids are crazy."

Annie relented. "They're not crazy. They just have difficult parents." She flashed Jana a grin. "They're not as lucky as you, that way."

"So what do we do?" Jana asked. "By seventh period everyone was talking."

"They'll be talking about something else by tomorrow."

"No, they won't," Leigh said. "It was sounding like a soap opera. They'll want to know what happens next."

"Nothing happens next, because nothing happened at all."

"That's not what the kids think," Zoe said.

Annie was skeptical. "They believe Will? Who just said the kids thought he was a dork?"

"I did," Leigh admitted, "but once the rumor spreads, people forget who started it. You wouldn't *believe* how many people came up to me at lunch and asked whether my parents were getting divorced."

"Tell them no," Annie said.

"I did, so they asked if Michael had seen them doing it."

"Tell them *no.*"

"I *did,* so they asked how I knew, and I didn't have an answer. No one knows what Michael saw but him, and he's not telling."

Zoe leaned even closer. "Has he said anything?"

"No. He's still unconscious."

"I kept calling to ask," Leigh said. "The nurses must know my voice by now."

"Can't they *do* anything?" Jana asked. "Can't they zap him with something to snap him out of it? All you read about is the high cost of medical care. What *are* we paying them for?"

Annie had to smile. Jana was so much like J.D. sometimes, so imperious, so expectant. "We're paying them to keep a close eye on your brother, so that when he reaches a point where they *can* do something to snap him out of it, they'll be there."

The girls quieted down, and Annie blessed them. They were more concerned about Michael than about Will Clinger's big mouth.

Annie shared those priorities, but she did worry about the mouth, and she wasn't thinking of Will's. Virginia's was worse. Virginia talked wherever she went, and she went places—the beauty shop, the manicurist, the health club—where people listened. And those people went every which way, spreading the news. The woman had to be stopped.

Idle gossip was an ugly thing. It planted doubts. If Annie didn't have total faith in her husband, she might be wondering at that very moment if there was any truth to Virginia's claim. She might, indeed, be wondering why Sam had been half-dressed at midday. She might be wondering if his upset was purely for Michael or whether there was more to it. She might be wondering about those three long showers.

But she had total faith in her husband. Total faith.

Sam arrived at the hospital to find Teke dozing on a chair by Michael's bed. He didn't risk waking her by talking aloud to Michael, simply stood looking down at the boy.

He remembered when Michael had been born—Teke's little surprise, they had called him, though no one had ever ascertained whether the surprise had been fate's on Teke or Teke's on everyone else. J.D. believed the first. He had wanted to stop at two children and blamed Michael's creation on a faulty birth control device. He would have sued Teke's gynecologist if Sam hadn't called him an asshole. When Michael had proved to be a boy, all misgiving was forgotten.

Sam suspected Teke had planned that third child. She loved mothering and did it well. She hadn't ever been interested in working outside the home as Annie did and was perfectly content to sign for UPS deliveries, run to school in the middle of the day when the kids got sick, referee backyard squabbles, and provide lemonade, oatmeal cookies, and Band-Aids.

He studied her as she slept. She was a striking woman, no denying it. Homebody she might be, but there was an earthiness to her that men found attractive. J.D. had been captivated when Sam and Annie had fixed them up, though on paper Teke had been all wrong for him. She came from nowhere, had two duffel bags filled with clothes, a thousand dollars in the bank, and little else. Marrying her had been J.D.'s first major act of rebellion.

No. That was wrong. J.D.'s first major act of rebellion had been befriending Sam, who had been nearly as unacceptable to the senior Maxwells as Teke. That thought haunted Sam now. He wondered if they had had a telescope to the future, if they had somehow known years before what would happen.

He couldn't believe it. He and Teke. Looking at her now, he felt no desire whatsoever, but then, the desire he had felt hadn't been for her. He loved and desired his wife.

Total faith.Annie repeated the phrase once more when she turned into Michael's room a step behind the girls and saw Teke dozing on the chair with Sam nearby.

"How is he?"

"Is he awake?"

"Any change?"

With the hushed chorus, the girls gathered around the bed. Annie slid an arm around Sam's waist. He did the same and kissed her, though she felt an odd tension in him. But of course he was worried about Michael. She echoed the girls' questions with a look.

"He's holding his own," Sam said.

Teke stretched, opened her eyes, and gave the girls a thin smile. "How was school?"

"Okay."

"Hard."

"Boring," came the assessment from Zoe, Leigh, and Jana, respectively.

"It's be better if we could be here," Zoe said.

"Michael?" Leigh coaxed, leaning over him. "Come on, Michael, it's us. Time to wake up and say hi."

Jana propped her backpack on the railing and opened one of the flaps. "I have cards, Mike." She took out a huge handful. "They're from the eighth-grade class. The twins ran them over at lunchtime. Homeroom this morning was dedicated to you."

Leigh was looking at Teke. "Are you okay?"

Teke repeated the same thin smile and nodded.

Annie was looking at Teke, too, though without a return. "Have you eaten?" she asked, trying for eye contact.

Teke darted her a quick glance before closing her eyes and resting her head against the back of the chair. "A little. The nurses bring me things."

"Can I bring you something more? A sandwich? A drink?"

Teke gave a tiny head shake. "But thanks."

Annie kept trying. "Why don't I drive you home for a shower and a change of clothes?"

Teke opened her eyes to Michael's inert form in a way that said she couldn't leave him that long.

"Annie and I are going for a walk," Sam said quietly. "We'll be back." He slipped his fingers through hers and drew her out of the room.

Annie's heart beat faster. Something about Sam seemed strange. He's heartsick about Michael, she told herself. Twice.

Holding tightly to his hand as they walked, she said, "Poor Teke. "This is a mother's worst nightmare." She looked up at him. "How is J.D.?"

"He's upset. He feels a little better when he's threatening legal action, but that's only to compensate for his helplessness here."

Annie tried to put herself in his shoes. "Maxwells don't like feeling helpless."

"No one does." Sam pushed the elevator button. While they waited for it to arrive, he turned Annie's hand over in his, tracing her fingers, touching her wedding band with his thumb. It was narrow, gently squared, and studded with tiny diamonds, actually a tenth-anniversary gift to replace the plain gold band that had been all he could afford for their wedding. Annie had loved that plain gold band. She still wore it sometimes.

The elevator opened. Two hospital attendants filed out, followed by a man in casual clothes—jeans, a plaid shirt, and a corduroy blazer with lapels wide enough to date it. He looked freshly showered and shaved, but somber. Annie wondered whom he was visiting.

"Do we know that man?" Sam asked as he guided her into the elevator.

She tried to see back down the hall, but the elevator door was closing. "I don't think so."

"He looks familiar. I guess I've passed him here." He leaned against the elevator wall, holding her close by his side.

She raised her face. "Are you okay?"

He shrugged.

"Worried?"

"Ohhhhh, yes."

"Have you been here long?" That would explain his needing to take a walk.

But he said, "Nah."

The car stopped at the floor below, then at each successive floor. It was jammed with people by the time it reached the ground. Sam led her down the corridor and through a swinging door that opened onto a patio strewn with tables and chairs. When he found no two chairs free, he grabbed one from one table, one from another, and set them down as far as possible from the rest. Once Annie was seated he sat beside her, but he was up a second later, shifting the chair on the grass so that it was closer, more head-on, to hers. He sat again, straightened his back against the chair, found that uncomfortable. So he came forward, set his elbows on his thighs, and studied his hands.

She touched his shoulder, hoping to calm him some. "I'm sorry I missed your calls. After Teke and J.D., this has to be hardest on you. You and Michael spend so much time together."

"It's not the time," he said, "it's the closeness. I love the little guy." He frowned. "Funny thing about love. Sometimes it screws you up."

It was a strange statement coming from the Sam she knew. The Sam she knew was positive to a fault. And he rarely studied his hands. "What do you mean?" she asked uneasily. Her thoughts took off in a wayward direction. She reined them back.

"It makes you unable to think straight sometimes." He raised his eyes. "Know what J.D.'s latest cause is?"

Annie felt a wave of relief. So it was *J.D.* he was talking about. "What's his latest cause?"

"He's after the driver of the truck. The man spent time in prison once, so he is condemned forever in J.D.'s eyes." His voice rose. "But that isn't right. Hell, we all make mistakes. We all do things in the heat of passion." He let out a breath and lowered his voice. "Anyway, J.D is sure we can get him for some violation of the law."

"Can you?"

"Not if he hasn't broken any laws, and it sounds like he hasn't. I called the police department before I left the office. They can't find anything other than this one prior conviction. They'll bring the man in and talk with him to appease J.D., but they can't charge him without cause. I feel bad for the guy. He was at the wrong place at the wrong time, just like Mike."

He looked off across the lawn, then at Annie, then down at his hands again.

Her unease returned. "Was that what you wanted to talk to me about?"

He shook his head and continued to scowl at his hands.

What is it, Sam? Tell me, please? I have faith in you. Total faith. "Virginia Clinger stopped at the house this morning right before I left," she began.

He looked up too quickly for Annie's peace of mind.

She swallowed. "Virginia's a difficult woman. I've never liked her. She loves goading people and making them uncomfortable."

"What did she say?"

Annie rolled her eyes to make light of it. "She said—made a *point* to say—that Teke was wearing a bathrobe and that your shirt and belt were undone when you ran into the street after Michael. She would love to think you two were having an affair." Which, of course, was not true. "She actually told the kids that you were, and they happily carried the news to school. Will Clinger has been shooting off his mouth all day. The girls were *livid*."

Sam closed his eyes.

Cold fingers touched Annie's heart. She rushed on. "They denied it, of course. Jon nearly got into a fistfight with Will. It's difficult when kids feel they're the object of whispering. They were insulted for us. I'm not sure what to do, Sam. I'm thinking I ought to go to the Clingers' tonight and confront Virginia. Maybe we ought to go there together. What she's done isn't right. It wouldn't be right under any circumstances, but with Michael in a coma, it's doubly wrong. Doesn't she know that rumors like that cause pain?"

Sam didn't speak.

The cold fingers encircled her heart. "There are explanations for everything," she said, nervously searching his face for a denial. "Teke was in her robe because she'd been doing housework. You were coming apart because you'd been in the bathroom. Everyone knows that the Maxwell house is an extension of ours. We walk in and out. We have each other's keys on our key chains. The idea the Virginia would try to make something out of nothing is infuriating." *Agree with me, Sam. Tell me she's an evil woman. Say something.* "It's not right that she should be spreading rumors." Her voice cracked. Fearful, she stopped speaking.

Still with his elbows on his thighs, Sam took her hand and sandwiched it between his. Her hands felt cold. His hands felt cold. The one around her heart was frigid, making breathing harder.

"Yesterday morning was incredible," he said, eyes down. "I got the call from the clerk of court that the decision was in, so I raced over for a copy. I barely saw the words, I was so excited. By the time I was done, I had one thing in mind."

Look at me, she begged silently. But he didn't.

"I wanted you. I always want you at times like that, and I thought it was so perfect that it was a Tuesday and you'd be at the house. So I drove home, and I was getting more aroused, and then you weren't there. I thought Teke might know where you were, so I went through the woods. She was just sitting in the living room drinking coffee. When I told her my news, she was happy for me. We hugged— we always hug—but then something happened. I was wanting you, and she was there, and it was like I forgot who she was and made love to you—"

"What?" Annie asked in a tiny wisp of breath that escaped the chill spreading inside.

"It was unreal and bizarre—"

Annie started to shiver. She tried to pull her hand away, but he held it fast, tremors and all. Her entire body was shaking. She felt she was splintering apart.

He raised his eyes beseechfully. "I keep asking myself how it happened and what I was thinking and feeling, and how could I have *done* something so stupid, but, so help me God, I was thinking and feeling for you. It happened in a flash and was over, and then the door slammed. Michael must have come in and seen us and raced back out. Then we heard the squeal of brakes. It was a mistake, Annie. I love you, not Teke. What happened in her living room meant nothing."

It was true? But it *couldn't* be. Sam loved her. She had *total faith* in him.

It was *true?* Her eyes filled with tears.

"Say something," he whispered. "Tell me I'm a louse. Tell me I'm a cheat. Tell me I don't deserve my family. Tell me I'm a worthless shit. But say something."

Needing to escape and blot out what he'd said, she tried again to pull her hand back, but he wouldn't release it. So she let it go limp. It shook more than ever.

He kept talking. "I'm so disgusted with myself that it's hard for me to bear my own company for more than a few minutes a sitting. I walked all over town this morning. I kept stopping at phone booths to call you." He paused. "Talk to me Annie."

She felt one tear fall, then another, hot and unreal against the coldness of her skin. "You made love with Teke?" she asked in a disbelieving whisper. Sam wouldn't do that. Not *her* Sam. "Teke's my best friend. She's your best friend's wife."

"I made love with you, but it was her body I used."

Annie struggled with that thought. It didn't make sense. "But *how?* There's no confusing the two of us. Her body's nothing like mine."

"I wasn't looking. So help me God, I didn't see a thing. I was only thinking that I'd had a great victory and that I was sharing the excitement with my wife."

"But it wasn't me, it was *Teke*," she cried. Her chin quivered. *Her* Sam wouldn't do that. "I don't understand. I thought we had it all."

"We do," he pleaded. "The problem isn't our relationship, it's *me. Me.* I'm the one who blew it. I'm the one whose brain wasn't working the right way. I'm the one who let my desire for you spill over into another woman."

She made a face at the *absurdity* of it. *"Teke?"*

"I came home wanting you, Teke was there wanting someone else, and it happened."

"How *could* it happen?"

"I—don't—know."

She sagged into herself. When she tugged at her hand this time, he let it go. She wiped the tears from her cheeks, then wrapped her arms around her middle, rocked a little, stared off into the distance. The cold hand around her heart was spreading a wash of despair. She was stunned and confused. "I never thought this would happen. Not to me."

"It was a mistake. My mistake."

"And Teke's," she said, feeling a spasm of pain. "How *could* she?"

"She's being punished for it."

"She was my best friend."

"She still is. She loves you. *I* love you."

Annie met his eyes, but they looked different. He was different. A stranger. Surely. Her Sam would never hurt her this way. Distancing herself, she asked rationally, "Does J.D. know?"

"No."

"Will you tell him?"

"That's Teke's job."

"She'd better do it before Virginia does." She closed her eyes and put a hand there. She continued to hug herself with the other. It seemed the only thing holding her together. The distancing wasn't working. "Oh, God," she whispered, "I feel sick."

"No more than me."

"What do I do?"

"You give me a chance to make things right."

She felt a quick, raw fury toward this man who was

her Sam, but not. Lowering her hand, she stared at him. "Make things right? You betrayed me *and* your best friend by screwing my best friend, and now their son is fighting for his life, and you want to *make* things *right?*" Unable to sit a second longer, she bolted from the chair and strode angrily across the grass.

"Where are you going?" Sam called, coming after her, sounding frightened. "To see Michael?"

"No. I don't want to see Teke." *Teke.* Her *best friend.* And *Sam. Her husband.*

"Are you going home?"

"I don't know." She turned to him then, with fresh tears in her eyes and a world of a hurt in her voice. "I have to think. I don't—this isn't—I haven't had any experience with—I don't know what to do."

"I'll come."

"No!" She knew that much. "I don't want you!" She ran off.

He followed. "You're upset. You shouldn't be alone."

"But I *am* alone!" she cried, and whirled on him a final time. She was shaking again. "That's what's so *awful* about this. From the day we met, I felt there was someone who knew all I was thinking and feeling. I gave you everything that was me. I trusted you completely. *Trusted* you." She started to cry.

"Annie—"

She whirled around and ran on.

"I *love* you, Annie."

She ran faster, then faster still, uncaring about the sobs that came from her throat or the tears from her eyes. She only knew that if she could outrun all he'd said, it might not be true after all.

Distraught, Sam started after her, then stopped. She was petite, vulnerable looking, and sometimes prone to the dramatic, but she had a grip on herself. She might walk around for a while, or get in the car and drive, but she wouldn't do anything rash.

He wanted to be with her. Desperately so. But he was the last one she wanted to see. He was the offending party. He had to respect her wish.

Feeling a great heaviness inside, he started walking slowly toward the hospital. Halfway there he stopped. Parked where he hadn't noticed it during his dismal confession to Annie was a police car from Constance-on-the-Rise.

His first thought was that something had happened to Annie, but he could still see her, albeit growing more distant. His second thought was that they had come for him—he was feeling so guilty. His third thought was that something had happened to Jon.

His head was filled with visions of a football injury or a car crash. He was about to run over and ask when two officers from Constance emerged from the hospital. Between them was the man who had left the elevator earlier, the man Sam had found so familiar.

Only then did he identify that man as a cleaned-up version of the one whose pickup had collided with Michael.

four

LIFE HAD CONDITIONED GRADY PIPER TO expect the worst. He hadn't had any childhood to speak of, had never known a real home or experienced much by way of human softness other than the little he'd stolen with Teke, and even that had been taken from him. For years he had lived day to day, neither planning for the future nor dreaming. Without expectations he couldn't be hurt.

Or so he reasoned, just as he reasoned that having lived through hell, he could take most any grief. He was tough as nails. So he reasoned.

Fact was, he was totally shaken by what had happened. He was shattered when he thought of the little boy and devastated when he thought of Teke.

"The problem," the policeman explained as they sat in a borrowed interrogation room several blocks from the hospital, "is that Constance is a pretty exclusive place. Carpenters who drive through usually have a destination. We need to know what yours was."

Grady tried to stay calm. He told himself that he was only being questioned, that the cops were just doing their jobs, that he hadn't broken any law and couldn't be charged. Still, he felt the chill of a reawakening terror. Once, he had experienced the ultimate in law enforcement. The horror of it could surge back with as innocent a thing as the yellow VIOLATION tab in an expired parking meter.

"I had no destination," he said. He couldn't very well say he was looking for Teke. That would spark a whole new set of questions and might well cause Teke trouble. Lord knew he'd done enough of that. "I was just driving down the street."

"Looking for what?" officer asked.

"Work. Prosperous townfolk are always repairing and renovating."

"Why Constance? We're not on a highway, sure not on one coming from Maine. But you're right. We are prosperous. A thief might think he'd made a find."

Grady looked the man in the eye. "I wasn't looking to rob anyone. I was minding my own business. I was driving slowly. The boy ran out. I stopped best I could, but the damage was done. I talked with you at the scene and again at the station in Constance. I told you where you could find me, and you did. I haven't lied to you yet."

"The question is whether you told the whole truth," the officer said, and came forward. "You're an ex-con. We know that. And we know what you served time for. Now, don't you think we have a right to wonder what a murderer is doing driving around our streets?"

Grady had known they would find out. The chill inside him deepened. "I served my time. I been out fourteen years."

"Doesn't change what you are," said the second officer, who came toward him with his hands on his hips. One was tauntingly close to his gun. "We're a nice, peaceful town, Mr. Piper. Unemployed carpenters don't joy-ride round our streets. They don't sit in our coffee shops. They don't bed down in our park." Idly he tapped the leather holster. "Where'd you sleep last night?"

Grady had a feeling he knew; still he said, "The motel on the edge of town."

"Why?"

"I had nowhere else to stay."

"Why'd you stay at all?"

"Because of the boy. I told you. I couldn't leave without knowing how he was."

"So now you know. Are you leaving?"

Grady shook his head.

"Why not?"

For the first time Grady felt a flicker of anger. He might have murdered a man once, but he wasn't a coldhearted son of a bitch. "Because the boy's unconscious. I can't leave until I know if he'll make it."

"He could be unconscious for a while."

Grady shrugged. He'd stay for as long as it took.

"You got enough money to hole up at a motel that long?"

"I got money."

"Where'd you get it?"

Grady's nostrils flared. His anger grew, hot against the chill that pooled deep in his gut. "Am I under arrest?"

"Where'd you get the money?"

Grady asked the first officer, "Am I being charged?"

"No," the man said, and called off his partner with a look. When his eyes returned to Grady's, they were quieter. "You didn't break any law that we can see. But you have to understand our situation. Constance is a special kind of town. It isn't known for what happens, but for what doesn't happen. We don't have drug pushers on the front steps of the school. We don't have hookers on street corners. We don't have rape. And we don't have murder."

Grady didn't blink. That didn't mean he didn't wonder how many of the citizens of Constance cheated on their income taxes or on their spouses. He'd had many a wealthy customer over the years. He knew what they did.

"What happened to the Maxwell boy yesterday," the officer went on, "is upsetting to the whole town. They want to know how it happened, so it doesn't happen again."

"I told you how it happened."

"They also want to know all they can about the man driving the truck. Now, fine. We know who you are and where you're from. What we want to know is when you're leaving." He smiled. "The news that you'd gone back to where you came from would make our folks feel a whole lot better."

Grady's anger swelled far above his fear. *Fuck your folks,* he wanted to say. *This is a free country. I want to drive down your streets, I'll damn well drive down your streets!* But he had learned the hard way what back talk accomplished, especially back talk to cops. They could get you for pissing, if they were so inclined.

So he deliberately relaxed his mouth, deliberately took a deep breath, deliberately pushed the anger to the back of his mind, and in an even voice said, "I understand your problem, Officer, but I can't leave until I know about the boy. I won't cause your town any harm. I didn't mean any in the first place. If anyone's upset about what happened to that boy, it's me."

"You done worse," the second officer put in.

Grady leveled him a cold stare. "I was convicted of manslaughter. I served my time. I finished my parole. For fourteen years I've been clean. You want to know how I got my money?" He didn't mind telling, didn't mind telling at all, long as he was the one offering to do it. "I got my money working. I started in construction, sunup to sundown. Then I met a carpenter who took a liking to me. He was the first kind man I ever knew besides my father. For five years he taught me the trade."

"D'ya steal his customers?"

"I paid him referral fees," Grady said tightly. "Even when his cancer got so bad and I was getting the customers on my own, I paid him. Then I paid for his funeral. I've had a few other expenses, but not many, so I have money in the bank. I don't have to steal from your homes. I don't have to sell drugs to your kids. And if I want to stay in that motel on the edge of town for two years, I can pay the bill in advance. I wouldn't, though. That motel's not worth it. Even *I've* stayed in nicer ones." He rose and faced the first officer, who wore an amused look. "Any other questions?"

The officer shook his head.

"I can go?"

"We'll drive you back to the hospital," he said, and started to rise, but Grady held up a hand.

"I'll walk." Without so much as a glance at the second officer, he left the room. He walked down the hall holding his breath, half expecting to be called back. Tempering the urge to run, he walked down the stairs to the first floor, pushed open the door, and went through. He stood on the stone steps for a minute, drawing air into his lungs that was dirty with the pollution of thousands of home-bound cars, but fresh and free and his to draw in. Then, on legs that hadn't been steady since hitting his brakes hard the day before, he set off in the direction of the hospital.

He held his head high, kept his eyes straight

ahead even when the cruiser from Constance passed him. Only when it had disappeared, and the police station was too far behind for Big Brother to read his mind, did he think about the whole truth. The whole truth was that the boy's condition was only one of the reasons he couldn't leave. The other was Teke. He had come to see her. He wouldn't leave until he had done that.

In a ragged spill of moonlight, Annie wrapped her arms around her knees and rocked in her corner of the window seat. Moving helped. It fought the chill and distracted her from the pain. But the confusion lingered, and the disbelief. She was too weary to blot them out.

"Mom?" came a tiny voice from the door.

It startled her. Normally, even three floors up, she heard the sounds of the house, but she hadn't heard the garage door. Her mind was a cell padded with torment.

Soft as a zephyr, Zoe flew across the floor. "Where *were* you?" she whispered with a hug. "We were so worried."

"I had to leave," Annie whispered back.

"Daddy said you were upset."

"Things got to me. I didn't think I could help." She shifted so that she was the hugger rather than the huggee. "How's Michael?"

"The same."

She was about to ask how Teke was, but a slash of pain deleted the words. "How's everyone else holding up?"

"Okay."

"Did you have dinner?"

"Uh-huh. We went to an Italian place near the hospital. J.D. was in a snit."

Annie's heart went out to J.D. He had been betrayed just as she had. He would be in far more than a snit when he learned the truth. She couldn't begin to imagine his fury. And against *Sam.* They had been best friends for so long. It was tragic.

"Why was J.D. in a snit?" she asked Zoe.

"The guy who was driving the pickup came to the hospital to see Michael."

"What a nice thing for him to do!"

"That was what I thought, but not J.D. He was furious."

"Did he *say* anything to the fellow?"

"No. The guy was leaving when we were coming back from dinner. One of the nurses mentioned who he was—she thought it was nice of him, too. I think J.D. would have run after him, but the man was gone by then. So he started interrogating the nurse. When she said that it wasn't the first time the man has been by, J.D. hit the roof. But the nurse said that he just stands in the hall and looks at Michael. He never stays long, she said. He never goes into the room. She said she's seen it before in cases like this, that he's probably feeling terrible about what happened."

"What did J.D. say to that?"

"He said the man was a no good slime, and that he was only there for show. Jana thought so, too. She thought he should stay away."

"But it wasn't his fault."

"I told Jana that. She said that he may not have broken any laws, but that if he'd been watching where he was going, he wouldn't have hit Michael."

"He didn't hit Michael, Michael hit him," Annie said, and in the next breath felt an awful pain. Michael had hit the truck because he had run blindly from the house, because he had seen Teke and Sam making . . . making . . .

"That was what I said," Zoe went on, "and Jana got mad at me. She said I was being disloyal to Michael."

Making love? Having sex? Copulating? Annie didn't know what to call it. One word was as upsetting as the next. *Sam* and *Teke?* It hurt so much.

"Am I being disloyal?" Zoe asked.

Not you, honey, Annie thought as she looked into her daughter's upturned face. The moonlight on it was frail, painting even greater vulnerability there. Annie suspected her own face looked much the same.

"No," she whispered, pulling Zoe to her again. She felt herself start to cry, which was surprising. She had thought herself all cried out.

"Mom?"

Annie held her tighter. After a minute, brokenly, she said, "It's an upsetting time."

"Are you okay?" Zoe asked, sounding frightened.

"Just feeling raw."

"Mom?" came another, deeper voice, followed by Jonathan's materialization in the moonshine. "Why are you up here in the dark?"

Annie brushed at her tears with the back of her hand. "I needed thinking time. That's all."

"Why did you leave so suddenly?"

"Everything just hit me suddenly."

"We were all worried. Especially Teke. Dad said he thought you'd gone home, but he wasn't sure."

Annie hadn't been sure, either. She had left the hospital, driving blindly, crying freely, with no plan in mind but escaping the truth. More than once she had thought to keep driving and driving until she was lost in a world totally new. Increasingly, though, her hands took familiar turns until, eventually, she was home. Which was right. Because, severed as she felt from Sam, she still had the kids.

"I'm right here," she said with a teary smile. She held out an arm to Jon and slipped it around his waist when he gave her a hug. She was blessed to have children like these. Particularly now.

Particularly now. The tears came again, along with the image of Sam and Teke together. Her stomach turned, and for a minute she thought she might be sick. Except that she had been sick before. There was nothing left to throw up.

She sniffled and managed a watery, "I'm sorry. This is difficult for me."

"Michael will be all right," Jon assured her.

"I know." With final squeezes to Zoe and him, she said, "Go on downstairs. I'll be down in a bit."

Jon went. Zoe was slower in leaving. "Are you sure you're all right?"

"Uh-huh," Annie lied.

"You seemed okay in the car. I thought you were okay when we got to Michael's room. Then you went for a walk with Daddy. Was it the hospital that did it? The machines and all?"

"Something like that."

"Will you be able to take us there tomorrow?"

Annie tried to imagine getting up in the morning and carrying on as usual. But nothing was *as usual* now. Nothing would ever be *as usual* again.

"We'll see," she whispered, then felt so bad for causing Zoe distress that she added, "I'll try. Okay?"

"Okay," Zoe whispered back. "And Mom? About Jana? I know it's tough for her with Michael unconscious and Teke a zombie and J.D. uptight. But what she said wasn't fair. Maybe you could talk to her? Tell her I wasn't being disloyal?"

Annie smoothed the blond waves from her daughter's forehead. "I will."

Zoe gave her a kiss. She was halfway across the floor when Annie heard her say, "She's all yours."

Annie turned to the window. Without light in the room, there was no reflection on the glass. Beyond it, the night was clear and starry, cold as the chill she couldn't seem to shake, cruelly beautiful given the awful upheaval of her life.

"Are you all right?" Sam asked quietly.

She bit her lip to keep from crying again.

He waited. "I was worried."

Good, Annie thought. You deserve it.

"Did you come straight back here?"

"No," she said.

"Drive around some?"

She pushed the heel of her hand higher on her cheek, letting her fingers tangle with the waves framing her face. She wished he would leave her alone. With her wound so raw, his presence hurt.

"Did you have dinner?" he asked.

"I threw up lunch. Dinner would have been a disaster."

"Annie, I'm sorry. I am in absolute agony asking myself why I did what I did and trying to think of ways to make it all better. You have no idea how awful I feel."

Annie slid her palm to cover her eyes. She was could feel the beginnings of a migraine.

"Teke knows you know," he said. "She feels as awful as I do."

Teke. How could he have done it with *Teke?* Annie asked herself for the umpteenth time. At least if he'd had to be unfaithful, he could have picked someone she didn't know. Wasn't that what most men did, created a secret life for themselves, separate from home? That might have been easier for her to bear. Then again, maybe not. Betrayal was betrayal.

"Talk to me, Annie. Please? We always talk."

"We used to. We used to be faithful, too."

"One time. That's it. I did it one time. Five min-utes' worth, maybe less."

She grunted. "You always could be fast when you wanted."

"Annie—"

Her thoughts suddenly exploded. "How *could* you? We took vows, Sam! We swore to be loyal!"

"I didn't plan it."

"With Teke. My best friend. How *could* you?" She had been asking herself that over and over and over again. The thought that Sam might be in love—romantically—with Teke was too painful to consid-er, so she asked, "Was it her looks?"

"Of course not!"

"Some *scent* she has? Or just a curiosity that's been nagging at you for years, that you had to satisfy?"

"For God's sake, Annie, there's no reason to what I did. It was crazy. Insane. Ask me to describe the details of what happened, and I can't. There weren't any details. There wasn't any awareness."

"Did you come?" It was an ugly little fact, haunt-ing her, necessary to make the picture more com-plete.

"What?"

"You heard." If she had to repeat it, she would gag.

He snorted. "Yes, I came. I always come when I'm with you, and in my mind, I was."

"Don't *say* that!" she screamed. "It's an insult to my intelligence!"

"Shhhh."

She lowered her voice. "You should have been thinking of the children then, too. What will *they* think when they find out?"

Sam sighed. "They'll think I'm a louse, and they'll be right. They'll think all the same things you do. Annie, we have to discuss this. I don't know how to handle it. They'll be going back to school tomorrow calling the Clinger kid a liar. Should I tell them the truth now? Should I wait? What should I do?"

Annie didn't know. She struggled to separate her personal anguish from the rest of the problem. In a small voice she said, "They'll be so hurt."

"And angry and confused, just like Michael must have been. If I felt I could spare them that, I would. I'd tell Teke not to tell them. I'd tell J.D. not to tell them. But then there's Michael. When he wakes up, he's sure to say something."

If he wakes up, she thought fearfully. Aloud she said, "If he remembers."

"And then there's Virginia. She's a plague."

For the first time since learning the truth, Annie pictured Virginia chatting it up around town about Sam and Teke having an affair. It had been bad enough when Annie thought it was a lie. Now it was even worse. The whole town would know that Annie couldn't satisfy her husband. She was mortified.

Wrapping an arm around her head, she moaned. When Sam's arm came around her shoulders, she shrank away by flattening herself into the corner.

He took a step back. "I'll talk with her."

"That won't do any good. She'll think you're trying to cover something up. We'll have to talk with her together. That'll look better." She moaned again. "I never thought I'd be lying for the sake of how things look, but I don't see any other way out. Virginia has to be told that you and Teke aren't having an affair."

"We *aren't,*" Sam declared.

She shot him a look in the dark. Sadly she said, "Don't quibble over semantics, Sam."

"I'm not. An affair implies something ongoing, but I was with Teke once, for a handful of minutes. It was unpremeditated and ultimately abhorrent, and it won't ever happen again. Now, there's no way I can stretch things to call *that* kind of situation an affair."

Annie shrugged. "Call it what you will."

"Annie."

"It's disgusting by any name."

"Was. Past tense. It's over." He took a short breath. "Y'know, if you'd been home, it wouldn't have happened."

She gaped at him. "You're blaming *me?*"

"You were the one I wanted, but you weren't there. I raced all over the house looking for you. I called the school. When I ran through the yard, I had visions of your being at Teke's, but you weren't."

"And you couldn't wait? You were that desperate?"

"I could—but it happened so fast, it was done before I knew it had started, and then there was Michael."

Annie pressed her face to her knees. In the ensuing silence she pictured Sam running a hand through his hair, pictured that hair looking even better for the mussing. It wasn't fair. He should have looked like a monster. At least a little.

"What a mess," he muttered.

"Maybe it was inevitable."

"How so?"

"The closeness between our families." In her search for explanations, this one had cropped up. "Maybe it was unhealthy."

"We weren't *that* close."

"We're close enough to co-own two vacation places. What are we going to do about those?"

"I don't know." He paused. "I haven't thought about it." He paused again. "A lot depends on what happens between you and me. I love you, Annie. I don't want our marriage to fall apart."

The fear in his voice touched her. She told herself to ignore it, but she was cursed to love Sam too completely for that. Still, it didn't change the fact that he had betrayed her trust and that their relationship would never be the same.

With that thought, she began to cry again.

"Annie—" He reached for her.

She jerked away. "Don't!"

"I want to touch you."

"Like you touched Teke?" she sobbed.

"Like I touch *you*. You're different from any other woman, Annie. You look different, feel different, smell different, taste—"

She covered her ears.

He pried her hands away, coming down on a knee on the window seat. "Taste different."

"How do you know?" she cried through her tears. "I thought you said you didn't see or feel anything with Teke. How do you know I'm so different?"

"You're the only one who turns me on."

"That was what I always thought, but I was wrong. I thought one way, while you were feeling another."

"I *wasn't*," he swore, and sighed. Holding her wrists, pleading now, he said, "I'll do whatever you want, Annie. I'll sleep on the sofa if you can't bear lying in the same bed as me. I'll give you my keys to the Maxwells' house so you'll know I won't go in on my own. I'll see a *shrink*, if you want."

"*That* won't do any good," she wailed. "You're the most sane person I know. That's one of the things that's so *awful* about this. Your *profound sanity* makes what you did all the more absurd."

"Then, what? What should I do? Tell me, and I'll do it."

"Give me room. Let me breathe."

He immediately released her hands and withdrew to the end of the window seat. "Now what?"

She felt bereft, cold, confused. "I don't know."

"I love you. And you love me, don't say you don't, because it can't just have died in a minute, not a love like we have."

"I can't think," she cried. "I need time."

"How much time?"

"I don't know!" He was pressing her for direction, but she was treading foreign ground. Sam had never caused her pain or inspired this kind of anger before.

"What do we say to the kids?"

She wiped the tears from her cheeks. Foreign ground it was, indeed, but there were certain immediate problems, among which handling the children was foremost. So she groped her way on. "Nothing, I guess. Not yet." One part of her prayed they wouldn't have to know at all. Will Clinger's rumors were nothing compared to straight talk from Annie and Sam. She couldn't begin to assess the emotional damage that would cause. "It's too much, with Michael so sick."

"How do we act with them?"

"We focus our worry on Michael."

"Can I kiss you?"

"No."

"What about Virginia?"

"Kiss her all you want," Annie said bitterly.

"You know what I mean."

Yes, she did; still, the bitterness was there.

"We'll talk with Virginia," he said.

"Yes."

"Do you want me to move out?"

She looked at him then. His expression was hidden by the night, but she knew he was fishing for hope. Quietly, if a bit dryly, she said, "That would defeat the purpose of not telling the kids, don't you think?"

"Yes. Same thing with my sleeping in the den."

"You take the bed. I won't be sleeping much anyway."

"Annie, that's absurd—"

"What's absurd?" she cut in. "I rarely sleep through the night anyway, so instead of lying in bed, I'll be walking around or sitting up here. The kids know I'm upset about Michael."

"I don't want the bed if you're not there. You take it."

"So what'll you tell the kids?"

"That I'm upset about Michael."

"And when they wake up and find you sprawled on the sofa in the den?"

"Same thing. I was upset about Michael, walked around for a while, fell asleep there."

"Night after night?"

When he didn't answer, she knew she had made her point—both about keeping up a facade before the kids and about the extent of her hurt. *Night after night.* She wondered when it would end, *if* it would end. She felt as though the neat little bundle that was her life with Sam had been torn apart and the pieces strewn on the floor. Still stunned from the tearing, she didn't have the strength to start picking them up.

Sam rose from the window seat. As wearily as she felt, he said, "We can both take the bed. I'll just be careful not to go near your side." He was halfway to the door when he stopped and bowed his head. "Annie?" She was silent. "We're holding a press conference tomorrow morning. About *Dunn* v. *Hanover*. I canceled it yesterday and would scrap it for good if I had my way, but our public relations people are insisting."

"While Michael is sick?" she asked. Victory or not, a press conference seemed inappropriate.

"J.D. wants it. So does J.S. I'm going to have trouble doing it." He hesitated. "Will you come?"

Annie let her head loll against the window frame. In the past, she had attended Sam's press conferences. It had been her pleasure to be there, to be introduced, to beam at her husband. She couldn't do it now, though, couldn't possibly do it now. She couldn't produce a beam if her life depended on it, and the last thing she wanted was to be introduced. She didn't want people looking at her. She felt sure they would know the truth and stare, perhaps be amused or feel pity.

"I have school," she said.

"I know, but I thought maybe you could go in a little late."

That was what she had done in the past. Her silence said she wouldn't do it this time.

He stayed where he was for another minute, before whispering, "Okay," and going quietly down the stairs.

Annie was a chronic insomniac. She could function at peak level with five hours of sleep, which meant that, in theory, she could go to bed at midnight, wake up at dawn, and be fine. In practice her eyelids were often drooping by ten at night. She would sleep straight for several hours, then only on and off after that. Normally she made the most of the wakeful time to do creative thinking, read a book, grade exams. Often she simply fitted her body to Sam's and took pleasure in his warmth.

There was no warmth this night. She didn't go to bed at all but stayed in her office, dozing on the window seat, waking to a cacophony of thoughts. Once she ventured down to the kitchen for aspirin and herbal tea, but the fact that the kitchen looked so normal, when nothing was normal at all, upset her. She returned to her office, wrapped herself in an afghan, and shivered.

If she caught three hours' sleep, that was pushing it.

Nonetheless, she was in the kitchen the next morning when Zoe and Jon came down and saw them off with a promise to pick Zoe up after school. Yes, she would drive to the hospital, she had decided. She loved Michael—who was just the same, the nurse told her—too much not to go. Whether she would be able to talk to Teke was something she would face at the time.

Sam came down dressed for work, just as the children were leaving. Not knowing what to say to him, she went up to shower. The bathroom was filled with steam by the time she turned the water off. She was reaching for the towel draped over the door when she saw his tall, gray-garbed figure.

"Yes?" she asked in alarm, and covered herself with the towel.

"Can we talk a minute?" he asked.

"I'm not dressed."

"Come on, Annie."

She knew he was thinking that she was his wife, that he'd seen her undressed thousands of times, that he knew every inch of her body. But what he had done had made him a stranger. She felt self-conscious.

She didn't move. She didn't speak. She simply stared at his blurred form until he got the message. As soon as he left, she toweled herself off and put on a robe. Then she opened the bathroom door. "Yes?"

He was sitting on the edge of the bed with his

elbows on his knees. His suit looked formal against the rumple of the sheets, not so formal against the other side of the bed, the neat, unslept-in side. Either way he looked handsome. She resented that tremendously.

"What are your plans for the day?" he asked with due humility.

"I don't know."

"You'll be at school?"

"For a while."

"Are you going to the hospital?"

"I'll take Zoe and Jana there after school. Jon will drive in with Leigh after practice."

Sam looked at his hands. "Can we meet for coffee?"

"I won't be staying that long."

He looked up. "Then an early dinner? In town? Here?"

She shook her head. Her insides ached every which way around her heart. "I can't, Sam," she said.

"Won't."

"Can't. There's a war going on inside. I'm bleeding in places I haven't found and won't be able to find until the dust settles a little."

He considered that. After a minute he pushed himself up and stood, so straight and resignedly Sam that Annie was tempted to throw herself at him and beg his forgiveness. Only she wasn't the one to be begging forgiveness. She hadn't done anything wrong. At least she didn't think she had.

She was so confused.

She watched him go, thinking she should wish him good luck in his press conference but refusing to speak, thinking that she should be pleased at having turned him down for dinner but feeling no pleasure at all. Lest she start crying again, she busied herself getting dressed, but by the time she was done she knew that she couldn't go to school. She couldn't stand before two hundred freshmen and discuss D. H. Lawrence.

D. H. Lawrence. Right there in the syllabus. *Sons and Lovers.* One man and two women, one earthy, one introspective. She couldn't possibly talk about that.

Cursing fate, she called in sick. Then she changed from her suit into a pair of jeans, threw on sneakers and a sweater, and climbed into the car. Thirty minutes later she was in Rockport, at the small, time-worn cottage she had called home for the first twenty-one years of her life.

The drive was rutted, not so much from the weather as from neglect. Peter Huggins couldn't be bothered with things like repairing pavement, mowing lawns, or maintaining picket fences. He was an artist. He let things flow. With a small, sweet, sheepish smile, he gave nature its run of the place.

Annie parked behind his rusted old station wagon and let herself in the side door. The kitchen was chaotic. Pete didn't believe in washing dishes until there was nothing clean left in the cupboard. He didn't believe in putting away staples only to have to take them back out for the next meal. He didn't believe in throwing junk mail into the trash when it could be used for drawing on. Ahhhh, but what drawings he made. Annie might fault him for the littered countertops, but never for his drawings.

Pastel Pete, they called him for his artistic preference. He supported himself by selling watercolors in local galleries, but he was best known for the seasonal murals he drew on the south wall of the bank in the center of town, and for his eccentricity. He rarely obeyed rules, yet he was so sweet, with his pink cheeks and his blond-white hair and beard, that no one minded. It was generally accepted that he was an endangered species, to be protected by an indulgence of his need for space.

Annie left the kitchen. Originally there had been three other rooms in the cottage, a living room and two bedrooms. Soon after Annie had married, though, Pete had taken a sledgehammer to the walls, and the end result was a single large studio with jagged edges where walls had once been. One coat of thick white paint—deemed a suitable canvas by Pete—on everything in sight, and the redecorating was done. Eighteen years later the walls were a treasure of drawings, of landscapes, seascapes, and portraits, running the gamut from whimsy to realism. Annie shuddered to think of the time when her father would be gone and those walls might come down.

"Pop?" she called when she didn't see him.

Seconds later his head appeared around one of the jagged-edged walls. He smiled and waved her close with a hand. He was sitting on the floor working on yet another section of wall. Though the colors were characteristic of his style, Annie couldn't make out what he was drawing. She saw sparkles— pale yellow, green, pink ones on a field of blue—but the sparkles weren't Fourth of July–type sparkles. They had life to them somehow.

"They're from another world," he said in a voice that got softer and more gravelly with each year that passed. He was seventy, making his voice soft and gravelly indeed.

"Ahhhh." She squatted beside him to better study the patch of wall.

"They wilted a little during the trip to earth. Thirteen hundred light-years is a long time. But they're reviving."

"Why are they here?"

"Just visiting."

"That's a long trip for just a visit."

"They need comfort. Their home planet is shaky. They're wanting to know that life exists somewhere else, just in case."

Annie smiled. She leaned toward her father and let him fold her in his arms. He wasn't a large man— five nine, tops—but he was solid. That solidity was familiar and sure.

"Something shaky with you?" he asked.

She made a sound that said yes.

"Need a little comfort?"

She made another sound like the first.

"Want a brandy?"

She smiled. Brandy was her father's weakness. "You swore you never touched the stuff until dinnertime."

"I swore I never drank alone. Dinnertime's when I'm with Peter Jennings. Now I'm with you. Want one?"

She shook her head against his shoulder.

"Tea?"

She shook her head again.

"Cocoa?"

She sighed. When she'd been a child, cocoa had been a panacea. Somehow she didn't think it would do the trick now. "I'll just sit a while, I think," she said, but she didn't move from his arms.

"Jock-o'-my-Jon okay?" he asked cautiously.

She smiled at the nickname, which he'd been using since Jon had been six and a T-Ball star, and nodded.

"Pretty little Zoe?"

She nodded again.

"Big bad Sam?"

Her smile faded.

When she didn't answer Pete said, "Uh-oh." He paused. "What'd he do?"

She sighed. "Something that upset me."

"He doesn't often."

"No."

"I like Sam."

"So do I."

"Then it'll get better," he said in a soothing way.

Annie took full measure of the soothing, but it was an ephemeral thing. When it was gone, she eased herself from his arms and got to her feet. While Pete went back to work, she wandered around.

For the most part, the walls of the house were a random assortment of thoughts. Like his kitchen, the assortment was chaotic, until one reached the back wall.

Most families had picture albums or, increasingly, videocassettes to document their lives. Pastel Pete had a full wall of his house. Sketched right on the flat white paint were drawings of Annie as a child, a teenager, a teenager, a young woman. There were drawings of her as a bride, of Sam, of the children at various ages. There were also drawings of Annie's mother, who had left when Annie was two. The images on the wall were all Annie had to remember her by.

Annie studied them. By Pete's hand her mother had been small and fragile, with long dark hair and a gentle smile. Had it not been for her eyes, she would have looked the part of the innocent. But eyes were Pastel Pete's forte. If there was feeling there, he captured it—indeed, often captured it elsewhere and put it there, though no one ever called him on it. That was one of the things people indulged in Pete, in large part because they couldn't fault the accuracy of his insight.

In Annie's high school graduation picture, he'd captured excitement and fear in her eyes. In her college graduation picture, he'd captured headiness; in her wedding picture, utter bliss.

Annie's mother's eyes were spirited. They spoke of a woman who wouldn't be tamed, a woman who needed continual change and challenge. Peter Huggins had been a colorful, if brief stop along the journey of her life. Annie's arrival had prolonged that stop, but not even she had been enough to prevent the inevitable moving on.

Annie couldn't say that she had been an unhappy child. She had adapted to her mother's absence, and Pete was as dear as a father could be. It wasn't until she became a teenager that she'd felt the loss. That was when, grappling with her own nascent womanhood, she'd begun to blame herself.

If she were more beautiful, her mother might have stayed. If she had long, flowing dark hair. Or green eyes. Or a heart-shaped face. If she was *different* somehow, more interesting somehow, her mother might have stayed.

Through those teenage years, Annie felt inferior to almost everyone around her. She grew introverted. She took to reading and writing poetry in her journal. Her father, a man of few words and much soul, was her very best friend.

Then came Teke. And Sam.

Annie thought of him now, pictured him in his office with clients on either side, a bouquet of microphones gathered in a cluster on the desk, and beyond it a circle of the Boston media's elite.

Did you expect this victory, Mr. Pope? one of the reporters would be asking.

A lawyer never expects a victory, Sam would answer modestly. *He does his homework, plots his case, and argues his heart out, then stands back while our system of justice has its way.*

Do you see this decision as affecting other states?

I see other states ruling similarly, though not because of this case. The concept of making allowance for the trauma of crimes like sexual abuse is one whose time has come.

From the far side of the room, another reporter would call, *Will you be representing other women's groups?*

Perhaps.

And another. *Would you say that you were better able to argue this case because you have a wife and a daughter?*

By all means. I would want my wife and daughter protected in the very way these women here have been.

Where is your wife, Counselor? *yet another reporter would ask.* She usually attends your press conferences.

She couldn't make it, *Sam would say.*

Why not?

She works.

Does she get jealous when you work with groups of women, like this one?

No, *he would say, but smugly now.* She knows what she has to do to keep my attention.

What is that, Counselor?

She has to be beautiful, seductive, and interesting. She has to bring in her share of the money. She has to dress up when I want her to dress up, and dress down when I want her to dress down. She has to wash my socks and pick up my shirts from the laundry. She has to dust the house every morning. And she has to have a homemade meal, hot and ready on the table, every night.

But she doesn't do all that, *a reporter in the image of Virginia Clinger would point out.* She doesn't do half that. She may have a career, but she's a sham of a wife. She mismatches your socks, serves you ready-made from the market for dinner, and she's far too pale to be pretty. It's a wonder you haven't strayed before. Or have you, Mr. Pope?

Not wanting to hear the answer, Annie turned from the wall of drawings and went for cocoa after all.

five

STANLEY WALLACE HAD BEEN A CLIENT OF Maxwell, Roper and Dine since the days Roper and Dine had been alive and John Stewart had been the only Maxwell in the firm. Stanley had made a fortune in zippers. Though the fortune had shrunk in recent years, it remained impressive enough for Stanley to be coddled by the firm.

That was why J.D. ignored the pressure he felt to race back to the hospital after the press conference Thursday and took Stanley to lunch instead. J.D. had been handling the account for years. He had a solid rapport with Stanley and a vivid understanding of the kind of money the firm stood to reap as the executor of his estate. Clients like that weren't put off unless the circumstances were dire. Nor were they taken to Dino's Sub Shop for lunch.

J.D. took him to the Federal Club. Over crab bisque and medallions of lamb, they discussed Sam's case and Stanley's estate. Stanley saw them as related. Chauvinist that he was, he feared that the ruling in Sam's case would give license to women to complain, which was what his own daughters did all the time. He was convinced that they would spend him into the poorhouse if he didn't guard his money well.

J.D. let him talk, which meant suffering through the long lapses between sentences that typically punctuated Stanley's speech. His mind didn't work as quickly as it once had. Neither did his body. At eighty-six it protested most movement, which meant that the walk back to the law firm—Stanley didn't believe in taking cabs—was accomplished at a snail's pace.

That was actually fine with J.D., who could ratio- nalize not being at the hospital as long as he was with a client. Besides, he could afford to walk as slowly as Stanley wanted. He billed by the hour.

"Shouldn't happen to a boy," Stanley tsked, turn- ing to talk of Michael as they ambled along. "To someone my age, maybe, but not to a boy. Has there been any change?"

"They took him off the respirator this morning."

"Ahhh. Now, that's a good sign."

J.D. wished he could see it that way, but all he could see was Michael's deathly pale face. It was never far from him. "Actually," he told Stanley, "they felt he probably hadn't needed it in the first place. His vital signs haven't changed any since they removed the tube. He's still in a coma."

Stanley tsked again and lapsed into silence. After a bit he said, "And Theodora? How is she?"

J.D. felt a flicker of annoyance. "She hasn't left the hospital since it happened. She just stands by his bed." He didn't know what he expected, but it wasn't that. Her paralysis was unsettling—not only to him, but to Jana and Leigh. They had been impos- sible the night before, bickering with each other in ways Teke would have known how to handle. Lord knew he didn't.

"Poor Theodora," Stanley mused, and lapsed into

another silence. By the time he emerged, they had reached the law firm. J.D. guided him to an empty conference room, where the old man promptly stretched out on a sofa and dozed off.

J.D. returned to his office with the intention of calling the hospital, but he had no sooner picked up the phone than Virginia Clinger appeared at his door. He had known she was coming. She was Stanley Wallace's daughter. In return for a check each month to supplement her alimony, she filled in as his driver when neither of her sisters could make it.

"Hey," she said with a bright smile, "got a minute?"

He didn't, and Virginia wasn't his favorite person. As an old family friend, she was a nuisance. As his neighbor, she was a snoop. Unfortunately she was also one of three beneficiaries to the Wallace estate and, as such, was an investment in his future. So he nodded, set down the phone, and gestured her to a chair.

She was wearing a suit with a short skirt the likes of which J.D. would never have allowed Teke to wear. He had to hand it to her, though. She did have great legs.

Wrapped in a cloak of sweet perfume, she crossed those legs, folded her hands demurely in her lap, and faced him with wide-eyed concern. "I keep ringing your doorbell and missing you. How is Michael?" When J.D. told her about the respirator, she gave a huge sigh. "Thank goodness for that."

"It doesn't mean all that much."

"It certainly does," she scolded. "It means he can breathe on his own, which you didn't know before. Is he moving at all?"

"Randomly. The nurse says they're muscle spasms."

"What does the nurse know," Virginia scoffed. "She doesn't know what's going on in his mind. Just this morning I was using the stair machine with a friend at the health club, and she said that her sister in Omaha had a similar experience with a child of hers several years ago. It was a little girl. She was hit coming home from school when a car failed to stop for the school bus. She was in a coma for *nineteen days.*"

J.D. wasn't sure if he trusted anything Virginia said. She was a known embellisher of the facts. Still, he listened. He was hungry for hope. "Did she wake up?"

"Uh-huh," Virginia said smugly, "but only after my friend's sister got involved in a radical form of therapy. She is *convinced* that's what brought her daughter out of the coma."

J.D. wasn't into radical forms of anything; still, he wanted to hear more. "What kind of therapy?"

"It's called coma arousal. For hours at a stretch, they banged wood blocks together by the little girl's ears. They shined bright lights in her eyes. They scratched her skin. They say that when a person is in a coma, he is lost somewhere inside his body, and the therapy is designed as a beacon to guide the person back. You should look into it, J.D. I bet Michael's doctors haven't suggested it."

"It's only been two days," J.D. reasoned. "They're concentrating on keeping him stabilized."

"They're too conventional," Virginia said with a twitch of her nose. Coaxingly she added, "This wouldn't hurt. My friend said that her sister would be glad to talk with you. Or with Teke. How is she, by the way? I keep an eye on your driveway, but I haven't seen her coming or going."

J.D. pictured the front window at the end of Virginia's house. It was a large bay and looked out from the breakfast room, where it seemed Virginia spent most of her time. Many a morning he had seen her at that window watching him leave for work.

"Teke stays at the hospital with Michael," he said.

Virginia looked surprised. "All the time? But, what's happening at the house?"

"We're managing."

"She's put all that responsibility on you?"

One part of J.D. was pleased to know that someone else thought Teke could be doing more. The other part felt called upon to say, "She's staying with our son, who is in a coma."

Virginia dropped her eyes. She looked at her hands, turned them in her lap, looked up unsurely. "I'm worried about her, J.D."

"She'll be fine."

"No, not just about Michael. In general. I think Teke is going through something else."

J.D. shot a fast look at the ceiling. "Like what?"

"A personal crisis."

"Come on, Virginia—"

"I'm serious, and I wouldn't say anything if I didn't mean it, because I'm in an awkward position. It's no secret that I was irked when you married Teke. Our families have known each other for years. They had hoped we'd marry each other, and I'd have married you in a minute, but you picked Teke. It was done, I accepted it. I tried to be a friend to her."

J.D. shrugged at the impossibility of that. "You're very different women. She's a homebody, you're a social butterfly."

"We're not so different."

"She loves kids, you love adults."

"I like kids, too."

"She's a one-man woman; you're looking for husband number four."

"Are you sure about that?"

"Is it five?"

"About Teke."

J.D. had no idea what she was talking about. He glanced at his watch. He had a client due in at three-thirty and had been hoping to get to the hospital and back in time.

Virginia sat forward. "I think she's having an affair."

"What?"

"An affair."

He laughed. "I thought you'd gotten over me, Gin. Why the sudden bad-mouthing of my wife?"

"I *never* got over you, which is why I'm worried. She's going to hurt you, J.D."

"Having an affair," he said as though it were the most preposterous idea around. Teke wouldn't have an affair. She wouldn't dare.

"With Sam."

"Are you kidding?" He felt the stirrings of impatience. "Sam is my best friend. He's my law partner. Be real, Gin."

But she wasn't backing off. "I saw them."

"When?"

"Tuesday."

"The day of the accident?"

She nodded. "When they ran out of the house after Michael, they were barely dressed. Teke was tying her robe, and Sam looked guilty as sin."

J.D. stood. Her perfume was suddenly cloying, and he had heard more than enough from her mouth. Aware that he was toying with future business, he kept his voice civil. "I think you ought to leave."

"Ask Sam."

"I won't ask Sam. I won't insult him that way."

Still she didn't back off, which annoyed J.D. all the more. "It makes sense," she insisted. "Why did Michael run blindly into the street that way, if not to escape something upsetting that he'd seen? Think about it, J.D. You'll know I'm right."

J.D. started for the door but stopped when a thought struck. He speared Virginia with a look. "Who have you told this to?"

She rose. "That's not the point—"

"It *is* the point!" he shouted. In sudden fury he swung the door shut and faced her again. His voice shook. "You're right. Our families have known each other for a long time, which means that I know you and what you're capable of. You meddle, and you gossip." He raised a finger. "I'm going to say this once and only once. You—saw—nothing. If Michael ran out of the house, it was for a good reason and *not* because my wife and my best friend were doing something they shouldn't have been doing. Give me a little credit, Virginia. I can satisfy my wife." His voice hardened. "I also carry a little weight with your father, who is beginning to begrudge supporting the cosmetic surgeons of Boston. Stanley could easily be convinced that you have plenty of money without his contribution each month. I promise you—spread your little story around, and there'll be trouble."

More meekly Virginia said, "I'm only trying to protect you."

"By wreaking havoc on my marriage?" he yelled. "No wonder you can't keep a husband." He pointed to his head. "Loose screws. How would sabotaging my marriage possibly *protect* me? That's the *last* thing it would do. *Particularly* with Michael so sick."

"I only wanted to help."

"You want to help? Fine. You can clean house

and do laundry and make dinner, like my wife would be doing if she weren't at the hospital with my son. You want to clean and do laundry and make dinner? Of course you don't. You want hired help to do all that, while you go to the health club and sweat a little in front of the trainer. The *trainer.* For God's sake, Gin, he's ten years younger than you are. His biceps dwarf his brain. Can't you do better than that?"

"I'm not—"

"Let's get Stanley. He's napped long enough." J.D. threw open the door and strode angrily down the hall, but whereas the boiling should have stopped the instant Virginia and Stanley left, it didn't. A whistle of alarm continued to shrill in his mind.

Carried by the momentum of that alarm, he went into Sam's office, shut the door behind him, flattened his hands on the desk, and, heedless of the fact that Sam was on the phone, said, "What were you doing at my house Tuesday?"

Sam held him off with a finger. "That's right," he said into the phone. "Six defendants in a class action suit." He shot a look at the ceiling while the person on the other end of the line spoke, then said, "No, I don't believe there has been a similar ruling in another state yet. Look, Hank, can we finish this up later?" He listened again, said a quick, "Right," then hung up the phone.

"Well?" J.D. prodded. When Sam didn't speak he said, "My house. Tuesday. Were you there when Michael ran in?"

It took a long time, but Sam finally nodded.

J.D. had an awful, awful feeling that had to do with the resigned way Sam looked. "What were you doing there?"

Looking for Annie was the obvious answer. But Sam didn't say it.

"Simple question," J.D. prompted, his voice now dangerously low. This was Sam, his trusted friend and law partner. "What were you doing there?"

Still Sam didn't speak. J.D. tried to read the look on his face, but he only saw red. "Want to know what Virginia just told me?" he asked, and was prepared to go on when Sam spoke.

"Probably the same thing she told her kids, who told our kids yesterday in school. She's probably told half the town. Annie and I are going to talk with her later—"

"No need," J.D. cut in. "I just told her to keep her mouth shut. I threatened that I'd influence her father against her, which is an unethical thing to do, but, so help me, I will if she so much as *hints* again that you and Teke are having an affair." But that wasn't the end of it. J.D. had a need to lay it all out. "Want to know what she said? She said that when Teke ran out after Michael, she was tying her robe, and that you were looking guilty. She said Michael must have barged in on the two of you." He paused, breathing uneasily. "Deny it, Sam. Tell me she's wrong. I need to be able to say that you unequivocably deny it."

Sam looked at him for another minute, then rose from the desk and went to the window. "Teke and I are not having an affair."

J.D. waited. "Go on," he finally said. He knew there was more. It was the missing piece of the puzzle.

"I was with Teke when Michael ran in. He saw us before we saw him. He must have misinterpreted."

"Misinterpreted what?" J.D. demanded.

Sam scratched his mustache. It wasn't a typical gesture, which made it all the more meaningful. Sam Pope only scratched his mustache when he was unusually nervous. Not uneasy, or unsure, but *nervous*. As in *guilty*.

J.D. gritted his teeth. "You did it, you bastard."

"Not like you think."

"You either fucked her, or you didn't. Or are you trying to tell me it was kinky? For Christ's sake, Sam!" He wrapped a hand around the back of his neck and turned away. He couldn't believe it. His best friend and his wife. He wheeled back. *"Why, Sam? Jesus.* It never even occurred to me to think of it, that's how dumb I am, but it makes sense. It explains why Michael ran out without talking to her, and why she won't look me in the eye." He tried to grasp the meaning of it. "How could you do this to me? Teke is my wife. After all I've done for you, all I've *fought* for you—is this how you pay me back?"

"You're jumping to the wrong conclusions."

"Okay. Set me straight. Yes or no, did you screw her?"

"There was nothing personal—"

"Were you or were you not having intercourse with my wife when my thirteen-year-old son caught you at it?"

"Easy, J.D."

"Yes or *no."*

"Yes, but—"

"Christ!" J.D. was seized by a fury so raw, his head spun. His first thoughts were that he wanted to hit Sam. His next thought was that it wasn't worth the effort. So he made for the door.

Sam was fast beside him, saying under his breath so that the ears of the firm wouldn't hear, "It wasn't her fault."

"She can tell me that," J.D. muttered as he stormed down the hall.

"She won't. She blames herself."

"Maybe justly."

"No." Sam grabbed his arm. "Don't hit her with this now. She has enough to deal with without it."

J.D. shook him off and strode on. "What about me? Don't I have enough to deal with? I'm the one picking up the pieces. I'm the one trying to keep my family functioning."

"You won't do it this way."

J.D. stopped short and glared at him. "I'm supposed to forget it? I'm supposed to condone it? Is that what Annie did? My God, poor Annie."

"We'll work it out."

"She's too good for you, Sam." He set off again.

Sam kept pace. "I won't let one stupid mistake ruin my life."

"It ruined Michael's."

"Not yet."

"He loved you," J.D. argued in a hoarse whisper as he swung past the receptionist.

Sam caught the door in the middle of its neat MAXWELL, ROPER and DINE and followed J.D. into the lobby. "He will again."

"Not if I can help it," J.D. vowed. He jabbed the elevator button and, when the door didn't open, continued to jab.

"That would be too bad."

"Yeah, well, that's the way it is. I don't forget it when friends stab me in the back."

Sam thrust a hand through his hair. He was agitated and upset, which pleased J.D. immensely. As far as he was concerned, their friendship was over. He stared at the digital readout above the elevator door, refusing to demean himself by paying Sam further heed.

In a quiet voice Sam said, "It was one time, J.D. My mind was off somewhere between *Dunn* v. *Hanover* and Annie, and Teke was thinking of you, not me. It was over before either of us knew what was happening, and we're paying the price, believe me, we are. If you think I'll ever forgive myself, you're wrong."

J.D. kept his eyes where they were. He refused to react.

"Annie and I thought it better not to tell the kids."

"I disagree. They should know what they're dealing with."

"Don't say anything, J.D. It'll make things worse."

"They have a right to the truth."

"The whole truth?" Sam asked. There was warning in his voice. "You want them to know about those little trysts you've had?"

J.D. glared at him. "You bastard."

"Does Teke know about those?"

"You know she doesn't." He had worked damn hard to make sure of it. He liked being able to satisfy himself with other women. It made up for the monotony of his relationship with Teke. "Are you threatening to tell her?"

Sam shook his head, but there was an anger in him that infuriated J.D. all the more. He didn't know what Sam had to be angry about. *He* was the one who'd been cuckolded.

But Sam was angry indeed. "I'm saying you're a fine one to be getting up on your high horse over this. You haven't been faithful to Teke all this time, but she's been faithful to you, and I've been faithful to Annie. What kind of hypocrite are you?"

"I didn't make it with my best friend's wife," J.D. said as the elevator arrived. He stepped inside, half expecting Sam to follow and argue his case in front of the people there. But the door slid shut, leaving him with those three people, no Sam, and a headful of rage.

Teke felt as though she were in a netherworld of unhappiness. Not having slept more than a handful of hours in the past two nights combined, she was dead on her feet. She had changed clothes and freshened up with the toiletries J.D. had brought, but she needed a shower. Worst of all, despite the removal of the respirator, she was growing more discouraged. Michael's condition hadn't changed.

Increasingly, in the hours she spent by his bedside, talking to a body that wouldn't respond, she found herself thinking about what would happen if he never woke up. Or if he woke up paralyzed. Or if he woke up with the mind of a three-year-old.

Thought of any one of those possibilities set her to shaking. So did sight of Sam. And Grady. He was the worst, *the worst!* He kept coming, standing there in the hall, reminding her of another life. But, damn it, that life was over. He had no business haunting her.

Grady had been her strength once. Now she had none. What she needed was Annie, but Annie didn't want her, and Teke couldn't blame her for that. Teke had been a friend of the very worst kind.

"Hi, Mikey," she said weakly. She ran her fingers along his arm. "How're you doing?" She had said the same words, asked the same question, hundreds of times. Her voice was like a broken record, sounding more warped with each repetition. "Your mouth looks good, honey," she tried now. For lack of anything more intelligent to do, she was starting to speak all her thoughts aloud. "I'm glad they took the respirator away. You didn't need a tube in your throat. Now you won't be frightened when you wake up. There'll just be the IV needles, but they'll come out as soon as you can eat. Aren't you hungry? Wouldn't you like a Double Whopper?"

She took a weary breath and fell silent. Talking was a strain. If only Michael would show that he heard, she could talk forever, but he refused to do that.

Her head flew up when J.D. burst into the room. "I just had a swell time at the office," he said.

She wasn't so exhausted that she didn't hear his sarcasm. It coated his words, the same way something terrible controlled his features.

He grasped the rail and faced her across Michael's still form. "First, I had a little visit from Virginia, who said she thought you were having an affair with Sam. Then I confronted Sam, and he confirmed it. You *tramp.*"

She felt a sudden, odd calm. Fatigue, perhaps. Or numbness. Most surely relief. It was better that he know the truth.

"How could you do this to me?" he cried, sounding more angry than hurt. "Didn't I treat you well? Didn't I give you a house and clothes and children and food? Didn't I please you in bed?"

Technically he did, if reaching orgasm was the measure. If foreplay and afterplay counted, there was little pleasure. Their love making had lost its glow years before.

"How often?" he asked sharply. "How often did you do it?"

"Once."

His eyes narrowed. "With Sam, maybe, but with other men? Were there little bang jobs in the woods with the landscaper, or backstage with that bearded high school drama teacher?"

His words cut to the quick in that they painted the picture of a whore, which she didn't consider herself at all. Still, she welcomed whatever insults he wanted to throw. She deserved the punishment. She was guilty of betraying him with Sam. He had a right to be angry.

"Huh?" he prodded. "Or didn't I hit on the right scenario? Was it in the bathroom of the gas station while the car was being serviced? Or, goddamn it, in my own bed with the exterminator?"

"You know it wasn't," she murmured.

"No, I don't. I don't know anything! You're in Constance all day long, doing what I assumed were perfectly innocent things, while I'm in Boston earning the money to support you. I trusted you, Teke."

Her eyes dropped to Michael. It occurred to her that they shouldn't be talking this way within his earshot. Then she realized the folly of that. He hadn't appeared to take in anything she had said before. She didn't think that would suddenly change. And if it did? If harsh, frank, even crude words could bring him from his coma, she was all for it.

"Well?" J.D. asked. "Aren't you going to defend yourself?"

She raised one shoulder and let it fall. That was all the energy she could muster. "How?" she asked. "What I did was wrong. It was only one time, but it was wrong."

"Damn right it was, and look at the consequences."

Her eyes were on Michael. "I've been doing that every single second since it happened."

"You put him here." When she nodded, he amended that to, "You and Sam." He straightened and took an audible breath, the kind Teke had come to associate over the years with the passing of judgment. She wasn't surprised when he said, "My parents were never wild about you. From the very first, they had doubts. They thought I was marrying beneath my station, and they were right. You never did fit in as well as I'd hoped you would. Oh, you looked pretty enough when we went places, you never did me any harm, but you weren't an asset, not like some wives. Some wives help their husbands' careers. You never did."

Of all the little digs he'd gotten in over the

years—*I think your hair needs another combing,* or *The children should have new sneakers if we're going to the country club cookout,* or *Don't you have a dress that's a little more elegant?*—that was a new one. "How was I supposed to help your career?"

"By talking to people. Impressing them."

"You've aged well," J.D. went on. "I'll give you that. I can understand how you turn men on."

She had never defined herself that way. "I don't—"

"I can even stretch my imagination to see that with the kids in school all day, it must get lonely for you sometimes. I mean, the company of other women might be fine for planning little to-dos, but the rest of the time you're home and I'm at work. If you'd said you needed something else, I might have accommodated you." His voice turned cruel. "But to go behind my back and do it with my best friend, how *low* can you go, Teke? How *desperate* can you get? Was he good? Did you like it with him?"

The discussion was starting to sicken her. "I wasn't—"

"He's athletic, is that it? He's taller and more coordinated than me. Was it a challenge? Something you'd been thinking about for years? All those times in Maine when we were sitting around in bathing suits, were you thinking about it then? Did you once stop to think about *Annie?*"

I wasn't thinking at all, she wanted to cry, but he was ranting on, and she let him. The doctors and nurses were elsewhere. The sooner it was all out, the better.

"When we made love, you and me, were you thinking about him? Or about someone else? Well, I wasn't, Teke. I was thinking of you every time we made love"—his voice grew tighter and lower—"which wasn't all that often lately, was it? If I didn't suggest it, we didn't do it. So why was I always the initiator? Because you were putting out for other people."

She had already denied there had been anyone but Sam. She didn't have the strength to do it again.

"What a bitch. You're a lousy wife, Teke. You're a lousy *mother.*"

That stirred her. Mothering had always been her strong suit. It was what she had wanted to do from the time she had known mothering existed. "I've always done everything right until now," she said in her own defense.

"But you blew it!" J.D. told her. "None of the rest counts now. Look at Michael. Look what you've done to him. You betrayed him, just like you betrayed me. Face it, Teke, you're a *lousy* mother."

She couldn't let it stand. "No. I made one mistake."

"You're a failure."

"One mistake, and I'll make up for it. I'll spend the rest of my life at it, if need be."

"May not be too long, if he dies."

She felt a sharp pain in her middle. "*Shhh,* J.D."

"He could. Or be a vegetable for the rest of his life. How you gonna handle that? They don't stage art auctions for patients in long-term vegetative states!"

"He won't be!" Teke cried. It was one thing to think the worst, another to hear it said aloud.

"How do you know?"

"I won't let him be!" she vowed.

"You're into playing God now? Come off it, Teke. You're not doing anything but standing here in an endless daze. What good are you doing Michael?"

Fighting for composure, she swallowed hard. "He knows I'm here. I'm showing him I love him."

"You're showing him what a waste you are. You could be doing something to help him wake up. You

could be asking the doctors about alternative thera-
pies. You could be prodding them to do more. You
could be trying some of those techniques yourself.
But no, you'd rather stand here like an upright
corpse. You look like death warmed over," he muttered.

Teke barely heard the last. Her eyes were on the
part of the sheet beneath which lay Michael's
uncasted leg. Her heart was beating faster. "Did you
see that?" she whispered excitedly.

"See what?"

"He moved his leg."

J.D. looked that way, but the sheet was still.

"Come on, baby," Teke urged, leaning close to his
face, "do it again. You can do it. Try it again."

"Nothing," J.D. said after a minute, but Teke
wasn't accepting that. She ran around the bed and
out to the nurse's station.

"He moved!" she said to the nurse there. "It was
his leg, just for a minute, but I'm sure he moved!
What does that mean? Can we make it happen
again?"

The nurse returned with her to Michael's room,
where J.D. quickly said, "There's been nothing. My
wife must have imagined it."

"I did not imagine it," Teke told him. "I've been
standing here so long with nothing, that even the
tiniest movement would look huge." To the nurse
she said, "My husband and I were arguing. Michael
must not have liked what we were saying. Could
that have done it?"

"Could have," the nurse said, but she didn't
sound overly sure.

"It was probably another muscle spasm," J.D.
said.

"No," Teke insisted, refusing to be denied this ray
of hope. "I've seen those. This was different. It was

more purposeful." She leaned down. "Come on, Mikey. Do it again. I know you can. Do it for me."

J.D. snorted. The minute the nurse left the room, he said, "You're the last person he'd do it for."

"Then *you* try," she cried, discouraged all over again and, at that moment, feeling an intense dislike for her husband. "You accuse me of doing nothing. Well, you're not doing much of anything yourself."

J.D. straightened his shoulders. His eyes were cold. "I'm working—I'm making the money to pay for your mistake. I'm also picking up the pieces for you at home. Nothing gets done there while you're here. In case you've forgotten, you have two daughters, too." He looked disgusted. "You've made a mess of things, Teke. A real mess." With that he turned and left.

"I haven't," she protested, but with no one to hear, the words sounded empty. She looked down. Michael wasn't moving. She was *so sure* he had responded. *So sure.* But he looked exactly the same as before. "Yes. I have."

Her eyes filled with tears, and she was suddenly too tired to fight them. So she cried softly while she held Michael's hand and thought about all the things she had wanted for him. She had wanted him to play basketball, and make videos, and call girls. She had wanted him to sail around the world in schooners like the one he had fallen in love with on Labor Day weekend. She had wanted everything good to happen to him, because he was her son, he was an incredible kid, and she loved him.

She was weeping softly, thinking that none of that might ever happen, when a movement at the door caught her eye. It was Grady, as wavy now through her tears as he had been through that long-ago storefront window.

"Go away," she whispered, and made a sharp

shooing motion before wiping her cheeks with her hand.

Every other time he had gone. This time he didn't.

"Go away," she whispered again, but more feebly. She began to shake as she hadn't when J.D. had come. Struck by the fact that her marriage was endangered, her son in a coma, and her life generally in tatters, she covered her face with her hands, backed up, and slid down the wall to the floor, where she sat crying, not caring who came and saw and pitied.

Grady's arms circled her. She hadn't heard him approach, but she knew they were his. They had a special shape. He had a special scent. Twenty-two years hadn't changed either.

"Go away," she sobbed.

"Can't do that," he whispered hoarsely. "I never could, when you were hurting."

She tried to think of all the reasons she should hate him and make him leave, but all she could think about just then was how tired she was, how sad, how heartsick, how frightened, and how solid and reassuring he felt.

So she indulged herself this one pleasure in the midst of hell. "Oh, Grady. I've botched things up."

He tightened his arms around her but said nothing.

"You told me to do good when you sent me away. I thought I had. Now I've ruined Michael's life."

"I was the one driving down the street."

"But he ran out because he saw me with Sam. I was with Sam, Grady. Sam is my husband's best friend. I'm a horrible person, not what you wanted me to be at all. You shouldn't come near me. You shouldn't have anything to do with me."

He stroked her head, as he had done when she was ten.

"J.D. hates me. Michael hates me. The girls will hate me, too, when they find out." Her voice rose to a wail. "What am I going to do?"

"Get some sleep," he said into her hair. "You're worn out."

"All I ever wanted was a family." A husband, children, a home, security. "Now I'm losing it."

He ran a hand over her back. It was a gesture that said he had known her intimately once and still cared. She knew she should reject his comfort, just as he had once rejected hers. She should stand up, walk away, and show that she could live without him.

But she couldn't just then. She needed his caring. She was feeling at sea in a storm.

"You lose friends," he said in an anchoring voice. "Maybe a husband. But not children. They're your blood."

"My blood," she whispered, but her eyes were closed and her damp cheek lay against Grady's chest. His heartbeat was rhythmic and firm. It lulled her.

From a great distance she heard a voice ask, "Is Mrs. Maxwell all right?"

"She's very tired," Grady said. "I'm going to drive her home. Will someone call her there if there's any change?"

"Of course."

Teke stirred enough to murmur, "I can't leave."

But Grady seemed to know what he was doing. He helped her to her feet and, supporting her with an arm around her waist, started her walking. He stopped for just a minute at the side of the bed and said, "That's a fine name, Michael is. He's a fine-looking boy."

Teke felt a pang. Of all the secret times she had thought of Grady over the years, all the times she had wanted to show him her children and the life she had made for herself, she had never thought it to be under circumstances like these. "I want him to live and be all right, Grady."

"Tell him that."

"Michael, do you hear?"

Grady touched Michael's hand. "Your mom needs some sleep. She'll be back in a little while."

Teke said nothing more. She let herself be led from the hospital and seated in Grady's pickup. No matter that it was the same truck that had hit Michael. She was too tired to care. She was asleep by the time they left the parking garage and didn't wake up until they reached her house.

He didn't walk her to the door. She didn't ask him to, nor did she turn and thank him for driving her home. Talking to him would mean facing him and the conflicting emotions he evoked, which she didn't have the strength to do.

So she went to the door and let herself in without a look back. She didn't listen for the pickup's growl but went upstairs and started the shower. For an eternity, it seemed, she stood under the scalding spray. She scrubbed herself, then scrubbed herself again. She washed her hair until it squeaked. Then she left the shower, put on a nightgown, and climbed into bed.

That was at four in the afternoon. She slept until seven the next morning and awoke to find J.D.'s side of the bed neat as a pin, which was fine. Given what he thought of her, sharing a bed with him would have been as distasteful to her as to him. *What a bitch,* he had said, and considering what she had done with Sam, he was probably right. Likewise when he'd called her a lousy wife.

The lousy mother part bothered her, though. She had been, and still was, the most conscientious mother she knew. So she made a full breakfast for Jana and Leigh before sending them off to school, spent an hour putting the house in order and gathering the things she wanted, then set off for the hospital.

She was done standing by Michael's beside doing nothing. He was in that mind of his, she knew he was. She intended to get him out.

six

SAM COULDN'T SEEM TO MUSTER THE ENERGY to get himself off to work. He had shaved, showered, and dressed. His briefcase was on the floor by the door, his keys on the counter nearby. Still, he lingered. Once in the office, he knew, he would be bombarded with phone calls relating to *Dunn* v. *Hanover.* The press wanted statements; well-meaning friends wanted to offer congratulations; other victims of abuse wanted to hire him. It might have been flattering, if it weren't so embarrassing. In light of the way he had abused his own wife, he felt like a fraud.

Annie had left soon after Zoe and Jon, but signs of her were everywhere. Handwritten notes were tacked to the kitchen bulletin board, a scarf was hooked through the refrigerator handle, a pair of earrings lay on the windowsill at the end of a row of small potted plants. The plants were wilted. He took a glass from the cabinet, filled it with water, and worked his way down the line.

Time had calmed Annie some. When he spoke to her she gave brief, quiet answers. But always answers, never questions or unsolicited remarks.

This was his punishment, he supposed. The cold shoulder. A loathsome formality. Severence of the soul-wire.

And no Annie to hold. That was the worst. He could live without talk if he could hold her—not make love, just hold her. There was something about the way her body fit his, something about her warmth and her softness, that had become requisite to his existence.

Setting the glass on the counter, he began to wander from room to room. At the den he stopped. On impulse he opened the cabinet that held the VCR, selected one of the family cassettes, and put it in the machine. Remote control in hand, he leaned against the broad leather arm of the sofa.

The tape opened with a game of Trivial Pursuit. It was a recent tape, he remembered the game, but it might have been one of dozens of others. The Maxwells were paired against the Popes, which was very much the norm. J.D. was the detail man and hence the strongest player of the four, Teke the weakest simply because she was always leaving the game to fix snacks. Annie and Sam pooled their varying strengths, and the kids played both sides.

Sam studied Teke on the screen. She seemed comfortable playing second fiddle to J.D., exchanging looks, laughs, and whispers with him while he came up with his answers. She exchanged her share of looks with Annie and the children, too. And with Sam. He scrutinized those for something either of them might have felt but suppressed, a hidden desire, a pent-up hunger. He saw nothing remotely suggestive. For his part, he was totally engrossed in Annie, who had an arm around his waist and a cheek to his shoulder. He loved it when she nestled against him that way.

He sighed. The Maxwells didn't touch the way the

Popes did. But they always won the game.

Wondering if there was a perverse lesson in that, he fast-forwarded the tape. This time he found the Popewells celebrating New Year's Eve. They were wearing ragtag costumes—Teke had dragged out a trunk filled with goodies from Halloweens past—and eating nachos and blowing horns. The television was tuned to Times Square. The Big Apple slowly dropped. Everyone counted, louder, louder, and exploded with excitement when the new year arrived.

There were kisses all around. Sam watched once, rewound the tape, and watched again. He saw himself kiss Annie, then the kids and Teke and the kids and Annie again, where he lingered. Teke kissed J.D. but went on to the others and didn't return. Not that J.D. was lonesome. He was dancing around the room with a rabbit and a chipmunk, Jana and Zoe respectively.

Another fast forward brought him to a Sunday afternoon of car washing. Soap and water were everywhere, most noticeably on the women of the house, who never could win in a water war but took it all in stride. Annie and Teke were laughing hysterically. Their T-shirts and shorts were drenched and clinging. Little was concealed of their shapes.

Sam studied Teke. Her breasts were full, her hips curvy, as she squirmed to avoid the spray of the hose. Annie's body was smaller and sweeter and so much more enticing to Sam that he wondered how he had ever touched Teke and stayed hard.

Disgusted with himself all over again, he tossed the remote control on the coffee table, left the room, and climbed the two flights to Annie's attic office. Sinking onto the window seat, he fingered the afghan that lay in a haphazard heap. He knew she was sleeping here, using the afghan to keep warm.

He drew it to himself to ward off the chill he felt.

He had committed one stupid act, with ramifications that seemed to grow worse by the hour.

J.D. paced his office. Folders were piled neatly on his desk, along with a schedule of the day's meetings, but he couldn't get himself to look at either. It had been bad enough trying to concentrate when Michael was the only thing on his mind, but now Teke and Sam were there, too. He didn't know how he was going to work.

"What's the story on Michael?" his father asked from the door.

J.D.'s stomach jumped. He stopped pacing. "He's the same."

"Mary said you slept here last night."

Mary McGonigle had been with John Stewart for twenty-odd years. In addition to being his secretary, she was, as needed, his paralegal, his private courier service, his travel agent, his bank teller, and his personal shopper. J.D. wasn't sure if she was his lover. He wasn't sure if his mother was, either. He wasn't sure if John Stewart still had those kinds of urges. He was a very cold man.

The major difference between Mary McGonigle and Lucy Maxwell, as far as J.D. could discern, was that Mary was groomed and at work by seven each morning. That was how she had managed to catch J.D. Not that he had anything to hide—well, he did, but his having spent part of the night in the office was explained away easily enough.

"Teke went home for a break," he said, "so I stayed with Michael for most of the night. I came here to catch an hour or two of sleep." When Mary had woken him up in the middle of the fourth, he'd thanked her and gone back to the hospital, waiting there until he felt sure Teke would have left the house. Then he had driven to Constance, showered and changed clothes, and returned to the office, where he was good for absolutely nothing.

"I need your help with Ben Meyer," John Stewart said now.

Wait till you hear what Teke did to me, just wait till you hear. Shooting for nonchalance, he slipped his hands into his pockets and steadied his voice. "What's the problem?"

"He's giving us trouble on the university bequest." Ben Meyer was a multimillionaire and the major contributor to a new sports complex. John Stewart had been negotiating the gift.

You'll hit the roof, but only until you find out whom she did it with. All hell will break loose then. "I thought it was a done deal," J.D. remarked.

"It was, until Ben got to looking around at the sports complexes at other schools. He wants his to be like theirs. He wants his *full* name on the outside of the building. He says the Meyer Sports Center isn't enough."

You'll say you told me so. You'll say it's my own fault. I'll never hear the end of it. "I thought it was a whole package, with the name on each side of the building and a formal portrait and plaque in the foyer," J.D. said. *You'll tell me to boot them out, both of them. You'll want Teke out of the house and Sam out of the firm.*

"He wants the full name," John Stewart told him. "The university doesn't."

But she's the mother of my kids, J.D. argued. *They need her. I can't do what she does for them. I don't want to.* He shifted one tense shoulder in a way that made it look like a shrug. "It's his money."

John Stewart's eyes said John David was pitifully shortsighted. His voice reinforced the impression.

"It's our money lost if he's displeased with the arrangement and goes to another firm. I want you to talk to him."

"Why me?" J.D. asked. *And Sam, what in the hell am I supposed to do about Sam? He brings good money into the firm. And he does the storm windows for me. I don't know how to do the storm windows.*

"You have children nearing college age," John Stewart said. "You can make the argument that using his full name would be unwise. He'll believe you, more than me, when you tell him what the kids will do with it."

Blowen Meyer. It was really quite funny—or would be if the whole situation didn't suddenly strike J.D. as being petty. *One time? Okay, even if it was, it was a cheap shot. I was the one who gave them their tickets to the big time. I was the one who stuck my neck out for them.* "Everyone calls him Ben," J.D. grumbled. "Why can't he use that?"

"He wants his real name. And there's no middle initial."

"That's what he gets for being only half Yankee. Why in the hell does he need his full name on the wall? What'll he want next, a crown?"

"Take care of it, J.D.," John Stewart ordered as he turned away. "I want this settled."

Annie sat at her desk with her forehead in her palm. The headache was back, partly, she was sure, from the strain of fighting back tears. She tried to keep her mind occupied, but it wouldn't cooperate. It insisted on running to Sam.

"Knock, knock," came a voice from the door.

She looked up and mustered a smile. "Come on in, Jason. I was just thinking."

Jason Faust was a graduate student in the department. He was working toward his degree slowly. Coming from wealth gave him the luxury of doing that. It also gave him an arrogance that some of the others resented. Annie wasn't bothered by it. She found him to be bright and hardworking. This was their third year together. She relied on him as a guide for the newer teaching assistants.

"Must be heavy thoughts," he said. "Want an aspirin?"

"Already took three."

"A cup of coffee?"

She demonstrated the fine tremor in her hand.

"Some weed?"

She shot him an admonishing look. Then she sat back in her chair and ruffled the papers on the desk. "I'm a little behind. That's all."

Jason leaned against the wall just inside the door. In a quiet voice he said, "I was sorry to hear about your friend's little boy."

She frowned. She hadn't told anyone at work. She rarely involved colleagues in her personal life. "How did you know about that?"

"Susan." The department secretary. "When I couldn't find you yesterday afternoon, I asked. It must be difficult, running back and forth to the hospital. If I can help with anything here, I'd be glad to."

"I might take you up on that. God willing, Michael will come out of the coma soon. If he doesn't, if he's still in the hospital later in the semester when we get into the crunch of exams and paper, things could get hairy."

"I can handle hairy."

"That's because you're younger than I am. Youth has a resiliency that fades the older you get."

"You're not very old."

"I'm old," she said. She felt old and ugly, unappealing enough for Sam to have been tempted by Teke.

Granted, Teke was no younger than she was, but a different body was a new one and might have a certain appeal. Why Sam had been susceptible was another matter. Annie had been so sure of his love and loyalty. She didn't know where she'd gone wrong.

"Funny," she mused, "you get so involved in living that you sometimes forget what really matters. I worked so hard to build a career. I squeezed courses in while the kids were little, and increased the load as they got older. Then I got my degree and began teaching, and it seemed so important, and when I won tenure, that was the *best.*" She caught her breath. "Now something like this happens, and you realize that none of the scrambling up the ladder matters half as much as you thought it did."

"Do they think the little boy will pull through?" Jason asked.

Annie had been reflecting on Sam and Teke and marriage and friendship. Poor Michael was on the periphery of all that. "I think so." She tried to sound encouraging. "He's breathing on his own now."

"How's his mother—your friend?"

Annie wasn't sure. Teke had been gone from the hospital by the time she had arrived the afternoon before. Annie had been relieved, for more reasons than one. She knew she would have to face Teke sooner or later, but later helped. She needed more time to gather herself and her thoughts.

"She slept home for the first time last night. It's good, if not for her, then for her kids. She has two others." Annie took a tired breath. "I worry about them."

"Are they close to their brother?"

"He's thirteen to their fifteen and seventeen. Growing up, the girls always played with each other more than with him, but, yes, they're close. We're all close."

Were, she corrected, and wondered what was going to happen.

"I could teach for you, Annie."

"Hmmm?"

"You look so unhappy. Go on home."

She picked up a pen. "It's worse there."

"To the hospital, then. It might make you feel better. All you have left today is Brit lit, which I know like the back of my hand."

She crinkled her nose and began doodling.

"Then call your husband. Make him take you to lunch."

That was the worst suggestion of the three. She put more pressure to the pen, which wasn't making a mark.

Jason came toward the desk. "Do something, Annie. I hate seeing you upset."

She tried to form a smile, but it came out skewed. "I'll be okay."

"Isn't there anything I can do?"

"Yeah. Get the department to buy decent pens." She tossed hers aside. "These stink."

"I'm serious."

She looked up then. Jason Faust was known as the department hunk—this, from women of widely varying preferences. Annie couldn't argue with their assessment. He was blond-haired and silver-eyed, reminiscent of a younger, looser J.D.

"You're sweet," she said.

"So are you. What can I do to help?"

She sighed. "Nothing you're not already doing. It's nice having you around. You're more normal than some."

"Does that mean I get to teach a course next year?"

"It's only October."

"It's never too early to put in a bid. If I don't, someone else will."

"Someone else will anyway," she reminded him gently, "someone who has completed the degree that you're ambling your way through."

"But I'm brilliant," he argued with a grin.

She grinned back. "True. Still, it's not my decision to make."

"And not the time to discuss it anyway," he said resignedly as he turned to leave. "Will you let me know if there's anything I can do to help you out?"

"Uh-huh."

"Promise?"

"Uh-huh."

He winked and left.

"So, Mikey, what do you think?" Teke asked in a full voice as she stood back to admire her handiwork. The wall opposite his bed, stark white before, was now alive with a colorful assortment of the get well cards that Teke had taped there, along with a bright red banner that read GET WELL, MICHAEL. That the banner clashed with his T-shirt, which was turquoise and had his name plastered across the front in bold orange letters, was so much the better, as far as she was concerned. She wanted people to notice. She wanted everyone who walked in the room to know what her son's name was and the fact that he was a living, breathing human being.

"It looks great, Mrs. Maxwell," said a nurse who came in to check the needles in Michael's arm. He had dislodged one the night before, the result of an increase in random, sometimes agitated movements. No one was calling them a prelude to consciousness, but Teke prayed they were. At least she knew for sure that he wasn't paralyzed. Something in his brain was connecting, if in no orderly fashion.

She planned to work on that, too. She had made

an appointment with the physical therapist, so that she could learn how to exercise Michael's arms and legs. She was determined to keep him in shape and to remind his body of how it was supposed to behave.

"Those colors are bright enough to wake the dead," the nurse went on good-naturedly, "and it isn't just the wall, Michael. You should see the lady herself. She's wearing a hot pink sweater and tights. Of course, she's got the figure for it. If I tried that, I'd look like a blimp. Is she always this way?"

Michael didn't answer.

"She's also been baking. I see M&M cookies, and"—the nurse looked around—"I smell brownies. There they are, in a basket on the dresser, right beside the Hershey's kisses. I take it someone's a chocolate fiend?"

"Michael," Teke said. "Definitely." She passed the basket of brownies to the nurse. "Please have one."

Tempting Michael with his favorite treats was only half the point; the other was tempting the hospital staff to take a personal interest in him. On the chance that such an interest would result in more enthusiastic care, which in turn might help end Michael's coma, she could play dirty.

Anything for her son. No one was accusing *her* of being a lousy mother again.

"Oh, Lord," the nurse moaned, "she brought music, too. Don't tell me—Guns N' Roses, U2, Aerosmith."

Teke smiled. "You have a teenager?"

"Oh, yes." To the silent boy on the bed, she teased, "And it's a lucky thing for you that I do. I'm used to that noise. Watch out for the doctors, though. Shoot one of those songs at them when they're not expecting it, and they're apt to run for cover." She patted his arm. "See you in a bit."

Teke took Michael's hairbrush from the large

satchel she'd set on the floor by the bed. "Someone around here has to know how to wash the hair of a bedridden patient." Careful to avoid his stitches, she brushed his hair. "That'll be next on the list, right after food. Aren't you hungry, baby? I know you don't like me nagging, but you've got to wake up for a meal once in a while." She stroked his throat. "I'll spoon it in if you open your mouth. What would you like? A chocolate milk shake? Pudding with whipped cream? A hot fudge sundae?"

"There must be ways to get food into him."

The voice was quiet, but recognition was instant. Teke didn't have to look up to know that Grady had come, and she wasn't even sure his voice had done it. Her skin was suddenly more sensitive. She guessed she could be blind, deaf, and dumb and still know the instant he entered a room.

As quietly as he, she said, "They can put a feeding tube down his throat."

"Why don't they?"

"They want to give him a little more time." She prayed he would wake up before that was necessary. "It's an awful thought, a tube. But he's lost weight. He hasn't eaten a solid thing in three days."

Grady came up on the opposite side of the bed. He didn't say anything, just looked down at Michael.

Teke put the brush away. She took a breath that was remarkably steady, given the momentousness of the introduction she was about to make. "Michael, this is Grady Piper." *A face from my past, the great love of my life.* "He's the man whose truck you hit." Keeping her eyes on Michael, she said with resolve, "You shouldn't have come again, Grady. There was no need." He had driven her home when she had fallen apart the afternoon before, but she was fine now. If he wanted to help more, he could leave town. She had an angry husband and a very ill son. Grady couldn't change either fact. Years before he had opted out of her life. He had no place in it now.

But he said, "I can't stay away. I have to know how the boy is."

"A phone call will tell you that," she suggested. When Grady was silent, she took a different tack. "My husband blames you. He doesn't want you here. He'll make trouble."

"He already has. The police watch every move I make."

"Then *leave*," she whispered with urgency, and finally raised her eyes. She wasn't in shock now. She wasn't in tears or so tired that she couldn't see straight. For the very first time in twenty-two years, she took a good look at Grady Piper.

He was six feet three and as hard of body as he had been so long ago. He was wearing an open-necked shirt and jeans, but it was his face that drew her. It was tanned, with the squint marks he had earned at the docks as a teenager embedded more deeply now. His hair, once black as the paint he put on tug hulls, was lightly flecked with silver, but he looked well, too well for her peace of mind. She had spent years trying to hate him. She was trying still. "Damn it, Grady," she cried, "why did you do it? Why did you write to me? Why did you come?"

"I told you in the letter."

"You said you wanted to see me. But why?"

"I just wanted to see you."

"You had *no right!*" she cried in a burst of anger. "You were the one who made me leave Gullen! I would have stayed and waited for you, but you told me to go. You said you didn't want me. You said you wouldn't come back for me. You said you wouldn't come back *at all* if I was there."

"I wanted something better for you."

"Well, I thought *you* were something better, but you turned me away. So I did what you said, I got my education, and my husband, and my better life, and I was perfectly happy with it, until you sent that letter. You shouldn't have done that, Grady! You can't waltz in and out of people's lives. It isn't fair!"

"Life isn't fair."

She looked away. "Swell."

"It isn't. I saved you, so I lost you. Where's the sense in that?"

Facing him again, she saw his tension. It was wire tight in his jaw and as heartrending as the pain in his eyes. But she refused to relent. "You wouldn't have lost me if you hadn't sent me away."

"You don't understand," he ground out. "I'm a murderer. I'll be that for the rest of my life. I'm an ex-con. People know that right away, they can smell it on a man. Know what it's like to go through life with the kind of stink?"

"You're being overly dramatic."

He gave her a disparaging look. "I'm good at what I do, but for every job I get, there's three I lose because of my record. You wanted to be muddied by that?"

"I wouldn't have minded."

He snorted. "That's a nice house you've got. Nice car. Nice ring on your finger. I couldn't have given you those."

"As if I cared."

"Well, I did. I wanted the best for you." After a minute he lowered his eyes to Michael. "I wasn't even planning to see you that day. I just wanted to see where you lived. I wanted to see if you'd gotten the best. Looks like I botched things again." In a voice rife with self-disgust he muttered, "What a fuck-up I am."

Teke's anger dissipated. She sighed. "Oh, Grady.

If you're that, then I'm ten times worse."

He met her eyes. "Because of what you told me last night?"

She nodded. She had half hoped he wouldn't remember, though she supposed it was just as well. He wasn't the only fuck up. Indeed, where Michael's accident was concerned, he was nothing more than a victim of circumstance. He shouldn't be wallowing in guilt.

"Is Sam a good friend?"

"My husband's best."

"How long has it been going on?"

"Tuesday was the one and only time."

"Why did it happen, then?"

She rubbed Michael's chest. If he was listening, he was getting an earful, but she didn't care. "I had gotten your letter and was upset. He came. It happened."

"Isn't your marriage good?"

"My marriage is okay." She paused. "Was okay. I don't think J.D. will ever forgive me for what I did. It was treason of the first degree." When Grady said nothing, she dared look up. "It was, Grady. I've never done anything as awful in my life."

He looked confused. "Where I've been, they talk lots about patterns of behavior. I didn't have one, not so far as murder went, which is why they let me out after eight. I hadn't done anything, other than that one big crime, and I didn't do that one for kicks. The prison shrink talked about an anger that had been growing for years. He talked about a highly charged emotional situation that exploded, like a key of dynamite hit by a match." His gaze grew more direct. "We know why I exploded. Why did you?"

Teke didn't follow.

"You cheated on your husband once," he said. "Just once. You must have had good reason."

"I did," she snapped, throwing caution to the winds. Her relationship with Grady had never been pasteurized, as suburban ones were. It had been naked and unadorned. "I was sitting in that chair, remembering everything we'd had, everything I'd been pushing out of my mind for years. I had tried so hard to forget you. But it was useless right then. Your letter was real. It all came back. I found myself wanting you, the passion we had together, and getting angry about that. Sam came. I wanted to be swept up in his excitement. I hadn't counted on my body being so ready for you."

Grady didn't blink. "What's wrong with your husband?"

"Nothing's wrong with him."

"Why didn't you call him?"

"I didn't think to call him."

"Why not? He could have come home."

"He was at work. He wouldn't have left. But that's not the point. The point is that I wasn't thinking *at all.*"

Grady focused on Michael. After a time, in a voice hard with conviction, he said, "You'd have called him if your marriage was good."

"It was," she protested. She was desperate to believe it.

"It couldn't have been, or you'd never have done it with Sam."

"If that was true, why did Sam do it with me?" she asked. "He adores Annie. They have a terrific sex life, a terrific marriage.

Grady raised his eyes. "I wouldn't have cheated on you if you were my wife, and you wouldn't have cheated on me."

"But I'm not your wife!" she shouted and the anger was back. "You precluded that."

Her anger had no effect on the heat that entered

his gaze. "It was good between us, Teke."

She moaned and put a hand up to steady her heart. Her anger had no effect on her own heat, either. It was stirred by the smallest, briefest memory.

"Right from the first. Do you remember?"

She closed her eyes and nodded. She was suddenly breathing more quickly, just as she'd been doing that night. She had been fifteen, Grady seventeen, and she had worshiped the ground he walked on. They had been seeing each other whenever they could, meeting in dark, hidden corners of Gullen, innocently at first, then with greater purpose. Grady, whose body had been a man's for years, had been taught by the best in town, yet he had treated Teke as though it were all new. The hands that held her face for his kisses had shaken, same when he had lowered those hands and unbuttoned her shirt.

She had been shy, unsure of the new body she'd grown, but needful of him, and he had been so very gentle. She remembered the way he had cupped her breasts and the strangeness of the feeling. She hadn't understood how he could touch her there and she could feel it so much lower. But he had soothed her worry with small words and deepening kisses. He had made that lower feeling so commanding that she had been desperate to take off her jeans.

The hurt had surprised her, but he had kissed away her tears, teased her breasts with his tongue, and held himself still inside her until the sting had passed and the tingle begun. Then he had taken her to the stars. They visited one one night, and another the next. There was a whole universe to explore, and they had been determined to do it, until Homer Peasley had come in their way.

Covering her face with her hands, Teke took deep, gulping breaths. She had loved Grady so. She would have gone to prison for him if he had let her, or *died* for him if that would have spared him his fate. But he had told her to leave and never look back, he had *ordered* her to leave and never look back. When she had resisted, he had used even sharper words. He had spurned her attempts to visit and to write. She had been hurt and heartsick, young and naive. What choice had she had but to obey him?

"Not fair," she charged now. *"Not fair."*

"What in the hell is he doing here?" J.D. roared.

Teke swung around to the door, then swung right back when she felt Michael move. She blotted out all else but that. "It's your dad, baby. I told you he'd be here. Move again, honey. Let him know you know."

"Get out," J.D. said to Grady.

Grady held up a hand. "I'm going."

"You put my boy in this bed. I don't want you here."

Teke released a breath when she didn't see further movement from Michael. "It wasn't his fault," she murmured, but J.D. disagreed.

"He was driving down a street in a neighborhood he shouldn't have been in at all. He's got no business in Constance."

"Yes, I do," Grady said. His voice was quiet, but Teke heard his steel. When she saw it mirrored on his face, she felt an instinctive fear. She knew what that steel could do.

"Don't, Grady," she warned.

But he was focused on J.D. "I was hired this morning by a man named Charles Hart. His mother lives on Chadwell Street in an old Victorian with a carriage house behind it. He wants the carriage house turned into an apartment. I get to live there free while I do the work."

J.D. pursed his lips. "Obviously Charlie Hart doesn't know you're a murderer."

"Feel free to tell him," Grady offered, and set off.

Teke couldn't believe he wasn't defending himself. "Grady—"

"That's right," J.D. called, "and don't come back. We don't want you here. You upset my family. The police may have no cause to file a criminal complaint against you, but if I see your face around here again, I'll go for a restraining order, and if I have to do that, I'll slap you with a civil suit at the same time."

Grady moved, tall and smooth, past the window and down the hall.

"A civil suit for *what?*" Teke asked J.D., who looked at her with such dislike that she would have cringed, had she not been hot in defense of Grady.

"For being a public nuisance. For causing mental anguish. Hell, I'll sue him for trespassing, since we're paying so much for this goddamned hospital room."

"He has every right to be here."

"Are you kidding?"

"He's my friend."

J.D. nodded. "Ahhh. Your friend. What's the matter, Teke? Now that you know that I won't touch you and that Sam doesn't dare, are you desperate for somebody new?"

Her hand came up so unexpectedly that she was the one who reeled when it hit him hard across the face. She had never hit another human being that way. It shook her.

Hugging herself, she said, "Damn it, J.D., you bring out the worst in me."

He held his head high. She knew he wouldn't touch his cheek, though it had to be smarting. Her hand certainly was. But he wouldn't give her the sat-

141

isfaction. He was prideful that way. She had seen him hold his head high just like that any number of times, though never because of her. Through the course of their marriage, they had rarely argued.

"Maybe it's just the real you," J.D. said. "Another thing to learn about, along with your appetite for men other than your husband. Is there more?"

Pride, yes. And smugness. She could understand the first, but the second galled her. He was putting himself up to be perfect. But Grady was right. Something had to have been wrong with her marriage for her to betray her husband. *No way* would J.D. have run home if she had called, and she wouldn't have called. She would have satisfied herself before she'd have done that.

"Yes," she said in a moment's bravado, "there is more. If Grady Piper wants to come here, he's coming. He feels terrible about what happened. No matter that through no fault of his, Michael ran in front of his truck. Grady is suffering, too."

"Fat chance. He can't feel the way we do and still be capable of taking a life. He's a convicted felon, a murderer."

She was shaking her head. "He killed a man, but it wasn't intentional. He was found guilty of manslaughter, not murder one or murder two. If he'd had money enough to hire a good lawyer, he might have gotten off even that. I've seen Sam win acquittals when men have done worse. But Grady was dirt poor, like I was, so he had to serve his time. That's over and done. He's as much a thinking, feeling person as you or me or Annie or Sam."

J.D. was regarding her strangely. "How did you know it was manslaughter?"

"Because I was there," she told him. Keeping the secret no longer seemed to matter. Far more important to her was telling the truth. "I told you. Grady's my friend. I've known him all my life. He came from Gullen."

J.D.'s jaw dropped, then snapped right back up. "He came to see you, didn't he? That was why he was in our neighborhood. He came to see you. So this is even *more* your fault. If he hadn't come looking for you, Michael would have run across the street and been fine. Of course, that's not taking into consideration the emotional trauma of seeing you with Sam." He made a face. "You're disgusting."

"Maybe," she said and turned back to Michael, "but I'm still rational. Don't threaten Grady, J.D. If his being here bothers you, he'll leave when you come. But no lawsuits. Please. The only thing they'll accomplish is to embarrass us all."

J.D. wasn't one to take defeat lying down. That evening, after dropping the girls at home, he drove to see Charlie Hart. They were casual friends and sometime tennis partners, but the relationship had never evolved into more. For one thing, Charlie was a staff doctor at the small hospital in Constance and, as such, didn't run in the circles that merited J.D.'s interest. For another, he was something of a bleeding heart, championing causes that bored J.D. to tears.

J.D. was optimistic that he could make Charlie see the light. He calculated that all he had to do was to mention the word *murderer,* and Charlie's dedication to the preservation of life, as evidenced by his work, would take it from there.

His calculations were wrong on two counts. First, Charlie knew about the murder conviction. "He told me about it right off," he explained as they stood on his front porch in the balmy October night. "He told me about spending time in prison and about his parole. He said he had nothing to hide. He had impressive references."

"From whom?"

"Past employers. The pastor of his hometown church. His parole officer."

"Were these letters?" J.D. asked. Letters could be easily forged. Every lawyer knew that. Doctors, well, they weren't quite as astute.

"Yes, they were, but I followed them up with phone calls. Every reference vouched for him, except one. George Wiley." Charlie arched a brow. "That's George Wiley, as in representative to the U.S. House. I tried his Maine office, but they said he was on a fact-finding trip in the Baltics. His letter was authentic enough. Piper built a family room for him several years ago. He showed me pictures of it and of some of his other work. He looks to be quite skilled."

J.D. was beginning to feel thwarted. "He's the man who hit my son, Charlie."

"I know. That's one of the reasons he wants to stay around here. He feels responsible."

"He *is* responsible."

But Charlie scratched his head. "That's not what the police say. I called them after I checked out the references. They say he was going slowly and that he did his best to stop. Hell, J.D., this is a good deal for me. I pay for raw materials; he provides his labor and know-how in exchange for my letting him live there. He'll be cold, let me tell you. That place will be like a barn until he gets guys in with the heat. He says he's lived in worse."

Reluctantly J.D. said, "I'm asking you as a personal favor, Charlie. My family suffers every time we see him. The sooner he leaves here, the better. I'll help you find someone else, but I'd rather you didn't hire this particular man."

Charlie grew thoughtful. "What am I supposed to tell him?"

"That you've reconsidered and decided you'll be uncomfortable having a convicted felon working around your mother's house."

Charlie remained thoughtful. "I could. But that'd be wrong. I have no problem having him around."

"He could rob your mother."

"He could also protect her from a robber." He set his mouth and looked at J.D. apologetically. "I'm going to stick with it, I think. The guy's a straight talker. I like him. I like the idea of giving him the chance."

Which was, in a nutshell, J.D.'s second miscalculation. Bleeding hearts pulled for the underdog. No matter what.

seven

GRADY STAYED AWAY FROM THE HOSPITAL over the weekend. He respected the family's need to have their own time with Michael, and in truth he didn't relish another confrontation with J.D. Oh, he was up for the fight. He could out-lawyer-speak J.D. in a minute, he knew that much about his rights. But Teke would be the one to suffer, and he didn't want that.

So he settled for updates from the ICU nurse and, between those, moved his few possessions into Cornelia Hart's carriage house, began drawing up plans for its conversion to an apartment, and explored the offerings of local lumberyards and supply houses.

Midmorning Monday, when he figured J.D. would be at work, he went to the hospital. Michael was alone and unmoving in his room. Behind him the bank of machines bleeped steadily, but another sound now joined those, that of music from a boom box on the bedstand.

It was a nice touch, he thought, a way to clue Michael in to the familiar, another of the changes Teke had made in the room. The place had been humanized. It was brighter, warmer, more personal, even if—disturbingly—it implied the boy might be there awhile.

"Hi there, Michael," he said. "How's it goin'?" He wondered where Teke was. He had been hoping to see her, too. "I like your T-shirt." This one was white. At its center was a bright neon circle with a diagonal slash through pointy letters spelling DEAD-HEAD. "Don't agree with you about the Dead, though. They're cool." He sifted through the compact discs that lay by the boom box. "Not your taste, huh? Maybe it wouldn't have been mine, either, if it hadn't been forced on me. When I was in prison, there was a guy on my cell block who was a *real* Deadhead."

He studied Michael's face. It was totally impassive. "You knew I did time, didn't you?" He paused. "Can't keep a secret like that. People always find out. Better to tell them up front. They want to kick you out, they can, but it's less humiliating if they do it at the start."

He scanned the room. The wall of cards had spread to the floor. People obviously cared about Michael. He envied the boy his friends. When he was Michael's age, he'd had but a handful. Most were years older and wouldn't have known how to write a get well card, much less think to send one.

He returned to Michael's face. He wasn't sure what to say, didn't know what the boy heard. He figured the sound of his voice was probably more important than his words, so he talked about what he knew.

"Some people get nervous when you tell them where you've been. They think you're going to whip out a gun and blow their brains out." He made a sound. "Shows how much they know. One stretch in prison was enough for me. I'd kill myself before I'd do anything to put me back there."

His voice grew earnest. If Michael did hear, Grady wanted him to hear this. "That's why I know I wasn't breaking any law when I drove down your street. I've learned to be careful. Because of where I've been, cops watch me all the time. I keep my hands in clear view when I'm walking down the street. I pay the waitress even if the food is lousy. Light turns yellow, I stop."

He touched the boy's arm. Teke's son. Should have been his.

He sighed. "Boy, I would've done that if I'd seen you. I'm real sorry, Michael. If I'd had any idea you were coming through those trees, I'd have stopped. I just didn't see you."

He waited for the boy to open his eyes and say, "That's okay. It was an accident. I'm not angry." But he didn't, and Grady had a terrifying sense of déjà-vu. *Open your eyes, bastard. Open your eyes and hit me again. You're not dead. You're too hard to die. Open your eyes, goddammit.*

He shot an alarmed look at the machines, thinking Michael might have died on him, too, but they were happily humming away. Shaken, he clutched the bedrail. He bowed his head and gathered his wits. He was raising his head again when saw the giraffe. It stood in a corner of the room, looking worn. He guessed it to be a much loved relic of Michael's childhood and thought of his own.

"I would've bought your mom something like that, if I'd had the money. I knew her when she was a little girl, y'know. We grew up in Gullen together." He daydreamed his way back. "She was real pretty. First time I noticed her, she'd been bit by a dog—no, I noticed her before that. I used to see her in the schoolyard on the days they made me go. She stood out from the others with that dark hair of hers and that light skin and those scared eyes. But it was on the day she was bit by the dog that she had such a woeful look on her face that my heart broke right there. Her daddy was one mean son of a gun. Tough as rusted nails. He used to make her wait on him, then he'd knock her around when she didn't do things just right. He smiled. "She grew up nice."

The smile faded. He took a breath, let it out in a hoarse, "I loved her. We were going to spend our whole lives together." There was pain in remembering those dreams and knowing how awfully they'd been blown to bits. Still, fragments returned. "She wanted to have babies, that's all she wanted to do, have babies and me. But I wanted her to go to school before we had babies, because I hadn't been to school and I thought one of us should be educated if we wanted our kids to do better than us. Our kids were going to do good things. We used to talk about that a lot."

He slipped his hand into Michael's. He was her son, flesh of her flesh. Holding his hand was once removed from holding hers. It helped fill the hollowness he felt. "Then the jury said I was guilty. I knew I was going away for a long time and that from then on I was marked. I knew we'd never have the things we talked about. I knew I'd always drag her down. So I sent her away."

"You returned my letters."

His eyes flew to the door. Teke was leaning against its frame, holding a cup of coffee. He wondered how long she had been there.

"You didn't have to do that, Grady. They were just letters. You could have ignored them. But you deliberately returned them."

"No point in reading them. They'd only have hurt. Better to make the break."

"Not for me. It was devastating."

"It worked."

She studied her coffee, looking as though she were thinking of arguing. But she only sighed and took a sip, then asked, "What was it like, prison?"

"Hard," he answered. "Gray and cold."

"Were you scared when they first took you there?"

He nodded. "I'd known tough men at the docks, but none were like the guys on the inside."

Teke shivered. She held the coffee cup in both hands. After a minute she took another sip. "Breakfast," she said sheepishly.

"Didn't you have anything before you left the house?"

"I was here all night. I thought of going to the cafeteria, but I couldn't see myself sitting down with all those people in white. Besides, I didn't want to leave Michael that long." She crossed to the bed and touched his cheek. "Hi, sweetheart. Has Grady been keeping you company?"

"Boring him, most like."

"No. Michael's the curious kind. Videography's his thing. He's apt to wake up and want to do a piece on prison life."

Grady shrugged. "It's not real exciting. There's day after day of doing the same awful thing and feeling the same awful fear. Then you get out and the fear is just as bad."

"In what sense?" she asked, reminding him of the Teke of old, all questions about what he was doing.

He had always liked that. It made him feel important, like who he was and what he did mattered. So he said, "You're on your own once you're out. All of a sudden there's no one to tell you where to go when. There's no one providing your food and your clothes. You've got to do everything for yourself, only you haven't been doing it for so long that you're not sure how. The stores are selling different kinds of foods from when you went in. The machines in the Laundromats work differently. Your clothes are funny. You think everyone's staring at you. You feel out of place and unwanted."

"Did you go back to Gullen?"

"For a bit. Didn't know where else to go."

She whispered, "I was sorry about your father, Grady. The church ladies wrote me that he'd died. I grieved for him more than I ever did for Homer. I wanted to come back for his funeral, but I couldn't. It would have been too painful."

Grady looked down. He knew about that pain. His father had been a hard man with a soft spot for his son. For years the county authorities had thought he was abusing Grady by keeping him out of school and forcing him to work at the docks, but the truth was that he loved having Grady with him. The feeling was mutual.

"Those first two years," Grady said, "he visited me the first Sunday of every month. It was hard on him. He used to see the others in that visiting room and get a frantic look on his face, like he didn't know how his son could be there, like he had to do something, to protect him somehow. Then one Sunday he wasn't there when he was supposed to be. I knew there'd be only one reason he'd miss. It took them three days to tell me he was dead."

"Oh, Grady."

"Just as well," Grady rationalized as he had dozens of times before. "He was sick. His heart was getting weaker and weaker. If he'd been there when I'd come back, he'd have had to sit around watchin' me work, and he'd have hated that, too. It was the working side by side that he liked." He studied Michael. "Videography, huh? I don't know anything about videography."

"I do," said the nurse as she entered the room with a gurney and a trail of attendants. She looked at Teke. "All set?"

Teke had a suddenly frightened look in her eye—the same kind of look she had worn as a little girl, which had so affected Grady—but she stepped aside so that they could transfer Michael. "They're taking him for a brain scan," she explained.

Grady went to her side. "What are they looking to find?"

"Patterns of brain waves that may or may not be normal."

He watched the technicians deftly shift monitors, bottles, and tubes. He was wondering how long it took to do a brain scan and whether J.D. would be coming to wait with Teke.

Reading his mind, she said, "My husband isn't a good waiter. He'll talk with the doctors once they've had a chance to look at the results of the scan." Behind the fear in her eyes was a warning. "He comes in at lunchtime. That, and before and after work."

Grady nodded. While it wasn't exactly an invitation, it was an improvement on the you-shouldn't-have-come-here then. He could live with that for now.

The scan said that Michael's brain was working fine, which made his coma all the more frustrating for Teke. She soared high one minute when he moved an arm or a leg or his mouth, fell low the next when he was as still as a corpse.

His care dominated her time; her day was taken up with working his good arm and leg, massaging his muscles, bathing him, combing his hair, and talking to him, lest he forget who he was. But there were other times—times when J.D. glared at her, when Annie avoided meeting her eye and Sam gave her wide berth, when the children—worse, John Stewart and Lucy—came, and there was a pretense of normalcy to uphold.

"Upset about Michael" became the catch-all to excuse bad moods and incommunicativeness, but Teke knew it wouldn't work forever. At some point the girls were going to wonder why their parents avoided each other, why Annie wasn't talking to Teke, why the foursome had split.

Of that foursome, she missed Annie the most. She missed their phone conversations each night, their shopping trips, their lunches when one or another of them needed a lift. Annie had always steadied her through life's shakes, and, Lord knew, life was shaky now.

Teke needed steadying. That was why she hoped Grady would visit again—but for every minute of hoping, she spent another one in self-reproach. Grady was her past. There was no room for him in her present, certainly no room for the pain he had once caused. She couldn't live through that again. She wouldn't survive.

Still, she felt something small lighten up inside her when, within minutes of J.D.'s lunchtime departure, Grady walked in carrying a paper sack that smelled of something greasy and hot.

"Pastrami with cheese and peppers," he said, and handed it to her. "Five to one you haven't eaten."

He was right. She took the bag and held it a minute, thinking that she should hand it right back, but that she was very much in the mood for greasy and hot she was. Shooting him a fast, "Thanks, I'm starved," she sank onto a chair, unwrapped the sandwich, and took a large bite.

Grady went to Michael's side. "How are you, pal?"

He tipped his head to read the T-shirt of the day. "Michael Maxwell's Gym. Super-Jocks Only." To Teke he said, "Is he one?"

She nodded. "A basketball buddy brought that in. Tryouts are coming up. It's going to be tough if he can't make them." She took another bite of the sandwich, but it wasn't as good as the first.

"I watched your husband leave. He looked upset."

"He's not very pleased with me," which was putting it mildly. He had been in a stew, railing on about the doctors' failure to wake Michael, Teke's failure to wake Michael, Teke's hair, her clothes, the bags under her eyes. "Things are beginning to pile up at home. He doesn't understand why I can't divide my time more evenly."

"Can't you hire someone to help?"

"I already have someone, but she only comes once a week. I don't think she has time for more, and I can't be there to train someone new. Besides, the girls can help with the cooking and the laundry. So can J.D. But he won't."

She took another bite of the sandwich and felt an intense annoyance. It wasn't that J.D. was suddenly refusing to do things, just that she was suddenly realizing how very little he had ever done. She hadn't thought to mind before. The house was her domain; she took pride in keeping order there. But she could have used his help now and, if not his help, certainly his understanding.

"How about this guy?" Grady asked Michael. "Does he help around the house?"

"Not much. But that's my fault. I spoil him. Oh, I tell myself not to do it. No thirteen-year-old girl today is going to grow up to want a husband who can't do for himself. Still, I spoil him. He's such a good kid, and if he isn't busy with school, he's playing ball or using the videocam. It's not like he's loitering on the street corner with a cigarette dangling from his mouth."

"I would have loved a spoiling when I was a kid," Grady mused. "I used to do whatever had to be done. We both did."

Teke picked out a strip of green pepper. Eating it, she thought back to those times. "There wasn't much easy about our lives. Maybe that's why I spoil my kids. I want them to know what carefree means." She thought of all Grady had said the day before. His description of prison haunted her, and while she told herself that it was none of her business, that she was better off not knowing, that in sending her away Grady had forfeited his rights to her concern, she found that she was curious about his life. So she said, "Tell me about after you got out of prison. You went back to Gullen and felt stared at and strange. Did you work at the docks?"

He shook his head. "Someone else was in charge there. He didn't want me." He was silent for a while, looking at Michael through faraway eyes. "My parole officer was just as glad. He thought I should do something different. He got me into boat-building school."

Teke smiled. That sounded like something she could see Grady doing. He loved boats and was good with his hands. Definitely boat-building school.

"It was nice," he confirmed. "Nice people. But hard work. I'd gotten my high school equivalency in prison. Took a few college courses, too. But the others were way ahead of me."

His high school equivalency. Teke was impressed. "What happened then?"

"My favorite teacher was a canoe buff. He was into making wood-and-canvas canoes and got me hooked. There was a simplicity to the work—and a beauty to the finished product—that appealed to me much more than learning about sophisticated aerodynamics and high-tech finishings. Every free minute I had, I was helping him."

Teke could see the pleasure he took in the memory. It warmed her. "Go on."

"He left to head his own school in Seattle."

She felt a stab of disappointment. "What did you do then?"

But Grady was watching Michael more closely. "I'd swear his eyelids just moved." He looked at Teke. "Has he done that before?"

She was on her feet and hanging over the bed in a second. "Michael? Was it something Grady said?"

"Maybe he was trying to open his eyes."

"Come on, baby," she urged, "do it again."

They watched, but there was no sign of activity.

She shook him a little. "It's been a week, Mikey, a *whole week.* I want you to do something. *Now.* Do you hear me?" she begged. "*Do* something."

When he didn't, she put her fingers to her forehead to control the hysteria budding there. "This is the worst part, the up and down. He's becoming more active—a finger, a foot, a chin, now his eyes."

"Maybe I imagined it."

"You didn't. He teases us, then stops, gives us hope, then dashes it." Her voice grew pleading. "I know you're in there, Michael. Blink for me. Make a face." She put her fingers through his. "Give me a squeeze. Just a little one so I'll know you've heard."

But she felt nothing. With a discouraged sigh, she straightened. "Okay," she murmured, recouping, "I can wait. I can wait." With measured movements, she returned to the chair and took another bite of Grady's sandwich. It had cooled off and tasted vile, but she chewed and swallowed. Determined to carry on, she cleared her throat and addressed herself to Grady again. "After your friend left for Seattle, what did you do?"

He had his hands in the pockets of his blazer. "I started working construction to earn money to fly out and offer him my services."

She continued to work to calm herself. "Did you?"

"No. I took to carpentry, and by the time I had the money, I was liking the work too much to quit. I make canoes sometimes, but it's just a hobby."

She took a calmer breath at last. "I'm glad."

"Of what?"

"That things worked out well." She tried to picture his life now. "Are you really living in Gullen?"

"Nah. I stop by sometimes, but I'm pretty nomadic. I have most of my stuff in my truck."

"But the letter you sent was from Gullen."

"I was there briefly. I never stay long because of the memories. They were worse this last time. I was feeling down. I thought it was time I saw you. So I sent the letter." Gruffly he said, "I should've waited a week. The timing would've been different then. None of this would've happened."

He was right, Teke thought. Once, he had returned the letters she sent. It was ironic that a letter *he* had sent should cause such havoc. But there was no taking it back. Her existence was unreal, her inner clock ticking from one endless twenty-four hours into the next. Life was the hospital. Michael was in a coma, J.D. scorned her, Annie hated her, and Sam was distancing himself as far as he could.

Grady's voice was near, low. "Teke?"

"It wouldn't have mattered," she cried softly. I'm the problem here. I'm the poison."

"Not true."

"Then what explains it? I'm the one common element in all these people's screwed-up lives." She suddenly found his arms braced on the arms of her chair. His face was inches away. "Take you," she went on. "If you hadn't known me, you wouldn't have committed murder or gone to prison. You would have had a nice business, a nice wife, a bunch of nice children. You deserved all that."

"Who said I didn't have it?"

She went still. He hadn't mentioned a wife and kids. She had just assumed there were none.

Straightening, he put his hands back in his pockets and faced the window. "I married. We had a little girl. My wife divorced me three years ago."

Teke was stunned. She had never imagined Grady with another woman. Foolish, and selfish, but she hadn't.

"But why?" she asked. The Grady she had known would have made a perfect husband and father.

"We attributed it to lots of things—different interest, different values, different life-styles. Fact was," he said with a dry stare her way, "one too many times it was your name I called out in bed. So don't think you have a monopoly on betrayal, b'cause you don't."

That gave Teke much to consider in the long hours that followed.

Annie took care to ensure that she never visited Michael alone. It was easily enough done. Even on the days when Leigh and Jana went later with Jon, Zoe was eagerly waiting on the school steps for her to drive up.

"I know I'm awful for saying this, Mom," she said on one such day. "I mean, we're going to the hospital to visit Michael, which is the worst thing in the world to have to be doing, but it's nice having you come for me. I like knowing you're here at the end of the day."

Annie reached over and took her hand.

"Am I awful?" Zoe asked.

"Not at all," Annie answered. She needed to hear things like that. She needed to feel she was doing something right. Of course, that didn't say much for what she'd been doing before. "Does it bother you that I work so much?"

Zoe considered that. "It doesn't 'bother' me. I'm proud of what you do, and you love your work. It's just that I wish I had you more to myself." She settled onto the passenger's seat with a smile. "This is nice. Just the two of us."

Annie felt a tugging at her heart.

"Maybe it would have been different if I was an only child," Zoe went on. "Then I'd have you to myself whenever you weren't working. Well, I'd have to share you with Daddy, but that's different."

The tugging Annie felt this time came from the agony of being estranged from Sam. They barely talked. Not that he didn't try. But she couldn't say much. She was angry, and hurt, and read into everything he said.

"Do you feel that Jon crowds you?" she asked Zoe.

"No," Zoe said with conviction. "Jana and Leigh do. Jana especially. I mean, I love Jana, she's my very best friend in the world, but she talks to you about all the things *I* want to talk to you about."

"Oh, baby. I'm sorry."

"Why can't Jana go to Teke with her problems?"

"Because she's used to coming to me, just like you're used to going to Teke when you need something to wear for a dance. She's good with clothes. I'm good with problems."

"There are times when I wish we weren't so close that way. I mean, it's fun being with the Maxwells— and Jon would scream if we went on vacation without them—but I'm telling you now, I wish we could

do that once, just once, go on our own family vacation, just us four." She paused and repeated, "Am I
awful?"

"You're not awful at all," Annie said, and felt a
new sadness. She had always thought they were
doing the right thing, sharing their lives with the
Maxwells. One big happy family, the more the merri-
er, one for all and all for one. Or was that the need
of four adults, none of whom had come from big
families, themselves? She wondered if the Maxwell
kids felt the same way Zoe did.

At least Zoe's timing was right, Annie mused.
Popewell vacations were very definitely on hold.

She sighed. "I'm glad you've told me this."

"Can I tell you something else?" Zoe asked quickly.

"Sure."

"I'm doing awful in math this term. I don't know
what happened, I must have missed something
early on, and I can't seem to get anything right
now." She raced on. "They're sending a pink slip
home to tell you that I have a D average, but I want
you to know that I'll bring it up, I promise I will. I
made an appointment for extra help Thursday afternoon. Is that okay?"

"Of course it is," Annie said, "and I'm not angry."
She was disturbed that Zoe had kept the worry to
herself. "Did you think I would be?"

"It's a *D,* Mom. That's em*barr*assing."

"Math was my worst subject, too."

"Jana's *so good* at it."

"So was Teke, but they both struggle with the
English courses that you and I breeze right though.
Don't sweat it, honey. Just do the best you can. And
by all means, go for extra help Thursday."

That was how Annie found herself driving to the
hospital alone. She might have waited and taken
Zoe in later, but Jon had offered to do it after prac-

tice, and since Annie had to stop at the supermarket, the dry cleaner, the library, and the drugstore before she turned in for the night, she figured she would visit Michael first, then do all the rest. Her life was hectic enough. She didn't need Boston at the rush hour.

Michael was nine days into his coma. The strain of it had begun to show on them all in short fuses and long faces, but it was nowhere more noticeable than in Teke. She was giving Michael a rubdown when Annie arrived. Her movements were tired, the voice that kept up a monologue strained.

Annie watched for a minute from the hall. For a split second she imagined Teke's hands on Sam. The image was so vivid that she might have actually turned and left if Teke hadn't looked up just then and seen her.

Trying to act confident when she felt awkward and unsure, she approached the bed. "How is he?"

Teke kept at her work. "He's moving more. In one breath the doctors say he may be trying to break out. In the next they say it may be nothing."

Annie was appalled by how thin Michael's leg looked. She guessed he had lost ten pounds since the accident.

Teke must have followed her thoughts, because she said, "As of last night, I've been feeding him some. I spoon ice cream and protein drinks into his mouth, and he swallows. Not that it's making much of a difference. He looks emaciated."

"You'll notice a difference in a day or two," Annie said. "Even if you can keep him from losing more weight, it's worth the effort."

Teke nodded.

Annie wondered what it was about her that had appealed to Sam. Yes, Teke looked cute in her celery-colored tunic and tights, but her face was drawn and gaunt. "You've lost weight, too."

Teke set Michael's leg down. "I can't eat much. I'm too upset."

Typical Teke, Annie thought. She had always been that way, unable to eat during final exams, or in the days preceding her wedding, or when the kids had chicken pox all at the same time.

She had an idea. "Why don't you leave." It seemed the perfect solution for them both. "I'll stay here with Michael. Go for a ride, go to a restaurant, go home for a rest."

Teke ran an arm across her forehead. "I'm all right."

"Go on. I'll stay with him."

"I want to talk with you, Annie. I want to explain, apologize."

Annie shook her head. "No—"

"There's so much to say. You're my best friend. I need you to listen."

"I can't," Annie begged. "Not yet. But I can talk with Michael. Go. Please."

"I'm so sorry—"

Annie put her hands over her ears. She didn't want to hear an apology. She wasn't sure she would believe one.

After a long, beseechful stare, Teke took her bag from the floor and left. In her wake, Annie felt worse than ever. One stupid mistake, Sam had called it, but what harm it had done, and the harm kept compounding itself. She wondered where it would end.

Turning to Michael, she said, "Why is it we hurt the people we love? Can you tell me that?" She sighed and scrubbed his arm with her fingertips. More softly she said, "I'm sorry. It's just that it's so difficult out here. Part of me envies you, lying in there with your eyes shut to the world. Why must things be so complicated?"

Michael didn't answer. He didn't blink. He didn't try to escape the scrubbing of her fingertips.

"I always wanted a career. From the earliest, I loved literature and poetry. When I was a little girl, I used to have discussions with my local librarian, then with my teachers, then, at college, with friends. I knew I wanted to teach. That meant getting an advanced degree, and Sam agreed. He was totally supportive. So I did it, Michael—slowly, granted, when you kids were little, but I did it. I got the degree, then I started to teach. The older you guys got, the more I increased my load. Then I was given tenure. What a coup for the woman juggling a family and a career."

She gave a self-derisive snort. "I had it all, I thought. Now my daughter says she's been missing me. She says she's flunking math, and I didn't know anything about it. She couldn't tell me, because she couldn't get me alone for a minute. That's terrible, don't you think? And then there's Jon, who is always out of the house at football practice or with Leigh. Is he there because I'm not around? Sam came right out and said it. He said I should have been home that Tuesday. He said none of this would have happened if I'd been home.

"That hurts," she whispered. "I really thought I was doing things well, and what I couldn't do, Teke could, what J.D. couldn't do, Sam could, and vice versa. The relationship between our families was unique. It was practical and efficient, a neat little package. I thought it was perfect."

She moaned softly. "Well, let me tell you, that neat little package has fallen apart. Your house is a mess, my house is a mess. My office is a mess, I can't concentrate on work. My *life* is a mess." She caught sight of Sam at the door and went still. He was looking as tired as everyone else, but so dear and familiar and concerned that the fact of his betrayal was all the harder to believe.

"Are you telling him something good?" he asked. A slight hesitation in his voice kept his words from being glib. He paused on the threshold, as though caught by a moment's fear, before entering the room.

"I'm complaining," she said, returning her eyes to Michael. His expressionless face was easier to take than Sam's vulnerable one.

"Complaining about what?"

"Feeling overwhelmed. I hadn't realized how much I depended on Teke. I have a list of errands a mile long. I was going to run them later, but now that you're here to stay with Michael, I'll go."

"Don't," Sam said quickly. "Visit Michael with me."

"He does as well with monologue as with dialogue."

"Then talk to me, Annie. Please. Don't keep running away."

She took a shaky breath. Being with Sam like this was an agony, but for the life of her, she couldn't meet him halfway. The wound was still too raw. "You've already apologized. There's nothing more you can say that will help right now."

"There's years' worth of thoughts."

"None of which relate to what I'm feeling."

"They should."

Angrily she raised her head. "How so? They had to do with love and caring and feeling, not bitterness and anger. We never talked about hurting each other. That was supposed to be impossible."

She thought she had him when he ran a hand through his hair, but he came right back with, "Right, which was why I wasn't prepared for what happened. Don't you see, Annie? It never *occurred* to

164

me that I could touch a woman other than you. I was as shocked as anyone else."

"After the fact," Annie reminded him. "You weren't so shocked at the time."

"In my mind I was with *you,* which was why it happened like that," Sam said firmly. "I couldn't have made love to Teke. I'm not attracted to her that way. Did you ever see signs that I was?"

"The wife is the last one to see things like that."

He let out a breath. "You don't believe me."

"*I* sure don't," J.D. said from behind him, and strode into the room. "I'd say that hindsight gives new meaning to all the hugs and kisses and hand holding you've done with Teke over the years."

"That was fondness for a good friend," Sam declared. "You'd have done the same to Annie, if you were the demonstrative type."

J.D. looked at Annie. "Are you all right?"

Annie felt a quick pique. She didn't like the way J.D. assumed command. There was an argument to be made that if he had been the demonstrative type, Teke wouldn't have been susceptible to Sam. There was further argument to be made that some failing in their marriage had driven Teke into Sam's arms.

"I'm fine," she said, and gathered the strap of her purse to her shoulder. "Just going, now that you two are here." She didn't care to spend time with either of them just then. "I sent Teke off for a break. One of you should stay until she gets back."

"I can't stay long," J.D. said. "I have an appointment at four."

"You always have an appointment at four," Sam barked, "or three, or two. Whenever you don't want to be somewhere, you have an appointment. This is your son"—he jabbed his finger Michael's way—"lying here. Doesn't that affect you at all?"

J.D. recoiled. "Of course it affects me. But I won't

do him any good pacing the floor here for hours."

"Have you talked with him like the rest of us have? Or, on the chance that he doesn't hear, does that offend your good sense?"

J.D.'s eyes went from Sam to Annie and back. His frown deepened.

"What's with you? *I'm* the one who's been wronged."

"And you won't let me forget it. You look through me, you walk past me, you talk around me. When are we going to *deal* with it, for Christ's sake? You and Annie, both, running away from the problem like it might disappear on it's own. Well, it won't! Sooner or later, we have to *face* it."

"That's easy for you to say," Annie put in. "You're not the one feeling the hurt."

"True," Sam admitted, "but I'm the one who caused the hurt, and, I swear, it's worse. What can I do? Tell me. I want to make amends, only neither of you will allow that."

"Make amends?" J.D. scoffed. "The damage is done!"

Sam snapped his fingers. "And that's it? The friendship is over? The partnership is over? The *marriage* is over?" The last he said looking at Annie, but she didn't have a chance to reply because at that moment a feeble sound came from the bed.

Michael's eyes were half-open. They closed again, then reopened, still only halfway, but that was more than they'd done in nine days.

Annie leaned close. "Michael," she called urgently, "can you hear me?" His eyes focused directly above him at first. Slowly they shifted until they met hers. "Are you with us?" she whispered, half-afraid to hope.

After a pause, during which she had blood-chilling visions of his mind being gone, he gave a nearly imperceptible nod.

Sam gripped the boy's shoulder. "Do you know where you are?"

Michael's eyes moved slowly. They met and held Sam's, crept to J.D., who was leaning in beside Sam, inched across the room, then returned to Annie. "Hos-pi-tal," he mouthed.

Sam grinned. "All riiiiiight!"

"I'm getting the doctor," J.D. said excitedly, and raced out.

Annie smiled through tears of relief. She moved her hands around Michael's face, through his hair, over the bright pink scar from which the stitches had newly been removed. "Thank God. Thank God! Oh, Michael, we've been so worried! How do you feel?"

His eyes slipped shut.

She shot a terrified look at Sam, who looked as terrified as she. "Don't go," she begged Michael. "Come back. Come back."

Michael dragged his eyes back open. His tongue skimmed his lips. "Thirs-ty," he whispered.

A nurse and a doctor come in on the run. Annie's sole thought was to give Michael anything his heart desired. "He's thirsty. What can he have?"

The doctor leaned over him. He arced a light in front of his eyes, then, appearing satisfied with the results, snapped it off. "Do you know who you are?" he asked.

Michael gave another faint nod.

"Who?" the doctor prodded.

It was slow and weak, but distinct. "Mich-ael Phillip Max-well."

Only then did the doctor allow a smile. "Got the whole thing in there. I'd say that deserves, what, a chocolate milk shake?"

Michael shook his head.

"I thought you liked chocolate."

"Coke," Michael whispered, and produced a lop-sided grin.

The nurse left the room at an excited run, calling the news to any attendants in sight.

Annie straightened. Leaving a hand around Michael's arm, she took a deep, relieved, grateful breath. It was half out when she gasped. "Someone has to get Teke."

"Don't look at me," J.D. said.

What Annie heard was, *If she saw fit to leave his bedside, she can just wait until she gets around to returning to find out he's woken up. Besides, she doesn't deserve to share the excitement. She was the one who put him here.* But Annie didn't agree. As hurt as she'd been by what Teke had done, Teke was Michael's mother. She had been living his coma with him for nine long days. She had to be found.

Annie thought to send Sam, then thought again. She didn't want Sam going after Teke. She didn't trust them together.

"I'll go," she said, and set off.

eight

SAM HAD NEVER BEEN AS RELIEVED IN HIS LIFE as when Michael opened his eyes, identified where he was, and offered the doctor his full name. Winning *Dunn* V. *Hanover* paled by comparison, both with regard to heartstrings and consequence in his life. While Michael had lain in a coma, Sam carried a ponderous burden of sorrow and guilt— and might well have carried it the rest of his life, had Michael not awoken. He saw Michael's awakening as the beginning of the end of the nightmare. What the boy remembered of the accident was unknown and at that moment irrelevant. The most important thing was that he would live.

He drifted in and out of sleep. Between a pervasive weakness, and the fact that his right arm and leg were in casts, it was hard to assess what effect the brain injury had on his motor ability. J.D. wasn't pleased with that; after waiting in limbo for so long, he wanted to know exactly what was what and pestered the doctors accordingly. Sam was simply grateful that Michael was awake and aware.

By five-thirty Jon arrived with Leigh, Jana, and Zoe. Their excitement filled the small room and spilled into the hall, but no one seemed to mind. On a floor devoted to head injury patients, one's recovery gave hope to the families of others.

Annie ran in at six, followed closely by Teke, whose face was streaked with tears. She couldn't say a word, just stood smiling at Michael through those tears before sitting down, slipping her arms around him as best she could, and crying into his pillow.

As he watched, Sam's throat was tight. He prayed Michael would remember how much his mother loved him when and if memory returned.

Determined to make a celebration of the awakening, Sam took Jon to a nearby pizza parlor and returned with four huge, gooey pies and a bagful of sodas. The smell permeated the room in a dramatic change from its earlier sterility. Everyone dug in as though they hadn't eaten in days, while the one boy who truly hadn't dozed on and off. The kids didn't seem to mind when his eyes were closed. He opened them at appropriate times, which was all that mattered. He was the guest of honor at their party. They kept a constant stream of chatter aimed his way.

"What did you *feel* all that time?" Jana wanted to know.

"I'll bet it was like floating," Zoe speculated, "all white and light and airy."

Jana shook her head. "Not light and airy. Dark and heavy. Like his limbs were weighted down. Like a gray cloud was smothering him. Like he wanted to get up but something kept him down."

"I've read about out-of-body experiences," Jon told Michael, "where you're here, but you're not. Was it like that? Could you hear things?"

"Or feel things, or smell things?" Leigh asked.

Michael opened his eyes. They fell on Leigh, who,

sitting beside him on the bed, was the nearest. He frowned—Sam loved the expression after days of no reaction at all. "Floating," he said in a raspy voice, and tacked on, "I guess," before closing his eyes again.

"Floating," Jana mused. "That's incredible. Did you know where you were the whole time?"

Eyes closed, Michael nodded.

"Did you want to talk, but couldn't?" Zoe asked.

He frowned again. After a minute he moved a single shoulder in a shrug.

Leigh asked, "Could you feel what they were doing to you—moving your arms and legs and stuff?"

Michael's eyes opened to her but were distant. He looked confused. "Sometimes."

Jon leaned against Leigh. "I'll bet you were lying there thinking some of the things we said were pretty stupid. But you run out of things to say, you just babble on and on when someone doesn't answer."

Sam thought back to some of the things he had told Michael. The boy wouldn't have to recall the accident to know what had happened. One look at Teke, and Sam knew she was thinking the same. She was standing against the wall now, and though there was a flush on her cheeks that hadn't been there in nine days, she looked frightened.

He caught Annie's eye. The way hers skipped to Teke, then to the floor, was telling. Likewise the way she kept her head bowed. He wondered what she had told Michael during her private times by his side. He could see that she felt awkward, even embarrassed. He guessed she was apprehensive, too.

J.D. returned from making another round of phone calls, helped himself to a piece of pizza, and asked, "How's my boy doing?"

"Okay," Michael whispered.

"Not eating pizza?"

The boy moved his head in the negative. His eyes slid from J.D. to Teke, several feet away, then several feet more to Annie, then to Sam. Sam didn't like that perplexed look. It suggested Michael was remembering things.

"Well, *well*," boomed John Stewart, striding into the room with Lucy in tow, "there he is. You had us worried, young man."

Lucy set a small foil box on the bedstand. "Fresh truffles for my chocolate lover," she said. She touched a hand to her mouth and patted a kiss on Michael's cheek.

He managed a feeble half smile.

Zoe clapped her hands together. "We'll have to call Terry and Alex. They've been here nearly every day. They were *so scared.*"

"And Josh, Tommy, and Nat," Jana added.

"And Kari Stevens," Zoe finished with a heart-throb sigh. "She keeps asking about you, Michael. I think she likes you."

Leigh grew stern. "What were you guys doing, leaving school like that?"

"MTV," Michael mouthed.

"One stupid concert was worth all this?" Jon asked. "No way, man. That was a dumb thing to do."

"You could have been suspended," Zoe said.

Jana grunted. "So instead you were hit by a truck! Didn't you see it coming?"

"How could he?" Jon asked. "The trees block the street."

"Or *hear* it?" Jana pressed. "It's not like there's so much traffic on our street that you wouldn't hear a motor. What were you *thinking?*"

Sam was growing uneasy. He wished she would leave it, but Jana was so like J.D., and J.D. had never been one to leave well enough alone.

Zoe put a tempering hand on Jana's arm. Softly she said, "His mind was on the concert."

"But Mom taught him not to run into the street without looking. That was rule number three, right behind keeping his fingers out of light sockets and putting the toilet seat down after he peed."

"Jana Maxwell," Lucy scolded, "such language!"

"It doesn't matter," Zoe whispered to Jana.

"It *does.* If he'd looked where he was going, this wouldn't have happened."

"He wasn't thinking."

"Why *not?*"

"Mom and Sam," Michael murmured, drawing all heads back his way.

Sam's gut twisted. He racked his brain for a way to stop what was coming but couldn't think of a thing. He looked at Annie. She had her head down and her arms wrapped around her waist.

"What?" Leigh asked, leaning closer to Michael, who seemed perplexed again.

"I saw," he whispered, and shut his eyes.

"He saw what?" Leigh asked Jon.

"Mom and Sam?" Jana asked no one in particular.

Zoe turned in confusion to Sam. "What did he see?"

But before Sam could offer any sort of answer, Leigh gasped. "Oh, my God! Will Clinger!"

Jana's eyes widened. "*Virginia* Clinger!" She turned on Teke. "It's true!"

Zoe shook her head. "No."

"But Michael said!" Leigh argued.

"Jesus." This from Jon, who was staring at Sam as though he were alien.

Sam held up a hand. *It's not what you think,* he wanted to say, but there was nothing more trite than that. He didn't think "I was hard for Annie, so I screwed Teke" would do. Nothing else came.

"Mom?" Jana asked, pale now. "Is it true?"

John Stewart's frown deepened as he looked from one face to the next. "What are they talking about?"

"A mistake," J.D. said. His jaw was like stone as he stared at Sam, who at that moment felt that the future of everyone in the room rested on any words he might say. He was used to thinking on his feet—that was part of being a trial lawyer—but law school hadn't trained him for *this.*

"Mom?" Jana prodded, her eyes glued to Teke's ashen face. "You and Sam?"

"Say something, Mom," Leigh begged.

"Your father's right," Teke managed in a shaky voice. "It was a mistake."

"I don't like what I'm hearing," John Stewart warned.

"Did it *happen?*" Jon asked Sam.

"Something happened," Sam conceded. "It remains for us to define what it was."

Jana turned on him. "Did you—fuck—my—mother?"

John Stewart's face went purple. Lucy gasped. Zoe cringed. Annie cried, "For *God's* sake, Jana!"

"*Did* you?" Jon asked Sam.

There was a split second during which Sam might have denied it, but he kept hearing his warning to clients. "I need to know it all, the whole truth," he always said. "Tell me that, and we can work with it. Tell me only half of the truth, or lie to me, and when I'm surprised down the road, I'm gone." Instinct told him that if he lied now, he would pay ten times over.

"Ah *hell,*" John Stewart exploded, "I knew he was trouble. I knew they *both* were. Good job, John David, good job."

Before the last was out, J.D. had taken his parents' arms and was urging them toward the door. "I think you'd better leave. We have things to discuss."

John Stewart wasn't budging. "I warned you."

"Not now, Dad."

"'Trust me,' you said. 'I know what I'm doing,' you said. Now look what's happened."

"Dad—"

Sam wasn't waiting to hear what J.S. would say next. Crossing the floor in two strides, he said in a low voice, "We have a difficult situation here. Michael still has a ways to go before he's out of the woods, the others are upset, and quite frankly, I'm not sure what to do or say myself."

"You should have thought—"

"Enough, J.S. Say what you want, but later. We need to be alone now." He appealed to Lucy. "Take J.S. home, please? Give us a little time. We have to try to find a way to deal with all this."

"He's right, John," Lucy said in an anxious voice, and plucked at her husband's arm. "John David will call us later, won't you, John David?"

J.D. ushered them through the door without answering.

"Call me," J.S. ordered.

"Fine," J.D. said.

Sam should have felt relief when the elder Maxwells moved on down the hall, but the worst was ahead, he knew. Thrusting a hand through his hair, he stood facing the door for another minute before turning around slowly.

All eyes were on him—Leigh's and Jon's from beside the bed, Zoe's and Jana's from the middle of the floor, Annie's from the window, Teke's from the wall. J.D. walked in and took up position against the hall window with his arms crossed over his chest. The pose said he would be no help at all.

Jana broke the silence in a voice with a hostile

edge. "That was why Michael ran out of the house, wasn't it?"

Sam reminded himself that Jana was little more than a child, that they were all little more than children—granted, modern children who were used to frank discussions, but children nonetheless. They had just learned that two of the most trusted adults in their lives were flawed. Hostility was to be expected.

He chose his words with care. "Michael saw something he didn't understand."

Jon was as hostile as Jana. "He's not two years old, and he's not dumb. You knew what they were doing, didn't you, Michael."

Michael kept his eyes shut.

"Right," Sam said. "Now if he thought I was raping his mother, he would have jumped on me, hit me, done something to get me away, but he didn't do any of that, so we have to assume that *he* assumed that his mother and I were having an affair. But that's wrong. We were not having an affair."

"Then what was it?" Jon asked.

"A onetime lapse of judgment."

"You always said monogamy was best."

"It *is*—"

"And that we should be loyal to the people we love, so now you screw fidelity when you get the urge."

"I didn't 'get the urge' to be with Teke," Sam argued, "any more than she 'got the urge' to be with me."

"Then why did you do it?" Leigh asked, turning bewildered eyes on Teke.

Teke put her fingers to her lips, as though holding back words until the right ones came. Finally she said, "Yes, a lapse of judgment. I have never been unfaithful to your father at any other time in our marriage."

"But how could you have done it now?" Leigh asked.

Before Teke could answer, Jana said, "I knew there was something wrong. You weren't looking at each other, or talking to each other." She turned to J.D. "You've known for a while, haven't you?"

J.D. nodded. His arms remained folded over his chest, his feet crossed at the ankles.

Zoe, who had inched her way toward Annie's elbow, whispered, "You too?"

Annie's head remained half-bowed. She hesitated, then nodded.

"How could he *do* this to you?" Jon asked in horror.

Sam felt the cutting edge of his question. It made him want to wrap a protective arm around Annie. But he feared that if he tried, she would slip away. In front of the children, that would make things worse.

Annie shot a teary look at the ceiling. She sighed raggedly. Finally, with a self-deprecating smile she said, "I'm still trying to figure that out."

Zoe came closer and slipped a hand through hers.

Sam tried to make eye contact with Zoe, but she refused to look his way. As much as it hurt him to see Annie in pain, this hurt him, too. He and Zoe had always been close. She was his little girl, would always be his little girl. But she wouldn't look at him.

"Look," Sam said sadly, "what happened is over and done. The past nine days have been hell. Michael is still our first priority."

All heads flew to the bed. Michael's eyes were closed.

"Is he all right?" Zoe whispered.

"Michael?" Leigh called, shaking his shoulder gently.

Michael opened his eyes enough to let her know that he'd heard, then he faded out again.

"Maybe he doesn't want to see you," Jana told Sam with an inclusive glance at Teke.

Sam refused to blink. "Maybe he doesn't, but I'll still be hanging around, doing my best to help him get back on his feet."

"Maybe my father doesn't want that," Jana had the gall to say.

Sam wondered if she had always resented him or whether she was simply reacting in defense of J.D. Either case spelled trouble for the future, but again he refused to balk. "Maybe he doesn't," he said, "but I like to think he'll put Michael's welfare above our differences."

"What about Will Clinger?" Leigh asked.

J.D. spoke at last. "I took care of the Clingers. They won't be spreading any more rumors."

Jon put his hands on his hips and muttered, "Shit."

"What does that mean?" Sam asked.

"It means that the rumors were true, and that half the school knows, and that it's *disgusting*."

Sam's nerves were beginning to fray. "Oh, come off it, Jon. It's only as disgusting as you make it. We all make mistakes. The key to character is whether we learn from them."

"So we're supposed to just forget it? Just go along like it never happened?"

"No. Even if Michael weren't lying in that bed, there's still the matter of Teke's relationship with J.D. and mine with Annie. There's also the matter of the way you guys see me, which I care about a lot, and the way I see myself. I'm not feeling real good about myself."

Jon was untouched. Turning to Annie, he said, "I'm going home. I can't stand this."

"Jon, please," Annie begged.

"How can *you?*" he asked her.

Sam straightened. "That's enough, Jon."

But Jon wasn't done. "And you tell us not to fool around! You tell us to wait! You tell us not to give in to momentary urges! What a *crock!*" He grabbed Leigh's hand. "Let's go."

"Jon!" Annie cried. "Jon, wait!"

Jon was nearly at the door when Leigh tugged him to a stop. "What?"

"Take Zoe and Jana."

Jana protested instantly, "I want to stay with Michael."

Zoe looked at Annie. "I want to stay with you."

To Jana Annie said, "Michael should rest, and you should cool off." Taking Zoe's face in her hands, she whispered, "It'll be better if you go on home. I won't be long."

"Will you be okay?"

"Of course."

But Sam wondered. Annie looked shaky and pale. He had been worried about his standing with his children; it suddenly occurred to him that she was worried about hers. Her shoulders were slumped, her chin dragging. She struck him as a shadow that would disappear if the light grew much brighter.

But that was wrong! his mind screamed. She had nothing to be ashamed of. *He* was the one with the guilt, and the more he watched her, the more it grew.

Jon waited stiffly in the hall while Leigh, Jana, and Zoe kissed Michael good-bye. Zoe cast lingering looks at Annie, finally following the others only after Annie shooed her with a hand.

The silence they left behind was sudden and complete. There wasn't even the bleeping of machines to break it; the machines had been turned off after Michael had woken.

Sam looked from face to face. There were just the four of them in the room. And Michael. He went to the bedside. Michael's eyes were shut, but not comatose slack. Nor was his face expressionless. He might be dozing on and off, but Sam suspected he was aware of what was going on.

"I've been trying to explain what happened," he said in a quiet voice, "and none of the explanations seem to be going over real well. The bottom line is that I'm sorry. I'm sorry." He focused on Annie, whose eyes were downcast. "I have never regretted anything in my life the way I regret this. I would do anything to make amends, but I need direction."

"You've never needed direction before," J.D. said.

"That's not true. You've given me lots."

J.D. snorted. "Don't kid yourself. You've taken what you wanted and left the rest. You've had your own agenda all along."

Sam drew back. "Why do you say that?"

"Because it makes sense. You saw a vehicle in me. I had ins that you didn't. You used my contacts for recommendations to law school—"

"You *offered* those."

"You used my brains to get you *through* law school—"

"On the dry courses that were boring as hell, but who coached you through trial practice?"

"It was my contact that got you into the DA's office and my pull that got you into Maxwell, Roper and Dine."

"You haven't lost money on me yet," Sam put in in self-defense.

"Ahhhh. Which brings us to *Dunn* v. *Hanover*. Was that what put you over the top? Big money fuels big egos. Did you think that bringing a fee like that into the firm gave you rights to your partner's wife?"

"J.D.—" Teke tried.

He glared at her. "I'd keep my mouth shut if I were you. You're as bad as he is."

"But he didn't mean to do it. *I* didn't meant to do it, and I'm just as sorry as he is." She looked at Annie, whose head remained bowed. "Just as sorry, for what it's worth."

Annie was huddled against the wall. Unable to bear seeing her that way, Sam went to her, but when he reached out, she took form and slid past him. "I'm leaving now," she said brokenly.

"Annie?" came a froggy sound from the bed.

She gasped and hurried there. "What is it, sweetheart?"

Michael's eyes were more open than Sam had yet seen them, but his voice was rusty and thin. "I didn't mean to say it."

She stroked his hair. "Oh, Mike, it's not your fault. You didn't say anything that didn't need to be said."

"Everyone is angry."

"Not at you. Never at you. All you have to think about is getting better."

He closed his eyes. She kissed his forehead. When she straightened she caught sight of an empty soda can on top of one of the monitors and reached for it. "They'll be moving you to another room soon. We'd better clean up."

Sam came alive then and took the can from her hand. "I'll do it."

"That's not necessary," she said without looking at him.

"It is," he insisted, and there was suddenly a deeper message he had to convey. "I made the mess, I'll clean it up." He looked from J.D. to Teke to Annie again and repeated with conviction, "I made the mess, I'll clean it up. I'll put things right. I swear it."

* * *

Annie drove straight home. She went right to the attic, curled onto the window seat, and brooded.

"Are you okay, Mom?" Jon asked.

Startled, she gave a high-pitched, "Um-hmm."

He came into the room, went to the desk, and without turning said, "I'm sorry if I made a scene, but I'm not sorry for what I said."

Not knowing how to answer, Annie was silent.

"I can't believe what he did."

"It wasn't only his fault. It takes two."

"But he should have been stronger. He should have been in control. It shouldn't have happened unless he'd wanted it to." He lowered his head. His voice came out muffled. "Do you think he did?"

Annie had asked herself that so many times, the repetition was driving her mad. "I just don't know."

"And with *Teke.* I mean, that's the worst! She's been like a second mother to us. How could he do it with *her?*"

"He says it only happened once."

"Do you believe him?"

"It would hurt less if I did."

"But do you?"

"I don't know what to believe, Jon. I'm as stunned as you."

He was silent for a time. Then he moved from the desk to the cork board that hung on the wall. On it, between favorite family snapshots, Annie had tacked scrawled germs of thoughts.

"When did you find out?" he asked.

She took a steadying breath. "The day after it happened."

"And you're still stunned?"

"Very."

Jon swore. "What a *dick!*"

"Please, Jon."

But it was as though the control he had been exerting for her sake simply snapped. "He is. And a phony." He made a disdainful sound. "After all the times he stood there lecturing to us about doing the right thing. The crusading lawyer. The man with a heart to match his drive. Know the razzing I've taken on that? What a *joke!*"

"Please, Jon. He's not all bad."

Jon whirled around. His eyes were dark and as impassioned as Sam's could be when he was arguing a point. "How can you *say* that? He tells you he loves you, then he turns around and makes love to another woman. It wouldn't have been so bad if he'd picked up a twenty-five-year-old looker—I mean, it would have been *gross,* but at least then we could've said he was going through a midlife crisis or something. But Teke?"

"You're making it worse, Jon," Annie warned. She didn't need reminders of her age or of the young and attractive women Sam saw every day of the week.

"Well, I'm angry, even if you're not!"

"I *am* angry, but when I tried calling your father names, it didn't help."

"So what *will?*"

"I don't know!"

"Mom?" Zoe asked, sounding frightened. "Why are you yelling?"

"I'm yelling because Jon's yelling," Annie cried. "What do you want me to *do,* Jon?"

Jon stormed toward the door. "I don't know. Maybe you should divorce him. That's what he deserves." He was gone down the stairs before Annie could respond.

"Are you going to, Mom?" Zoe asked in a tiny voice as she came to Annie's side.

Annie held her close. One of them trembled, perhaps both did, though the line between them blurred. Annie knew for a fact that the word *divorce* shook her.

"Are you?" Zoe whispered.

Annie kissed her soft blond waves. "I haven't thought about that."

"Because you're too upset to think about it, or because you don't want one?"

"I don't want one," Annie said, knowing it was the truth.

"Even after what Daddy did?"

"What Daddy did was unthinking and unkind and very, very wrong. I'm hurt and I'm angry. I want to strike back, but divorce isn't something to be done out of vengeance. Daddy and I have been married for nineteen years. I don't know as I want to throw the whole thing away."

"Can you forgive him?"

Forgiveness was one issue to be tackled, trust was another. "I don't know."

"But if you can't, how can you live with him?"

"I may not be able to," the furious part of her said.

"Will you get a divorce then?"

Annie recalled dozens of times over the years when Jon or Zoe had come home telling of a friend whose parents had split. "Tragic" had been one of the buzzwords they'd used to describe it, "difficult" another, "heartbreaking" a third. Annie had identified with those children and, because of that, had taught Jon and Zoe to be extra-understanding and supportive of those friends. The Popes were, after all, secure in the knowledge that divorce would never hit them. How smug they had been.

Annie could understand why Zoe was so frightened. She was, too. "I don't want a divorce, sweet-

heart. It's not a word I ever dreamed I would associate with your father and me."

"Do you still love him?"

"Yes. One afternoon can't kill half a life of loving."
Her voice cracked. Her eyes filled with tears, again.
"That's why this all hurts so much," she managed in
a broken whisper.

"Does he still love you?" Zoe asked.

It was a while before the knot in Annie's throat
eased enough to let her speak. "He says he does."

"Do you believe him?"

Taken at its most innocent, his explanation of what
had happened with Teke was plausible. "I want to."

"How will you find out for sure?"

"I don't know. Time, I guess."

Zoe was quiet then. She began to rock against
Annie, and even with tears still threatening, Annie
had to smile. When Zoe had been a baby, Annie had
rocked her for the soothing, the comfort, the sheer
pleasure of it. If the rocking stopped, Zoe had
always started it up just this way. So now Annie
rocked with her, wondering as she did just who was
giving the comfort and who was receiving it.

"What is it about us, Mom?"

"Hmmm?"

"Aren't we pretty enough? Or *sexy* enough?"

Annie felt a squeezing around her heart. "For
whom?"

"Men. Look at Jana. I always thought I was just as
pretty as she is, but she's the one the boys want to
take out."

"Who says?"

"I *see*."

"But she doesn't have a boyfriend. ... " Unless
Annie had been so preoccupied with work that she
hadn't noticed. "I thought you guys went out in a big
group."

"Yeah, and the boys in the group all crowd around her. Like Daddy crowding around Teke. What's wrong with *us?*"

Annie moaned. "Oh, sweetie, nothing's wrong."

"Then why does it happen?"

"Maybe because we're quieter."

"Maybe because our breasts are too small."

"Zoe."

"I'm serious. Boys like big breasts."

Time evaporated. Annie was Zoe's age again, telling her father the very same thing. "Know what Papa Pete used to tell me when I complained about that?"

"What?"

"He said that big breasts would sag in time. He said that in the long run, I was far better being me."

"Well, that's just fine," Zoe said with a gutsiness that Annie hadn't had at her age, "but what about the short run? Jana shouldn't be the only one with guys after her. And Daddy should want you the way he wanted Teke."

Annie agreed. "Know what else Papa Pete said?"

"What?"

"He said that good things come to those who wait."

"Meaning that if I'm patient, I'll have guys after me, but what about you? You were supposed to already have your good thing. Are you supposed to wait until he decides he wants you again? What do you do in the meanwhile? Will you sleep in the same bed with him? Will we all go out to dinner together?" She gasped. "And what about Thanksgiving? We always spend it with the Maxwells. And Christmas? And New Year's? And *skiing?* Mom, what are we going to *do?*"

Annie didn't know, she just didn't know.

* * *

"John Stewart is waiting," the message read. It was written on a small MAXWELL, ROPER and DINE memo sheet in Mary McGonigle's script and was lying on his desk when J.D. reached the office the next morning.

He stared at it for the longest time, wishing he could ignore it, knowing he couldn't. John Stewart might have been put off the day before, but he wouldn't be put off again.

J.D. crushed the paper into a ball and threw it in the wastebasket on his way out the door. He strode down the hall, determinedly keeping his pace steady, and turned into John Stewart office with his head held high.

"It's about time," John Stewart boomed, tossing a chin toward the door.

J.D. would have shut it even without the hint. He had no intention of the office grapevine in general, or Mary McGonigle in particular, picking up any of what was bound to be said.

John Stewart wasted no time getting to the point. "Well? Are you going to divorce her?"

J.D. walked to the window. Absently he rubbed the brass telescope that stood there. "Why did I know you were going to ask me that?"

"It's the most appropriate question, isn't it?"

"Actually, the most appropriate question is how Michael is doing." He put his eye to the telescope's lens. "In case you were wondering, they moved him to a private room early this morning. He's still sleeping most of the time, but he wakes up when you call to him. The doctors say that as he eats and regains his strength, he'll be awake more. As for his motor ability," J.D. went on, thinking of Sam and Teke and feeling anger, thinking of Grady Piper and feeling anger, and all the while looking through the tele-scope at the Ritz-Carlton Hotel, "there seems to be some minor impairment."

"What does that mean?" John Stewart growled.

J.D. had put the same words to Bill Gardner no more than thirty minutes before. "It means that he doesn't have full control of his limbs. He can't direct them and make them respond the way they did before the accident." He wondered why the tele-scope was focused on the Ritz. "The prognosis is good. He will eventually regain most of what he had, but how much will depend on how much he wants it and how hard he works." Basketball was out for the year. Probably baseball, too. "The next step is ther-apy. They'll move him to the rehabilitation center in about a week."

John Stewart grunted. I won't have my grandson lolling around with old men who foam at the mouth."

J.D. saw a sheer drape being drawn open and a scantily clad woman appearing. Feeling like a voyeur, he straightened and turned around. "Old men who foam at the mouth do not go to rehab centers, at least not the one I have in mind." Gardner had recommended it. "It's a notch above the rest."

"Why can't he come home?"

"We aren't equipped for the kind of intensive rehabilitation that he needs."

"Of course you aren't now, but you can be."

"He'll do better in a center. He'll have people all over him there."

"And Theodora? Will she be there?"

"Probably. Michael has become her personal cause."

"That's guilt speaking."

"And maternal instinct," he said because he

188

didn't like it when John Stewart belittled Teke. Even now.

"Guilt. Believe me. Guilt. That brings us to the matter of divorce. She'll take you to the cleaners if you're not careful."

J.D. slipped his hands in his pockets. "She can't do that. She was the one who had the affair."

"Still, we'll need the best lawyer possible. I think Hammond over Mittleman. I've been hearing that Mittleman lets his associates do most of the work. That's not for us. Hammond may cost more, but it will be worth it in the long run. I don't want that gold digger to get a penny more than is absolutely necessary."

J.D. walked to the bookshelf and fingered the spine of a leatherbound reference book. He doubted Teke would ask for much. She never had, J.D. had to say that for her. She accepted what he offered, but she wasn't a thief. She hadn't been stockpiling jewelry, as some women he knew did. "Don't call Hammond," he said.

"Why not?"

"Because I'm not ready."

"To divorce her? But she admitted to adultery. What greater evidence do you need?"

"I'm not going to a lawyer yet."

"If it embarrasses you, I'll call—"

"What embarrasses me," J.D. said, turning around, "is your wanting to be involved in something that isn't your business. This is my marriage. I'll decide if and when I want to end it." More quietly he added, "If and when that time comes, I'll find my own lawyer."

"Yes." John Stewart cleared his throat loudly. "We've seen how well you do things. Honestly, John David, you would be so much better off in life if you would listen to people who know more than you do.

Marrying Theodora Peasley was a mistake from the start. She wasn't your type."

J.D. remembered some fun times they'd had. He had thought she was hot stuff when they'd first met, and the attraction wasn't only to her body. It was to her simplicity and her naiveté, which he'd found to be a refreshing change from his usual dates. Once married, she had taken the role of wife seriously. She had dressed for him and undressed for him, had kept the house neat, had dinner ready for him when he walked in the door.

"Not your type at all," John Stewart continued. "You had a far more genteel upbringing. You lived in a beautiful house. You had the nicest clothes and well-bred friends. From the time you were old enough to sit through a meal, you were taken to fine restaurants, not only here, but in New York and Washington, too. You had an exposure to culture—fine arts, the theater—that Theodora couldn't conceive of, and that, before we even mention private school. Do you remember your classmates there?"

J.D. certainly did. Among them had been a senator's son who was into selling drugs, a millionaire's son who was into buying them, and a Nobel Peace Prize winner's son whose idea of peace was making love to his roommate. "They were nothing to write home about," J.D. said, but his father snowballed on.

"You had horseback riding lessons, ice-skating lessons, and ballroom dancing lessons, and all that at a time when we didn't have the financial comfort we have now. But we were willing to sacrifice because we wanted you to mix with the kind of people who had something to offer the world. Theodora had nothing to offer, nothing at all."

The devil made J.D. say, "She was great in bed,"

which had been true enough before the novelty had worn off.

"If that's the only reason you married her, then you have no one but yourself to blame for what has happened. Honestly, John David, is sex that important to you?"

It wasn't. Increasingly he and Teke had stayed on separate sides of the bed. He wasn't sure what it was, whether they had become bored with each other or whether his tastes had changed, but she didn't turn him on the way she once had. It had been a while since he had reached for her in the night. In that sense, Sam could have her.

"You're a fine one to downplay sex," J.D. remarked. "I'll bet you see some great stuff through that telescope of yours. Does some high-class call girl rent the suite you're focused on?"

John Stewart's neck turned pink. "I have no idea what the telescope is focused on. I never use it."

J.D. didn't believe that for a minute. Nor did he believe, at that moment, that John Stewart wasn't carrying on with Mary McGonigle. He would have said as much if good sense hadn't prevailed.

"Divorce Theodora," John Stewart ordered.

But this time around J.D. wasn't being ordered. "I'll decide what I want to do in my own time."

"She is an embarrassment to this family. So is Sam Pope. I want him out of this firm."

J.D. wasn't surprised by that demand, either. John Stewart was a punisher, and more than anyone else, J.D. was in a position to know that.

John Stewart would probably suggest keeping Sam in the firm but giving him little work and even less compensation, if that were something he could control. Since it wasn't, he would naturally want Sam out.

"It's not a wise move, J.S. Sam is one of our biggest money winners."

191

"We can do without him."

"He has one of the highest profiles and the best reputations of any lawyer in the state."

"Fine. Let him run for public office. He won't get *my* vote, I can assure you. I don't vote for men of dubious moral character."

J.D. thought of Mary McGonigle. He often thought of her during John Stewart's self-righteous tirades. Usually those tirades were directed at public officials, other lawyers, or even a client. They had never been directed quite this way at Sam before.

"And I don't relish the idea of calling a man of low moral character my partner," John Stewart went on. "I don't care how many people like him. What he did was about as low as any man can get." He scowled at J.D. "For the life of me, I can't figure out why you want to share a letterhead with the man. I can't figure out how you can stand *looking* at him. Don't *you* want him out?"

J.D. returned to the window. Yes, he wanted Sam out, just as he wanted Teke out. They had betrayed him in the worst possible way. But he had to think about what his life would be like without them. He was resisting doing that, and he had a funny feeling he knew why. Sam—Teke, too, for that matter—stood for everything that John Stewart was not. J.D. feared what his life would be like in their absence.

"I asked you a question, John David."

His father's indignation snapped a tiny thread of control in J.D. Recklessly he turned and said, "Will you get off my back?"

"Excuse me?"

"What Sam said last night was true. My family is going through a crisis. Your interference makes things worse."

"I'm responsible for the only stable things in your life!"

"Does that include Teke?" J.D. burst out. "Because I have to tell you, there are times when I wonder whether the main reason I married her was because you were so against it. Interesting thought, huh?"

He left the office savoring the fact of John Stewart's mouth open but silent.

nine

ANNIE HAD ANOTHER DIFFICULT NIGHT. SHE had actually started out in bed, confident that Sam wouldn't risk touching her, but the sound of his breathing, the shift of his body, even his scent, stirred the upset she felt. So she took haven in her office, dozing off in the wee hours, only to come awake at seven with Sam hunkered beside her.

"You should have come back to bed," he said. "You need more sleep than you're getting."

She wondered how long he had been there. He was wearing nothing but shorts, and with his hair mussed and his jaw stubbly around his mustache, she guessed he had come straight from bed. She wished she looked half as good as he did. But she was sure that her hair was sticking out every which way, that she had marks on her cheek from where she'd been lying on her shawl, that the vile taste in her mouth was visible on her lips.

"I'm fine," she murmured, pushing herself up.

"You have shadows under your eyes. And you've lost weight."

Wrapping the shawl around her nightgown, she made for the door. "Thanks."

"I worry about you, Annie." He followed her down the stairs.

Too little, too late, she thought crossly. "Well, don't."

"Keep this up, and you'll collapse in the middle of a class."

"If that happens, my friends will be there to help me. I'm not totally alone, or helpless." She closed the bathroom door in his face and pushed in the button to lock it. Then she turned on the water and felt foolish, on top of ugly.

By the time she reached the kitchen, Jon and Zoe were on their way out of the door. "The fall formal is in two weeks," Jon reminded her. "You wanted me to buy a tux this year. Can we go soon?"

"This weekend," Annie promised, putting a cheek up for his kiss. "And college applications. Let's look them over so you can start thinking about the essays."

Zoe nudged him out and gave Annie a hug. "I need a haircut, Mom."

"Didn't you just have one?"

"It doesn't look right." She tugged at the chin-length blond waves that were so much like Annie's. "You said we could try someone new, but I don't know who. Will you ask Susan Duffy?"

Susan Duffy was the secretary in Annie's department. She had spectacular hair. Zoe oooed and ahhed each time she saw her.

"I'll ask," Annie said, though she knew Susan had the kind of hair that would look great regardless who did it.

"Thanks," Zoe said, and kissed Annie's cheek. "Jon will run me in to see Michael after practice, so you won't have to see Teke. We'll be home in time for dinner, okay?"

Annie nodded. She would risk seeing Teke anyway, because she wanted to see Michael, but being able to do it earlier in the afternoon would ease the rush later.

She watched Jon back out of the driveway and waved when he drove off. Tux. Haircut. College applications. A trip into Boston to see Michael. Dinner. Two classes today, two hours' worth of student conferences, another several in preparation for tomorrow's classes—and damn, she'd forgotten, a department meeting at six, which meant that dinner would have to be on the stove, ready to be dished out before she left the house at five forty-five.

A week before, Teke might have helped with the tux and the haircut and the dinner, and there wouldn't have been any trip into Boston to see Michael. Without her as a backup, Annie's life was hectic. Yet as she stood at the side door staring at the empty driveway, all she could think about was that her children were growing more independent and would soon be gone, which would leave her either alone with Sam or alone with herself. Neither thought buoyed her spirits.

Those spirits sank even lower when she inadvertently rear-ended the car stopped in front of her at a traffic light. The car was a silver BMW not unlike Sam's black one. There was no damage, but that was ascertained only after the driver of the other car bent his nattily suited, well-built, thirtyish-looking self over the front of the BMW and studied it with a caressive eye that cooled the instant he looked at Annie.

"You lucked out, lady. I'd have your eyes checked if I were you. If you couldn't see me stopped there, you have a problem." He climbed back in his car and drove off before Annie could come up with a clever answer. But then, cleverness had never been her thing. She envied people who were fast on their feet. She especially envied *women* who were like that. They had an edge on the others. They were tougher. They got what they wanted.

Determined to toughen up herself, she went into her first class with a chip on her shoulder. It was an advanced seminar on the works of Jane Austen and consisted of twenty students, most of whom were either seniors or graduate students. If their participation in the discussion was telling, few had done the assignment, which was to consider the relevancy of *Mansfield Park* to Austen's own life.

"Am I in the wrong class?" Annie asked, looking around the room puzzledly. "Was there some kind of campus celebration last night that kept you all from giving Jane Austen even the smallest amount of thought?" She looked at her notes, then at the class. "I could lecture you as though you were freshmen, but I would have thought you'd moved beyond that." She wore her disappointment on her face, but most eyes in the room were downcast, depriving her of even that small satisfaction. She took a breath. "Okay, let's make it a paper. For tomorrow, I want five pages on *Mansfield Park* vis-à-vis Jane Austen's life and times." Ignoring the ensuing murmurs, she gathered her notes and left the room.

But that was only the start. By noon she was beginning to wish she had stayed home. The first of her conferences was late, throwing off all the others, and when she finally sat down to work at her computer, it died. She was in the process of discovering that the entire building had lost electricity, when the fire alarm sounded, a false alarm, no doubt tied in with the electrical problem, but enough to send her outside with the others. And there they waited, while precious minutes ticked by.

She studied Natalie Holstom, whose specialty was wartime literature, and Monica Pepper, whose newly released book on young American writers had been critically acclaimed. Both women were bright, aggressive, and attractive. Both were younger than Annie. Both had, on occasion, shown up with men just Sam's age.

After an hour Annie gave up the wait and drove into Boston. She had to take a detour when her normal exit off Storrow Drive was closed for repairs. That set her back another ten minutes. Then the garage she normally parked in was full, so she went to the next and wound her way up six floors until she finally found a space. She got lost trying to find Michael's new room and reached it only to discover that he was sound asleep.

Teke had gone home for a few hours, the nurse told her. While she waited, J.D. stopped by, but being with him was awkward. She didn't want to talk about Teke, didn't want to talk about Sam, didn't want to *think,* much less talk about what kind of interaction the two families would have in the future. So she wrote Michael a note, which she set on his bed tray, then retrieved her car and returned to school.

The electricity was back on, but rumor to the contrary must have spread through the campus, because her Romantic poetry seminar was sparsely attended. There was nothing more depressing to Annie than a sparsely attended seminar. She wanted to be so admired that students would *die* before they would miss one of her classes.

The minute this one was done, she raced back to her car, drove to the supermarket, and raced home, only to find that she had forgotten to buy lasagna noodles. She raced back to the market and was in the process of racing home again when a local commuter train stalled on the tracks. Again it was a situation of expecting things to be cleared any minute and opting to wait, rather than take an alternative route that would add fifteen minutes to the drive home.

It was twenty minutes before the train was moved, and by that time Annie was in a sweat. So she finished the race home and prepared a fresh salad and the lasagna, which she barely had time to put into the oven before she was off on the trip back to school.

Even then she arrived late. Fifteen pairs of eyes turned to her when she walked into the room. Fifteen pairs of eyes followed her to the only free chair, which as fate would have it was directly beside the department head. Charles Honnemann was an older man, kind enough, traditional enough—and it wasn't that she minded sitting next to him, just that she wasn't of a mind to sit where everyone was looking.

Annie was a teenager again, feeling self-conscious and downright odd. She was sure that she looked a wreck. Her blouse bunched at the waistline of her skirt, her stockings were snagged from a close encounter with a stack of dog food bags at the supermarket. She hadn't had time to comb her hair or gloss her lips, her hands were shaky, and beads of sweat kept popping out on her nose. And she had shadows under her eyes. And she had lost weight. And her husband had thought so little of her charms that he had taken comfort from her best friend, who had long dark hair, full breasts, and a sultry laugh.

She barely heard what was said at the meeting. The instant it was done she made a beeline for her office, where, shielded by the dark, she collapsed onto the side chair, put her head in her hands, and took great gulps of air.

She heard something at the door, then footsteps

leaving. Lacking the strength to either call out or haul herself from the chair and close the door, she stayed where she was. She wasn't frightened. Campus security was tight. Chances were slim that a robber or rapist have gotten into the building, or someone intent on taking hostages and making demands, though that thought captured her imagination. She wouldn't have minded being locked in a room for three days, unable to run anywhere or do anything or think about anything but the one issue of survival. That would certainly put other things into perspective.

"Here," came a gentle voice. It was Jason Faust, urging a plastic cup into her hand. "Wine. Drink up." When she hesitated, he nudged her hand. "Go on. It's all right."

She took a sip of the wine. When it went down just the right way, she took a more healthy swallow. Then she let her head rest against the back of the chair. "What a horrible, *horrible* day."

"I guessed that when I saw you hurrying down the hall. You looked beat."

"I am beat. And old and ugly and unpopular," she said without thinking. When she did, she took another good drink of wine. "Are there ever times when you feel that there's a conspiracy against you? When you feel that the world is one big, happy cholla ball that pricks you every time you try to catch hold?"

Jason chuckled. "Where did that analogy come from?"

"A desert tour during a family trip to Arizona two years ago." It had been a Popewell trip, now a collector's item.

"Ahhh. Yeah, I know what you mean."

"*Everything* has gone wrong today."

"I heard about the Austen seminar."

"Mmmm. I shot myself in the foot with that little flare of temper. Who's going to have to *read* through those five-page papers? Me! As though I don't already have enough to do."

"I'll do it."

"As though you don't already have enough to do."

"I'd be glad to help you, Annie. I'd be honored."

She sighed. He was a kind boy. More than a boy. An adult. And a big help, if not physically, then emotionally. She wondered whether he had a girlfriend. "You're sweet, for a filthy-rich guy."

"Ahhh, money. 'The sixth sense which enables you to enjoy the other five.'"

W. Somerset Maugham. She knew the quote. "Is it?"

"Sure. It lets me do things like keeping vintage wine stashed in my desk."

"Not just vintage wine, I'd wager." She remembered when he had offered her a smoke. She didn't want to *think* of what else he kept in his stash. Yes, she was straight. She was also the older generation.

"Does it bother you?" he asked.

"What you keep in your desk is your affair."

"Does it bother you that I have money? It bothers some of the others in the department. They don't take me seriously."

Annie was feeling the first effects of the wine, a warming on her cheeks and in her stomach. It helped to soften the echo, *older generation ... older generation ... older generation.* "If they don't it's only because they haven't had a chance to work with you like I have. You can hold your own with any one of them."

"Not yet," Jason said, "but thank you. Your opinion is the one I value. You're the cream of the department."

The cream of the department. How nice that

sounded. She wished she did feel like cream, all sweet and silky and smooth. "I wonder sometimes," she mused sadly. "I try—Lord, I try—but I seem to be botching things up lately." She drained the plastic cup. "It was the women's movement that did it, told us we could be everything, but we can't. We can't be mothers and wives at the same time that we're professors. It just doesn't work. Someone always gets gypped."

"Who's getting gypped in your case?"

"My kids. I'm not always around when they want me." She knew she should head home to them now, but she couldn't muster the energy to move. This was the most relaxed she had been all day. The darkness helped. And the wine. "My husband, too."

"How does he get gypped?"

"He wants me, and I'm not there."

"Does he come looking for you?"

"Sometimes. But he's busy, too."

Jason sighed. "If you were mine, I'd court you forever and love every minute."

"You'd get bored before long," she said, and took another swift drink. The wine was down her throat before she wondered when he had refilled her cup, but she didn't ask or complain. Feeling light-headed wasn't all bad.

He sat back on his heels. "Why are you so down on yourself?"

"I'm just being honest."

"Modest is the word. Don't you know how appealing you are?"

"I am not appealing," she cried. "I'm pale and too thin. I have wrinkles on my neck and my hands, my eyes are too close together and when they get shadowed they look even worse, my mouth is too small, I could go on and on." Her voice caught. "There is absolutely nothing exciting about me." If there had been, Sam would never have been drawn to Teke.

Out of the blue, she started to cry.

Jason rose to his knees and drew her down so that he could hold her. She tried to pull back, but he wouldn't let her go. After a minute she didn't want to. His arms were a comfort.

Sam's had always been that way. They were a haven, waiting to envelope her at times of upset and joy alike. She could sink into them, as she did now, and cry or laugh or simply *be,* and the reward was always there. A kiss, a touch, a caress—he knew her body as no other man did.

Jason's lips touched her forehead. "You are beautiful," he whispered.

She shook her head against his throat. He smelled different from Sam, but the difference wasn't bad. And his warmth felt good. She had been missing Sam's warmth. And his words, *You are beautiful.*

"'Beauty is not caused. It is,'" he quoted. "That's Emily Dickinson. She's your favorite, and she's right. When beauty exists, it exists. It doesn't need artificial enhancers. Life enhances it. Time enhances it. The kind of beauty that comes from within lasts forever."

Annie gave an uneven sigh.

"You are beautiful," he whispered, nuzzling her neck, "inside and out." He kissed her jaw, then her lips.

She wanted to be beautiful. She wanted to be wanted and needed and so sexy that Sam couldn't *begin* to think of touching another woman.

"I want you, Annie," he whispered more roughly, and even that change in his voice felt good. Every woman wanted to be wanted. Every woman wanted to know that she could pump a man up so that he trembled with the need for release, and he was trembling now.

Every bit of the wine she had drunk had gone to her head, because she was suddenly feeling not warm, but hot and trembling, herself, with a need that arched her closer to him.

He whispered a triumphant, *"Yes!"* against her ear, then drew back and reached for the buttons of her blouse. Annie heard a tiny ping of warning, but it was in the very back of her mind. In the front was a fascination with the way he was looking at her, perhaps imagined in the dark, but as real as the way Sam always looked at her. She saw pleasure on his face when he opened her blouse. It made her feel so pretty that when he struggled with the catch of her bra, she released it herself.

He caught her mouth with his at the same time that he covered her breasts with his hands. He began to knead them with an eagerness verging on the rough, but that spelled appeal to Annie. It was like a balm, so badly needed that she let herself be drawn onto his lap.

She gasped when she felt his hand between her legs.

"I've wanted you for so long," he whispered, and began to stroke her. Again she gasped, this time when the ping came more loudly in her mind, but it faded. She felt pretty. She felt feminine and sexy. She felt wanted. His whispered words, the ragged sough of his breath, the strain of his muscles, all built her up.

Then she heard the rasp of a zipper, too real against the headiness of her illusions. She tensed.

"It's okay," he said, "okay, just touch me here."

"I can't—" But he put her hand where he wanted it. She protested, "Please, this isn't—"

"I love you, Annie."

She tried to pull her hand away. "I don't—"

"I have a condom, it'll be so good, you'll see."

"My God, *no!*" she cried, because it suddenly hit her that he wasn't Sam, wasn't Sam at all. She scrambled backward with such abruptness that he was taken off-guard. "My God," she whispered more to herself this time as the enormity of what she'd almost done hit her. She clutched at her blouse. In a shaky voice she said, "I'm sorry, Jason, but this isn't right. It's not at all what I want, and it's not what you want."

"Like hell it's not," Jason said, but he had hauled himself to the opposite wall and was fixing his pants. "It's what we both want."

"I'm married."

"What difference does that make?"

"I'm committed to someone else."

"Is that why you let me kiss you? And open your bra?" His glare cut through the darkness. "Were you thinking of your husband then? Or do you want to blame what you did on the wine?"

Blaming the wine would have been taking the easy way out. Annie refused to do that. Rather, she buttoned her blouse with raggedy fingers and said, "I *was* thinking of my husband. That's the problem. I was using you, but you shouldn't be a stand-in for someone else. You deserve more."

With a snort of disdain, he rose. "That's an honorable remark coming from an honorable woman. Excuse me if I don't stick around for more. I might just gag." He pulled the door open and left. The door slammed shut behind him.

Annie thought about that door as she sat on the floor in the dark. She guessed he had closed it when he had come in with the wine and wondered whether he had had seduction in mind from the start. Had it been seduction? Or simply each his own need? She feared the last. She had been vulnerable as could be.

She should have been impressed by the fact that she had stopped, but she wasn't. More important—and incriminating—and *humbling*—was the fact that she had started at all.

Grady approached Michael's room with more hesitancy than ever. It was a new room, a new floor, and there was no window to preview what was happening inside. He had to go right to the door.

Teke was sitting on the chair with her head bowed. High on the wall the television was on, but Michael's eyes were closed.

He entered quietly. It was a minute before Teke looked up. He saw something in her eyes, but he wasn't sure what it was. He wished he did, because she looked different. Wearing a silk blouse and tailored slacks, she was far more Constance than Gullen. She intimidated him a little.

"Hi," he said. "How are you?"

She nodded, shrugged, said a soft, "Okay," and looked at Michael.

"I was glad to hear he woke up." It was the understatement of the year. Grady had been breathing sighs of relief all weekend, had actually gone to church Sunday morning for the first time since he'd been a boy. "How's he doing?"

"Not bad. He's eating. They've been giving him tests. He's lost strength and the range of motion he had before, but the loss isn't permanent. They're working on a therapy plan."

Grady saw that Michael's eyes had opened. They were focused on him. "Hi," he said with a smile that he hoped hid his nervousness. He was the man whose pickup had taken the boy down. He didn't know what kind of welcome he would get. "It's good to see you awake," he said. "I was real worried."

Michael stared at him for the longest time. "Grady?"

Grady didn't see any anger. "You remember I was here?"

"A little. I ran into your truck."

No anger. Grady was relieved. "'Fraid so."

"Did I dent it?"

"Nah. Truck's a lot harder than you. How're you feeling?"

"Okay. I want to go home, but they won't let me."

Not wanting to side with the bad guys, Grady asked, "Why not?"

"They want me to go to the rehabilitation center first. They say my arms and legs aren't working right, but what do they know. I'm just weak."

Grady suspected "they" knew more than Michael did. "The rehab center will help you get your strength back."

"I want to go home."

Grady felt at a loss. He sought Teke's help, but she looked bewildered, and when he returned to Michael, the boy's eyes were closed.

The television was tuned to a soap opera. Grady watched for a bit, but his mind wandered. He was surprised when seemingly out of the blue, Michael asked, "Were you really in prison?"

"You remember that, too?"

"Were you?"

"'Fraid so."

"For what?"

So he didn't remember everything. "Murder."

"Awesome."

"Not really. It was pretty bad. Both doing it and being punished for it. I don't recommend either."

"Did you have a trial?"

"Sure."

"Who was your lawyer?"

"He was court-appointed. You wouldn't know him."

"Sam does murder cases. Too bad you couldn't have had him. He's *awesome.*" He stopped abruptly, tacked on, "Was awesome," and stared at the television for a minute before asking, "How long were you in prison?"

"Eight years."

"That's not so much. Not for murder."

"It's enough," Grady said.

"Did they let you out early for good behavior?"

"They let me out because I served the minimum of my time and because they needed my bed. I don't know about the good behavior part. I spent my time in solitary."

"Wow."

"Why?" Teke asked.

"There were times when I had to fight to defend myself."

"Solitary must have been horrible," she said.

"It was safe. After a while it felt too confining."

"That's just like what I felt," Michael said with an animation so much like Teke that Grady felt a swell of affection for the boy. "I could see out sometimes, but I couldn't talk to anyone or go outside this tiny little area. Then Sam snapped his fingers. Like someone turned a key in the lock."

The animation died. It struck Grady that Michael was angry at Sam. And at Teke. He hadn't looked at her once while Grady had been there.

"Do you remember my telling you that I knew your mother when she was little?"

Michael thought about that with his eyes closed. "Maybe," he finally said.

"The one thing she always wanted was a family. She loves you a lot."

"Hmmph."

Figuring that if he pressed, he would blow his credibility, Grady simply said, "Gotta get back to work now. Can I visit again?"

"Sure."

"Can I bring something? Candy? Soda?"

Michael did shoot a look at Teke then, but it was a defiant one. "I want a Ring-Ding. She says they don't have enough nourishment."

"Ring-Ding it is." With a wink and a thumbs-up, Grady left the room. He paused in the hall, hoping that Teke would come out to talk. When she didn't he started slowly toward the elevator. He glanced back from time to time, but she didn't appear.

Increasingly, Teke needed to talk with Annie. She waited for a time when they might be alone, but it seemed that if the children weren't there, J.D. was, or Sam, or Michael's friends. Come midweek she was desperate enough to take Annie by the arm, hustle her out of Michael's room, and usher her down the hall.

"Just to talk," she assured her.

Annie protested, "There's nothing to say."

"There's too much, all long overdue. The air is *festering* with everything that hasn't been said. I need you, Annie." She knew Annie would pick up on her urgency, even tired as she was and bruised as she looked. Annie was sensitive to people's feelings, and though Teke felt like a rat preying on that, she neither slowed her step nor spoke until they were shut in the private bathroom at the end of the hall. Leaning against the door so that Annie couldn't escape, she said, "There are certain things I have to say. I want you to listen."

Annie frowned at the floor. After a minute she leaned against the handicap rail and raising her head. She looked so fragile that Teke nearly backed off. But she couldn't. She was too desperate to repair the harm she had done.

"I am very, very sorry for what I did, Annie. I know I've said that before, but I don't know if you heard. I can't tell you—I just can't tell you how much I regret it. I'm embarrassed and appalled. I'm disgusted with myself—and I do blame myself. I was the one who took the first step."

"Why did you?" Annie asked sharply.

Teke hesitated for only as long as it took to fill her lungs with air. "Because of Grady."

Annie's sharpness became confusion. "The man who was driving the truck?"

She had to make Annie understand her state of mind when Sam had come to the house. "I grew up with Grady. I adored him. We were lovers from the time I was fifteen until the time they put him in jail."

Annie gasped. Her confusion turned into hurt. "You never said. You never talked about your past. I always assumed there wasn't anything there."

"I couldn't talk about it. It was too hard. I was trying to forget that I had a past. Grady was my whole life, until he was sent to prison. I woke up thinking about seeing him and went to bed smelling him on my skin. We were going to be married. We were going to have babies. We were going to be together forever and ever. Suddenly all that was impossible."

"Did you know the person he murdered?"

Teke nodded. "He was my father."

Annie gasped again.

"Shocking, huh?" Teke asked, feeling a touch of hysteria. "Well, it is for me, too. This is the first time I've ever said it out loud. But it was more than shocking at the time. It was a nightmare that was just as awful as this one."

"What *happened?*" Annie whispered.

Teke's eyes filled. She looked at the ceiling. "My father used to manhandle me. Grady told him not to. One night he caught him at it and they fought. That's it. Two lives down the drain—three if you want to count my father's, but I don't." Her voice hardened. "He was a drunk who didn't want to work even to support his family. His life wasn't worth two cents."

At the look of horror on Annie's face, she said, "Does that sound harsh? Are you appalled that this woman you thought you knew can say such callous things about her own father? Well, maybe I am cold and harsh and callous, but do you know that my mother and sisters died because he wouldn't get the doctor? They were sick, but he refused to spend the money. *He* was the murderer, far more than Grady."

"Oh, Teke," Annie said in a nearly inaudible voice, "why didn't you tell me?"

"If I couldn't allow myself to think about it, how could I tell you? I blotted it out. I separated myself totally from my past. That was the only way I could survive. And I don't want your sympathy now. All I want is for you to understand what Grady meant to me and what it was like for me to think about seeing him again."

"Then you knew he was coming?"

"He wrote that he was, though I didn't know exactly when. I was furious at the thought of his showing up again, but that didn't keep me from repeatedly touching where his pen had touched and holding the paper where his hands might have held it." Her throat knotted as she remembered the past. In a whisper she said, "I loved him so much. You can't imagine."

Annie studied her hands.

"What are you thinking?" Teke asked.

Without looking up she said, "I'm thinking that I

can too imagine. I love Sam that same way, so maybe you can understand the hurt I'm feeling. I'm also thinking that if you loved Grady so much, you should never have married J.D."

"Grady was convicted of murder and sent to prison. Before he went—the last time I saw him—we had an awful argument. He said he didn't want to see me again, ever. I was devastated. I tried to write, but he returned my letters unopened. I tried to visit, but he refused to see me. Same with phone calls. So what choice did I have? He sent me away. He ruled out a future. He told me to make my family with someone else, because he didn't want me. So I did the only thing I could. I put Grady behind me. I met you and Sam and married J.D. and had Leigh and Jana and Michael. They've been good years."

"But not good enough?"

"*Good* years." Teke was trying to understand it herself, which was one of the reasons she had so needed to talk with Annie. It wasn't that Annie had all the answers, but she helped with the sorting out. "When I got Grady's letter, I was taken off-guard. Suddenly all the things I'd refused to think about all those years crowded back." She hesitated, then pushed on. "My relationship with Grady was very different from my relationship with J.D."

"In what ways?"

"We were both poor. We were soul mates in a harsh world. We comforted each other in a life with few other comforts." She lowered her eyes. "And then there was sex. Things with Grady were hot. Things with J.D. were tepid."

"Even at the start?" Annie asked.

"It was okay then. I was turned on by the kind of life J.D. and I were going to make together. As the years passed, though, the novelty of it faded. I tried not to make the comparison, but after a while I couldn't help it. It got worse the more I realized that things would *never* be what I wanted them to be with J.D."

Annie said a quiet, "I didn't know."

Teke smiled sadly. "It's not something a woman brags about, even to her best friend. I feel like I'm betraying J.D. saying it now." She grimaced. "As if I hadn't already betrayed him worse. And you."

There was a knock at the door.

"Just a minute," Teke called. In a lower voice she said to Annie, "Nineteen years of marriage, and I never cheated on him. I didn't mind the lack of passion. I had a home and a family and all of you, and it was so much more than I had as a kid that I used to go to bed thanking my lucky stars that I was where I was. Then, damn it, I got Grady's letter, and I wanted him, just like I had when I was a kid. It was like I was suddenly *starved* for what I hadn't had all those years, and that *terrified* me. Because I *do* have a *good life.* I didn't want to give it up. So help me God, if I could have gone to my grave without ever seeing Grady again, I would have been fine."

She let out a breath. Using both hands, she scooped her hair to the top of her head, wound a long piece around it, and tucked it in. Absently, nervously, she pulled a few wisps down to shield herself from total exposure.

"It was like the murder," she said. "It was unpremeditated and over and done so quickly that it was hard to believe something so fast could create such havoc with people's lives. I was distracted thinking of Grady when Sam came in. I was *overwhelmed* thinking of Grady, so much so that I don't remember a thing of what I felt with Sam. It was about as intimate as the four of us skinny-dipping off Sutters Island on a moonless night."

The image made her smile. Skinny-dipping had

always been Sam's idea. The thrill had been doing it without the kids finding out. She wondered if Annie remembered, too—but if so, there was no pleasure in the memory. She looked defeated. And she remained quiet.

"Tell me what you're thinking," Teke coaxed. "I need to know."

Annie gave a tiny moan. She drew in a deep breath, wrapped her arms around herself, looked every way but at Teke. "There's one part of me that says 'It's over and done. Let's forget it,' as though we can go back to the way it was before." Pleadingly she looked at Teke. "But I don't think I can *do* that. It hurts every time I think of it. I'm feeling things about myself, and feeling things about you and about Sam, that are very new, and it's *hard*."

"You and Sam had so much. All that can't be ruined."

"It may not be, but it's changed. There won't ever be that kind of blind trust again. It's gone."

"I'm sorry," Teke said. "I think that's what haunts me the most, you and Sam. Okay, so if you and I aren't ever friends, I can accept that as my punishment, but if things fall apart between you and Sam, that'll be too much. It shouldn't happen. He loves you, Annie."

Annie raised her eyebrows in a shrug.

"He does. And you love him. Don't let it fall apart because of a stupid move on my part."

Annie gave her a dry look. "You didn't rape him, Teke."

Another knock came. "Just a *minute*," Teke called, and added quietly but crossly, "Why are people so impatient?"

"Some needs are urgent."

Teke let out a breath. "Okay." She leveled a look at Annie. "But that was only part of what I wanted to say. I need your help. Jana refuses to talk to me. Leigh does only when absolutely necessary. Neither of them can talk to J.D., which means that emotionally they're on their own. I'm worried about them. I have no idea what they're feeling about all this, besides anger. You're the one they've always talked to, and in this case, you're the most innocent of the parties. Can you talk with them, Annie? Please?"

Annie looked uncomfortable. "That's putting me in an awkward situation. I won't talk badly about you in front of your daughters, and I can't talk badly about Sam even though there are times when I'm sure that I hate him, and I have no idea what's going on between you and J.D. What am I supposed to tell them?"

"I don't know," Teke wailed, hit by the same panic that had been hitting her on and off since Michael had slammed the door and run out of the house. "*I don't know.* But I'm losing them! Tell me what to do!"

Annie must have sensed her panic, because she straightened and said, "I'll talk with them. I don't know as it'll do much more than buy time—"

"They need a outlet, an adult they can talk to—"

"They need *you.*"

"But they've always gone to you," Teke said. "I know you're angry at me, but I'm begging you, for old times' sake if nothing else, help my kids."

Annie was suddenly angry. "God damn it, Teke, if I talk with your kids, it won't be for old times' sake. I've known them since they were born. I *love* them. Of *course* I'll talk with them. All I'm saying is that in the end you're going to have to talk with them yourself."

With the sound of another, sharper knock, Annie nudged her aside and pulled open the door. Teke had no choice but to follow her back down the hall.

ten

O N THURSDAY, ONE WEEK AFTER MICHAEL woke from his coma, he was moved to the rehabilitation center J.D. had selected. It was a forty-minute drive from Constance, but J.D. felt that the quality of the facility and the care there would more than compensate for the distance.

He drove his car while Teke went in the ambulance with Michael. Once at the center, Michael was whisked away for evaluation by the staff. It would be an hour or more, they were told, before he would return to his room. That gave J.D. the time he needed.

"Let's get coffee," he said to Teke.

They went to the cafeteria, where it seemed much of the staff was on break, but the setting was still preferable to home for what J.D. had in mind. He found a table in a far corner where they might have a measure of privacy.

"What are your plans now?" he asked once they were seated.

Teke looked uneasy. He could understand why. It was the first time they had been alone together since all hell had broken loose. He wasn't feeling terribly comfortable himself, and he was the one in the right!

"My plans?" she asked.

"You've been spending most nights at the hospital. Now that Michael's here, will you be sleeping at home?"

She fingered her coffee cup. "I don't know. I haven't thought that far. I want to do what's best for Michael."

"What about Leigh and Jana?"

"They don't seem to want me very much right now."

"Does Michael?" he asked with reason. He had seen the boy with his mother. It wasn't what Michael did as much as what he didn't do that suggested his anger. He avoided looking at her. He spoke to her only in brief answers to questions she posed. He smiled for others, but the smile faded when she came into view.

Michael was the same way with Sam. That gave J.D. a measure of satisfaction.

Teke raised the coffee cup to her mouth, then put it down without a sip. "He may not want to see me, but his situation is different from Jana's and Leigh's. He's younger, and he's hurt. The doctors say he'll spend several weeks here, then months in therapy at home before he'll have the kind of mobility he had before."

"At least he'll have it," J.D. reminded her. He had been infintely grateful when Bill Gardner had finally assured him on that score. "It could have been worse. I wouldn't complain about therapy if I were you."

"I'm not complaining. I'll do whatever has to be done, but it won't be easy on Michael. Therapy is hard work. It's painful and frustrating. He's already down in the mouth about not being able to play basketball, and it'll get worse when the season starts. And he isn't looking forward to being tutored."

"Have you arranged for that?" J.D. asked. He had told her to the week before.

She nodded. "I have someone coming here every afternoon for two hours."

He was instantly skeptical. "Is two hours enough?"

"It's all they advise. Michael still fades in and out. His level of concentration isn't what it was. Besides, he can't write with the cast on his arm, and even when it comes off, he'll need therapy before he'll be able to handle a pencil."

"What if he had a laptop computer?"

"That would help."

J.D. took out his date book and made a note to call Dick White. Dick was a client who owned a large chain of computer stores. He would know which machine to buy and would give J.D. a deal. "This tutor, is he good?"

"He's been highly recommended. He was agreeable when we talked on the phone."

J.D. pictured her greeting a tutor at the front door of the rehab center, walking him to Michael's room, having coffee with him after the sessions were done. "What does he look like?"

"I don't know," Teke said innocently enough, then stiffened when she got his drift. "Please, J.D.," she whispered, "don't insult me that way."

"Why not? You insulted me."

"And I'm paying the price. You can be sure I won't do it again."

"Not even with Grady Piper?" he asked, and could see by her sudden pallor that he had touched a raw cord. That gave him pleasure. He pressed on. "You didn't just 'know' him in Gullen, did you? You were lovers."

Her gaze met his and held. "You knew I wasn't a virgin when we met."

"I knew. I imagined that you had a naughty past, but that was kind of exciting. I thought I was the one who would straighten you out, only I wasn't able to, was I? Once a whore, always a whore."

Her skin remained pale. The cup shook slightly when she raised it for a drink. She set it down on the saucer with great care.

"No argument?" he goaded. He wouldn't have minded repeating the accusation.

"If calling me names makes you feel better, go ahead. You know how childish it is, though, don't you?"

"What I know," he said in a voice that was low but vibrating with the anger that was never quite gone, "is that Virginia Clinger did serious damage before I shut her up. I can't tell you how many men have teased me about you and Sam. Thanks to you, I feel like a fool. So if I want to call you names, I will."

She didn't flinch. Looking more weary, she said, "We have to talk about where we're going, you and me."

That was supposed to be his line. He resented her saying it first, but as long as she had, he figured he would give her a chance to make a fool of *herself* for a change. So instead of telling her what he wanted—as he knew she was expecting him to do—he sat back in the plastic chair. "Where do you want to go?"

To her credit, she didn't hem and haw. She composed herself much as she did when they were at functions where she was clearly outclassed. Then she said, "My first choice would be trying to see if we can patch things up. That would be best for the kids."

"Forget the kids. Another five years and they'll be

out of the house. What about us? Do you honestly think patching things up will work after what's happened?"

"It was *one time,* J.D.," she countered. "My *God,* you'd think I'd been picking up men right and left for years. One time. Either you're blowing this out of proportion—or you're using it as an excuse to extricate yourself from a marriage that you've been tiring of for a while." Her eyes sharpened. "I'm not thick, J.D. I know our marriage isn't exciting. It's been pleasant, and it's functional, but I never had the kind of relationship with you that Annie has with Sam."

"So you were jealous? Was that why you went after Sam?"

"I didn't go after him. It just happened. And there wasn't a stitch of jealousy involved. Annie and Sam have played such an important role in my life that I had nothing to be jealous about."

J.D. leaned in angrily. "Sex, Teke. Were you jealous of them in that department?"

"How could I be?" she cried. "I don't know what they do."

"You and Annie don't talk about that?"

"Of course not."

He wanted to believe her. He had been bothered by the thought of their making comparisons. He and Sam didn't talk, precisely because they knew each other's wives so well, but women were different. "You talk about everything else. Why not that?"

"Because it's private. Intimate. Embarrassing."

He snorted. "Which brings us back to the nitty-gritty. Sex isn't great between us. It never really was. Patching things up wouldn't do a thing to change that. It's either there or it isn't. In our case it isn't. We might have tried to fool ourselves for a while, but the chemistry just isn't right."

"But the marriage has worked. We share values when it comes to basic life-style. We don't argue about money or the house or the cars. Or the kids. We have a lot going for ourselves."

"A month ago I would have agreed. That was before the sex thing got too much for you."

"One time, J.D."

"The first. There'll be others. You'll see. It's like taking drugs. You resist and resist because you're totally clean, then for whatever the reasons you try it once. Suddenly you're not totally clean, so it doesn't make much difference if you try it a second time, then a third and a fourth. My good friend Sam learned that from his clients and passed it on during one of our evening talks." He sat back. "You didn't know about those, did you? The nights when we stayed in the office shooting the breeze from five to seven, then raced home so our wives wouldn't be upset." J.D. had spent some of those early evenings with women, but he wasn't telling Teke. He wasn't giving her dirt to use against him. "Well, Sam and I don't have those talks anymore. In fact, if John Stewart has his way, Sam won't be in the office at all."

Teke caught her breath. "Oh, J.D., that's not fair. He's done well for the firm."

J.D. raised a remedial finger. "Done well for *him*. His name is the one in the lights, not the firm's."

"But he brings in huge fees."

"That was the only thing that swayed John Stewart from bringing Sam's place in the partnership to an immediate vote. But he says it's only a delay. He wants Sam out. He wants you out, too. He thinks I should get a divorce."

Teke caught another, sharper breath.

"Didn't it occur to you that that might happen?" J.D. asked in disbelief. She was either more naive than he had thought or just plain dumb. "Didn't it occur to you that if you cheated on me, I might say, What the hell, it's not worth a damn, why should I make the effort to keep it together? Hasn't the thought of divorce entered your mind at least once in the last few weeks?"

"It has," she said, pushing her hair off her face, "but it isn't what I want. Marriage is something to fight for."

J.D. felt a stab of impatience. "Is it worth the fight? Face it, Teke, we're night and day, you and I. Know what's made our marriage work? Annie and Sam! They make us look attractive to each other. If it weren't for them, and for the kids, we'd probably have been disillusioned long before now. So now we won't have Annie and Sam, because I can't trust you around him, and Annie can't trust him around you, and the kids will be gone soon, so what's left? Do you think the sex will suddenly improve? Do you think I want to be worrying about how I compare to your other lovers? Sorry, lady, I don't compete that way."

She lowered her chin. Her hair slid forward.

"So I've put down money on a condo in Boston," he said, proud of himself for taking decisive action, particularly when her head flew up in alarm. "It's a big place, so the kids can visit, and it's furnished, so I can move in whenever I want. That's why I have to know your plans. If you'll be staying here with Michael, I'll stay at the house with the girls until he comes home. If you'll be sleeping home, I'll move to Boston now."

She had a hand on her chest. "You put money down. So fast?"

He shrugged. "It's a buyer's market."

"Didn't you want talk about it with me? Didn't you want to think about the effect it would have on the kids?"

"I've thought about the kids. What I'm doing seems far more honest than if I were to stay in the house and pretend we still have feelings for each other."

Teke blinked. "Don't we? We're married. I respect your work. We have a past together and so many memories. We share children."

"But we don't love each other." He would never have said that a month before. He had thought he loved her. But the speed with which his feelings had changed suggested something else. "Maybe we never did."

"There are different kinds of love," she argued, but he knew she was groping. "Not all are heavily passionate."

He couldn't hold back a bitter laugh. "Baby, we barely did *lightly* passionate." He sobered, thinking about the sham of his bragging and about the other women he had known over the years. "And you weren't the only one who felt the lack, Teke. Many a time I've needed more."

That seemed to stem any further argument she might have made. She scooped her dark hair away from her face again—it was the kind of gesture he had thought sexy once, the kind other men probably still thought sexy—and stared at him for a minute. "Is this the end, then?" she asked shakenly. "Will you be filing for divorce?"

"Not immediately. This is a trial separation."

Her face lightened. "Then you think there may be hope for us?"

"Not much."

The lightness faded. "So why a trial separation? Why not go right into divorce proceedings?"

Why not? Because J.D. wasn't in any rush. Because there was a sense of power in keeping Teke dangling. She deserved it. Anyone who betrayed him deserved that much and more. "Maybe," he said, "because I want to keep you tied up until Annie and Sam decide what to do. If you're free, you're apt to try to grab him."

She made a face that said she thought he was crazy, but he didn't care. He was in control. He was calling the shots. He would file for divorce when it suited him—not when it suited John Stewart or Teke or Sam—and not a minute sooner.

Annie was trying to put together a last minute dinner when Jana came through the back door and asked, all breathless and upset, "Are they getting divorced?"

Annie looked up from reading the directions for a pasta mix. "What?"

"I think they are. Mom's been sleeping at the center and Dad's been sleeping at home, and that might be just fine because of Michael, except that I went into the den a little while ago and saw a pile of change-of-address postcards on the desk. Dad is sending them to credit card companies and magazines, and he lists a place in Boston that isn't his office. *Are* they getting a divorce?"

Annie set down the box. Jana looked devastated. "I don't know," she said softly. She wished she knew better what to say to the girl. "It's not my business to ask."

"Well, wouldn't you think it someone's business to tell us? Don't they think we're old enough to see things are wrong? We know what she did. We know Dad is furious. We know that marriages fall apart over things like that."

Annie grabbed the lapel of Jana's blazer and gently tugged her along to the phone. She hung on while she used the other hand to punch out the office number, but she connected with the answering service. "He must have already left. Is he coming home to have dinner with you and Leigh?"

"He said he was. He said we were going out. Again." She tossed her hair back from her face. "I'm getting so sick of eating out. I never thought I'd say that, but it takes time to get seated, time to give your order, time to get your food, and then it's never done the way you want." She gave Annie a look of dismay. "Then Dad gets impatient and complains to the waitress, but when Leigh and I tried making dinner last night, it was a disaster."

"The chicken wasn't good?" Annie asked in surprise. She had given them a foolproof recipe.

"The chicken was great, but we didn't start the rice on time, so he had to wait for that, and by the time *it* was done, the chicken was overcooked, and the peas were all puckered."

"I wish you could eat here," Annie said, feeling awful that they couldn't, but J.D. never would come. Fortunately she didn't have to say that. Jana knew, and Jana knew why. Jana didn't want to be with Sam any more than J.D. did.

"So, is Dad moving out?" she asked.

"Your mom didn't mention it when I talked with her the other day."

Cautiously Jana said, "I didn't know you two were talking."

"We're beginning to," which was probably stretching it, because Annie hadn't talked with Teke since that day in the bathroom. But the stretching had a point. Annie felt that Jana was wrong for turning away each time Teke approached.

"Well, you might be able to forgive her, but I can't. What she did was selfish and cruel."

"She didn't intend to be selfish and cruel." Annie had come to believe that. "She wasn't thinking."

"Then she's an airhead."

"Oh, Jana," Annie said, tugging the lapel of Jana's blazer again, "sometimes people do things because they're confused. It doesn't mean they're airheads."

"You *are* forgiving her." It was an accusation now.

Annie thought of her close call with Jason Faust. It haunted her, wrapped her in guilt, made her head pound and her stomach turn. It also gave her an insight she hadn't had before. Looking back on those few minutes with Jason, she could begin to understand what Teke had been feeling if she was thinking about Grady Piper and wanting to feel feminine and loved. If what Teke had done was wrong, what Annie had done wasn't much better.

"Who am I to play holier than thou?" she asked Jana. "I've made mistakes in my life. We all have."

"But she *hurt* you. She cheated on you nearly as much as she did on my dad. How can you forget that?"

"I didn't say I could forget it, but the hurt will lessen in time. I'm not saying things are back to normal, Jana, just that I'm trying to keep an open mind."

"About Sam, too?"

That was harder. Sam was her husband. She expected different things from him than she expected from Teke.

"I'm trying to keep an open mind," she repeated, though her voice was harder.

"And I'm supposed to?"

"If you can."

Zoe burst into the kitchen, crying, "Mom, I can't do this math—Jana! Thank God you're here! Can you help me? This does—not—make—sense."

Jana held up a hand to ward Zoe off. Of Annie, quietly, she asked, "Will you find out what you can?"

"About what?" Zoe asked.

Jana scrunched up her nose. "Nothing." She was watching Annie.

Annie nodded. "Give Zoe a hand, and I'll be forever grateful." She sent Jana off with a squeeze and was looking up the number of J.D.'s car phone with a thought to catching him there and clueing him in to Jana's upset, when Leigh came through the door, looking lost in Jon's varsity jacket.

"Is Jana here?"

"Upstairs."

"Dad just came home. He wants her there. I would have called, except that the minute he came in he picked up the phone himself, and besides, I had to get out of the house. He's angry. One of his clients is giving him trouble." She went past Annie and slid her arms around Jon, who had appeared in the doorway. Annie guessed he had seen her come through the backyard from his bedroom window.

"Can Leigh eat with us?" he asked Annie.

"Not tonight. J.D. is taking Jana and her out."

"He wants to talk," Leigh told Jon. "Jana thinks he's moving out of the house. That's the first step in getting a divorce."

"Not necessarily," Annie put in, trying to calm Leigh, who had the same tendency as Teke to panic about high-priority items like home and hearth. "Often people take breathers from each other so that they can think things through. Often they need to separate to realize that they *don't* want to get divorced."

Leigh might have heard, but she was still talking to Jon. "So much for having a big happy wedding. We can forget that if they get divorced."

"That's not true." Annie went to them. "You'll have a big happy wedding regardless."

But Leigh was shaking her head. "Melissa

Weber's sweet sixteen was a nightmare. Her parents fought over the restaurant, the invitations, and the guest list, and then they stared daggers at each other the whole night. Even if Mom and Dad don't get divorced, after all this our wedding will be a mess."

"No, it won't—"

"We'll elope," Jon told Leigh.

"But we want to be there," Annie argued. "Besides, it's too early to be making wedding plans. There's college and graduate school—"

"We're not waiting that long," Jon said.

"And I'm not going to graduate school," Leigh added. "It's a waste of time and money, if I don't want a career, and I don't."

"Look," Annie said, taking a breath, "there's time to talk about all this. *Jana!*" she called, then said to Leigh, "Run back and tell J.D. that she'll be right there."

"I want to talk to Jon first."

"*Jana!*" More softly, "Talking with Jon won't help, if your dad is in a lousy mood."

"Would you call him, Annie?" Leigh begged, turning Jon toward the stairs. "Tell him I'll be there in a minute?"

"But it wasn't an hour ago that you saw Jon—" Annie called after them, then gave up when the door that led to the garage opened and Sam came in. "I have no control here," she said, throwing a hand in the air. It came down on the phone and punched out the Maxwells' number. The line was busy. "Swell." She shot a warning glance at Sam. "Dinner will be a little late."

He put his briefcase and trench coat on a chair and came to stand by the counter. "Bad day?"

"Busy." She focused on the pasta directions, took butter and milk from the refrigerator, measured the proper amounts of those ingredients and water into a saucepan, and set it on the stove.

"How are things at school?" he asked.

Gradually add pasta. She eased it in. "Getting busier."

"Midterms?"

"Uh-huh." *Bring just to a boil—*

"For all three courses?"

—and simmer for four minutes to desired degree of doneness. "Only Brit lit. The others have papers due."

"Won't the TAs help with the grading?"

Jason Faust would help with anything. He might have stormed out of her office in a huff that day—that embarrassing day, that *mortifying* day—but he had been solicitous ever since. He seemed willing to forget anything had ever happened. She wished she could.

She lit the gas under the saucepan. "The TAs will do the exam. I'll do the papers myself."

"That's a lot of work."

She gestured him aside so that she could reach the cabinet. "It's what my students are paying for," she said. She took out dishes and glasses, then opened the drawer that held the silverware, and all the while she tried not to be aware of Sam, but it was impossible. Forget the fact that he was a large physical presence. There was also the chemical thing. More than once since Annie's talk with Teke in the bathroom, she had wondered whether some sly little muse had given Sam and her their own chemical attraction, plus the chemical attraction that should have gone to Teke and J.D. So Teke and J.D. were without, while she and Sam had twice as much.

She felt it now. She always felt it. Sam Pope was the quintessentially magnetic male animal, where she was concerned.

"You don't have to work, you know," he said.

She shot him a dry look. "If I wasn't working through all this, I'd be a basket case."

"But if you're overwhelmed . . ."

"I'm not overwhelmed."

"You just said things were out of control."

"I said I had no control, meaning of a situation involving Leigh and Jon and Jana and J.D. that will be resolved any minute—" She broke off when the phone rang. "Don't answer that," she warned Sam, and reached for it herself. But one of the children beat her to it. "That will be J.D. wanting the girls home." She took napkins from the holder just as footsteps could be heard above.

"What's the problem?

"Jana is convinced J.D. is moving out. Do you know anything about it?"

"No."

"Leigh is convinced Teke and J.D. will end up divorced." With a look she asked Sam what he knew on that score.

But he answered, "I'm the last one J.D. would share his feelings with right now."

"Have you talked about it with Teke?"

"Come on, Annie. She wouldn't tell me. You're her friend."

"You're her lover."

"Was," he stated, "in the most remote sense of the word."

Jon barged into the kitchen. "Mom, J.D. invited me—" He stopped when he saw Sam. More deliberately he directed himself her way. "He invited me to go with them for dinner. Do you mind?"

"Of course not."

"I mind," Sam said. "I was hoping the four of us could have dinner."

Jon's jaw was set. He stared at Sam for a minute

before putting the burden on Annie. "Mom?"

"Go," she said softly. "Your being there may make things easier for Leigh and Jana."

Jon bolted back to get the others.

"What about us?" Sam asked.

The part of her that still wanted to punish ignored the hurt in his voice. "His being there will make it easier here, too." She piled everything on the plates. "He isn't a happy camper when you're around." When she turned to set the table, Sam took the plates from her hands and went there himself. She expected him to set the things down, turn back to her, and argue. Instead he started to set the table.

As she watched in surprise, the part of her that loved him cried. She knew how much his children meant to him, knew how much it hurt him when Jon looked at him the way he had. "Give him time, Sam."

He nodded and went on setting the table. He put the forks on the wrong sides, but Annie didn't have the heart to tell him, and in the next instant Jon, Jana, and Leigh were cutting through the kitchen to the door. Annie got kisses in passing from all three, but they went out the door without a word.

Sam lunged for the door before it could slam. "Don't be late, Jon," he called. "It's a school night." He seemed so forlorn as he stood looking out that Annie might have actually gone to him if Zoe hadn't chosen that moment to wander in looking down at the mouth.

"Wasn't Jana able to help?" Annie asked.

Zoe shrugged. She leaned against the wall by the phone, but when it rang she made no move to answer it.

Annie picked up the receiver. "Hello?"

A soft woman's voice said, "I'd like to speak with Samuel Pope, please."

Annie didn't recognize the voice and was instantly wary. "Who's calling?"

"Teresa Heskowicz."

Annie didn't recognize the name, either. If Sam had mentioned it, she would have remembered. Possibly Sam had *chosen* not to mention it. With a sharp look she held the receiver his way.

He took it. "Yes?" He paused. "I'm that Samuel Pope." He frowned and rubbed the back of his neck as he listened. "I may be able to help, but you've reached me at a bad time. Perhaps we could talk tomorrow. Do you have my office number?"

A potential client, or so it sounded to Annie. Sam didn't look embarrassed, only annoyed to be disturbed, or so it seemed to Annie. So she hoped. Once upon a time she wouldn't have had a second thought when a female called her husband on the phone. She wished she could turn back the clock.

But she couldn't. And Zoe's eyes were still on the floor. "What's wrong, babe?" she asked, touching the girl's cheek.

"She might have asked me to dinner, too. I'd have gone."

"I have a feeling Jon invited himself. Besides, we want you here."

Zoe inched her eyes up only enough to see that Sam had hung up the phone. She went to the table. "I'll finish this."

"Daddy's doing it."

"He's doing it wrong." She switched the forks.

"That side?" Sam asked contritely.

Zoe nodded.

Annie took salad makings from the refrigerator and was closing the door when Zoe was there. In a low voice she said, "Jana's seeing Danny Stocklan."

"Seeing?"

"Dating. Saturday night."

"That's okay," Annie said. "You can be with the other kids without her."

Zoe sucked in a corner of her mouth in a way that said she wouldn't do that.

"Why not?" Annie asked softly.

Zoe shrugged.

"Why not?" Annie coaxed.

"They want Jana, not me. She's the life of the party, not me. I just go along because she's there."

"That's not true, honey," Annie said, wanting to cry. "They *like* you."

Zoe began chewing on the inside of her cheek.

"Why don't the three of us go to a movie Saturday night?" Sam asked.

Zoe shook her head.

"Then to dinner. Or bowling." When Zoe shook her head again, he said, "We could go to the observation deck at the airport and watch the planes taking off."

Annie remembered Zoe loving that as a child. But she wasn't interested now.

Sam kept trying. "We could go to the mall and play with the dogs at Paul's Puppy Palace." When that suggestion prompted yet another head shake, he said, "I could put you under my coat and smuggle you into an adult movie."

Annie had to smile at that one, it was so typically Sam—and so thoroughly bogus—but Zoe didn't smile.

So, gently, he said, "I'm open to other suggestions."

"I'll stay home," she told Annie, and whirled around and left the room, but not soon enough to hide the tears in her eyes.

"Oh, dear," Annie whispered, and set down the salad makings. She couldn't bear it when Zoe was upset this way. She was such a gentle child, such a vulnerable child. Annie identified with her so strongly.

Sam reached the door first, but Annie slipped past him in the hall. At the base of the stairs, she turned and put a staying palm on his chest. "It'll be better if I go."

"Because she's angry at me?"

"Because she needs a woman."

"I used to be able to help."

"Okay, because she's angry at you. Time, Sam. They *both* need time."

"How *much* time?" He raked a hand through his hair. "I can't stand this, Annie. I want to talk with them, and I want to talk with you. I want to start repairing things, only no one will let me. When does the anger start to fade? How long does it take?"

She tried to take her hand back, but it was reluctant to leave his chest. So she left it there a little longer, just as long as it took for her eyes to tell him—to beg him—to be patient.

"I love you," he whispered with such a look of longing that she nearly forgot who she was, where she was, why she was there, and what all had happened to their lives of late.

But she didn't forget. She couldn't. Taking a shuddering breath, she turned and went on up to Zoe.

Grady was armed when he went to the rehabilitation center to see Michael. "These are for you," he said, pulling a tin from the bag he carried.

"Saltines?" Michael asked warily.

Grady opened the tin and tipped it to display the Ring-Ding cakes inside. "No one'll steal a saltine, so they're safer in here."

Michael gave a small grin. "What else is in the bag?"

With a little less confidence, Grady pulled out a battered old baseball hat. "It's my good-luck charm," he said. "Found it caught on my fence post when I first went back to Gullen after I got out of prison. Don't know whose it was." He straightened the visor enough so that Michael could see an A with a halo around it. "I was never an Angels' fan, not living in Maine, but I figured it stood for a new life, so I put it on my head. I came to think it was keeping me out of trouble." He looked for a place to put it, finally hooked it on the back-most of the beams that formed a therapeutic apparatus over the bed.

"Not there," Michael said. "On my head."

Grady put the hat there, feeling warmed from top to bottom. Then he reached into the bag again and, more surreptitiously this time, took out a heaping handful of bubble gum packs and slid them into the bedstand draw where Michael might reach them.

"I saw that," Teke said.

"They're for him," Grady told her. "This is for you." He pulled out the last of his gifts, a plastic bag filled with scraps and remnants, different-colored pieces of twine, and wire and fabric. "They're the best of my jobs. It's like my personal signature, stealing a souvenir." To Michael he said, "Your mom used to make the prettiest things with scraps like that. I thought she might like something to do with her hands while you're with the therapist."

Michael didn't look impressed, and what had seemed such a good idea to Grady back in the carriage house suddenly lost some of its sparkle. This Teke wasn't the penniless girl he had known in Gullen. She was married to money. She wouldn't be excited by a bag of scraps, regardless of how many years they had been in the collecting.

So he mumbled to her, "You were baking cookies for the people at the hospital. I thought you might make earrings for the nurses here. Dumb idea, I guess." He started to put the scraps back in his bag.

"Wait." She studied the scraps, looking torn. Then, with the tiniest shadow of smile, she held out her hand.

Grady's heart flipped in his chest. He passed her the bag of scraps, wishing they were diamonds, she was so pretty. For all the imagining he'd done, all the wondering about what she looked like twenty-two years later, she filled his highest expectations. She always had.

He took a breath, forcing his eyes from Teke to Michael. "Are they treating you okay here?"

"I guess," Michael answered less enthusiastically now.

"No?"

"The exercises stink."

"That's okay, as long as they help."

"I want to go home."

Grady sought Teke's guidance, but she looked as helpless as he felt. "When do they say you can?"

"They say it depends on how hard I try, and I *do* try, but it doesn't help."

His discouragement cut into Grady, a sharp reminder that it was Grady's truck that had caused the damage. He struggled to be positive. "You haven't been at it for long."

"Nothing's working."

"Then you'll have to try harder. Especially if you're going to wear my hat."

"My dad won't like the hat," Michael said.

Grady had figured as much. He had also figured that he had given the boy his hat as much out of defiance as fondness. Thanks to J.D., the police stopped by several times a week to let Grady know they hadn't forgotten he was there.

That defiance kept Grady from offering to take back the hat. "Tell your dad it's your good-luck hat and that you do better when you're wearing it. But if he's going to believe it, you do have to do better when you're wearing it."

"How old is your little girl?" Michael asked.

Grady drew back. He shot a look at Teke, but she didn't seem to be any more aware of where the question had come from than he was. "Six," he answered cautiously.

"What's her name?"

He paused. "Shelley."

"Where does she live?"

He took a breath. "With her mom in California, last I heard."

"Don't you keep in touch?"

Grady frowned at his boots. "Her mom doesn't want that, and she has custody."

"Why does she?"

Grady met Michael's gaze. "Because the judge thought a little girl needed her mother more than her father, especially since her father is a convicted murderer."

Michael was silent then. Grady was beginning to think he was leaving the subject behind—and happily so, it was a painful one for him, when the boy asked, "Does that bother you?"

"Yeah, it bothers me. It bothers me a whole lot."

"Is that why you keep coming to see me? Because you miss her?"

"No."

"Because you feel guilty about what happened?"

"Sure, I feel guilty. But it's not the only reason I'm here."

"If you're here to see my mother, I don't want you coming."

Teke rose from her chair. Grady stayed her with a hand. "Why not?" he asked quietly. If there was one thing he had learned from the prison counselor, it was to talk out his anger. Michael clearly had anger. Unless it was understood and channeled, he wouldn't have a chance in hell of running down a basketball court again.

"Because she isn't worth it," he cried, sounding wounded and not a minute older than thirteen. "She cheated on my father."

Grady nodded. "She told me. She told me right in front of you, and she also said it was a mistake and she felt awful about it. So are you going to hold it against her forever? Me, I can't do that. I need people to forgive me. I killed a man. I took his life. He's dead and gone because I hit him too hard. In my book, that's worse'n spending one afternoon with the wrong person."

Michael turned his head away and closed his eyes. In a voice that was suddenly younger than thirteen and much more vulnerable, he asked, "So are you here to see her, or me?"

"You," Grady grunted, "though don't ask me why. At least she's a fighter. Her life fell to pieces, but she went on to make something of it. You gonna do that?"

"But I can't move my legs," the small voice said.

"You can move them. You just can't move them right. So you'll have to learn how again."

"What if I can't?" Michael asked, on the verge of sudden tears.

"Hey," Grady said gently, and before he knew what he planned, he was sitting beside Michael, lifting him, holding him close. "You can learn how to walk again," he said while the boy cried quietly against his chest, "you sure as hell can. God knows you got enough people waiting here to help, and that's a head start, boy. It's more'n some people have. You can learn to walk again. You just have to make up your mind to do it."

eleven

J.D. OVERSLEPT. HE HADN'T DONE THAT SINCE college, and then only on the mornings after the nights Sam had gotten him drunk. He had an internal alarm clock that worked three hundred and sixty-five days a year. It would have worked this day, too, if he hadn't been up absurdly late the night before trying to put his belongings in some sort of order in the bedroom and bathroom, and *that* after making dinner for himself, then cleaning up the mess the kitchen had become. Sure, he could have eaten out. But making his own dinner on his first night in his own apartment had struck him as a decidedly ... *independent* ... thing to do.

No one had told him that spaghetti sauce spattered all over the place if the heat wasn't kept low. No one had told him that cooked pasta picked up speed as it left the pot and was apt to slide right over the plate onto the counter if care wasn't taken. And that was the *second* batch of pasta. He had lost most of the first down the disposal when he had tried to drain the water from the pot by tipping the works while holding the lid slightly ajar. The maneuver had only succeeded in burning the heel of his hand.

But that wasn't even the worst. The worst was the bottle of olive oil his elbow had inadvertently sent flying. He had had to wash and rinse the floor five times, and even then it looked oily, which didn't speak well for the grease-cutting claim of the dish-washing liquid he had used.

Now, not only had his internal alarm betrayed him, but so had the one on the nightstand. He still didn't know why it hadn't gone off at seven. It was eight-thirty now, and he was racing around a strange apartment trying to remember where he had put things the night before. He was certain that he had brought along his charcoal Harris tweed suit, a sure harbinger of November, on the first of the two trips from Constance that he had made the day before, but he couldn't find it in the closet. Ditto for half his ties. Not that he was reaching the getting-dressed stage fast. His razor blade had turned dull halfway through his shave, and he didn't have a spare. So he gave his chin a nick or two, which he might have done anyway since the shower had steamed up the mirror so that he couldn't see what he was doing. Now he had to wait to get dressed until the bleeding stopped or risk getting blood on his shirt or tie. So, with tiny pieces of tissue stuck on his chin, he went to make breakfast.

The good news was that the newspaper he had ordered was right at his door as promised. The bad news was that he had forgotten to buy milk for his breakfast. So he dumped the cereal back into the box, swept the overflow into the sink, and put second best, a bagel, into the toaster while he read the paper. He was barely past the first page when the toaster started to smoke. He pushed up the handle; the bagel stayed down. Smoke continued to curl toward the ceiling, setting off the fire alarm. Swearing broadly, he silenced it by knocking it down with the handle of the mop that had come in so handy the night before.

By that time he was determined that no bagel would get the best of him. So he took a fork and began to pry pieces of it from the grillwork on the inside of the toaster. He ended up with several quarter chunks and lots of crumbs that couldn't be spread with cream cheese—which was just fine, since he had forgotten to buy cream cheese, too.

That was when the full force of what he had done hit him. For the very first time, standing there in his new kitchen with his feet sticking to the floor and the ruins of breakfast before him, reality came into focus.

He had left Teke. He had left the house and the children. His nineteen-year-marriage was on the verge of breaking up. His future was suddenly open.

The part of him that had depended on Teke, that liked being a Popewell and appreciated the constancy of the house in the suburbs, was terrified. That part wondered whether he had acted hastily.

Not so the part that had dabbled with other women, thought his law practice boring as hell, and resented every word John Stewart Maxwell said. That part was determined to make breakfast better tomorrow.

Sam sat on the sleek upholstered chair assigned him. His legs were comfortably crossed at the knees and his elbows propped casually on the arms of the chair. To the television audience, he was a man of easygoing confidence. Inside, he was suffering.

He would never have agreed to do this show had he not turned down half a dozen others since winning *Dunn* v. *Hanover*. Only when his partners and the public relations firm had thrown up their hands in unanimous despair had he capitulated. One show, he had allowed. Preferably midmorning when no one he knew would watch, he had thought to himself. As fate would have it, early morning was what they had arranged, and he was hating every minute of it.

"I think the court decision was *all wrong,*" an admitted abuser was saying. "I don't think I should be held responsible for something I did twenty years ago. I've changed. I don't do those things now."

"But you did them *then,*" an avowed abusee argued. "What was done to me has affected my whole life. I'm suffering now for what my father did to me then. Shouldn't he suffer, too?"

"Mr. Pope," the moderator prompted, "isn't that your major argument?"

Sam struggled to focus in on the discussion. "Not exactly, not if revenge is the goal—"

"It's not revenge," the abusee charged. "It's *justice.*"

"It's a waste of time," the abuser retorted. "I live a good life now. I work hard, I earn my money, I pay my taxes, I treat my family well. Bringing me to trial for something that happened so long ago is a waste of everyone's efforts. What good'll it do? Life goes on. People put things like that behind them."

"But *I can't,*" the abusee cried. "I live with it every day of my life."

"Mr. Pope?" the moderator prompted again.

Sam cleared his throat. He was struggling to separate his own situation from that being discussed, but although he sided with the victim, he felt he had "perpetrator" written all over him.

"Our system of justice rejects the concept of an eye for an eye," he said slowly, "which is why revenge for its own sake is no good. Paying reparation for wrongs done is something else." He would *gladly* pay reparation, if that would make things right with Annie, with Teke and J.D., with the kids. He would *gladly* pay Michael's medical bills, foot the bill for his tutors, buy him whatever, if it would help. "If the person abused has suffered—and continues to suffer—mental and physical pain for wrongs done, such that normal living is disrupted, he or she has a right to sue for restitution."

"It's greed, pure and simple," the abuser stated. "They want the money."

Sam was wishing that something as simple as money would solve his problem when the abusee made him feel even worse by saying, "No amount of money could *possibly* make up for what I've gone through."

And back and forth it went, with emotions running high, just as the producers wanted. Sam's emotions were running high, too. He was feeling guilty. And fraudulent. And unworthy of entering a single viewer's living room, all the more so with each reference to him as an authority in defense of the abused. He was infinitely grateful when the show ended.

A short time later, returning to the office, he spotted J.D. in the restaurant in the ground-floor atrium of their building. There were others at other tables, men and women in business suits, their intermittent conversation punctuated by the genteel ring of silver on china. J.D. sat alone with the newspaper and what looked like a huge breakfast that he was just starting to eat. It seemed the perfect opportunity. Sam had been trying to catch him relaxed and idle for days.

Not about to ask and be turned down, he dropped onto a chair. "We need to talk," he said.

J.D. turned a page of the paper and folded it back. "I'm taking a break. Can't it wait until later?"

"The office is no good for this kind of talk. J.S. has ears in the walls."

J.D. forked up a mouthful of Belgian waffle. He chased it down with fresh-squeezed orange juice.

Sam motioned the waitress for coffee. "How's the apartment?"

"Great," J.D. said, and started on a rasher of bacon.

"All settled in?"

"Um-hmm."

"Do you need help with anything—hanging pictures, mounting tie racks, hooking up the VCR?"

"It's done."

Sam nodded. He supposed supers did that kind of thing, but it felt odd. He had helped J.D. with more mechanical nuisances than he could count. "If there's anything I can do, just yell. New places can be depressing as hell until you get them fixed up the right way."

J.D. wiped his hand on a napkin before turning a page of the paper. "This place is furnished. There isn't much fixing up to do."

"You like it, then?"

"I wouldn't have taken it if I didn't."

Sam smiled a thank-you to the waitress who brought his coffee. "It must be weird, quiet after all those years in a full house." He tried to picture his own house that way, with the kids off to college, their rooms empty and dark. The only good part of it would be that he had Annie all to himself. They could make love where and when they wanted. If they were making love. Which they hadn't yet. Not since Teke.

J.D. kept eating and reading.

Sam watched for a minute. Then he took a frustrated breath. "Either you're still angry, or you're scared, or starved, or that paper's more interesting than I am. Come on, J.D. Put the goddamned thing down and talk to me."

J.D. set the paper aside. He draped his arm over the spare chair to his left, leaving his right hand free to lift his toast. "Scared?" he asked curiously.

"That I may say something tough."

J.D. swallowed a bite of toast. "Like what?"

"Like, did you really have to move out of the house? Like, do you know what that's done to the kids? Like, is it really over?"

J.D. didn't blink. "Yes; yes; I don't know."

Sam looked away, swearing under his breath. "Christ, is that what twenty-some years of friendship boils down to?"

"You tell me. You're the one who destroyed the friendship."

There was the guilt again, back as strongly as it had been on the television show. "Does it have to be destroyed? Isn't there a way to salvage something of it?" He held up a hand. "Don't answer if you're going to toss out more angry platitudes." He came forward and lowered his voice. "Listen to what I'm saying. That afternoon is over and done. I have apologized as best I can, I don't know how else to do it. Now I'm trying to move beyond it, which means trying to envision the future, but that's hard to do, because suddenly you're out of the picture. I don't want that, J.D. None of us does."

J.D. was quiet, brooding in the direction of his plate. He had stopped eating.

Taking encouragement from that, Sam argued his case. "Your moving out of the house has hit everyone hard. Michael may be in rehab, but we can look forward to the time when he'll be home and back to normal. Your leaving is something else." He raised that same quelling hand. "Forget the anger. Forget the smart one-liners. Talk to me, J.D. Tell me what you honestly, deep down inside, feel. You may say that I don't have the right to know, but it isn't just me. It's Annie, and it's the kids."

J.D. set his mouth in a flat line. When he raised his eyes to Sam's, they were surprisingly direct, which was the first indication Sam had that he was getting through. The second was the absence of anger in J.D.'s voice. "Honestly? Deep down inside? I think the move may be permanent."

"But *why?*" Sam burst out. He couldn't conceive of a life without J.D. an acre away. J.D. lent an order to the things they did. He was the restraining force when whimsy threatened to overtake reason. Now it seemed he was being taken over by whimsy himself. "On the sixth of October you loved Teke, on the eighth of October you stopped?" Sam snapped his fingers. "Just like that? It doesn't make sense."

"It does," J.D. said, "if the love was less than love all along. I'm beginning to think my marriage may have been flawed from the start. Did I have a relationship with Teke, or was it with Teke and Sam and Annie? Think about it, Sam. It's been a bizarre arrangement."

"It worked."

"Bizarre," J.D. insisted. "The very first date I had with Teke was a double with you and Annie, and we did that through most of college. We got married within two months of each other, we took vacations together, we rented apartments in the same building, bought first houses in the same neighborhood, bought second houses that abutted each other. Hell, our children are nearly interchangeable. People looking at us are hard-pressed to tell which are the Pope kids and which are the Maxwells. So"—he took a breath—"the question becomes whether I fell in love with Teke or with the foursome."

"You had to have felt something for Teke."

"I did. But it can't sustain us as a twosome."

"You haven't given it a chance!"

"I gave it nineteen years. In the past, the slack between Teke and me was filled by you two. Now it can't be, because you're part of the problem. So there's just Teke and me. Through this whole trauma with Michael, we've been no help to each other, no help at all. If not now, when? My relationship with Teke is empty. Trying to hold on to something without substance is dumb."

"What about the kids?"

"They'll visit."

"What about Thanksgiving?"

"Teke can have it. No one's stopping her."

Sam was feeling depressed. "Sure, she can have it. She always has. She makes Thanksgiving like no one else does. But the fact is that Annie won't do it like we have in the past, which means that we'll be having separate Thanksgivings for the first time ever. That means Teke will be making turkey for the kids and no one else."

"Let her invite friends." On a more sour note he added, "Let her invite Grady Piper. They were lovers once, did you know?"

Sam knew. Annie had told him that much. "It was a long time ago."

"He's still carrying the torch. That's why he came in the first place, and that's why he's staying. Just wait. He'll cause more trouble yet."

"Our men in blue haven't come up with so much as a misdemeanor. He looks to be doing a fair enough job on Cornelia Hart's place."

"Yeah, well, I'm thinking about the job he'll be doing on Teke. He'll screw her. Just wait."

"And who's given him a perfect opening? If you didn't want him to have it, you shouldn't have moved out of the house. Either she's yours or she isn't. Either you stake a claim or you pull it up and move on."

"Have you done that with Annie, staked a claim?"

"She knows I'm not leaving," Sam said, though it suddenly sounded like a pretty passive claim staking. Words he had used earlier that morning—"reparation" and "restitution"—came to mind.

"Has she forgiven you?"

"I'm working on it." Hard enough? He wondered. He was still giving her time to come around on her own, and in the meanwhile he was trying to be home more. Since *Dunn* v. *Hanover* he had been bombarded with calls from victims seeking representation but was farming out many of those cases to other lawyers. He had even let ongoing work slide to allow more time for Annie, yet it struck him that he could be more aggressive about winning her back. "At least there isn't another man in the picture," he reasoned aloud. "You can be sure I'd be doing more if there were." He refocused on J.D. "So don't complain about Piper. You left. That's abandonment. Teke is fair game."

"She's still married to me"—he wiped his mouth with a napkin and tossed down the linen—"but Christ, he can have her. What I don't like is his being around my son."

"Michael needs someone," Sam said. The thought broke him up, as always. "He won't look at me, and you're not around."

"I visit the center."

"Does he know you moved out of the house?"

"I haven't mentioned it. I assume one of the girls has told him. Jana says she wants to move in with me. God only knows what Leigh says. She's never home when I'm talking with Jana. She's always with Jon."

"They're inseparable."

"That's nothing new."

"Well, it's worse than ever," Sam remarked. Jon and Leigh had banded together in the crisis and become a unit to the exclusion, it seemed, of everyone else in both their families. Annie might benefit from having him around more. So might Zoe.

"So talk to Jon," J.D. said.

"Lotta good *that*'ll do. He isn't of a mind to listen to anything I say. He thinks I'm a two-faced liar. You'd have better luck talking with Leigh."

J.D. grunted. "Leigh and I aren't confidantes."

Sam thought of his own daughter. His relationship had had its confidante moments back in the days when she used to talk with him. Now she wouldn't. "What a mess," he muttered.

"Yeah. Well."

Turning sideways, Sam dropped his elbows to his knees. His hands hung limply between them. "Okay." He took a breath. "No point in rehashing. Let's talk about the ski house. By the end of the month the mountain'll open. How do you want to handle it?"

J.D. frowned. "Hell, I don't know how to handle it. How does Teke want to handle it?"

"I haven't asked. She'll only defer to you. Your moving out of the house has hit her hardest. It makes things very real."

J.D. tipped back in his seat. "What if she's pregnant?"

Sam was startled. "By me?"

"Did you use something? Of course not, and she wouldn't have run upstairs for her diaphragm."

Sam clamped a hand on his arm, bringing J.D. and his chair forward with a thud. "She is not pregnant."

"But what if she were?" J.D. asked in what Sam could have sworn was amusement. "That'd throw an interesting wrench in the works."

"She's not pregnant," Sam repeated, but he was suddenly sweating. He hadn't considered pregnancy. He should have. But he hadn't.

"What about AIDS?" J.D. asked. "Have you thought about that?"

"No," Sam stated, angry now, "but if that proves to be a problem, it won't be Teke who's at fault, it'll be you." The thought made him sick. Having had just about enough of John David for the moment, he rose. "While I'm thinking about that, you can think about the ski house and about Sutters Island. If you're divorcing us, we'd better negotiate a separation agreement. But I'm warning you, I'll fight for my fair share. I'll take the blame for what I did with Teke and for what subsequently happened to Michael, but that's it. It's gone far enough. You want to move out, fine. You want to divorce Teke, fine. You want to convince yourself that you're too good for the rest of us and shouldn't dirty your hands any longer, fine. But we've given you a goddamned good twenty years. Leave us, and you'll go right down the tubes."

"I don't believe that."

"Believe what you want. Without us, you'll be another John Stewart in no time. That what you want?" Disgusted with himself, with J.D., with the whole unhappy situation, he stalked off.

Teke was at the rehabilitation center working with Michael and his therapist when a nurse tracked her down. "You have a phone call, Mrs. Maxwell. He says it's urgent."

"Must be your dad," Teke said. Hiding a rise of nervousness, she she gave Michael's shoulder a squeeze. "I'll be right back."

The nurse waited until she was in the hall to

scold, "It isn't your husband. It's Sam Pope. I explained that you were busy and that I didn't have the time to hunt around for you, but he was insistent."

Teke grew frightened. She imagined a dozen urgent messages Sam might deliver, none of them happy. Her heart was pounding by the time she reached the phone. "What happened, Sam? Is it Jana, or Leigh?"

"No, no. They're fine."

"Annie?"

"She's okay. Teke, are you pregnant?"

Teke's mind drew a momentary blank. "Excuse me?"

"Lots of women conceive in their forties. If you did, you should have already missed a period."

Pregnant? From their one, aborted, ill-fated time together? She made a high, slightly hysterical sound and said a small, silent prayer that none of those other urgent things had come to pass. "I didn't miss. I'm not pregnant."

Sam sighed in obvious relief. "Thank God. There could be a helluva lot of worse things than our producing a child, but under the circumstances I can't think of many. Sorry, Teke. I didn't mean to scare you, but J.D. put that bug in my ear, and it was buzzing so loud I couldn't hear a damn thing."

"That's an Annie analogy," Teke said with a fond smile. She missed Annie. She couldn't *begin* to think of what Annie would have felt if she had become pregnant with Sam's child.

"How's Michael?" Sam asked more calmly.

"Cranky. But more for me than for anyone else. I wonder if he'll ever forgive me."

"I'll talk with him about that."

"It won't be easy. You're pretty high on his shit list, too." Thank *God* she wasn't pregnant! That would have been a *disaster* where Michael was concerned.

"I can try. You just keep up all you're doing. Sooner or later he'll realize how much you love him."

She was counting on that. At times it was all that kept her going.

"Hang in there, Teke. If you need anything at home, just yell."

She really did love Sam, for just that kind of care. "Annie may not like that."

"Annie feels as badly as I do that J.D. moved out and left you alone. She made me promise to stay in town late tonight so that she could invite your girls over for dinner without my presence spoiling things."

"Oh, Sam."

"I can live with it. So you'll stay later with Michael?"

"Uh-huh." It was one immediate problem solved. She was grateful for every little bit of help. "Please thank Annie for me."

"I will. Take care, Teke."

Annie had finished a meeting with a student and was returning several books to the bookshelf when Sam arrived at her office. At the sound of a noise at the door, she turned with a start. Her first response was pleasure, but it was quickly tempered.

"Sam. I didn't expect you." She glanced her watch. "Didn't you say that you had a lunch meeting?" Of late he had started giving her a rundown on his schedule before he left the house in the morning. "In case you need to reach me," was the excuse he offered. She suspected it was his way of saying "I have nothing to hide."

"I canceled it," he said now. "It hit me that I hadn't been out here in a while, and that in another few weeks you'll be tied up with exams, and that since I won't be home for dinner, I really wanted to take you to lunch. How about it?"

She shot another look at her watch, then one at a small paper sack that rested on the file cabinet. "I was planning to have a sandwich here while I work. I have a class at one-thirty."

"Just to the coffee shop. I'll have you back in time."

She would have gone with the old Sam in a minute, but the new Sam had slept with her best friend. She was still feeling the hurt of it.

"Please, Annie? It's time, don't you think?"

He was right, she supposed. She couldn't avoid him forever—even if she wanted to—which she didn't.

Without looking at him, she took her purse from the bottom drawer of the file cabinet. He had her coat waiting when she straightened.

The coffee shop was the most intimate of the eating places on campus. It was shabby in the way of an old and adored pair of shoes. It was also, just then, crowded and loud. After two minutes of standing in line waiting to order, Sam was scowling. "This place is a pit. Maybe we should go somewhere else."

But she was comfortable on her turf. "Be patient. We're moving."

"I wanted to take you somewhere nice. Why did I suggest this?"

"Because I said I didn't have much time and this is the closest. It's fine," she assured him. It was functional, atmospheric in a campy college way, and not romantic in the least.

"I wanted a place that was sparkling white, with fresh flowers on the table and waiters with gloves and empty tables all around us so that no one would be embarrassed when I started whispering sweet nothings in your ear."

She shot him a quelling look. She didn't want him saying things like that.

"Another time," he murmured as they moved forward.

"What'll it be, Dr. Pope?" the young man behind the counter asked.

Annie ordered tuna salad and tea. Sam ordered a double bacon-cheeseburger with fries and a Coke.

"That still gives me a little jolt," he said, leaning down to her ear while they waited for the burger to cook.

"What does?"

"'Dr. Pope.' I don't hear it often enough to get used to it. It sounds so formal. My first thought is to ask who in the hell Dr. Pope is, then I realize it's you. It makes me proud."

She blushed, but she said nothing as she watched the young man behind the counter scoop tuna salad onto a bed of shredded lettuce.

"*You* make me proud," he said, still by her ear. "You're the most normal-looking person here."

Easy enough to be, she mused with a glance around at the motley assortment of collegians. She could have said the same for Sam. She could have said he was the most *handsome* person there. Or the most *sexy*. "Some of these not-so-normal people are geniuses."

"I'll take normalcy over genius any day." He grunted. "I'd take normalcy over most *anything* right now."

She thought of recent events and nodded, then shook her head when the man behind the counter asked if she wanted chips.

Sam turned sideways so that he was facing her. "I

talked with J.D. this morning. He really thinks this is it for his marriage."

Her heart fell. "So quickly? So *finally?* No second thoughts? No *counseling?*"

"Can you see J.D. in counseling?"

She thought about it for half a second. "You're right. He'd never do it. But, boy, a therapist would have a time with him. Forget his relationship with Teke or with us. The dynamics between him and his father could fill five years' worth of sessions."

"I think he knows that," Sam said, and reached for her tuna salad plate before she could. He beat her to her tea, too. When his lunch had joined the rest on the tray, she led him to the only free table. It was smack in the midst of the fray. Which was fine, she mused. There was safety in visibility. Sam couldn't try anything, and she couldn't succumb.

He didn't start to eat immediately. Folding his arms on the edge of the table, he watched her until, feeling self-conscious, she begged him to stop.

"I can't help it," he said. "You are not only the most normal-looking person here, you are also the prettiest. I love you, Annie."

She rolled her eyes.

"I do."

"I'm sure."

"What does that mean?"

"It means that I believe you."

"But?"

"But you have a funny way of showing it sometimes."

"One time, fast falling into the past."

She picked at her tuna. "If only. The repercussions keep coming. Poor Teke."

"You're not angry with her anymore?"

"Sure I am. But she and I have been best friends for so long that I'd have to be inhuman not to sym-

pathize. Her husband just left her. She must be feeling deserted." Annie would have been *devastated* if
Sam left her.

"How much of a comfort do you think Grady
Piper is?"

"Some. Then again, one part of her is furious he's
here at all. He hurt her badly when he sent her
away."

"J.D. is convinced they'll be sleeping together
before long. Do you think so?"

"I think she may be too angry for that. Or too
frightened."

"Frightened?"

"Of involvement with Grady again. It was disaster-
ous once. Besides," Annie added, looking him in the
eye, "she slept with you, and look what happened.
Instant pain, incredible sorrow, prolonged
heartache. The thought of going to bed with *any*
man may terrify her."

Sam returned her gaze without a blink, but as he
did, his eyes grew smoky. Annie knew that look. It
said he was picturing *her* in bed. As flattering as it
was, it wasn't what she wanted just then.

"Please, Sam," she whispered.

He straightened, cleared his throat, shifted on his
seat in a way that confirmed he had been growing
aroused. With a determined look, he bit into his
cheeseburger.

"Besides," she went on, "one of the most basic
things Teke and I had in common was coming from
dysfunctional families. Getting married and having
kids was high priority for both of us, but for Teke
even more so than me. I had dreams of teaching.
She never had dreams of being anything but a wife
and a mother. Whether it was an illusion or not, she
thought she had an anchor in J.D. I think she'll cling
to her marriage until it dissolves in her hands."

"I hope not."

"Why not?"

"She deserves more." He hesitated, looked torn, finally said, "J.D. wasn't always faithful to her, Annie. It was never anything prolonged, and I never learned about it until after the fact. We'd be at a law association breakfast and a lawyer who had always been pleasant before would go out of her way to avoid us. J.D. would make a comment about the trouble women have with mornings after."

Annie was appalled. "Are you serious?"

He nodded.

"You never told me that before!"

"What good would it have done?"

Not much, she supposed. But she was stunned. "What did you say when he told you things like that?"

"I told him it was wrong. I said it wasn't fair to Teke. What else could I do? I couldn't very well tell her about it, and I knew that if I told you, you'd think less of him. I thought less of him. Still, he was my best friend." He grew thoughtful. "Funny how one indiscretion on my part evoked such scorn from him." He held up a hand. "I know, I know. My indiscretion was with his wife. Still, if you want to generalize, what I did wasn't any worse than what he's done more than once. Not that I'm trying to excuse it. Nothing does that. Cheating is cheating, and it's wrong. But I'm saying that if J.D. gives up on his marriage so quickly and easily, Teke has a right to see an old friend, and if he makes her happy, I'm all for it."

"Would you do that?" Annie asked.

"What?"

"If I said that I wanted a divorce, would you get together with Teke?" It would be easy for him to do. They knew each other so well. *So* well.

His face lost color. "Do you want a divorce?"

"It's a hypothetical question. The issue is Teke."

He seemed not to hear. "I don't want a divorce, Annie. I've told you over and over again. I love you. I want to work things out."

"*If* I gave up on you, would you go to Teke?"

He made a face. "God, no. What would I want Teke for?"

His distaste was real, giving Annie a marginal sense of relief. Still, she could think of dozens of things Sam might want Teke for. "Home cooking. Clean laundry. Familiarity. Sex."

"Teke is a good friend, but she doesn't turn me on, and as for the rest, I'd hire someone before I went to Teke."

"Dr. Pope?"

She looked up. "Hi, Georgia. Jason." To Sam she said, "You met Jason at last year's Christmas party. Jason Faust. And this is Georgia Nichols. She's a first-year TA." To the two, and with a deep inner satisfaction where Jason was concerned, she said, "My husband, Sam."

Sam stood and extended a hand first to Georgia, then to Jason.

"I'm sorry for bothering you," Georgia said, returning to Annie, "but I'm supposed to meet with you at three, and I can't make it. Can I reschedule for tomorrow morning?"

Annie took an appointment book from her pocketbook. "Tomorrow morning's tight. I couldn't do it much before noon."

"Noon is fine with me."

Annie wrote it in. Closing the book, she studied Jason. "You look peaked. Are you feeling okay?"

"I'm fine. Just giving Georgia moral support. All set, babe?" he asked Georgia, who nodded and waved her thanks to Annie as the two moved off.

Annie watched them go. Jason walked and talked fine, still ...

"What?" Sam prodded.

"Jason doesn't look right."

"He normally looks *better* than that?" When Annie turned to him, he said, "He a great-looking guy, whether you say he's peaked or not. Is he gay?"

'No, he's not gay."

"How do you know?"

"I know." Oh, yes.

"How?"

"Because the grapevine says he isn't," she prevaricated, "and the grapevine doesn't lie." She checked her watch. Time was running out. Fork in hand, she began to eat in earnest.

"If I was the suspicious sort," Sam said, "I'd be jealous. Your Jason is not only great-looking, he's young. Some women have a thing for young flesh."

"Some men, too," Annie replied.

"Have you never been tempted?"

She fought the urge to squirm. "I'm married."

"That doesn't mean you haven't been tempted."

She continued to eat for a minute before setting down her fork, folding her hands in her lap, and raising her chin. "Prior to October sixth, I had a husband who satisfied me in every respect, including the sexual. He had an endless hunger. He kept me sated so that I couldn't begin to think of other men. Then his hunger got out of hand. Unfortunate things happened. We're still trying to recover."

Sam whispered, "Give me three hours in the nearest motel and we'd move a long way toward that recovery."

She felt a frisson of something warm tickle the base of her spine, and she ignored it. "I'm not talking about sex, I'm talking about trust. Besides, I keep picturing you with Teke. I couldn't bear it if we were together and she was there, too."

"She wouldn't be," he whispered more urgently.

"I'd make sure you couldn't think of anyone but me."

But she shook her head. "It's no good. The images are too strong."

"What if we went away? Just the two of us, somewhere we've never been. Would the images follow?"

"I don't know."

"Let's try it."

"With everything else that's happening?" she asked, feeling sadness, frustration, and fatigue. "I can't, Sam. The kids are having a horrendous time trying to cope with the changes in our lives, and so am I. There are times when I'm awake in the middle of the night shaking with fear thinking about basic things to do with running a household that most women do with their eyes closed."

Sam looked dismayed. "Why didn't you say something?"

"Because it's humiliating. Here I've been walking around feeling so good about myself, feeling *superior* in my way because I have my Ph.D. and tenure and a family. Well, looking the other in the face now, I'm in *awe* of the women who do it." She sagged from the inside out, thinking how poorly she shaped up. "I want to do everything well, but I don't, know if I can, because there's so much to do. I swear, I've cooked dinner more nights in the past month than I have in the past three years, and I'm not complaining, I choose to do it, but it's more work on top of everything else."

"You *should* have complained," Sam argued. "We can eat out more."

"No, we can't, because everyone comes home at different times, and then the kids have homework, or they're on the phone, or Jon's rushing to finish at home so he can run over to Leigh's. Trying to corral them for an hour to go to a restaurant would be a nightmare. My cooking dinner is the path of least resistance. Same thing with Thanksgiving. Sure, we can make reservations somewhere, but it isn't the same. I want to have Thanksgiving dinner at our house. I think it's crucial that we do it for the kids' sakes. But do you know how intimidating the prospect is? Thanksgiving is a soup-to-nuts extravaganza. Taking shortcuts would be defeating the purpose, so that means poring through cookbooks, planning a menu, making things ahead of time and freezing them. We're talking a major meal, and that's not counting fresh flowers and candles and munchies."

"I'll help," Sam said.

The offer won him a tiny smile. "We'd be the blind leading the blind."

"So? I'm game."

"Sam, you can't cook."

"Maybe it's time I learned."

"When? You don't have any more time to browse in the cookbook section of the bookstore than I do."

"I'll make time."

"John Stewart would just love that."

"Fuck John Stewart," he said, scowling. "I'm a full partner in the firm. I'll work when I want."

Annie looked at him in amusement, amazement, affection. She couldn't help it. Until she glanced at her watch. "You may be able to do that, but I can't." She slipped her arms into the sleeves of her coat. "If I don't leave now, I'll miss my class." She hitched her chin toward his half-eaten burger. "You stay here and finish."

But Sam slipped into his own coat, grabbed a handful of napkins, the burger, and her hand. Then, as he had done when they had been young and innocent and so very idealistic, he walked her to class. Against her better judgment, she was snowed.

twelve

T EKE STOOD ON ONE SIDE OF MICHAEL IN THE waist-high water, his physical therapist on the other. While they held him afloat, they rhythmically manipulated an arm or a leg, bending it, rotating it, straightening it, ever gently, but ever more. The goals were flexibility and strength.

Michael was still recovering from the removal of the casts. Despite warnings to the contrary from the doctors, he had been hoping that the casted parts would emerge in perfect working order. Teke had been hoping it herself, she was that desperate for a miracle. But it wasn't to be, which caused another emotional slide.

"How's that feel?" the therapist asked him.

"Dumb," was Michael's muttered response. "If my friends saw me doing this, they'd laugh. I feel like a baby."

"It'd be easier if you were," the therapist remarked. He was a gentle giant with a dry wit that had boosted Teke's spirits more than once. Now he said, "Babies are eager to learn things. They try and try, over and over again. When they fall, no sweat, they get up. They don't know about embarrassment.

Big people do. They get hung up with their image. They don't like the idea that they have to learn at all. Their attitude holds them back. What they don't realize is that with a big people mind and the right attitude, they can learn twice as fast, with half the falls." He paused. "So, what'll it be, big people? Want to get dried off and hit the machines for a while?"

Since the machines demanded more from Michael than the pool, the pep talk was well timed. Michael grunted, to which the therapist responded by easing him to the stairs, carrying him up, and setting him into a wheelchair.

"I'll see you guys soon," Teke said, and headed for the women's locker room. Twenty minutes later, showered and dressed, she returned to Michael's room. She had barely settled onto the easy chair there when Grady walked in carrying a large bag with twin arches.

"Lunch," he said with a glance at the empty bed. "Not back yet?"

"It'll be another little while," Teke said, but she didn't move. She had been on the go since five that morning, when she had bolted out of bed to whip up a double batch of cookies, and that had been just for starters. Now, half a hectic day later, she was too exhausted to be annoyed with herself for not telling Grady that he shouldn't have come. "They're working with the machines. Since I can't help there, I thought I'd take a rest."

Grady reached into the bag, unlidded a cup of coffee, and passed it to her.

Her tired mouth slipped into a smile. "Thanks. I need this."

"Need lunch, too?"

"In a bit." She settled more deeply in the chair, tired enough to welcome the cushions, the coffee, and, yes, Grady. He was a friend—more than that, if she thought of the past. But even in the present, he was distinguishing himself. He was kind, he was caring, he was *there.* She was having trouble sustaining anger toward him.

Indeed, she was still married to J.D., still thinking that for the children's sake, they might reconcile, and in that sense Grady's presence was a risk. But she couldn't send him away.

"What're you thinking?" he asked.

She sighed. "I'm thinking that you really shouldn't be here, but that the company's nice. Back at the hospital, people used to drop by more. They've gone back to their own lives now."

"You must have lots of friends."

She raised the cup and savored the aroma of the coffee. "I'm active around town. I know 'most everyone." She took a sip. The warmth was heavenly going down after a swim and a shower. "There are some very nice people in Constance. And some very conservative ones. They always thought I was a little kooky." She arched a brow. "Wonder what they think now." She took another sip.

"Mrs. Hart likes you."

Cornelia Hart wasn't quite the gossip some of the others were. She probably hadn't heard about Teke's faux pas with Sam. "She's a sweetie. Is she being kind to you?"

"Very. She said it was too cold for me to live in the carriage house. She made me move into her basement."

"Wasn't she brave," Teke teased, though she was relieved to know that Grady would be warm. He had finished putting a new roof on the carriage house and was reshingling the outer walls. He hadn't gotten around to insulation or heat.

Grady grinned. "Gave the cops a scare all right. They saw me coming out of the house one too many times. They thought I was robbing the place."

Teke closed her eyes. "Thank you, John David."

"Actually, it's gratifying when they think they've caught me and then find that they haven't. One of the guys is okay. The other is into intimidation. He's the one who gets mean when he goes away empty-handed."

"That would be Connors," Teke said "His son was on Michael's Little League team for a while. He's the first one to say that the coach stinks and the last one to volunteer to coach himself. Let me know if he touches you. Sam will remind him of your civil rights. He's big on those."

"Sam sounds like a decent guy."

"He is."

"Would he really speak up for me at the same time that his partner is speaking against me?"

"Sam doesn't blame you for what happened. He knows that if Michael hadn't seen what he did, he wouldn't have run into the street that way." She tipped the coffee to her lips, but it wasn't much of a shield to hide behind. And anyway, hiding was pointless. Grady knew what she'd done. Everyone knew what she'd done.

"Do you love him?"

She blinked. "Sam? I love him like I love Annie. They're dear friends. I miss them both. They come to visit, but it isn't the same as it was. We were all so close." She thought of Sam's phone call several days before and had to smile. "Poor Sam." She could share this with Grady. "It suddenly occurred to him that I might be pregnant. He had quite a scare."

Grady looked none too calm just then either. "Are you?"

"Thank goodness, no. My carrying Sam's baby would have been one trauma too many. Not that I don't love babies. I loved being pregnant. I loved having little ones around. I loved watching them grow." Memory took her back to when the children were small and their problems correspondingly simple. Then it went farther. Looking at Grady, seeing the spikes of dark hair that touched his forehead, reminded her of the teenager she had loved. She remembered the dreams they had shared of the children they were going to have. She guessed from the stricken look on his face that he was remembering, too.

"Do you have a picture of your daughter?" she asked softly.

It was a minute before he reacted. Then he drew out his wallet and pulled out a dog-eared snapshot. "She was three."

Teke couldn't take her eyes from the little girl's face. "She's beautiful." The child had Grady's eyes and mouth and his raven hair. "So much like you."

"Not in personality. She's talkative and outgoing. Always jumping around, smiling at people." He stopped short. "At least she used to be that way. It's been a while since I've seen her."

"Wouldn't you like to?"

"Nah. She's older'n that now, and the older she gets, the more she'll see me for what I am."

"There's nothing wrong with what you are."

"Her mother didn't think so."

"Then why did she marry you?"

Grady rubbed the back of his neck. "I've asked myself that a lot. Don't have the answer."

Teke tried to picture the woman. She had known that Grady would have female companionship over the years—he was too virile not to—but in her mind those women were always fleeting shadows with neither faces nor names. The child's face was Grady's. It said nothing about his wife. "Tell me what she was like.""Sharon?" When Teke nodded he said, "She was five seven, slender, had light skin, brown eyes, and long, dark brown hair."

"She looked like me," Teke concluded quietly.

He sighed. "'Fraid so."

"Did you do it deliberately?"

"As the prison therapist would say, I must have known it on some level, but it wasn't one I clued into at the time."

"Was she nice at least?"

"Very nice."

"Did she make you a nice home?"

"*I* thought so. She thought the place was a hole. Fact was, I owned it, and I felt good about that, but she wanted something more. She thought I had potential. I guess that's it, why she married me. She thought I'd keep moving up and up and up in the world until I owned some big furniture manufacturing plant. Instead I went from job to job, taking each one for what it was. In my free time I'd be building canoes or taking finished ones up the river. Just me and a paddle. I loved that. Sometimes I'd be gone for three days. It used to drive her crazy. That, and your name."

"Oh, Grady."

"I didn't mind her leaving. I miss Shelley, though."

Teke studied the snapshot before handing it back. It was bent at spots, much handled, and, in that, heartrending. Grady would have been a wonderful father, she knew. "You can borrow my kids, if you want," she said. "Any one of the three. Of course, you might have trouble prying Leigh away from Jon, Jana will best you in every argument, and Michael will keep you constantly on the go, but they really are great kids."

"I'll take Michael for now," he said, grinning. "Thanks." Against her better judgement, she grinned right back.

268

*   *   *

Grady stayed only long enough to have lunch with Michael and Teke, but even that was five minutes too long. He was pulling out of the parking lot, his old blue pickup a dead giveaway of his identity, when J.D. pulled in. All the way home Grady thought about Teke and the flak she would be taking, which wasn't what he wanted at all. He went to the rehab center to see Michael and do what he could to cheer the boy, but even more, he went to give Teke a break. He went to bring her coffee or a sandwich. He went to do small somethings to make her life a little easier. No one else seemed to be doing that.

Annoying J.D. wouldn't help her, but what choice did he have? He couldn't leave town until he knew that both Michael *and* Teke were walking again.

Back in Constance, he took his frustration out on the cedar clapboards he was mounting on the outer rear wall of the carriage house. He was several hours into it, high on a ladder, when the police officers he was coming to know materialized below him.

He looked once, hammered two more nails, looked again. They hadn't moved. He told himself to stay calm, but it was hard when he wanted to yell. He was sure J.D. had sent them, too coincidental, the timing and all.

"Yes?" he asked the nicer one, whose name was Dodd.

"We have to talk, Mr. Piper," Dodd said.

Dutifully, because he hadn't done anything wrong and didn't intend to, Grady dropped the hammer into his carpenter's apron and backed down the ladder. On the ground he tucked his hands in the pockets of his parka against the chill of a gray November day.

"About what?" he asked.

"The Molson place."

"What's that?"

"Don't take us for dummies," Connors warned.

Grady kept his eyes on Dodd, who said, "The Molson place is a mansion on four acres just a bit down the road. It was robbed sometime between ten and eleven this morning. Where were you then?"

Grady felt his insides tighten. Ignoring them, he hitched his head toward the new patch of siding.

"The whole time?" Dodd asked.

"'Til ten-thirty."

"Where did you go then?"

"McDonald's."

"How long were you there?"

"Five minutes."

"He's a quick eater," Connors muttered.

"I didn't eat there. I got stuff from the takeout window."

"Did you come back here to eat?" Dodd asked.

"No. I went to see Michael Maxwell."

"What in the hell did you do that for?" Connors barked. "You looking for trouble? You know the boy's father doesn't want you around. What do you have, shit for brains?"

"Look, Mr Piper," Dodd said calmly, "we need to find people to verify that you were where you claim. Mrs. Hart says she can't imagine you'd rob anyone, since you haven't taken anything from her even though you've had plenty of chance to, but the last time she saw you was seven-thirty this morning. Did anyone else see you working here?"

Of course not, Grady thought. That would be too easy. "Someone might've seen the truck out front, but they wouldn't have seen me unless they drove around back."

"How about at McDonald's?" Dodd asked. "See anyone you know?"

"I didn't get out of the truck."

"I trust Mrs. Maxwell will vouch for your being at the rehabilitation center?"

"Her, or her boy," Grady said, adding to Connors. "He hates the food at the center. But he loves McDonald's. If his father is annoyed I brought him lunch, it's only because he didn't think to do it first."

Connors said to Dodd, "Let's take a look inside."

"Do you have a search warrant?" Grady asked. He knew his rights, and although he wasn't out to antagonize these two, he wasn't having those rights denied.

"This carriage house belongs to Mrs. Hart," Connors told him. "She gave us permission."

"The carriage house is mine while I fix it up. I'm her tenant."

"You paying rent?"

"The work I do is the rent I pay. So this is my home. Without a warrant, any search will be illegal."

Connors looked at Dodd. "He's hiding something."

"But he's right," Dodd said.

"We leave here to get a warrant, and he'll have everything stashed somewhere else by the time we get back."

"Not if we take him with us," Dodd said. "I'm sorry, Mr. Piper, but I'm afraid we'll have to ask you to come to the station. We'll want to ask you a few more questions."

Grady felt the old, familiar terror come to life. "Is there any reason for it, other than that I have a record?"

"That's reason enough," Connors said, taking him by the arm. When Grady pulled his arm free, he asked, "You rather have cuffs?"

Grady took a deep breath and straightened. He

looked at Dodd. "I get a phone call. If I make it from here, my lawyer can meet us at the station."

"I told you he had something to hide," Connors said.

Dodd spoke more kindly. "You don't really need a lawyer. No one's charging you with anything."

"I want a lawyer," Grady repeated. He'd had it with being watched and followed and questioned. "Do I call from here, or from the station?"

Dodd led him into Mrs. Hart's kitchen, where he made his one call. Forty-five minutes later, with apologies for taking so long, Sam Pope walked into the interrogation room of the Constance police station. The officers left them alone.

"Teke told me to call if I ran into trouble," Grady said. "I wasn't sure you'd come, but she said you were an expert when it came to a person's civil rights. That's what I need. They're questioning me about a robbery."

"Did you do it?" Sam asked.

"No. I've never robbed a thing in my life. Murder's my thing, or hadn't you heard?"

"I heard."

"Problem is, there are people in town who don't want me around."

"J.D."

Grady appreciated his bluntness. It made things easier. "They're searching my place, my truck, too, I guess. I told them they needed a warrant, so they're holding me here while they get it. For all I know, they're out there planting something in my truck. What's to protect me from that?"

"Me," Sam said, and went out the door. When he reappeared he motioned Grady out of his chair. "We'll meet them there."

"They said they wanted to question me more."

Sam's expression said they were full of it. "They

have no reason to haul you in here, other than that J.D.'s been driving them nuts. If they can convince a judge to give them a warrant, fine. But we'll be there during any search." Hands in his pockets, in a pose of utter confidence, he cocked his head toward the door.

It was nearly five when Sam returned to the office. He had barely started down the hall when J.D. fell into step beside him. "What in the hell are you doing, Sam?"

Sam controlled a flare of annoyance. "What?"

"Defending Grady Piper."

"I'm not defending him. There's no defense necessary. The man hasn't broken any law." He took the messages Joy handed him and turned smoothly into his office.

"That man is not our friend," J.D. stated slowly, as though to a child. "He is not good for Teke. He is not good for Michael. He is not good for me. The sooner he leaves town, the better."

Sam scanned the messages. "He's a free man, J.D. He can live where he wants."

"That's fine, as long as he doesn't live in my town."

"You live in Boston. Constance isn't your town anymore."

"I'm still a homeowner and a taxpayer. I have a say about what happens there."

"Not," Sam said, raising his eyes but not his head, "when it causes the violation of a man's rights." He did raise his head then. "You can't do that, J.D. You've been hounding the police to hound him ever since the accident. But they can't get him on anything. He's clean. He's doing just what Cornelia Hart hired him to do. Why don't you leave him alone?"

"Why doesn't he leave my son alone?"

"He feels guilty about the accident. He feels badly for Michael, and, hey, it's damn good that he's there. Michael is a man's boy, but who does he have now? You're too angry at Teke to help him, he's too angry at me to let me help him, so Grady's left. You should be grateful." He singled out one of the message slips and tossed the rest on the desk.

"He's after my wife."

"Why should it bother you if he is? You left her."

"She's still my wife."

Sam picked up the phone. "You can't have it both ways, J.D. Either you want her or you don't." He poked out the number on the slip. It was that of Bill Kneeland, whose appeal on a mail fraud conviction Sam was handling.

"Well, what about you?" J.D. asked. "You want it both ways. You claim to be my friend, but you drop everything and run to Constance the minute my enemy calls."

"Grady Piper is not your enemy," Sam told him, then spoke into the phone. "Hi, Bill. Just got your message."

"We're talking loyalty here," J.D. said. "Can't he get another lawyer?"

Covering the phone with a palm, Sam whispered, "He's new to town. I'm the only lawyer he knows besides you." He removed his hand and said to his client, "We'll be filing it first thing Monday morning. I have the motion right here." He searched the top of his desk, lifted files, pushed others around.

"Is he paying you?"

"There's nothing to pay for yet," Sam whispered with his mouth away from the phone. To Bill he said, "Right. I think our chances are good. The judge made some poor calls." He flipped through the papers on the other corner of his desk.

"Your time," J.D. said. "You left this office, drove all the way to Constance to represent him when the police took him in for questioning, then you negotiated his release."

"It'll be a while, Bill. I wouldn't expect a decision for two months, maybe three." He turned and sorted through the files on the credenza. "The reason we're rushing to file now is on the off chance that we'll benefit from the rush to clean the boards before Christmas, but I wouldn't hold my breath if I were you. Just relax. Once the brief is filed, it's out of our hands. Let me talk with you next week."

"Your time is worth money to this firm," J.D. said.

"Sure. Take care." Sam hung up the phone. "I didn't negotiate anything," he told J.D. while he turned back to the desk and went through the files on top a second time. "All I did was warn the cops that they were inviting a civil suit for harassment. It may come to that, if they keep on him the way they've been, and let me tell you, if it comes to a suit, you'll be named. So back off." Having worked himself into a small temper, he growled, "Where is that goddamned file? *Joy?*"

J.D. went out the door as Joy came in.

"Where's the motion on the Kneeland case?" Sam asked her. "Vicki was finishing it up. It should have been typed and ready by now."

Joy looked confused. "Vicki went to Providence."

That was the first Sam had heard of it, but then he'd been more out of the office than in it of late. "When?"

"Wednesday morning." Two days before.

"What's she doing in Providence?" He tried to remember if she had said something about going on vacation, but he was *sure* she hadn't. They had talked in depth on Monday about the Kneeland motion. He had outlined everything he wanted done.

275

She had planned to spend the week on it.

"Uh, I think she's doing something for J.S.," Joy said.

"But Vicki works with me, not with J.S." And it was an unwritten rule that partners didn't steal each other's associates. He looked at the mess he had made of his desk. "Do me a favor and straighten this up, Joy? Maybe I'm looking for it too hard to see the damn folder. I have to talk with J.S."

He went down the hall at a clip, gearing up to give John Stewart hell if he had secreted Vicki Cornell away. She was head and shoulders above Tom or Alex or any of the other associates. He knew that when he gave her an assignment it would be done well and on time. He relied on that.

John Stewart was leaning back in his desk chair with his fingers laced over his middle. He looked as though he had been expecting Sam.

"What's the story on Vicki?" Sam asked, forgoing any polite preliminaries. They would have been a waste of breath. John Stewart had been ignoring him since the day Michael had come out of his coma.

Without moving a muscle, J.S. said, "I needed Vicki's help on a case of my own."

Sam was incredulous. "You had her just *drop* the work she was doing for me? Didn't she tell you what she was working on?"

"She told me. I told her to give it to Tom."

"Tom doesn't know this case. You had no right doing that."

"I had every right. I'm the managing partner in this firm. I have the final say in things like this."

"You had *no right*." Sam thrust a hand through his hair, on the near edge of panic. Tom Mackie didn't know his ass from a hole in the ground when it came to writing briefs. Sam didn't know what he was going to do. "Do you understand the potential of the Kneeland case, J.S.? Bill came to us from one of the megafirms. If I get a ruling for a new trial, we'll be handling it. That's big bucks coming in."

"Oh? You're concerned about money?" John Stewart asked. "This is something new. Your billable hours have been pitiful."

"What are you talking about?"

John Stewart must indeed have been waiting for him, because he had the papers right there on his desk. He picked up the sheaf, dropped it again. "Billable hours. Way down for the last month. That's not the way this firm runs."

"*Dunn* v. *Hanover* brought in *six million dollars.* That's money for the firm before it's money for me."

"Not all profit, I might add. You didn't get a penny all those years when you did the work, and we haven't seen a cent of the six million yet."

"Right, because the defendant's insurance company has to pick up the tab, and insurance companies take forever to fork money up. But it's coming, and it'll go a hell of a long way toward putting this firm in the black for the year. Now you're complaining that my billable hours are down? What kind of crap is that?"

Innocently John Stewart said, "It's right here on the time sheets."

"Time sheets covering a period of intense personal crisis. Or have you missed that?"

"How could I miss it? You haven't been in this office more than four hours a day, if that."

"And when I'm not here, where am I? I'm at the hospital, or the rehab center, visiting your grandson."

"Or at the college taking your wife to lunch. Is that what you do with the draw you take from this firm each month?"

Sam was about to rake a second hand through his hair when he caught himself. He wasn't a lowly employee. He wasn't some raw kid who needed a taking-down. He was an experienced lawyer and a full partner in the firm. He could do what he wanted, when he wanted, with whom he wanted.

But there was more. He could feel it, could *smell* it in this office, and it wasn't the smell of the antique map of Boston that hung in its precious gold-leaf frame on the wall.

"Spit it out, J.S. What's on your mind?"

"What's on my mind is your role in this firm. I let you be voted in as a partner because John David convinced me it might be good to have a litigation department here, but I don't think so anymore. I don't care whether you bring in *ten* million on one case, you don't have the kind of image we want."

"You're angry about Teke."

John Stewart raised his chin. "I think that what you and she did was disgusting, though not surprising. Litigators are a different breed. They work with scum; they learn from scum."

"My clients aren't scum. I have a solid white-collar practice."

"I seem to recall that last spring you defended a prostitute who murdered one of her clients."

"It was self-defense. She was acquitted."

"It was not a white-collar case."

"I was appointed by the court to represent her. It took three days of my time. Where's your social conscience?"

J.S. shot a bored look at the ceiling. "Then there was the case that you tried last summer, where you defended a fellow who was charged with illegally distributing drug paraphernalia."

"Clean needles," Sam stated impatiently. "He was trying to save an addict or two from contracting

AIDS. Jesus, J.S., you're something else."

J.S. gave a shrug so subtle that it barely disturbed the smooth shoulder line of his Brooks Brothers suit. "The fact is that I am the sole living founding partner, the oldest partner, and the managing partner of Maxwell, Roper and Dine. And I want your resignation from the partnership."

Sam was dumbfounded. "What?"

"Your resignation."

"You're putting me on."

J.S. moved his head from side to side.

"I've given you twelve years of solid productivity," Sam argued.

J.S. pursed his lips in the direction of the records on his desk. "That's debatable, but what isn't is that we have irreconcilable differences. We look at the world, and the operation of a law firm, in very different ways."

"So?" Many a firm's partners had differences.

"I want your resignation."

"Well, you can't have it," Sam said in a flash of anger. "I'm a full partner here. I've invested twelve years of sweat and blood in this place. It's my firm, too. I'll fight."

"Fight all you want," J.S. said with maddening calm. "My reassignment of Vicki is just the start. I can make life very unpleasant for you, and if you're still hanging around after all that, I'll bring your partnership to a vote."

"You wouldn't win."

"I might."

"You wouldn't," Sam insisted, staring at J.S. in disbelief. Then he straightened and looked out the window but saw nothing of the view that was so prized. What he saw was another blow to the gut of the life he had thought so super little more than a month before. It boggled his mind. He was at the height of his career, and J.S. wanted to kick him out of the firm. Yes, they had their differences, but the fact was that Maxwell, Roper and Dine provided him with an established and respected base from which to operate. The thought of being forced to change that base at a time when the rest of his life was in turmoil was one upsetting thought too many.

"First things first," he said, and turned on his heel. "I have a brief to write by Monday morning. We'll have to discuss this another time."

Annie stopped at the supermarket on the way home and emerged with nine bags, a record for her, but the wave of the future, if her resolution to make one efficient, all-inclusive food trip per week held out. She had barely climbed from the car when Sam pulled into his side of the garage. The minute she saw the harried look on his face she knew something was wrong.

He started talking off his frustration and didn't finish until he had carried in every one of the nine bags, plus his own things, which consisted of an armload of books and two large portfolios filled with the Kneeland trial transcripts, the notes he had given to Vicki Cornell at the start of the week, and the half-finished, very raw brief that he had found on her desk. By that time Annie was staring at him, unable to believe what she was hearing.

"J.S. wants you out of the firm?"

Sam gave an agitated snort. "That's the long-range plan. The short-range one is to sabotage my work. Well, he almost succeeded there. I'll have to work all weekend, because this brief has to be filed by Monday or else. But I don't want to work all weekend. I want to take us all out for dinner tomorrow night. I want you and me to take off for the day

Sunday, maybe head over to Rockport and visit Pete, or drive north to Ogunquit. That's out of the question now. I'm not even sure how much of Jon's game I can make."

Annie was well familiar with the sixteen-hour-a-day, seven-day weeks that Sam put in when he was on trial and knew that without support in the office, he would put in the same kinds of weeks around important motion-filing times. Vicki Cornell had been a godsend. She shaved six hours off those sixteen, freeing Sam to work on other cases. She also freed him from the intense pressure that Annie saw signs of now.

Annie had an unwelcome thought. Vicki Cornell was young and talented. She wondered if Sam ever wondered what she looked like undressed.

"What a bastard he is," Sam ranted on, pushing his hand through his hair for the third time in as many minutes. "He could have told me on Wednesday, or left some kind of memo saying that he needed Vicki. Then I might have made other arrangements. I could have put Tom to work, and even though he wouldn't have given me anything finished, at least I'd have had something sketchy to refine."

"Why didn't Vicki say anything?"

"Probably because he snagged her while I was out of the office and sent her right off."

"She could have left a message for you, or called in from wherever she was."

"Yeah." Sam looked disgusted. "If she'd done that, she'd have put herself smack in the middle of a war between J.S. and me. Vicki Cornell wouldn't do that. She's ambitious. That's one of the things that makes her good, but it also means that she isn't about to antagonize J.S. He swings a lot more weight in this city than I do."

"You underestimate yourself," Annie said. She truly believed it and was relieved to say it, because she felt guilty on another score. She was actually pleased that Vicki had let Sam down. She wanted him to think less of the woman.

"J.S. has been around longer," Sam insisted. "His contacts are more dug in, and they're loaded." He sank back against the counter. "Whoever said 'When it rains, it pours' got it right."

Annie thought of John Stewart's threat to vote him out. Of all Sam had told her, this angered her the most. "Do you think he would ever actually bring your partnership to a vote, or is it all hot air?"

"He'd do it in a minute and with great pleasure. He didn't want me there in the first place. He feels his initial qualms have been validated. I'm not part of the 'image' he has of himself and his firm."

Annie was offended on Sam's behalf. "Will J.D. stop him?"

"Who knows? J.D. is a loose cannon. Some of the things he says are straight out of John Stewart's mouth. Others aren't. I don't know which way he'll turn or when he'll go off. The irony of it is that if my partnership comes to a vote, J.D. will be the swing man. Of the five partners, J.S. and Martin Cox will stand against me, and Will Henry will stand with me. That's two to two. Enter J.D."

Annie pictured such a meeting, such a vote. She pictured Sam standing up, pleading his case, and the thought of that rankled. "Damn it, you've done well for that firm. You've upheld your end of the bargain. They've made money on you for every one of the twelve years you've been there. To hold a vote to decide your future is an insult. I think you should resign."

He braced his hands on the edges of the counter by either hip. "I thought of that while I was driving home. I nearly missed my turn off."

"Resign, Sam," Annie repeated with greater conviction, and began unbagging groceries. "It's the only solution to an untenable situation."

"Resigning is easier said than done."

"I might agree if you had a corporate practice," she said. "Corporations want full-service firms. They want the security of numbers. When they form an affiliation with a law firm, it's akin to a marriage. Continuity is the name of the game, but that isn't so with a litigator. Your clients are rarely repeat clients. They don't keep you on retainer. New clients come as new indictments are handed down. Your practice is portable. You could hang out your shingle anywhere you wanted and do fine."

"In a slow economy?" he asked doubtfully. "I have a family to support."

"Your practice is *immune* to the economy. Look at what you've done this year. Here we are approaching Thanksgiving, and you probably have your next six months booked solid. True?"

He shrugged. "Four months."

"*Six* months. I've lived through enough years of your work to know that. You're too modest, Sam. You've established a fine reputation, and that was before the Dunn case. New clients have come out of the walls since that one. If you ever let it out that you were looking to move, you would be *bombarded* with offers from other firms, and you'd be able to name your price. They'd fight over you. Signing you on would be a coup."

She stopped what she was doing. He was watching her quietly. "Thank you," he said. "After what I've done to you, the vote of confidence means more than you know."

Whenever he looked at her that way she started to melt, and this was no exception. Betrayal or not, she was a sucker for honesty, for vulnerability, for humility. In a strong individual like Sam, those traits were intimate.

"I've never questioned your legal ability," she murmured.

"Just my ability to be faithful. Do you still? Do you worry that I might do what I did again?"

She took the egg tray from the refrigerator and began to fill it. "With Teke, no, but I wonder sometimes. You're a dynamic man. You work with women all the time."

"No more so than I ever did."

"I never thought twice about it before. It never occurred to me that you might be interested."

"I'm not," he vowed as he had numerous times before. He curved a hand around the back of her neck, brushing a thumb along her jaw. "I miss you, Annie."

She kept on with the eggs, but the warmth she felt increased. It spread from her mind to her chest, crinkling and curling. With each brush of his thumb, it moved lower. She fought it. Something said she shouldn't give in, but she couldn't think what it was. Pride? Punishment? Distrust? Anger? None made sense at that moment; still, she fought the urge to turn and bury herself in his arms.

"Annie?" he whispered, coming closer.

"Don't, Sam," she managed in a strained voice.

"I love you. Let me show you how much."

Warmer and lower, still she fought its pull. "It's just sex."

"It's love."

She had believed that once. When they had been nineteen and twenty and first meeting, falling into bed together had meant falling in love. She had come to know his body before she had come to know his mind, but they were older now. Annie was acutely aware of her own body now. It wasn't as young as it had been once. It would *never* be as young as it had been once. But there would always be younger women out there trying to snag Sam's eye. She needed to know that she had him so securely that he would be hers no matter what.

"I can't, Sam," she cried.

"I love you."

"But enough?" The egg in her hand broke. Swearing softly, she swung it to the sink before it dripped. At the same time the sound of footsteps on the back porch heralded Zoe and Jon's return from visiting Michael.

Zoe came in first. One look at Sam standing so close to Annie and she seemed unsure. With a soft, "Hi," she escaped to her room. Annie would have called her back had not Jon come in then.

"How's Michael?" Sam asked. If anything, he moved even closer to Annie. She knew that he was making a statement and wondered if it would cause a blowup. She wasn't in the mood for that. She was getting tired of living with a simmering ill will.

"He's coming home," Jon said.

Annie turned in excitement. "When?"

"Next Friday, if he can handle crutches by then."

"Crutches," she breathed. After the endless time when they hadn't known if Michael would come awake, much less walk, crutches sounded like a miracle. She turned to Sam. "*Crutches.* That's terrific!"

"He hates the center," Jon said. "They thought he would do better at home, but I don't know. Once he's home, he'll be dependent on Teke. He's pretty angry at her." The last was an accusation aimed at Sam.

"It might be for the best," Sam pointed out. "They'll be forced to talk things out. They'll have to confront the anger head-on."

"You think that'll help?" Jon asked. "Dream on."

"Jon—" Annie stopped when Sam touched her arm.

"Maybe it's time for us, too," he told her. "Okay, Jon, say it. Tell me what you think of me. Again."

But Jon only snorted and started for the door. "You know what I think of you."

Sam caught his arm. "Hold it. I'm giving you free rein to get it all off your chest. It isn't every father who gives his kid carte blanche that way."

"It isn't every kid whose father—who he practically *worshiped*—cheats on his mother with the person who is practically his second mother. That's *incest,* almost."

"Good," Sam goaded, gesturing more words out with his hand. "Incest is good. Come on. Let's have it all."

"Sam ..." Annie tried, growing frightened. Sam was upset about what had happened in the office. He wasn't in any shape to take on Jon.

"You're a phony," Jon said. "You've made a mockery of everything you've told us."

"More, come on, more."

"You've blown your credibility. It's gone. Your word isn't worth shit."

"Jon—"

"And there's no hope of redemption?" Sam asked. "Remember when you were six and threw a ball through the front window after you'd promised not to throw against the house? Or when you got your driver's license and promptly backed out of the garage into the mailbox after you'd promised you would be so careful?"

"It was an accident."

"Precisely. Accidents happen. Because of that, and because you felt awful, and because I loved you, I forgave you. Well, what about me? Don't I deserve the same?"

"You're my father. You're supposed to set an example."

"Well, I'm human," Sam declared. The instant he dropped his hand, Jon started off. "What time is your game tomorrow?"

"I don't want you going," he said from the hall.

"What time?" Sam called.

"You'll jinx my game!"

"What time?"

Annie heard an ascending clatter on the stairs. It was followed by the slam of a door, then silence. Sam dropped his chin to his chest. He stood that way for a long time, during which Annie's heart nearly broke. When he looked back at her, there were tears in his eyes.

Drawn by those tears and the pain she knew he was feeling, she went to him and took his hand. "Time heals all wounds, Sam."

He nodded. Then, with an unsteady breath and a look of defeat, he freed his hand from hers, gathered his books and papers, and left the room.

thirteen

SHEER EXCITEMENT HAD TEKE UP AT DAWN on the day Michael was due home. Having cleaned the house from top to bottom the night before, she now cooked his favorite beef stew, made his favorite fruit salad, baked his favorite black forest cake. As soon as the stores were open, she sent off Jana and Leigh, who had refused to go to school, to buy fresh flowers, a huge balloon bouquet, and a WELCOME HOME, MICHAEL poster, which they hung between the pillars straddling the front door. While the girls wove streamers through the entire first floor of the house, Teke showered and dressed. She put on her funkiest tunic and leggings and tied her hair up with the leftover strip of a streamer. She barely needed any makeup. Her face was alive for the first time in weeks, which was very much how she felt inside. In the excitement of preparing Michael's return home, the resentment that the girls had shown toward Teke seemed momentarily forgotten. She was their mother again, which was all she had ever wanted to be.

J.D. had insisted on driving Michael home, which pleased Teke as well. She wanted Michael to know

288

that his father would be involved in his life, regardless of where he lived.

The plan was for J.D. to arrive at the center at ten, pick up Michael and a therapist who would be helping out for the day, and arrive back in Constance by eleven. All week Teke had been bringing Michael's belongings home. There would be nothing more than a small duffel for J.D. to handle.

Leigh and Jana were at the window from ten-thirty on. By ten forty-five, when Teke joined them there, they were growing impatient.

"Dad must have been late," Leigh said.

"Not your dad," Teke quipped.

"Promptness is an asset," Jana said in his defense.

Leigh envisioned another problem. "Maybe they changed their minds about letting him go."

Jana scowled at her. "You sound like he's in an institution. He isn't *committed.* They don't have the *right* to change their minds."

"Maybe he fell," Leigh went on. "Maybe he hurt himself."

Teke was wondering the very same things, but she forced herself to be calm. "They would have called."

"He may not like sleeping downstairs," Jana warned. "Does he know?"

"He knows everything," Teke said. She had made sure of that. She had gone over everything with Michael, his therapists, and the center social worker. That way, she had reasoned, if he didn't like the arrangements, he might as easily blame the therapists and the social worker as blame Teke. He already blamed her for enough. "He knows that we converted the den into a bedroom. He knows that we converted the sunroom into a therapy room. He knows that a therapist will be here every morning and a tutor every afternoon. He knows that three times a week he'll be using the health club pool."

"When can he go back to school?" Jana asked.

"He'll have to walk well enough to handle the stairs. My guess is March."

"Not 'til then?"

Teke was thinking that everything was relative— that the thought of Michael missing five months of school was nothing compared to his being a paraplegic or worse for the rest of his life—when Leigh caught her breath. "There they are!" She left the window on the run and was out the front door, neck and neck with Jana.

Teke trailed behind. Her heart thudded with excitement and more. It was an emotional time.

Jana and Leigh fussed over Michael for as long as it took him to arrange his crutches and push himself to his feet. Then they stood nervously to the side while, falteringly, he started forward. J.D. walked on one side, the therapist on the other. Each step was a major undertaking—the placement of his crutches, the small push to shift his weight to them, the uneven swing of his legs. Teke knew the drill. She had been there, hour after hour, while the therapists had put him through it, but she saw something now that hadn't been present before. His face was a portrait of determination.

Teke felt pride. She felt excitement and nervousness. She felt intense hope and love and more than a little sorrow that her baby wasn't running up the walk the way he always had before. But he was home. She was so grateful, so happy for that that her throat grew tight and her eyes misted. She grinned, then grinned more the closer he came. Her lips trembled. She brushed tears from the corners of her eyes. Then he looked up at her and gave her a grin, and she gave up the fight. Laughing through her tears, she wrapped him in her arms.

"You're wonderful, Mikey," she said, and for that long, happy, proud moment, all was right with the world. Michael might recall what she had done and hate her again tomorrow, but today he was her little boy coming home.

Sorrow. Betrayal. Pain. Annie studied the words she had scrawled on the flap of her notebook. A woman needed strength to overcome any of the three. She wasn't sure she had enough.

She could find all the reasons in the world why Jon should forgive Sam and why Michael—and even J.D.—should forgive Teke, but when it came to Annie's forgiving Sam, things were more confused. The hurt he had caused ran as deep as her feelings for him. She couldn't be objective. She wasn't at her best. Different emotions pulled her in different directions, wearing her thin, weakening her so that at times she wanted nothing more than to crumble, to forget, to make things the way they were before. She would imagine that return to happiness and smile, until an unbidden image of Teke, Vicki Cornell, or a faceless female client who might tempt Sam arose, and the smile disappeared.

Tossing aside her pen in frustration, she proceeded to bundle up her books and head for class. Down one hall and a flight of stairs, she thought ahead to the discussion of the day. It would center on the role of opposites in Jane Austen's work—in *Emma,* Emma as the voice of imagination, Mr. Knightley as that of sane reasoning; in *Pride and Prejudice,* Mary Bennet as rational, her sister Lydia as emotional.

Ah, the irony of that, Annie thought—opposites, the swing of the pendulum, the frustration of conflicting visions. She envied Jane Austen. She would have given anything to transform the events of the past two months into a work of fiction. No doubt she would shred it in the nearest machine.

Her steps faltered. Ahead, Jason Faust was talking with several other students waiting for class. Though her guilt remained, each time she saw him was less awkward than the last. He had cocky moments and quiet ones. She wondered if he was all right.

The group of students greeted her and turned into the classroom. "A quick question, Jason?" she asked, holding him back. When the others had gone through the door, she said, "You look washed out. You have for a while. Is everything okay?"

"It's November," he said with a crooked grin. "My tan's gone down the drain."

"I'm serious. Are you feeling all right?"

"I'm lovesick."

She refused to blush. "You are not. I'm not your style and you know it. Are you sure you aren't sick?"

"I'm sure," he said, but he looked troubled. "Can we talk after class?"

Annie had a long list of things to do, but she owed Jason the time. She felt a responsibility for him, after what had happened. "Sure. I haven't had lunch. Why don't we talk in the dining hall."

He nodded his agreement and opened the classroom door for her. Taking his place at the back of the room, he seemed distracted.

Several students had questions for her after class. She answered them, then motioned to Jason. They passed through the crowded halls and went next door to the faculty dining hall. Shortly thereafter they were seated at a table, Annie with cups of chowder and tea, Jason with a glass of milk.

"Nice place," he said, looking around.

"Haven't you been here before?"

292

"I have. Still, it's impressive."

"Something to look forward to?" She started on her chowder.

"That's one of the things I wanted to talk with you about. I'm worried about next year. I really want that teaching position. I need the money."

She was quickly skeptical. "I thought money wasn't an issue."

"It never was before." He turned the glass of milk between his palms. "My dad just filed for bankruptcy."

"Uh-oh."

"Yeah. And I don't just mean that the business ran short so he had to file for bankruptcy protection from his creditors. There are serious legal problems. He's about to be indicted for real estate fraud. It's like the floor just fell out from under us."

Stunned, she began, "But I thought—"

"There were megabucks?" He smirked. "Most people do. That was the image. Only it ain't so. Maybe it was several generations ago, but the wealth has been dispersed. My dad had a nice chunk to start with, and he built it up in the real estate boom, then the boom went bust, and he got reckless. So now everything he has has either been frozen pending the government's investigation or earmarked for legal fees."

Annie could imagine the trauma of it. "I'm sorry, Jason. That must be difficult for your whole family. How long have you known?"

"Just a few weeks. He was trying to maintain an image, too."

"I feel *terrible*."

"No more than I," Jason said with another smirk. "Out of the blue, I'm on my own. He says he's supported me long enough. He says he'll give me a small allowance, but I have work to make up the rest."

"Tuition won't be a problem," she assured him. "You're eligible for a waiver as a TA anyway, and you get a stipend for that."

"It isn't enough. I really want that teaching position. What are my chances?"

She wished she could be optimistic. "About the same as they were the last time you mentioned it. If you could have your master's by June, you might have a shot. Honnemann will be looking for someone with the completed degree."

"Think I can do it?"

"Finish by June? Sure, if you want. After all, what is will, but faith and persistency?"

Jason frowned. "Emerson?"

"Aldous Huxley."

He grunted and took a long drink of milk. When he set down the glass, he said, "Do you think I can teach?"

"You're my strongest TA."

His gaze grew more direct, his voice lower. "That's some consolation."

"Jason . . ." She sighed.

"Sorry. Couldn't resist. It really was a blow to my ego."

Speaking lower now, too, she said, "It was a blow to mine, too, if the truth were told."

"Why you? I think you're hot."

Her cheeks turned pink. "Not hot. Forty years old, and married. I thought I was above doing something like that."

"You didn't do anything."

"No matter. It made me see that I was fallible."

"You were unhappy. Are things better at home now?"

Since she had no intention of discussing her marital problems with Jason, she said gently, "They're better than they are at your house. I feel awful about what's happened. No wonder you've been looking so pale."

He cleared his throat. "That's the other thing I wanted to talk to you about. You were right. I haven't been feeling super. I thought maybe you'd have the name of a good doctor in town."

"What's wrong?" she asked, feeling suddenly the mother, a role she much preferred to that of Jason's lover.

"I'm tired. Weak. That kind of thing."

"Maybe it's mono."

"I don't think so."

"Have you gone to the campus health service?"

"McDiagnosis? No thanks."

She would have chuckled at the characterization if the situation hadn't concerned her. Whether it was maternal instinct, guilt over past sins, or worry about a bright young man, she was willing to do what she could to help. "I have an internist in Boston. My husband and I both use him. I'm sure he'd see you." She took a pen and paper from her purse. "Use my name. If they give you trouble, say you're a cousin. If they still give you trouble, call me and I'll call." She handed him the piece of paper on which she had jotted the doctor's name and number. "About the other, the teaching position? See what you can do about registering to finish your course work this spring."

"Will you serve as my thesis adviser?"

"You know I will."

"I wasn't sure, what with our involvement."

She fought another blush. "Our involvement is strictly professional."

"Right."

More quietly she said, "That's all it can ever be, Jason."

"Gotcha," he said, and drained his milk on a single long glug.

* * *

Be strictly professional, Sam told himself, but it was easier said than done. The weekly partners meetings at Maxwell, Roper and Dine had become tension-packed ordeals since Sam's falling-out with J.S. A hostility had entered the proceedings. At times it was more subtle, at times less so, but there was always an edginess in the air, a walking-on-eggshells approach to whatever matter was at hand.

The matter at hand this day, at Sam's request, was the assignment of support workers to partners. After waiting patiently through the usual analysis of new clients, new rulings, and billing procedures, he was anxious to speak. Sitting back in his chair, he looked from one to another of the four men spaced around the oblong conference table.

"I've been running into a problem of late," he began. "Associates have been diverted to other partners while they've been in the middle of doing work for me. Books I've needed in the library have mysteriously disappeared. Messengers have been late delivering papers to my clients. My own secretary has been 'borrowed' and therefore busy at times when I need her. I think we have to address the issue of the management of the firm."

"J.S. is the managing partner," Martin Cox said unnecessarily. "He's been the managing partner for twenty years. I've never had any problem."

"You wouldn't," Sam remarked. Martin and J.S. were pals. "But just because something's been done one way for twenty years doesn't mean it's the only way. The present management isn't working for me. Maybe we ought to rotate as managing partner, or hire a business manager, or more secretaries, or a librarian."

Martin frowned. "Additional staff costs money. We don't need the expense."

"We need something," Sam insisted. "I'm not getting the backup I need, and it's having an adverse effect on my clients. If I were the paranoid type"—he looked straight at J.S.—"I'd say someone was trying to undermine my practice."

"Is that an accusation?" J.S. asked with some humor.

Strictly professional, Sam urged himself, though he was seething inside. "It's an accusation only because the threat was made." He hadn't planned to spill it all, but the smirk on John Stewart's face egged him on. Turning to the other partners, he said, "J.S. made it clear to me that this kind of thing might happen if I didn't resign my partnership."

J.D. looked sharply at his father, but it was Sam's fellow litigation partner, Will Henry, who asked, "Is that true, J.S.?"

J.S. shrugged with his mouth. "In light of recent events, I don't believe Sam has the moral fiber to continue on as a member of this firm."

"Moral fiber?" Sam echoed in a tone that said he knew about Mary McGonigle.

"Moral fiber," J.S. repeated, but his smirk had given way to something meaner.

"That's one opinion," J.D. ventured mildly.

"It's more than one opinion. It's the opinion of half the legal community in Boston. Word spreads."

Sam sat forward. "Bullshit. I'm *golden* in the legal community right now. If word has spread about my private doings, it's gone from your mouth to the ears of a few of the ass-kissing cronies who buy your self-righteous crap."

"Ahhh," J.S. said, "so the gloves come off. I was wondering when that would happen. Scum always does revert."

"Damn right the gloves are off," Sam said, rising. He'd had it with J.S.'s games. "You want a vote? Let's take a vote! Let's see if you can get the majority you need to boot me outta here."

Before J.S. could respond, J.D was on his feet. "Sorry," he said with an eye on his watch, "no vote today. I'm late for a meeting already."

"Sit down, John David," his father said, but J.D. was out the door without a backward glance.

"There's your answer," Sam told J.S. "He won't vote against you, and he won't vote against me."

"Oh, he'll vote," J.S. said. "I promise you, he'll vote."

"Fine," Sam said. He went to the door and turned. "But in the meanwhile, back off my case, J.S. If I keep running into brick walls, I'll sue. What'll *that* do to the image of your firm?"

He stalked out and down the hall to his office, where he sank onto his chair and brooded. There was some solace in knowing that J.D. hadn't wanted to vote against him, but the solace was shallow. He had half wanted the vote to be taken. He was feeling in limbo, wanting to know where he stood. It seemed he was wanting to know where he stood on many scores lately.

His eye fell on the newspaper that lay folded on the corner of his desk. He picked it up, reread the obituary he had seen earlier that day. It was a glowing piece about a man, well-known and respected, who had been a judge on the superior court. His death would leave an opening on the bench that would be as hard to fill as it would have candidates scrambling to fill it. Even now Sam guessed there were men and women making phone calls, assessing their chances, putting in their bids.

Had Sam been ten years older, he might have gone for it. He and Annie had often talked of how ideal a judgeship would be when he was in his fifties and looking to escape the hustle of private practice. Not that the governor would mind his youth. Governors loved putting their stamp on the courts, and the longer their appointees lasted there, the better. But Sam was only forty-one. His career was flourishing. He wasn't of a mind-set, yet, to be a judge.

Too bad. It might have been perfect. Another time.

Had he been ten years older, he would have gone for it. And gotten it. And told John Stewart Maxwell, in no uncertain words, to go fuck himself.

Grady swore at the slick layer of packed snow on the pavement. A four-inch snowfall had startled Constance the night before. The plows had been by, but barely. Driving was iffy.

The last time he had been down Teke's street, his truck had collided with Michael. This time he practically crept. Snow crunched under his tires when he pulled into the driveway. He climbed out and stood for a minute, admiring the pristine beauty of the scene.

Gullen had been beautiful on the rare days when there had been snow, but it was a different beauty, a more raw one. This one was as cultured, as rich and privileged, as the citizens of Constance. The snow draped the arms of the firs like white mink. Or so it seemed to Grady, who was feeling outclassed. This was Teke's home. This was the place where she hung her clothes, raised her children, and slept with her husband. Okay, so the husband was gone, but this was still hers. Even from the outside Grady could see that it was head and shoulders above anything he would have been able to buy her.

Everything here pointed to the vast differences between them.

But he wanted to see Michael. And, differences and all, he wanted to see Teke.

The sound of shoveling drew him to the back of the house. He trudged through the snow around the garage in pursuit of that rhythmic scrape.

Teke was by the back door in the first stages of clearing the steps. The air was invigorating. The exertion felt good. Lately too much of her time had been spent indoors. She was grateful to Mother Nature for getting her out.

Grady's appearance didn't surprise her. It had been five days since she had seen him last, and that, at the rehabilitation center with no promise of the next, but she had known he would come. He seemed intent on sticking around, and for the life of her, she couldn't tell him to get lost.

Looking—gorgeously rugged, to her chagrin and delight—like a dyed-in-the-wool woodsman with his plaid flannel jacket and galoshes, he took the shovel from her hands. "This snow is heavy as hell."

"I don't mind." She flexed her back, looking anywhere but at him. "It's a gorgeous day—blue sky, white snow, warm sun." Her breath came out in a wisp of white. "I need the fresh air."

"You look good, Teke."

Her parka was hot pink, thigh length, and foreign made. She wore a matching wool hat and mittens and lime leggings tucked into kneehigh fur boots.

"How's your boy doing?" he asked.

She hitched her chin toward the sunroom, where Michael and his therapist were at work. Grady waved. He made a gesture suggesting that Michael come out to help shovel, to which Michael responded with a vigorous nod. His therapist said something. Michael pulled a comical face.

Grady chuckled. "Cute kid." He started shoveling.

"Being home is still a novelty," Teke said. "His friends stop by every afternoon. He likes that until the talk turns to basketball."

"How's the therapy going?"

"So-so. He improves in spurts, takes two steps forward and one back." She batted snow off a bench with her mitten, then sat and raised her face to the sun. Its rays were pure. Far more than she. She drank them up.

The sound of Grady's shoveling stopped. In its place, his voice was wistful. "You look so pretty. Could be eighteen years old, sitting there with rose on your cheeks and on the tip of your nose. I swear, Teke, just as pretty as I remembered you all those years."

She kept her face to the sun. "Don't say things like that."

"It's the truth."

But it makes me ache for what we lost, she thought. After a pause, and in an off-handed way, she said, "Did you think of me often?"

"All the time."

"Did you ever think of writing to me?"

"I did write, but I couldn't send the letters. It wouldn't have been fair."

She righted her face and leveled him a stare. "It's not fair now." When he stared back uneasily, she said, "Your coming around here, being nice to Michael and me. It's not fair. You had your chance with me, but you gave it up. It can't go anywhere now."

"No one says it should."

"It always did, with us. Right from the start. It was strong."

"Isn't that good?"

"Not now. Now it makes me dream about what might have been, but what might have been can't be. I have three kids and a marriage that's on the rocks. It's all I can do to hold myself together, and I have a feeling this is just the start. I have to get Michael back on his feet. I have to win back the girls' trust. I have to deal with J.D. somehow. I have to deal with Sam and Annie and whatever we're going to do about our families. So much has changed in such a short time. So much is uncertain. I just can't deal with something as intense as what you and I had once."

He stared at her a minute longer, then resumed shoveling.

But she had to make him understand. "I kept going back to what Sam and I did, and asking how it could have happened, how I could have been so frightened by that letter you sent. We hadn't seen each other or spoken in twenty-two years, and during that time I had a very good life. So why was I suddenly so threatened?"

Grady thrust the blade into the snow, lifted the load, tossed it aside, thrust, lifted tossed.

"I was threatened," Teke went on, "because deep down inside I knew that my marriage wasn't great. I hadn't ever admitted that to myself. I hadn't been able to. But it wasn't great, Grady. J.D. is nice, and handsome, and successful, and he's given me three of the most wonderful children a woman could want, but I was more of a mother than a lover to him. I fill his needs like I do for the kids—I see that he has clean clothes and hot food, I make his bed in the morning and pull back the spread at night, I put his socks away with the colors separated just so, the way he likes it." All of which was lovely. Then there was the humiliating truth. She forced it out.

"Am I his outlet for passion? No. I never was."

Grady thrust, lifted, tossed, thrust, lifted, tossed. The rhythm soothed Teke, allowing her to go on. "I knew it from the start. Maybe he did, too. Maybe, like me, he had a list of priorities. He liked enough of what I had to offer, so he could live without the heat. Same with me. Only in the end I missed it. I missed you. I was threatened by the letter you sent because my marriage was missing exactly what you had to offer." She was silent, but only for a minute. "Are you listening to me, Grady? Have you heard what I've been saying?"

He gave a final thrust, lift, and toss, then straightened. He dropped his head back. He filled his lungs with air. Then he met her gaze.

"I'm telling you all this," she said, losing her composure enough to send her voice higher, "because I don't know what to do." Her mittened hands were holding tight to the edge of the bench. She was torn between wanting him to stay and wanting him to go. "When I found out Michael was coming home, I figured you'd cool it, and I was relieved, because I like seeing you too much. But it's been five days now—" she was baring her soul and unable to stop, "—and I've been dying. Seeing you is the highlight of my day. And that *infuriates* me. I made my own life when you sent me away. I relegated you to the past. But now you're back, tormenting me in the middle of the night." Appalled by the confession, she caught her breath. But the damage had been done, and that angered her even more. "Damn it, you have no right making me want you again!"

Grady grunted. Planting the shovel in a snowdrift, he stalked off the cleared path into the deeper snow of the yard.

"*Grady!*" she shouted. He wouldn't walk away from her. Not a second time. Not when he'd been the one to return.

She went in hot pursuit, following the trail his boots had made, out to the far edge of the yard and into the woods. The snow was lighter underfoot, deflected by the boughs overhead. She found him in the pine grove, under the widest and tallest of the trees, with his back to her, his hand flat on the bark, and his head bowed.

She stalked right up to him. *"No right, Grady."*

He turned, drew her close, and covered her mouth with his own before she could say another word. Not that she would have. With his very first touch, her anger fizzled. This was what the hungry part of her, the part that awoke in the night so desperate for his touch, wanted.

He sucked her lips open and surged inside, and for the first time in twenty-two long years, Teke tasted all she'd been missing. It was a breathtaking, mind-blowing, bone-melting experience.

The first taste was the best when it came to fresh-steeped tea in the morning, raisin toast slathered with soft butter, or hot fudge over melting vanilla ice cream—but when it came to Grady, the taste started great and got better and better, deeper, wetter, hotter, until Teke was dying for more.

Grady seemed similarly affected. His body trembled with a cruder need. Tearing his mouth from hers, he crushed her close.

She buried her face in his sheepskin collar, drinking in his smell as she had devoured his taste. When he unzipped his coat, she pressed her face to his throat. She was startled by the familiarity of him, the newness and the delight. It didn't occur to her to protest when he pushed off her hat and buried his face in her hair. He had done that so often when they had lain together, and the gesture was as satisfying to her now as then.

"Thick and pillowing," he said hoarsely. "I used to

love falling asleep in this." Holding her face in his hands, he kissed her eyes and the bridge of her nose. He ran his mouth across her cheek, ate at her lower lip, then her upper lip, then both, as though he couldn't get enough.

Teke couldn't, either. Her breathing was ragged when he finally returned her face to his neck, but passion was only partly to blame. She was suddenly frightened. The war inside picked up steam. "I didn't want this, Grady. Oh, Grady . . ."

"Do you remember the first time we kissed?" he asked.

How could she not? It had been a turning point in her life, a commitment to something that was destined to go far beyond. "We were in Hiller Malloy's boat. I was helping you repair it."

"I didn't want to kiss you."

"You kept looking at me and looking away."

"It seemed I'd been doing that for years, looking at you and looking away, and all the while you were getting taller and filling out and I was wanting you more. So then you were fourteen, and I thought I'd die if I didn't kiss you. I knew you hadn't kissed anyone else, and I had to be the first, like I could put my sign on you, so no one else would ever touch. But I was scared to death, because I didn't think I'd be able to stop." He took a handful of her hair and moved it over his face, then took a shuddering breath. "Everything you did was pure. But you were a natural. You let me show you what I liked. You were malleable and strong."

She was so far under his spell that it was a struggle to think straight. "Aren't those contradictory terms?"

"No. When I build canoes, the cedar is like that. I shape it to my mold, then know that it will withstand all but the roughest of the rapids." He ran eager hands over her back in the process of tightening his hold. "I won't be able to build another canoe without thinking of that."

She burrowed more deeply into the collar of his shirt, wanting to hide from him in him. There was a contradiction in that, too, but she didn't care. Her thoughts raced on. We're finished, you and I. You have no place in my life. This is madness, what we're doing here."

"You're not moving away."

Her dilemma in a nutshell. "I *can't,*" she wailed against the spot on his chest where the second button of his shirt had come undone. Her breath stirred the crinkly hair there, cool against his heat. Between that heat, and his exquisitely male scent, and the fine tremor that snaked through his limbs, she knew that his arousal matched hers.

"Push me away, Grady," she begged. "Someone might see us."

"I'm watching. No one's coming."

"I shouldn't be doing this. Something bad will come of it, I know it will, but so help me, I can't control it." She slipped her arms around him, contradictory yet again. "Push me away."

He smiled into her hair. "I'm not pushing you away. Not after waiting so long to hold you."

She raised her face, thinking that the waiting had been an *eternity.* Her eyes moved over his features, then she tugged off a mitten and let her hand do the same. "This isn't making anything easier. Don't make me do it," she begged, still whispering, touching his mouth now. "You have that power, Grady. If you were to push the issue, I'd make love with you in a minute, but it'd be wrong. My life has been turned upside down and inside out. There are too many complications, already. I can't handle another."

"I only want to help."

"You want to make love." There was no mistaking his erection, with his hands on her bottom, hiking up her parka just enough to mold her hips to his. He felt stirringly hard.

"Yeah, I want to make love," he admitted, and caught her lips in a kiss that told her how much. It was a fierce kiss, with little to temper it, and she fed the ardor. Her mouth was open, her tongue as heavily involved in the mating as his lips, teeth, and breath.

He was the one to finally twist away. "Okay," he breathed unevenly. "Okay. I'll stop. I've waited this long, I can wait a little longer."

"Don't wait! That's what I'm saying! It won't work! I don't *want* it to work!"

"I'll wait."

"*Don't,* Grady."

He silenced her with a last kiss, a less fierce, even sweeter one this time. At its end, he drew his tongue along the length of hers and out. She was trying to recover from that when he put a chaste peck on the cheek, turned her, and with a small push sent her off.

She stumbled back through the woods to the house, more confused than ever.

fourteen

THE SNOW WAS GONE BY THE TIME Thanksgiving arrived, leaving in its wake a tableau that was cold and bleak and very much in need of the festiveness that the holiday customarily brought. Annie wanted the festiveness to be there this year, too, as a foil against the precariousness of their lives. It was a difficult time, what with their separation from the Maxwells, Sam's uncertainty about his place in the law firm, and Annie's uncertainty about her relationship with Sam. She wanted the holiday to be as much fun as possible.

Sam was a treasure. He came home Wednesday night with a bouquet of bright yellow roses for her, an armful of rented movies, and half a dozen lobsters, fresh off the boat, newly cooked, and ready to eat. Zoe and Jon loved the lobster. Annie loved the roses. The movies were a success, but not in the way she sensed Sam had planned. Rather than a family viewing session in the den, Zoe and Jon took them to the Maxwells to watch there. On one hand, Annie felt badly for Sam, who desperately wanted to be forgiven by the children. On the other, a family viewing session was out of the question for her. She had too much to do in preparation for Thanksgiving dinner. Once she announced that, though, Sam set aside his disappointment and became her shadow. He had promised to help her, and he did.

The help carried over to Thanksgiving morning, when he bolted out of bed at the same time she did. She knew he would have liked to linger. She knew he would have liked to make love, but she wasn't ready for that. Unable to help herself, she had begun curling against him in the middle of the night, but in the light of day doubts lingered.

Still, she and Sam worked together well. He transferred the twenty-pound turkey from the refrigerator to the sink and washed it while she prepared the stuffing. While he held the turkey open, she spooned the warm bread-and-chestnut mixture inside. He made a pot of coffee while she took cheese rolls from the freezer, sliced them into disks, and left them on the counter to thaw. He inserted two leaves in the table and put on a linen tablecloth. When that was done she laid out a single place setting. He laid the other ten to match.

Watching him, Annie leaned against the doorjamb and nursed her coffee. Her doubts weren't only about Sam; they were about herself, too. "Think we bit off too much by inviting guests?" she asked. They had invited Sam's newest associate and his wife, plus two faculty couples from Annie's school. "Teke can handle twenty without batting an eyelash. I can barely handle my own four on an everyday basis."

Sam warmed her with a look. "You've been handling your own four just fine."

She shrugged. "With lots of canned soups and ready-made foods."

"Am I complaining?"

Wryly she said, "I'm not sure you dare. You must

be grateful that I didn't kick you out. J.D.'s having an awful time on his own."

Sam stopped what he was doing. "Is he? I didn't know. I guess I'm the last one he'd share that with. Me and Teke."

"Teke must know, the same way I do. Jana and Leigh visited him in Boston last weekend. They say he was a little scattered. He tried to make brunch."

"Why didn't he just take them out?"

"He wanted to prove something." Annie could certainly identify with that. She was doing much the same thing herself. "My heart goes out to him. He's ill trained to take care of himself. For that reason alone, I'm glad he'll be with Teke and the kids today. It's too bad that J.S. and Lucy decided they had to go to Florida to be with friends."

"Would their presence have been a help?" Sam asked.

Annie knew the answer to that as well as he did. "It might have been nice for Michael."

Sam set two spoons neatly to the right of a knife. "But they're furious at Teke. Add that tension to the tension J.D. may bring, and it spells disaster for the kids."

She could picture it. "My heart breaks for them. Do you think their dinner will go okay?"

He gave a less-than-encouraging shrug. "J.D. is being rigid beyond belief. Teke made one mistake. Is that grounds for chucking the whole marriage? He must be going through a midlife crisis. I used to think he was relatively rational. Now I'm not so sure."

"He's rational," Annie said, "He's just angry."

"But in punishing Teke, he's punishing the kids. It doesn't seem fair."

"He agreed to go to the house for dinner today. That's a concession." She wanted to think the best of J.D. He was her friend, too. "Do you think he's testing the ground for a reconciliation?"

"I hope so. I miss the fun we used to have. Looking back on it—God, I've spent so much time doing that—I realize that J.D. always kind of went along on our ride, but that was okay. We had such good times. I miss those, and I miss the kids." He started on another place setting. "Today will be tough for them. For us, too. It's a change. That's why having guests is good. If there were just the four of us and Pete, we'd be even more aware of the Maxwells' absence." He straightened with a look of determination. "We'll do fine, Annie. Whether or not J.D. and Teke can make it as a couple, we can. I know it."

She gave him a tentative smile and for a minute wanted nothing but to dissolve in his arms and put her ear to his heart the way she used to do. But the minute passed, and thinking that loving him was going to be an agony if she couldn't learn to trust him again, she retreated into the kitchen.

Sam finished with the table, showered and dressed, and then drove to Rockport to fetch Annie's dad. He parked behind the rusted station wagon that looked to have taken root in the rutted drive. Sam wondered if it worked. He half hoped that it didn't. Pete was a distracted driver, a menace on the road, if the truth were told, which was one of the reasons Sam picked him up when he was coming to visit. On this day, Sam had been looking forward to it. He wanted to talk with Pete before sharing him with the others.

"Pop?" he called from the kitchen. He didn't look at the counters, which were cluttered with foodstuff, or at the stove, where a small percolator reeked of burned coffee, or at the sink, which was half-filled with dirty dishes. He concentrated on stepping around a bucket and mop, a large aluminum trash can, and a case of paint cans with yellow spatters and entered the studio. "Pop?"

Pete looked up in surprise. He was sitting on an overturned orange crate, sketching on a pad, and was wearing nothing but a pale yellow shirt, faded boxer shorts, and brown socks. "It's that time already?" he asked in his sandy voice.

"Nine o'clock," Sam acknowledged fondly. He had actually hoped to get there earlier, but however late, he could never be impatient with Pete. With his blond-white hair and beard, his pink cheeks, and eyes that were expressive in a childlike way, Pete was as much a work of art as his paintings.

Now the older man set down what he was sketching and scurried across the floor to the spot behind a jagged remnant of wall where a mattress and stacks of open shelves marked his bedroom. "Want some coffee?" he asked as he would a tie around his neck.

"No thanks." Sam slipped his hands in his pockets and looked around. For all the chaos of the kitchen, the studio was light and airy. "I had two cups before I left."

"Cocoa?"

Sam shook his head. He saw paintings on the front wall that were different from the ones he had seen there last time and guessed Pete had done some housecleaning. The background was a fresh pale yellow, nearly the same color as Pete's shirt and very much the color of the paint stains on the carton in the kitchen. Sam figured pale yellow was the color of the year.

"How about a brandy?" Pete asked.

Sam chuckled. "Not yet. I still have to get us back

to Constance to pick up Annie and Zoe, but you can bet I have a flask for the game." They were going to the annual Thanksgiving football game between Jon's team and its archrival. The kickoff was set for ten o'clock. "It'll help keep us warm."

"Jock-o'-my-Jon ready to play?"

"As ready as he'll ever be," Sam said. He wandered to the back wall where the family pictures were. "It's his last game. Makes it kind of emotional." He looked over the pictures of Annie, so like Zoe as a child, then so like herself as an adult.

"She isn't like her mama, that's for sure," Pete said, coming up from behind. "Neither in looks or personality. Her mama left, just picked up and went. Annie's a keeper," he said with a gravelly grunt as he hitched up the straps of his overalls.

Sam looked at the newest picture Pete had drawn of Annie. She was standing on what looked to be a beach, with her arms wrapped around her waist and her skirt and blouse billowing in the wind. Her hair, too, was blown back, leaving her face exposed and vulnerable. Pete had drawn her in profile, which was unusual for him.

Unable to take his eyes from the drawing, Sam asked, "How much do you know about what happened?"

"Just that she's unhappy. I take it Teke's involved, since we're not going there this Thanksgiving."

Sam released a breath. "Teke and I were found in a compromising position by Michael on the day he was hit by that truck. From start to finish, it was one tragic coincidence after another. Teke's marriage is messed up. I'm fighting for mine. Think I can win?"

Pete was silent for so long that Sam was sure he was furious. When he dared a look, though, he nearly laughed. Seeming lost in thought, the man was wearing a tie that was white with large orange hearts, neatly knotted and tucked into the bib of blue corduroy overalls. With the tabs of his collar sticking out at odd angles, he was a perfect caricature of the old geezer.

"She loves you," Pete said.

Sam prodded, "But she doesn't trust me."

"She doesn't trust herself. She has low self-esteem. She blames herself for what you did."

"But I've told her it wasn't her fault. Many times."

Pete tapped a drawing of Annie's mother. Annie was a baby, on all fours, appearing forgotten in the background. "It comes from this. Maybe I shouldn't have put it on the wall, but it was the way I saw it. I wanted Annie to know. I was angry. I felt rejected, too."

"I'm not rejecting Annie," Sam insisted. "She's rejecting me."

"Because she feels she isn't good enough for you. Build her up, Sam. You can do it. There's reason why she's on that wall half face. She's only half the person she should be without you. Make her whole, Sam. You did it once, do it again."

Whereas the Popes were planning a leisurely afternoon after the game, then a four o'clock dinner, the Maxwells were eating at two. Teke had planned it that way in deference to J.D, who had said that he wanted to be back in Boston for a late afternoon cocktail party. She didn't know who gave cocktail parties on Thanksgiving Day, but she wasn't challenging him. She was grateful that he was coming for dinner, since Michael and the girls had wanted it so.

Did she want it? She hadn't been sure after tasting Grady in the woods that day, but a part of her still did cling to the hope of saving her marriage.

She liked J.D., she really did. He had given her a nice life and the security she had always wanted. She owed him for that and for what she had done with Sam. More, she owed it to the kids to give the marriage every last chance.

But she was a nervous wreck. In the best of scenarios the meal would be pleasant from start to finish, in the worst it would be a nightmare of spats and indigestion. She prayed for the first, if only for the kids' sake. They were her first priority.

Jana and Leigh came home from Jonathan's game in time to give Teke a hand in the kitchen. Jon had played well, his team had won, they were all smiles and excitement. But the euphoria seeped away along with the fading of the chill blush on their cheeks.

"This is strange," Jana said, staring at the table set for five. "All alone. We're pariahs."

Teke had done her best to make the dining room look lively. She had fashioned large orange-and-brown bows from streamers and hung them at strategic spots, had cinched the napkins with shiny ribbons, had sprinkled the tablecloth with gold sparkles. For a centerpiece she had turned a pumpkin into a turkey with the help of a gourd, flowers, and bright bits of fabric. She thought the effect quite nice.

So she scolded, "That's silly. It'll be much better for Michael this way. Quieter."

"But Michael loves noise."

"Uh-huh, and if everyone was here, he'd want to be running around with the videocam. This way there will be less excitement, less temptation, and less frustration."

"That's a rationalization," Leigh murmured, and turned back toward the kitchen. "The fact is that we can't eat with the Popes because Daddy doesn't want to see Sam. That means Jana can't be with Zoe, and I can't be with Jon. It isn't fair."

Teke handed her a masher and the pot of boiled potatoes. "You're with Jon all the time. Where did you go last night, anyway?"

"There was a party."

"Where?"

"At a girl's. You don't know her."

Teke put mitts on her hands and lifted the turkey out of the oven. She left it on the counter while she set about unmolding a fruit mold, and all the while she was wondering if she should badger. Her relationship with Leigh was iffy enough not to ask for trouble. Still, "It does matter," she said, though gently. "You got in late. I was worried."

"You knew Jon had to be in by one."

"I know that he can't drive later than that, but I thought for sure he'd want to make it an early night, what with the game today."

"He slept at the party."

"Oh," Teke said. "Must have been an exciting party." Then she had a less facetious thought. "He wasn't drinking, was he?"

"Jon doesn't drink."

Teke shot a look at Leigh, who was mashing potatoes with a vengeance. Returning to her own work, she ran a knife around the rim of the mold, put a plate over it, and was preparing to turn it when Jana came in.

"The candy bowls are filled. What else do you want me to do?"

"Take that dip dish, and go help your father cheer Michael up," Teke said. "He's feeling blue. Basketball tryouts begin on Monday. He wants to be there." She waited until Jana had gone before saying quietly, "I'm not an innocent, Leigh. I know what goes on at high school parties."

"Her parents were home."

"On Thanksgiving Eve, very probably, but that doesn't mean anything. Many parents buy the beer for the party themselves. They would rather the kids get drunk under their supervision, and that's one view, I suppose. I have trouble with it."

Leigh kept mashing.

"I wouldn't be asking you about Jon if it weren't for the can of Amstel Light that I found in your wastebasket last week."

"I used it on my hair."

"*If* he drinks at a party, he *cannot drive*. Either you drive home, or if *you* can't, you call us."

"We're not drinking."

"Good," Teke said, and turned the mold. "That makes me feel better."

"But I want birth control."

The gelatin mold hit the plate with a thunk, in perfect time with Teke's stomach, which had been none too steady to start with that day. She could have used a shot of Grady—a thought that she quickly pushed from mind. As an alternative source of support, she set down the plate and leaned against the counter.

"Well, didn't you think I'd ever want to do it?" Leigh challenged.

"I thought you would wait!"

"I've been waiting for *years*. I *love* Jon, and don't say we're just seventeen, because we're turning eighteen this spring. Some kids get married at eighteen. Some kids have *babies* at eighteen."

Teke knew that all too well. She had been one of the few girls from Gullen to make it through high school, so many others had dropped out to have babies. She would have had a baby herself if Grady hadn't been so determined to wait. Then, she had objected to his reasoning, but she was the first one to use it now. She wanted her girls to get a college degree. She wanted them to have fun. Babies were big responsibilities. They had a way of limiting choices.

"I want more for you," she told Leigh.

"Then let me get birth control."

"Or you'll go ahead anyway? Oh, Leigh," Teke begged, "can't you use a little restraint?"

"Like you did with Sam?"

Teke's breath caught in the back of her throat.

Leigh resumed mashing, though more slowly now. "Anyway, it's too late to be asking for restraint. We've already done it."

Already done it. Already done it. Teke put a hand to her chest to quash a rising panic. *They've already done it, Annie!* she cried. She should have known, what with all the time Leigh spent with Jon, and it wasn't tragic, she reasoned as she tried to get a grip on herself. They loved each other. They would get married one day. Teke hadn't been a virgin at seventeen herself.

But Leigh was her child, and lovemaking was womanly stuff. That made Leigh a woman, the first of her daughters to become so. It was an emotional idea, one that took some getting used to.

"Well?" Leigh asked, looking anxious.

Teke put an arm around her shoulder and held her tightly for a minute. Her throat was knotted. She ran through the arguments in Leigh's favor again until she was sure she was under control. With surprising calm she said, "I'll call the doctor next week."

Leigh seemed wary. "You will?"

Teke nodded.

"Are you trying to win me back?"

"No," Teke said, though being rational and agreeable didn't hurt that cause. "I'm trying to do what

318

makes sense. If you and Jon have made love once, you'll do it again. I want you protected."

Leigh let out a small sigh. "I almost went to Annie. I thought you'd be furious."

"I'm glad you didn't go to Annie. I'm your mother." Perhaps blindly feeling her way through certain things, but her mother nonetheless. "I can handle it. And I'm not an ogre."

"You've been strange lately."

"*You*'ve been strange," Teke countered. She scooped a lock of blond hair back from Leigh's face. "You're angry at me for what I did with Sam, but we all make mistakes, Leigh."

"What I did with Jon wasn't a mistake. It was the best thing in the world. The *best.*"

Teke put her forehead to Leigh's shoulder. More than anything she wanted Leigh to know the excitement with Jon that she had known with Grady, because if Leigh and Jon had that, on top of all else they had going for them as a couple, they would be happy in life.

She raised her head. "I want the *very* best for you and Jon, and I didn't mean to imply that what you did was wrong, maybe just premature. But arguing about it is ridiculous, because it's done. Just like what I did with Sam. It's done. Now we have to deal with the consequences." It was a very adult, very Annie approach, Teke thought. "In your case, that means getting birth control."

"Do you have to tell Dad?"

It struck Teke, along with a spark of emancipation, that she didn't. Her responsibility to J.D. had changed with his move from the house. "I don't have to tell anyone."

"He'll yell and scream and say that Jon's just like Sam, but Jon isn't."

"Yes, he is," Teke argued. "Whether you'll admit it

or not, Sam is a wonderful man, a great husband, and a top-notch father. I like to think Jon will be the same. I think your father would agree. But he has a lot on his mind, so we won't tempt fate by telling him about something he can't change. But *promise* me," she said with a sudden, horrifying thought, "that you and Jon won't do anything else until you've seen the doctor. Promise me that, Leigh? I won't be able to keep your secret if you get pregnant."

Jana burst through the door. "They're hungry. Dad wants to know when we're eating." She looked from one face to the other. "What's going on here?"

Teke left Leigh's side. She put the mitts back on, removed hot hors d'oeuvres from the oven, and slipped them onto a serving tray. "Let them work on these. Tell them we'll be eating in ten minutes." She steered Jana back toward the door. "Leigh, add butter and milk to those, then put them in the oven to stay warm while you toss the salad. I'll tackle the turkey."

There was an art to turkey carving. Teke had perfected it over the years, to the point where she was able to get every last bit of meat from the carcass, arranging it beautifully on a platter as she went. This year the only thing that was missing was Annie, who normally stood watching in awe. She didn't miss the awe, just Annie.

But she had promised herself she wouldn't pine today, not over Annie, not over the way things used to be. She was determined to enjoy this meal with her most immediate family.

The odds were against her, it seemed. The first problem was the table. Teke had outdone herself. It held enough food—steaming bowls and platters, a tossed salad, a molded salad, a bread basket, jelled *and* whole-berry cranberry sauce, the last because J.D. preferred it, condiments of every imagineable sort—to feed an army of Popewells, which made it all the more obvious that an army of Popewells wasn't there.

"Who's saying grace?" Jana asked.

"Sam always did it," Leigh said, "but Sam's not here."

Michael looked at J.D. "You do it, Dad."

J.D. looked at Teke. "We can skip it."

But Teke, who had never been superstitious, had the sudden fear that if someone didn't say grace, they would all be damned forever. So, bowing her head, she said, "Dear Lord, it's been a rough year. You've given us the strength to make it this far. Please help us through the rest. We give thanks for love and forgiveness, and for this food. Amen."

J.D. cleared his throat. "That was humble enough, I suppose."

"I try," she said, and reached for Michael's plate, which she filled to overflowing while the others helped themselves. She then proceeded to cut Michael's food into manageable pieces, but all the while, in a silence that was filled with the click of utensils, she felt a deep sadness. The smell of cooked turkey mixed with the smell of defeat. By the time she sat on her own chair, she was afraid she would cry if someone didn't speak fast.

So she said, "Tell us about the game, Leigh."

Leigh told them about the game. Jana put in a word here and there. J.D. even asked a few questions.

Teke kept an eye on Michael. He could handle a fork, but neither smoothly nor efficiently. It was painful to watch. Teke would have helped if it were allowed, but the center personnel had been clear on that. Feeding himself was therapy. Every forkful that he brought to his mouth would improve his coordination. Teke kept telling herself that. It brought her little comfort.

Silence fell again. Teke moved down the list of

topics she had compiled for just such an eventuality. "Jana's been named to represent her class in the intertown debate in January. Did you tell your father, Jana?"

"I did. Last weekend."

"Then tell me. I barely got the gist of what you're debating."

Jana talked for a bit. She finished with, "Pass the black olives, Dad?"

J.D. passed the black olives.

"Do you have enough gravy, Mike?" Teke asked.

Michael nodded. "Dad says they'll let me play on the team next year even though I didn't play this year, but I don't think they will. Everyone else will be playing better but me. I won't survive cuts."

"You'll survive cuts," Leigh said. "You're the best player they have."

"Not now. Maybe not ever. What if I can't run?"

"You'll run if you want to," Teke told him. "That's what the doctors said."

"Is it warm in here, or is it me?" J.D. muttered, pushing away from the table. He went out into the hall. "This thermostat is set at seventy-two! No *wonder* it's like an oven!" He returned to the dining room and asked Teke, "Why was it set at seventy-two?"

She set down her fork. The little food she had eaten lay like lead in her stomach. "I've been keeping it there so that the sunroom stays warm. That's where Michael spends most of his time."

"Speaking of sun," Leigh asked, "since you're both here, there's something I want to discuss. A group of us wants to do spring break somewhere warm."

"Take the sunroom," J.D. said. "Mike'll be out of there by then."

"I'm serious. We're thinking of going to Nassau."

"No," J.D. said seconds before he forked a piece of turkey into his mouth.

"Why not?" Leigh asked.

He chewed, swallowed, asked, "Do you have a chaperone lined up?"

"No."

"That's why not."

Leigh looked to Teke for help, but Teke didn't know what to say. Somehow "Don't worry, Leigh will have birth control by then" didn't seem right. Nor did "Virginity isn't an issue" or "No sweat, she drinks *light* beer." She wished Leigh had broached this with her first. They might have thought up a better way of approaching J.D.

Unfortunately approaching J.D. was necessary. He was the money man. Aside from half a dozen good pieces of jewelry, a fur coat, a life insurance policy, and a joint checking account, Teke had nothing. Only now did that strike her as wrong, unfair, even a little frightening.

"This is my senior spring break," Leigh was pleading, having returned to J.D. when she realized Teke would be no help. "Everyone goes somewhere for senior spring break."

"And you will, too," J.D. said, "but when you're in college, not high school."

"What if I pay for it myself?"

"With what?"

"Money from my savings account."

He shook his head. "That money stays where it is until you're twenty-one."

Michael looked up. "I thought you said I could take some of mine to buy an editing deck and a controller."

"If he can, why can't I?" Leigh asked.

"Spring break isn't exactly an investment in your future."

"That's not fair, Dad."

J.D. shrugged. When the phone rang he shot a
testy look at Teke. "Who's calling in the middle of
Thanksgiving dinner?"

Jana jumped up from the table. While she dealt
with the call in the kitchen, Teke asked Michael,
"Where are the twins having dinner?"

"At their grandfather's in Springfield. They
always go there."

"How about Nat?"

Michael scowled. "He's home. His dad's taking
him to shoot hoop at the gym as soon as they're
done eating." He prodded a piece of lettuce with his
fork, dropped the fork, picked it up again, and prodded his stuffing.

Jana slipped back onto her seat.

"Who was it?" Teke asked to make conversation.

"It was for me."

"Was it Zoe?"

"No."

The silence that descended again was thick and
unhappy. Teke cut a piece of turkey and ate it, cut
another piece and ate it. It occurred to her that
attempts at conversation were as awkward as
Michael's movements. Like him, the family had suffered a severe blow. They, too, were trying to figure
out how to function in a debilitated condition.

She looked at J.D., wishing he would initiate some
harmless discussion. But his face was tense. He was
watching Michael's struggle to eat. She prayed he
wouldn't comment. She didn't trust him to be supportive.

Desperate to divert him, she asked, "Who are
your parents eating with today?"

The tense look remained on his face when he
returned to his food. "Sid and Beverly Wyatt. They
invited me, too. J.S. can't understand why I wouldn't
go."

"What's hard to understand?" Jana asked. "We're your family. You're supposed to be with us."

"Under the circumstances," J.D. told her in what Teke thought was an arrogant voice, "fathers often eat elsewhere. I wanted to be with my children. He could understand that. What he didn't understand was why I wanted to be with my wife."

Teke's stomach clenched. She shot him a look of dismay, unable to believe he had said that in front of the children.

"Does Grampa *hate* Mom?" Leigh asked.

"He's protective of me," J.D. answered. "He sees that I've been hurt, so he's angry at the cause."

"Protective of you or of himself?" Teke couldn't resist asking, because the thought of J.D. making J.S. out to be noble was too much to bear. "The fact is that I'm an embarrassment to him."

"Does that *surprise* you? He has high standards!"

"For everyone but himself," Teke argued.

"What does *that* mean?"

It means that I know about Mary McGonigle. So don't talk about those high standards in front of me, J. D. Maxwell, or I'll tell your children about them. Enough is enough. I do not have a monopoly on wickedness.

When she said nothing aloud, J.D. told Leigh, "Your mother can't stand my parents. She's threatened—"

"I am not!"

"—because they are who they are. They're established. They're influential. They're society."

"I am not threatened," Teke insisted. "I don't aspire to be like your parents. I never have."

J.D. turned on her. "No? I've heard you asking my mother for advice—"

"Because I thought it would *please* her. People like to be admired. They like to feel that other people respect them, and I *do* respect your parents, but that doesn't mean I want to *be* like them."

"You could do a hell of a lot worse!"

"This *sucks!*" Michael cried suddenly. His fork sailed halfway across the table before tangling in the spider mums that served as the turkey's feathers. "It's not any fun! You hate each other! I want things back the way they were! I wish I'd never seen anything! I wish I'd never *said* anything!"

Teke was up from her chair in an instant and leaning over him. "Oh, sweetheart, it's not your fault."

"It is," he said. His eyes were filling fast. "No one would've known if I hadn't run in. Grandma and Grandpa would be here, and Sam and Annie and Jon and Zoe and Papa Pete." He started crying into the back of his hand. "I—want—all—that—again."

Teke wrapped her arms around him. She buried her face in his hair and cried with him, partly because his unhappiness was breaking her heart, partly because she wanted everything he did, but mostly because, at that moment, she knew in her gut that her marriage was over. She could fight until she was bone-tired and blue in the face, but it wouldn't work again. The damage was too extensive. It couldn't be repaired.

For a woman who had always put home and hearth on a pedestal, that realization was a blow.

Much later that night, Annie stood at the kitchen sink washing the last of the dishes and feeling an overwhelming guilt. The Popes' Thanksgiving had been really nice. Granted, she thought the turkey had looked ragged and the table had lacked the extra sparkle Teke might have put there, but no one commented on either of those things. Everyone ate, everyone talked, everyone smiled—which, apparently, was the opposite of what had been at the Maxwells'.

Sam came through the back door, shook off the cold along with his parka, and reached for a dish towel.

"How is he?" Annie asked.

"Pretty glum. Seems like Jana and Leigh weren't exaggerating. Things started out shaky and went downhill. Poor little guy. His world has fallen in on him."

"Would he talk to you?" she asked, but she knew the answer. She could see Sam's distress.

"He needs a fall guy, and I'm it. I wouldn't mind so much if everything else in his life was running smoothly, but things are so awful. He needs the friend I was. Maybe he's finding it in Grady, but not today. Michael was hating 'most everyone today. I think they ought to see a family therapist."

"J.D. would never—"

"Not J.D. Teke and the kids. They're on their own." More quietly he added, "Makes me feel guilty."

Annie felt the same.

"It was fine today, Annie. You did everything so well."

"I had help." He had been by her side every step of the way.

"But you ran the show." He slipped an arm around her waist and warmed her temple with a kiss.

Annie allowed herself to rest a minute against him. She loved him. She wished she trusted him as much as she had once. She wished she trusted *herself* as much as she had once. But she did love him.

"We have so much," he whispered. "Not everything yet, but so much. I still have a ways to go with

Zoe and Jon, but that'll come, I know it will, because I won't give up. Then I look at Teke and J.D. and the kids, and I don't think it will come. It's very sad."

Annie moved her forehead against his chin. Sam had always been sensitive when it came to causes at work. Now, since Teke, he was more sensitive at home. At times she wondered if he was doing it deliberately to win her back, at other times she wondered if the why of it mattered, as long as he wanted her.

Zoe came in the back door, hung her jacket on the hook, sank onto a chair at the table, and sat with her shoulders hunched.

Annie drew back and exchanged a worried look with Sam. She left his side and slipped onto the chair beside Zoe's. "What's wrong?"

Zoe moved her head in a small, unhappy gesture. Her eyes were on the edge of the table. She picked at the oak with her thumb. "Jana and I got into another fight. She keeps blaming Dad for everything that happened, but it isn't fair. Teke's just as much at fault."

"Jana's upset. It was a difficult day for her."

"Does that give her the right to say that Dad broke up her parents' marriage? Does it give her the right to tell Leigh that she'll be asking for trouble if she marries Jon? Does it give her the right to call me a loser just because I stick up for my own father?"

Sam, who had come to stand behind her, put a hand on her hair.

"Jana hasn't been herself lately," Annie said.

"Maybe this is her real self," Zoe argued. "She's acting just like J.D. She's always trying to *blame* someone, but what good does that do except make me feel bad?"

Annie took her hand. It felt small and lonely,

which was very much how Zoe herself had seemed lately. "Misery loves company."

"It isn't *fair*."

Annie pulled her close. "I know, sweetie."

"She's turning the other kids against me."

"No, she's not."

"She is. She goes out with them and doesn't ask me along. She has to be giving them a reason for it, and it can't be good. So who's going to be *my* friend?"

"You have other friends. There's Amy and Lisa and Leslie."

"Jana was always my best friend."

"And she will be again. You both go back too far not to make it through this."

"Will you and Teke?"

Out of the mouths of babes, Annie thought. She glanced at Sam, who looked as if he were bleeding inside. "Teke and I will make it," she told Zoe.

"And you and Dad?"

Sam spoke then. "We will. I love your mother too much to let one bad time come between us." He bent over her, bracing his hands on the table. "But that's the difference between your mother and me and J.D. and Teke, and it's why Jana's wrong in blaming me for the bad time her parents are having."

Zoe looked at Annie. "Teke and J.D. never had trouble before."

"That doesn't mean their marriage was strong," Annie said.

Zoe thought about that for a minute. "If I say that to Jana, she'll *really* tear me apart."

"Then don't. It could be that Jana knows it, and that when she lashes out at you, she does it out of envy."

Zoe thought about that, too. "I guess. Know what she said tonight?"

"What did she say?"

"She said that she hoped we were using the ski house at different times this year, so that there would be plenty of room for her to invite friends."

Sam grunted. "She's angry, Zoe. Don't pay her any heed."

"That's fine for *you* to say," Zoe said. "You're not the one losing all the friends." She slipped from Annie's grasp, ducked under Sam's arm, and ran from the room.

Sam started after her but stopped. "I'll only upset her more. You'd better do it. I'll finish up here."

Annie went after Zoe. She sat with her, talking softly, repeating the things she had said before. She wished she had remedies, but she hadn't when she had felt ostracized as a child, and she didn't now. Telling Zoe that her parents and brother loved her was just fine—and Annie did it over and over again—except that family was different from friends. Teenagers wanted friends.

She stayed with Zoe until the girl was nearly asleep, then kissed her and crept out. The kitchen was dark. The den was empty. She found Sam in their bedroom, sitting on the edge of the bed, still in his turtleneck sweater and slacks. His knees were spread, an elbow on each.

"When does it end?" he asked with an anguished look. "When do the dominoes stop falling? When do the screams stop echoing?"

She didn't know, and it wasn't for lack of wondering. She wondered each time she saw Teke, each time she saw Michael. She wondered each time she saw Jon turn his back on Sam, and Zoe avoid his eyes. She wondered each time she saw Jason Faust and felt shame.

And she wondered each time she saw Sam. She wondered when she would be able to see him as the man she had fallen in love with rather than the man she was forgiving.

The only thing she knew for sure just then was that Sam was suffering and she couldn't bear to see it. Silently she crossed the carpet, came between his legs, and brought his head to her chest, and there, with his breath warm and his scent familiar and arousing, she knew one other thing. She desired him more than she was angry, or hurt, or ashamed.

The beat of her heart must have told him so, either that or his own desperation, because his arms closed around her. He held her tightly at first, then loosened his hold so that he might move his head against her breasts. She kept her face buried in his hair while he did that, while he unbuttoned her blouse and unhooked her bra, and she might have felt embarrassed, remembering Jason, if the brush of his mustache against her breasts hadn't excluded all other thought. She felt herself swell to him, heard herself sigh, let herself ride with the heat that surged in her blood.

Sam led the way. She sensed it was what he needed, knew it was what she needed. She needed to know that he found her attractive. She needed his mouth hot and his tongue wet. She needed—so much that each one stroked her inside—the soft, sexy words that he whispered against her skin.

He took his mouth from her only long enough to drag his turtleneck over his head. "Oh, baby," he whispered against her flesh once more. His hands were behind her, under her. They dispensed with her skirt and helped her free herself of her underthings.

Catching her face, he brought her mouth to his. He used his tongue to bind her to him while he unfastened his pants and released her only to push them off, but the moment was long enough to give

Annie a look at his body. He was magnificent, so much more so than she could ever be that she would have shrunk back if Sam hadn't lifted her then and set her gently down on the spread.

Her insides were trembling, making her fingers less than steady when she touched his mouth and his mustache, but she couldn't not touch, she had been missing him so much. In her eyes, his body was perfect. She ran her hands through the hair on his chest, over the broad swells where his nipples lay small and hard, and along the tapering line down his middle. Her palms felt hot and achy. They wouldn't stay still. So she let them loose on her favorite parts, those ones of his that tightened and grew on the outside while she tightened and grew on the inside. She loved touching him there, loved stroking him, loved feeling the way his whole body tensed when she did it, the way his breathing shallowed.

She wondered if Teke had touched him there.

With a small cry she squeezed her eyes shut.

"Oh, no, you don't," Sam said in a ragged rumble. "I can guess what you just thought, but I won't have it. There's no room for anyone else in our bed. Just you and me, and what we do for each other, because that's all there's ever been. Look at me, Annie." He laced his fingers through hers and anchored them by her shoulders. "Look at me." He eased her legs farther apart.

It was too much. Her body was on fire, the flame too hot to deny herself the pleasure of Sam's possession. Wayward thoughts went up in smoke when she opened her eyes. Seeing him above her, feeling naked and open beneath him, she clutched at his fingers. "Tell me you love me," she whispered.

"I love you," he said, looking into her eyes. His penetration was slow, smooth, and so divine that a great sound of relief slipped from her throat.

The relief was short-lived. Sam proceeded to love her with such exquisite gentleness that she was straining for release long before he allowed it. He seemed bent on showing her how high he could take her, how long he could hold back for the sake of her pleasure, how much he loved her, and if the quantity and quality of a man's passion was the measure, he loved her very much indeed. If dawn hadn't ever broken, Annie might have been satisfied to lie in Sam's arms forever.

But dawn did come, casting the proverbial light on all the problems that no night of passion, however long and blinding, could erase.

fifteen

"**J**OHN STEWART IS WAITING," THE MESSAGE read, and it came as no surprise to J.D. when he arrived at the office first thing Tuesday morning. His parents had returned from Florida the night before. He knew that his father would be wondering how Thanksgiving had gone and that his concern would be prompted not by love of his son or his grandchildren, but by dislike for Teke.

J.D. wished that once, just once in his life, it wouldn't be that way. He wished that John Stewart's motivations would be positive rather than negative, that his primary concern would be his son's happiness.

Cursing his jumping stomach, he crushed the message, dunked it into the wastebasket, and strode down the hall. John Stewart was reading *The Wall Street Journal.* He set it aside when J.D. walked in.

"You're looking rested," J.D. said, dropping onto a chair. "Tanned, too. You must have played a little golf."

"Some," John Stewart replied, sounding vaguely peeved. "I spent most of my time explaining why you weren't down there with me."

334

"Ahh. Well, that shouldn't have been too difficult. I was with my family." The thought of people talking about his misfortunes rankled. "Or was it too much to ask that you not announce to the whole of Palm Beach that I'm separated from my wife?"

"Why shouldn't they know? My friends have all met Theodora. They know what she is. They were pleased that you'd finally come to your senses."

"She's still my wife," J.D. said. He looked around the office, thinking that it was a perfectly stuffy place. "I resent your bad-mouthing her to strangers."

"These people aren't strangers. You've worked with many of them, and they like you, John David. Say the word, and they'll pair you up with a different woman every night. Moreover, they admire your legal ability. Should we ever decide to open a Palm Beach office, we'll have a loyal following."

J.D. wasn't interested in being "paired up." If he wanted a woman, he could find his own. Nor was he interested in opening a Palm Beach office. If he ever decided to work there, he sure as hell wouldn't put himself smack under his father's thumb.

"What if I decided to go back to Teke?" he asked. Curiosity or defiance, he wasn't sure, but the jumping in his stomach was becoming a ping. "What would you say to all those people who like me?"

"You're not going back to her," John Stewart informed him in a full, confident voice. "You're too much my son."

"You can say that again. But don't look smug. It isn't a compliment. I'm too *pompous* to go back to Teke."

"That was unkind, John David."

J.D. shrugged. "The apple doesn't fall far from the tree. I'm pompous all right. Arrogant, too."

John Stewart pursed his lips. "You're in a bad

mood. Aren't you pleased with your apartment?"

His apartment. Ahh, that was a story in and of itself. He had hired a cleaning woman, who had proceeded to lose his toothbrush and half a pair of sneakers. The local laundry did his shirts just fine but couldn't seem to keep the starch out of his shorts. And every time he turned around, the dishwasher was full. But he would be damned if he would give his father the satisfaction of knowing any of that, so he said, "I'm very pleased with my apartment."

"Are you having trouble with a client?"

"Should I be?" he asked guardedly.

"Something has to account for your mood."

J.D. stared in amazement. "Part of what accounts for my mood is my son. He's been through an ordeal—is still *going through* an ordeal. You haven't even asked how he is."

"I assume he's fine, or you would have told me differently."

"He's not fine. He having a lousy time trying to accept the changes in his life." The pinging in his stomach moved to his head, goading him on. "We had an awful scene at Thanksgiving dinner. I sat at that table, just as you would have, expecting everyone to please me, and when everyone didn't, I did just what you would have done, I blamed them. *God,* you've set an awful example," he exclaimed, and was instantly amazed that he'd done it. His reaction to his father was getting gutsy something new and interesting for him.

John Stewart's voice grew gruffer. "Don't blame your problems on me, John David. I wasn't the one who picked that woman for a wife."

"No, but it's everything that I inherited from you that's let her down." J.D. came out of his chair, seeming propelled by the words. "I couldn't satisfy her, sexually or otherwise, because I'm cold, just like you. I'm boring, just like you. I'm self-centered, just like you. She probably would have divorced me years ago if it hadn't been for Sam and Annie."

"Sam," John Stewart snorted. "Sam isn't worth two cents."

J.D. had heard that once too often. Facing his father with more force than he had ever mustered against the man, he said, "Sam is the only thing that has kept me sane around here. Without him, I'd have left this firm years ago—either that or jumped off a roof. Sam has been my saving grace. The good part of me comes from him, not from you."

John Stewart's eyes were like steel. "So you're siding with him. I figured as much. You're a traitor."

"I'm a realist."

"You're a coward. You've walked out of *two* meetings now at which I've tried to bring Sam's partnership to a vote. You won't vote with me, but you don't have the guts to vote against me."

"I'm getting there fast," J.D. warned. His head flew around when the door opened without a knock. He was prepared to scowl at Mary McGonigle for the license she took, but it was Virginia Clinger's face that appeared, along with a whiff of her perfume.

"Oooops," she said, glancing from father to son and back. "Bad time. See you later."

She was gone as quickly as she'd come, but J.D. was instantly wary. "Why is she here?" He knew that her father had already gone south for the winter, knew that other than through Stanley, she had no dealings with Maxwell, Roper and Dine, since her divorce lawyers were elsewhere.

"Stopping in to say hello, no doubt," John Stewart said.

"On her own? Just for kicks? That doesn't sound like Virginia, unless she has something up her sleeve." The thought that she hadn't knocked—and that J.S. hadn't called her on it—worried him. He thought of what she had seen in Constance on the day Michael was hurt, and his wariness increased. "Have you been meeting with her?"

"She drops in sometimes."

"And talks about what? Sam?"

"What would she have to say about Sam?" John Stewart replied with an innocence that J.D. didn't buy for a minute.

"Virginia would say whatever she thought you might want to hear, if it could help her cause, which is to get as much money from her father as possible. I'm the one handling Stanley's estate now, but you're his longtime friend. What's she telling you? That she saw Teke and Sam together? That she has evidence they had an affair?"

"He already admitted they had an affair."

"He admitted they were together once, which doesn't constitute an affair. What happened between them is no more Virginia's business than it is yours."

"It certainly is my business. It's my law firm he's soiling."

"Soiling? Thanks to the Dunn case, we're being talked up around town like never before. That's not soiling. It's great PR."

"And you've bought into it hook, line, and sinker. Sam's brainwashed you."

"He's been a damn good friend, a *damn* good friend."

"How can you say that," John Stewart boomed, "after what he did to you?"

But J.D. wasn't being sidetracked by that one afternoon's fiasco. Buoyed by anger at his father, he was feeling an odd sense of power. It enabled him to share the most personal thing he ever had with the man. "I have a nightmare sometimes. I dream that we vote Sam out, and that each day, each week, each month, without him I grow to be more and more like you. I get colder and more self-righteous, to the point that I'm standing on top of a pyramid alone, all alone, because there isn't another person in this world who wants to be with me. That's my nightmare. Pretty grim, huh?"

John Stewart rose slowly from his seat and drew himself to his full height. In the same impelling voice that had made many a strong man quail, he said, "Not grim. Childish. I've given you a life, John David. I don't deserve this kind of disrespect."

J.D. didn't quail. He simply stared at his father in disbelief. "You don't understand. You don't get the point. You don't *hear* what I'm saying, do you."

"I hear what I need to hear. But if I were you, I wouldn't say it again. I can vote you out of this firm right along with your beloved Sam Pope. Think of that next time you're in the mood for calling me names. This is my firm, John David, *mine.*"

J.D. drew his head back. He might have argued that he had his own following, that he carried his weight when it came to the bottom line, that with both Sam *and* J.D. gone, the firm might well struggle to survive. But he didn't bother. Suddenly there seemed more important things to do than bicker with John Stewart. The pinging in his head had a ring of independence to it. He wanted to see where it would lead.

At the other end of Maxwell, Roper and Dine, Sam was returning from a sentencing hearing for a client. The judge had granted him a more lenient deal than the prosecutor wanted, but his client still had to do hard time. Sam was discouraged. His client was neither young nor in good health. Sam wasn't sure he would make it through a single day in prison, and he liked the man. He believed him guilty only of a naive mischoice of business associates. Unfortunately a jury had believed him guilty of more.

Of course, there were still appeals Sam could file, but in his heart he knew they wouldn't go far. His client had received a fair trial.

He wished he could receive the same at Maxwell, Roper and Dine, but no matter how many complaints he lodged at partners meetings, he continued to get the short end of the stick. J.S. had involved Vicki Cornell deeply enough in his dealings so that while she might be back working with Sam, at any given time she was subject to a summons from the senior partner. Tom Mackie was catching on to what Sam wanted done—but slowly, which put greater pressure on Sam to do the work himself. He did. And was tired and annoyed and increasingly concerned for the future.

He had barely tossed his briefcase onto the desk when Joy buzzed him. "Adam Holt is on the line," she said. "Would you like me to take a message?"

Adam Holt was one of Boston's leading legal headhunters. He had called Sam occasionally over the years, but his calls had increased of late. Sam never initiated the contact. He never said he wanted to leave Maxwell, Roper and Dine. But he found himself listening to what Adam had to say.

They had talked the week before. Sam might have let Joy put him off, had he not have been feeling so discouraged.

"I'll take it," he said, and pressed into the call. "How are you, Adam?"

"Fine, Sam. Actually, not so fine. I'm getting more calls."

"From?"

"Malek, Hill and French. They want you, Sam. They're desperately in need of a litigator. They'll pay top dollar."

Sam closed his eyes and rubbed the tired muscles at the back of his neck. "It's not the money, Adam." He sighed. "I thought I explained that before. Malek, Hill is too big. I'd die in a firm that size."

"You'd have your own department, your own little corner of the firm."

But Sam knew how big firms worked. If one insulated oneself, one became isolated and eventually ostracized. He would be jumping from the frying pan into the fire. Besides, he knew many of the partners at Malek, Hill and French. They were driven in different ways from J.S., but driven nonetheless. He wasn't sure he would trust them far. "It's not for me, Adam. Really."

"Then Waterston and Bailey. Have you given that one more thought?"

"I haven't given anyone more thought. I'm not necessarily going anywhere."

"But your practice is limited at Maxwell, Roper and Dine. Since *Dunn* v. *Hanover* especially, you've been sending clients to other firms because you don't have a big enough litigation department there. That's a shame, Sam."

But Sam didn't miss a "big enough litigation department." He liked his practice just as it was. What he didn't like was the ill will that seemed to be lining the halls of the firm and closing in to choke the partnership.

His eye caught on a large manila envelope that lay on his desk amid the morning's mail. It was from Joe Amarino, an old law school friend currently serving as the governor's counsel. They had talked on the phone the morning before.

After finishing up with Adam, he opened the

envelope and skimmed the cover letter. It was brief. "This is the application I mentioned," Joe wrote. "I do wish you'd consider filling it out, Sam. Not only do I think you'd make a great judge, but I believe you have a solid shot at getting the appointment. I haven't discussed it with the governor yet, but my gut instinct is that he'd be thrilled to be able to name someone young and idealistic to the bench. Don't wait too long. He wants to fill the opening as soon as possible."

Sam glanced at the application, tossed it onto the desk, glanced at it there, then looked away. He didn't know what to do. On the one hand, he wanted to stay where he was, at least until things in Constance straightened out some. On the other hand, he was starting to feel like an outcast at Maxwell, Roper and Dine.

Talk to Annie, he told himself, but he hesitated. He didn't want to hit her with this, particuarly now that their relationship had taken a turn for the better. In her eyes he wanted to look wonderful and strong and totally in control of his life.

Grady could see the change in Teke now that Michael was home. While the boy spent time each morning and afternoon with the physical therapist and the tutor, she had the leisure to go to the drugstore, the supermarket, the library. She no longer needed lunch from MacDonald's or coffee in Styrofoam cups. She cooked and cleaned and kept fresh flowers in small vases all over the house. Grady was challenged to find ways to help her.

For that reason he was actually pleased to arrive at her house for a midday visit with Michael and find her in a dither. "You're a *lifesaver,* Grady. The high school just called about Leigh. She's flunking two courses. I have to go talk with the guidance counselor. Would you stay with Michael while I run over, just for a few minutes?"

"Take your time," Grady said. "I don't punch a time clock."

She threw on a coat, grabbed her keys, and started for the door, only to return to him and wrap an arm around his neck. "Thank you," she whispered, then was gone.

Holding in his nostrils the faintly flowery scent that was the present-day Teke, Grady went off in search of Michael. He found him in the den that had been turned into a bedroom. He was watching television.

"Hey, Grady."

"Hey, Mike." He held up a hand; Michael slapped him five. "You're watching *soaps?*"

"Sure. They're just like life around here, one crisis after another. Now it's Leigh. She'd rather study Jon than French or English or math. If Mom butts in, it'll get worse. Leigh hasn't been hot on her since she had her affair with Sam."

"She didn't have an affair with Sam," Grady said, but Michael had clicked to another channel and was pointing to the screen.

"See that guy? He was in a car that went over a cliff. He was in a coma for two months. When he woke up he couldn't remember a thing, but at least he could walk. That should've been me."

"You can walk."

"I look like a jerk."

"You won't once you're done with physical therapy."

Michael didn't answer. He stared at the screen. After several minutes he clicked to another channel and went on staring.

"Tough morning?" Grady asked.

"I hate therapy. It's the pits. *She* wouldn't like it if she had to do it. She *hates* exercising. Give her five years, and she'll look it."

"I think she looks pretty good."

"Just wait. She'll have flabby legs and flabby arms and a flabby chin, and she'll *sag,*" he tacked on as though that were the worst fate of all.

"Ahhhh," Grady said. "It's Dump on Mom Day."

Michael glowered at the television. "She bugs me."

"She loves you."

"Oh, yeah? So why am I here?"

"You're here," Grady said, feeling snatches of impatience, "because you ran into the street without looking."

Michael looked at him then. "I wouldn't have done that if she hadn't been doing what *she* was. She's the grown-up. She's supposed to know better."

"Well, she didn't. So she apologized. She's been suffering through all this right along with you. She was the one who agonized while you spent nine days in never-never-land."

"She's not the one who can't play basketball."

"But she's the one who has to stand by while *you* can't play, and if you think that isn't just as bad, then you're not as smart as I took you to be. She hurts when you hurt."

Michael returned to the television, mumbling, "Serves her right."

"No. No, it doesn't," Grady said because he felt it was time someone did. "She didn't hurt you intentionally. She doesn't hurt *anyone* intentionally. Fact is, it's a miracle she doesn't, what with all she learned from her dad. Did she ever tell you about that? Did she ever tell you about the times he threw her across the shack? She was younger than you, but she was cooking for him and picking up after him, and what did she get? She got smacked across the face when he didn't like the food. She got dumped on the floor if she slept too late. And when he was drunk, he didn't need any excuse to knock her around. Did she ever hit you like that?"

Michael was staring at him.

"Did she?" Grady repeated.

"No."

"I didn't think so. She's spent the last twenty years of her life trying to make something better for her children than she had for herself. So you watch what you say about her. If you're lucky, real lucky, you might grow up to be as good a person as she is." He turned his scowl to the window. "Problem with you is you're stuck in here. You're going stale." He turned back. "Did you have lunch?"

"She made me grilled cheese."

"Did you eat it?"

"Some."

"Well, I didn't have anything, and I don't want left-over grilled cheese. I feel like something spicy. Want to go for Mexican?"

Michael's face brightened. "Out?"

"I've driven you home from the pool. You sit in a car just fine."

"I haven't eaten out since the accident."

"I don't see any problem with going to a restaurant. You can eat a sandwich just like you can sit in a car, just fine. Unless you're afraid someone's going to call you a jerk because you have leg braces and crutches." Grady considered that. "Maybe you should be afraid. Anyone who does that will have to answer to me. Fact is, I've murdered a man. Now, maybe you don't want to be seen in the company of a murderer—"

But Michael was already reaching for his braces. Grady helped strap them on. He helped cover them with a pair of sweatpants, then waited patiently while Michael worked his way into a sweatshirt and pulled on Grady's old hat back side to. A short time later, having left a large, impossible-to-miss note for Teke on the kitchen table, they were in the pickup and heading for town. Grady could feel the little looks Michael shot at him every so often, but it wasn't until they were sitting at Taco Joe's with enough food for four on their trays that the boy said, "You're different, y'know."

"Is that good or bad?"

"Good. Kind of like Sam. He'd always be the one to come up with some crazy idea if we were bored." His face darkened. "Just as well I can't play ball. I wouldn't want him to coach me anymore."

"Why not? I hear he plays a mean game."

"Yeah. With my mom."

"From what I hear," Grady said, "neither of them enjoyed that game a whole lot. My guess, he'd be relieved to play with you again."

"Well, he won't."

"Are you going to hold what he did against him forever? Even I got time off for good behavior."

"You did not. You said you used to fight to protect yourself."

"For which I am not proud. I don't think Sam's proud of what he did with your mom. They call it feeling remorse, and it goes a long way toward making yourself a better person. It'd be real nice if you gave Sam a chance. I'm always grateful when people do it for me."

"I have an idea. *You* can coach me. I'll bet you played—"

"Never."

"Never?"

"When would I have played ball?"

"Sam played in college."

346

"I never went to college. Never went to school more than a handful of days a year, growing up. I didn't have time to play ball. I was too busy helping my dad with the boats at the dock."

"You're not so busy now. What do you do when you're not working on Mrs. Hart's carriage house?" As though a light suddenly went on in his mind, his eyes brightened. "You build canoes. You said that. It just now came back. Do you really?"

Grady nodded.

"How?"

Grady chuckled. The boy could be a cynical forty-year-old, a whining three-year-old, or a smart-mouthed eighteen-year-old. Grady liked him best as the innocent-eyed and curious thirteen-year-old he was now. "You shape a little wood to a mold, hammer a little, sand a little, take the thing off the mold, and cover it with canvas. Then you sand more and paint some. Then you put the thing in the water and paddle off to the deep nowhere."

"The deep nowhere?"

"The great outdoors. God's land. Miles of woods and water, where nature reigns and man is a guest."

"Is it scary?" Michael asked in a breath.

"Not when you know what the sounds you hear mean. There's a life in the deep nowhere that most people never see because they scare the natives away with their own noise, but if you don't go there to see the natives, what are you going there to see?"

Michael blinked. "Indians?"

"Birds. Muskrat. Beaver. Moose."

The boy's eyes widened. "Moose?"

"Moose."

"*Awesome.*"

That had to be the ultimate compliment. Grady wondered if Shelley used the word and, if so, whether she spoke it with the same wonder Michael did.

"Will you take me there?" Michael asked.

"Soon as you can walk."

"But if all I have to do is sit in a canoe and paddle—"

"All? Are you kidding? You want to spend time in the deep nowhere, you have to be able to paddle, sure, but you also have to be able to carry the canoe over dry spots, and gather wood, and cook food. You have to be able to sleep on the ground, and squat in the woods, and clean up after yourself so you leave nothing but footprints. It's no picnic."

"Then why do you do it?"

Grady thought of his favorite river, way north in Maine, and felt a sense of release. "Because it's peaceful and free, and because up there I'm just as good as anybody else."

They both went back to eating. After a time Michael said, "It's like that at Sutters Island. None of my friends are there. I don't have to be the best."

"Who says you have to be the best anyway?"

"My dad." Michael gave him a curious look. "Is it because you've done time that you think you're not as good as anybody else?"

"Oh, *I* think I'm as good. Other people are the problem."

"Because you're an ex-con?"

"And a carpenter. Not as much status in that as in what your dad does."

"But if you do it well, that's all that counts. That's what Mom always says. She says I can be whatever I want in life, as long as I do it with passion. Do you do your work with passion?"

Grady had to smile. He could see Teke saying all that. "Depends on how you define passion."

"Do you do it *well?*"

"*I* think so, but who am I to judge. Maybe you can. Want to see what I do?"

Michael's face came alive again. "Now?"

"Soon as I'm done eating."

In five minutes they were on their way. Five minutes after that Grady pulled up to the carriage house.

"Wow," Michael said, studying the place through the windshield, "this is neat."

Grady thought so. The large carriage doors had been replaced with windows and a more conventional double door. A huge arched window stood where the hayloft door had been. The clapboards were new and painted a Nantucket gray against the white that framed the windows and doors.

The inside was less finished. Though studs gave a vague picture of where walls would eventually be, it was basically a single large room with pink insulation lining the outer walls. "Still have a ways to go," Grady said, "but it's tight enough now so I can work in the cold."

"What's going over there?"

"That's the kitchen. That's a bedroom. We're standing in the living room."

"What's up there?"

"The loft. Bedroom or office, whatever."

"Is the stairway going to wind?"

"You bet."

"*Awesome.* What a *neat place.*" Michael moved forward—more deftly now with his crutches—stopping to touch the wood that lay over sawhorses, waiting to be cut.

"Watch where you go," Grady said just as the sound of sirens came from the distance. He had the awful image of the boy slipping on sawdust. "Don't want you hurting any of my tools."

The sirens grew louder. They were a rare sound for the neighborhood. Grady had visions of an elderly person having a stroke. When the sirens grew louder still, he thought of Cornelia.

"Stay put a minute," he told Michael. "I'm going to check on Mrs. Hart." But the sirens beat him to the carriage house door. He opened it to an array of blindingly bright, blinking lights. There was no ambulance, just three police cars crowded in to prevent the escape of his truck.

"What's going on?" he asked.

The doors of the police cars swung open, disgorging officers with the guns aimed his way. "Freeze, Piper," one yelled. "Put your hands on your head. Nice and slow. That's it."

Grady's stomach, which had turned over at the first show of the guns, sent a clenching message to the rest of his body. "What's the problem, Officer?" he asked as calmly as he could. He had pretty much gotten used to the Constance police force, but they had never drawn their guns on him before.

"Take five steps forward."

Grady took five steps forward. "Have I done something wrong?"

"Where's the boy?"

"Inside."

The police immediately fanned out. They kept their guns pointed at Grady, who was growing more and more alarmed. He didn't like guns, didn't like them at all.

"What's the matter?" he asked, singling Dodd out from the posse. He wished they would tell him what he was supposed to have done this time. Last time it had been robbery. This time the presence of guns said it was something worse. The thought that there might have been a murder in town gave him a chill.

"Get the boy," one of the officers called.

"There he is," another said.

"What do they want, Grady?" Michael asked from the door, sounding frightened.

"Are you all right, son?" the officer closest to him asked.

"I'm fine. But why are you here? What are you doing?"

The officers closed in. Grady might have known it would be Connors who gestured with his gun. The man looked to be enjoying himself. "Against the car, Piper. Hands on the roof."

Grady knew the drill. He also knew that one false move could set off a dumb-assed suburban police officer's gun. Moving slowly, he put his hands on the roof of the cruiser. His legs were immediately kicked apart and his person searched.

"What are you *doing?*" Michael yelled. "He hasn't done anything wrong. What's the charge here?"

"Kidnapping," Connors said, snapping handcuffs on Grady.

Grady was dumbstruck. "Kidnapping?"

"Who did he kidnap?" Michael yelled.

But Grady suddenly knew. A powerful anger rose in him. "Dodd?" he bellowed, finding the man several yards off. "Have to talk, Dodd."

"At the station, bud," Connors said, and opened the back door of the cruiser.

Michael lurched forward. "You can't put him in that car. He isn't a criminal. He didn't do anything wrong." When an officer tried to restrain him, he shouted, "Don't touch me!"

Dodd came to Grady's side.

With a great effort, given the fury he felt, Grady lowered his voice so that Michael wouldn't hear. "You know what this is about, don't you?" he told Dodd. "It's Maxwell. I left a note on the kitchen table saying that I was taking the boy out. He must have seen it. You know he hates me, and you know I didn't kidnap that boy. I'm his friend and his mother's friend. Call her. I was doing her a favor by baby-sitting the boy. She should be home by now. If you take me in for kidnapping, you'll be making fools of yourselves."

Dodd looked disgusted. "We got the call. We have to follow through."

"And upset the boy?" Grady asked just as Michael materialized by his side.

"They can't do this, Grady. Tell them they can't. You didn't kidnap anyone. You have your rights."

"He sounds like his father, don't you think?" Grady asked Dodd.

Dodd looked around. He made a disgruntled motion with his hand that sent the other officers returning to their cruisers. Then he said to Michael, "How 'bout you come for a ride with Grady and me? We'll check in at the station, get this all straightened out, then drive you back."

"He has a tutor coming at three," Grady said.

But Michael wasn't budging. "I'm going with you. There isn't any crime if there isn't any victim, and if those dorks don't know it, I'll tell them."

"Watch it, Michael," Grady cautioned. "Those 'dorks' are here to protect you."

"Protect me? You could protect me far more than they ever could." He turned on Dodd. "You're making a major mistake. Grady didn't kidnap me. Do I look coerced? Do I look *unhappy?* No! I'm here of my own free will, which you guys would see if you had any brains under those fancy hats of yours."

"*Jesus*, Michael," Grady said, then said to Dodd, "He must watch too much television."

"Soap operas," Michael corrected, "and this is just like one. It's *sick!*"

Dodd scowled at Connors. "Get rid of the handcuffs."

"If I do that, he'll—"

"Get the goddamned things off!"

Connors took them off.

Dodd put a warning hand on Grady's arm. "You drive the boy back home now. We'll give you an escort. Any doubts when we get there, and we'll take you right back to the station. Understood?"

Grady understood. He also understood that J. D. Maxwell wasn't stopping until he was run out of town, but he'd be damned if he was going to let that happen. He was staying until Teke didn't read him anymore. Come that day, and only then, he would be gone.

When Teke came home to a swarm of police cars, her imagination went wild. She lost ten years in the time it took to park and run into the house. Once she learned what had happened, she was livid. After the debacle of Thanksgiving, and on the heels of her dismal discussion with Leigh's guidance counselor, this deliberate troublemaking by J.D. was the final straw. As soon as the police and Grady were gone and Michael was tucked away with his tutor, she gave vent to her rage.

"What an *awful* thing to do, J.D.! A cruel, stupid, *malicious* thing! You knew Grady spent time with Michael. You saw the note he left on the table. You *knew* there wasn't any kidnapping. Why did you *do* that?"

J.D. looked perfectly composed, which fed her anger all the more. Rather than deny what she said, he shrugged. "I don't like Grady Piper. I don't like him spending time with my son."

"Somebody should, since you certainly don't, but that's beside the point," she argued, and raced on. "What *right* do you have to treat Grady that way? You've been trying to get him in trouble since the day he arrived. What did he ever do to *you?*"

"He hurt my son."

"It wasn't his fault!" she cried as it seemed she had done a thousand times. "He's *never* done anything to you, except know me when I was a child"— she paused—"but that's it, isn't it? You're jealous. You don't want me yourself, still you're jealous."

"I am not jealous."

She should have been flattered, but her anger wouldn't allow for that. "He comes over and shovels the walk. He stays with Michael while I run down to the school. He stops by for an hour of friendly conversation with me. He helps me out. He makes things easier for me. And all that makes you look bad."

"No, it doesn't. I don't live here anymore. Obviously I can't do those things."

She slapped the counter. "You *never* did them, J.D. Your work, your needs, always came first. You helped me out only if it was convenient for you. If you want to know the truth, living here without you isn't much of a change from before. I took care of most everything then, and I do the same now. And if you *really* want to know the truth," she went on, caught up in a purging of the thoughts that had been festering in her mind, "I have never been so relieved to see you leave here as I was on Thanksgiving. I thought you were doing me a favor by coming, but you weren't. You're dark and gloomy and troublesome. When you came, you brought a storm cloud with you, and you took it away when you left. So, if you *really* want to do me a favor, you can just stay away!"

Somewhere in the midst of her tirade, she had started to shake. She made no effort to stop it as she stood glaring at J.D. She had never been so angry in her life.

"I can grant you that favor," J.D. said with his

chin in the air in fine Maxwell form. "I can grant you other favors, too, but you're going to have to ask for every single one. That means money, the house, the car, new clothes. Can you support yourself in the style to which you're accustomed?" he asked, heading for the door.

"I don't want your money!"

"Amazing how you've changed your colors, Teke. What was all the talk about wanting to save our marriage? About wanting what was best for the kids? Thanks to Grady Piper, you're willing to chuck it all, and you wonder why I don't like the guy?" He swung through the door.

She went hot in pursuit with a point to make. "Grady has nothing to do with this. It's between you and me." She raised her voice when he slid into his car. "Don't keep trying to blame him. If our marriage is gone, it's because we blew it ourselves. *We* did it. So don't blame him, don't blame Sam, don't blame your father—"

He sped off, leaving her yelling into the cold air with no one to hear. After a minute she quieted, wrapped her arms around herself, and returned to the house. But the anger didn't fade. Nor did the frustration, or the fear.

So, that evening, taking advantage of the fact that Jon and Zoe had come to do homework with Leigh and Jana, and Michael was watching television, she left the dinner dishes in the sink, ran through the woods, and knocked—a first—on the Popes' back door. She wasn't sure she was welcome, but she was desperate enough to take the risk.

"Got a minute?" she asked nervously when Annie came to the door.

"Sure. We were just having coffee. Want some?"

Teke shook her head. Heart pounding, she came into the kitchen.

355

Sam was sitting there. "Everything okay?" he asked.

"I, uh, need to talk with friends. No one else fits the bill. No one knows me the way you guys do." She leaned against the counter with her hands buried in the pockets of her coat and spoke above the racket in her chest. "It's no good between J.D. and me. There's nothing left. It's done. Over."

Annie and Sam exhanged an alarmed look. "Completely?" Annie asked. "Are you sure?"

"I knew it on Thanksgiving. What a disaster that was." She still felt it in her marrow, the horror of that day, the horror of this one. "It was *such a relief* when he left. The house is more peaceful without him. My *life* is more peaceful without him—not that we fought, we never did that, but he likes things done certain ways, and I felt obligated to comply. When the kids were little, I used to run around madly picking up toys when I knew he was on his way home. He wanted the house to be spotless, so it was. It's not toys now, it's clothes and schoolbooks and junk mail, but I haven't had to worry about any of that for the past few weeks, and it's nice. Same thing with serving dinner at six-thirty rather than seven-thirty."

"But you've been married to the man for nineteen years," Sam said. "There must be something you like about him."

Teke hugged her arms to her body. With the steadying of her heartbeat, she was more aware of the twisting of her stomach. She was about to turn a corner in her life. Once around it, there was no going back. "J.D. is stable. He's predictable. He earns a good living. He's financially secure. He treats me with respect—or he did, until now. Same thing with being sweet. He had his moments. But no more. He's so angry at me that we can't do anything for each other, and if Thanksgiving was a sample of things to come, the kids will suffer each time we get together. We had an *awful* argument today. So what's the point?" She appealed to them. "*Is* there a point? I guess that's why I'm here. Do either of you see anything worth saving in my marriage?"

"Yeah," Sam said. "You've been good for J.D."

"No," Teke said with a new conviction, "I mothered him. Too much. If he'd been forced to do more as a father or a husband, he would have grown stronger, and if he'd been stronger, he would have been able to stand up to John Stewart."

"He'll be worse off without you," Sam argued.

"Without me he'll be free to find himself."

"He won't find himself. He'll find J.S."

"Then I should stay in the marriage to save J.D. from his father?" Teke asked. The thought of that set her off. She was suddenly as angry as she had been earlier that day. "But what about me? When do *my* needs become important? I wanted a family and financial security, and that's just what I've had for nineteen years, but it's like having a high-paying job that you detest, so what's it worth? I still want family, and I'll want financial security until the day when I can't remember what it was like growing up with none, but I need *more.*"

"Is it Grady?" Annie asked.

"No," Teke said with a speed that belied her doubts. "Grady deserted me once. I don't want a man who does that to the woman he loves."

"Do you love him?"

"I *worship* him. All my *life* I've worshiped him. But I could have lived without him, really I could have, if my marriage had stayed intact." She gave a tired sigh. "Right now my first priority is the kids."

"You've thought this all through, then?"

Teke nodded. "And I've tried to be rational,

believe me, I have." She gave a sheepish smile. "J.D. isn't the only leaner. I've leaned on you, Annie, maybe more than I should have. You and Sam have been our rock. So without you our marriage crumbles."

"I feel awful."

"Don't."

"I can still remember the night we fixed you two up. We thought it was the perfect match, remember, Sam? Your best friend and my best friend, opposites that were bound to attract?" She returned to Teke with a helpless look. "So we blew it?"

"Oh, no, Annie," Teke hurried to say, "J.D. and I had nineteen fine years. If I hadn't married him, I wouldn't have had my children—and I might have gone on for another nineteen years with J.D. if things hadn't changed. But they did change, so now I have to think about where I'm headed. As I see it, in my new, rational mode"—that, added in self-mockery—"I have four immediate worries. The first is how to deal with the kids. Do I tell them now, or do I wait? Do I talk about divorce, or do I stick to separation?"

"You talk to J.D. before you do anything," Sam said. "You have to make sure this is what he wants."

"What if it's what *I* want?" Teke cried, and her emotions flared again. "Maybe it's time I did what's best for me! Do you know that I have no idea how to balance a checkbook, or what our auto insurance or home insurance covers, or what information is listed on an income tax form? I have never received a paycheck. I have absolutely no credit to my name. Do you have any idea how helpless I feel? How dependent? How *terrified?*" Feeling chilled, she pulled her coat more tightly around her. "But I'm getting ahead of myself. I have to decide how to handle the kids. I'm thinking that I shouldn't say anything until I know for sure what I'm doing. Right?"

Annie nodded. "Unless they have the power to change your mind."

With the conviction that had come to her in the wake of the afternoon's fiasco, Teke said, "It's too late. J.D. doesn't want a reconciliation. Any more than I do." She turned to Sam. "Does he?"

It was a minute before Sam said a quiet, "No."

The pain of her recent encounters with J.D. had immunized her such that the truth didn't hurt now the way it might have a week or two before. "That leads to my second worry. Christmas could be another horror. I don't want it to be."

"I think we should all go skiing," Annie said.

Teke was startled. "All of us? You don't want me there."

"I do. But will it be a torment for Michael if he can't ski?"

"You want *me* along?" She would have thought that was the *last* thing Annie would want.

"Yes, Teke," Annie said in a teacherly tone. "I want you to be with your kids and my kids and us."

"But *why?*"

"Because we have to go on living."

Teke wanted that more than anything, but she had thought it a pipe dream. "Together? After what happened?"

Annie grew thoughtful. "We were too close. I think we all agree on that. We leaned on each other too much, so now we have to learn to stand on our own. But we also had good times. Do we have to throw those out, too? The kids want to be together, and we all know J.D. won't come, which means you'll be able to relax."

"But will you?" Teke asked with a quick look at Sam.

Annie seemed to struggle with the question. "I'm trying," she finally said.

In the weeks since Michael's accident, Teke had been aware of missing Annie. Only now did she realized how much she loved her. She would have hugged her if things had been different. Instead she brushed tears from the corners of her eyes and said, "Well, at least it's a relief to know that the girls can go, even if Michael and I have to stay here." She took a shaky breath and returned to her list. "The other things are technical and related. There's the matter of taking steps to protect myself. I have to establish credit, for starters. And I have to secure enough money from J.D. to take care of the kids. I need a lawyer." She faced Sam. "Do you know of anyone good?"

"God, Teke, I hate to do this."

"It's necessary, Sam. Believe me. There's nothing left of my marriage to save. I've come to accept that now. When I cry at night, it's not over J.D. It's over the kids' suffering. Maybe if J.D. and I can make a clean break of it, their suffering will be minimized. I wouldn't be asking you for a name—it's another betrayal of J.D.—but I don't know who else to ask. I need help. Just a name."

Ten minutes later she walked back through the cold night woods with the name and number of Sam's recommendation in her jacket pocket.

sixteen

ANNIE DISLIKED THE ENGLISH DEPARTMENT'S annual Christmas party. For one thing, it came too early, barely into the second week of December, when she still had the taste of turkey in her mouth. For another, it came at the hell point before term's end, which was fine for the faculty members who didn't have families, but for Annie, who did, it meant one more lost night at a time when too many others were lost. For a third, it was held in a lounge saved for the occasion, a room hemmed in by dark wood walls, filled with heavy velvet furniture, and lit by candelabras that Annie swore had been brought to the New World from a dungeon in the Old. Worst, though, the party was stag. Neither spouses nor significant others were invited. Annie would have liked Sam with her this year.

She arrived late, helped herself to a toothpick's worth of shrimp and a glass of wine, and looked around. Her first thought was that it was just as well Sam wasn't there. Susan Duffy was dressed to kill. Natalie Holstrom wasn't far behind. Annie's second thought was that the first thought was very sad. She never used to have thoughts like it. She wished she didn't now.

Joining friends in the nearest group, she tapped in to the discussion there. A bit later she moved to another group, where she stood listening to the talk with half an ear. She saw these people nearly every day, which was precisely why she had always felt that dates should be included. They added freshness and depth to discussions. Annie liked meeting her colleagues' better halves. She liked showing off her own.

"Bored?" Jason asked, coming from behind to zero in on her ear.

She moved aside with him. "Academicians, regardless how extreme their politics, tend to be parochial. We rehash the same things over and over again."

"It's called self-aggrandizement. It's the nature of the beast."

She smiled. "So now that you know, are you sure you want to join us?"

"Sure I'm sure," he said with a cocky lilt. "I'm into self-aggrandizement as much as the next guy. Maybe more. Besides," he added dryly, "I can't afford to turn back. I've come too far. It's either continue on or sweep floors for Grounds and Buildings at six fifty an hour."

"Any word on financial aid?"

"Not yet. I've filed the forms. Now I wait for them to decide if I'm needy."

Annie couldn't begin to imagine what it was like to go from riches to rags, so she indulged him his flippancy. She probably would have anyway. She liked Jason, respected his intelligence and his quickness. She still blushed when she thought about the way she had let him touch her, but it wasn't so bad now that Sam's touch was back.

It bothered her that she hadn't yet told Sam

about Jason, but she didn't know how to do it or when. She was afraid of rocking the boat of their marriage, which was tentative, finally beginning to steady. She liked Sam's attentions. She was feeling more sure of herself as a woman.

Until she looked at women like Susan Duffy. So she tried not to.

"How's your family doing?" she asked Jason.

"To talk with them," he answered, "you'd think everything was hunky-dory. It's only when I ask for money that Dad sets me straight. They have limited cash flow, he says, though I can't see that their lifestyle has changed any. Not outwardly. It looks like I'm the only frill they've cut."

"Jason," she chided, then asked more quietly, "How are you feeling?"

"Great."

"Did you see my doctor?"

"Yeah. Cool guy,"

"Did he find anything wrong?"

Jason grinned and winked at someone across the room. From the light-hearted looks of him, Annie guessed he was fine. She was startled when he said, "Diabetes, he thinks."

"Diabetes?"

"Shhhhh. It's our secret."

Annie whispered, "But you say it like it's a cold. Diabetes is serious."

"It runs in my family. I'm not really surprised. I just thought I might escape it, arrogant bastard that I am."

She let out a breath. "On top of everything else."

"Don't look so worried. I'll be fine." He grew serious. "It really is a secret. I have enough of a problem with Honnemann. He'll never hire me to teach if he learns that I'm sick. You won't tell him, will you?"

"Of course not," Annie assured him quickly. "It's

irrelevant. I just hope that you won't be taking on too much rushing to get the degree by June."

"I have no choice. I have to work next year."

"Do you give yourself shots?"

"I take pills."

'Are you seeing a specialist?"

"Ducan Hobbs. Ever hear of him?"

"No, but I'll check him out."

"Thanks, Mom."

Annie didn't take offense. "That's more appropriate, don't you think?"

He looked at her breasts. "I don't know. You felt damn good."

Her cheeks flamed. She sighed. "Let's make a deal, Jason. You won't make comments like that, and I won't tell anyone you're popping pills, okay?"

Jason smiled, then looked beyond her. "Ahh, my fans await. Will you excuse me, ma'am?"

As she nudged him off, she caught sight of Charles Honnemann's bright red bow tie. He was standing alone. She joined him.

"The department keeps growing," she remarked. "Last year's party wasn't as large as this."

"A weak economy works in our favor, since our tuition's less than some," Charles replied. "The admissions people say inquiries are up. Whether that will translate into an increased enrollment again remains to be seen."

"In any case, you'll have at least one instructor's slot to fill. Any chance of appointing Jason?"

"There's a chance," Charles conceded, "but I don't know how good it is. He doesn't have his degree."

"He will. I'm advising him on his thesis. It's an analysis of the works of James Joyce. It's going to be brilliant."

Charles watched Jason, who was on the far side

of the room, entertaining a group of his fellow teaching assistants. "You like the boy."

"Uh-huh."

"He has an irreverent look to him."

"Is irreverent any worse than bizarre?" she asked, and didn't have to elaborate. There were any number of weird-looking people in the room. "He's a hard worker. He hasn't once let me down."

"Is it on the up and up?"

"Is what?"

"Your relationship with Faust."

"Excuse me?" she asked in surprise.

"You're fond of him. He's obviously fond of you."

Jason wouldn't have said anything, Annie was sure of it; still, she felt prickles at the back of her neck. "I'm married, Charles."

"So was Lady Chatterley." He sighed. "Not that it matters to me what you do with him. That's your business, and you're right, we do have some unconventional people in our midst who, no doubt, are doing far more risqué things than having intradepartmental affairs. But if you're going to bat for Jason, I want to know the nature of your loyalty."

Annie simmered. "Jason has an outstanding grasp of literature and a special feel for poetry. He can write, he can communicate, and, quite honestly, he's a refreshing change from some of the members of our department who are avant-garde for the sake of being avant-garde."

Charles nodded. "I'll think about it."

"Do," Annie said, setting her glass on a passing tray. She circulated for another few minutes before pleading family commitments and leaving the party.

Teke knocked on the door that led into the basement of Cornelia Hart's house, then waited nervously, shivering in the cold, for what seemed an eternity until Grady opened up. He was wearing a flannel shirt open over a pair of jeans and looked cross.

"Can I come in?" she asked quietly. When he reached the darkness behind her, she said, "I'm alone."

"Then maybe you shouldn't. I'm not in a great mood, Teke."

She wasn't in a great mood herself. The last few days had been tense ones. She was feeling shakey. I've been driving around for an hour. At first I thought I might go to a movie. Then I thought I'd get something stiff to drink." She paused. "My car brought me here."

He wrapped a hand around the back of his neck and hung his head.

"Please, Grady." She hadn't seen him since the kidnapping episode. "I have to talk with you."

"This is a shitty basement."

"Is that supposed to bother me?" she asked, stepping past him with a flash of indignance. "I would have visited you in prison if you'd let me." She looked around. "Lord knows I've seen worse that this." The place was floor-to-ceiling concrete and smelled of age and dust. In the dark portions she saw what she assumed was stored furniture. The one lit corner, not far from the heater, held an old four-poster bed, a mahogany dresser, and a large, overstuffed chair.

Parka and all, she slipped onto the chair. The sough of the heater was the only sound until her thoughts bubbled out. "I'm sorry about what J.D. did to you the other day, Grady. It was just plain malicious. since he hasn't been able to *sue* anyone over what happened to Michael, he's settling for being a giant pain in the butt. He's given Sam and me both a rough time, but you're the one who really gets his goat."

Grady remained behind her. "Why me?"

"I guess because you were my lover. He knew he wasn't the first, but as long as any others were faceless, he could pretend they didn't exist. He can't do that anymore."

"What's it to him who you were with before? Hell, he was the one who got you."

"Only because *you* sent me away," she shot back, then lowered her voice. "Besides, he never had the whole me. He knew that. You did, so he's feeling bested, and for J.D. to be bested by someone he considers beneath him . . ." After nineteen years of marriage to J.D., she could understand the man, at least. "It's no wonder you bring out the worst in him."

"Well, he brings out the worst in me, too," Grady announced with a force that brought her head around. He was standing in the shadows, reeking of animosity. "I swear, if those cops hadn't been with me when I saw him at the house, I'd have strangled him. I haven't been so angry since I hit Homer, and look where that got me. I'm supposed to be rehabilitated. I'm supposed to be able to control the anger. I thought I could, but I was close to the edge then. I shake when I think of it."

Teke nearly left the chair and went to him, but she didn't trust herself that far. She wished he would button his shirt. Then again, she prayed he wouldn't. Looking at him was a pleasure. She craved the occasional pleasure. "Come sit," she said. "Talk with me."

Hands hooked low on his hips, he took a breath that shook with lingering anger. After what seemed an eternity, he finally crossed to sit on the edge of the bed, safely out of her reach. Which was good, she told herself.

"So I wanted to apologize for J.D.," she said. "I also wanted to thank you. Michael was invigorated after being out with you."

"I'll bet."

"He was. He had a great time."

"I believe you. No problem with that kid. You should have heard him telling off the cops."

She smiled wryly. "He's had great teachers in J.D. and Jana. I normally wouldn't approve of that, but it's good to see him showing spirit."

"He needs to get out more."

"That's what he told me, so I spoke with his physical therapist. We've switched all of his sessions to the health club. The aqua-treadmill helps most anyway, and the other exercise machines are there. So Michael will leave the house every morning like his friends do. If that helps, we'll drive him to his tutor, rather than the' other way around. The social worker keeps saying that his recovery hinges on his attitude." It made such sense. Teke wanted to kick herself. "I should have realized how bored he was and done something before this, but I thought being home would be enough." It wasn't. And she was new at handling the emotional problems accompanying a major injury. "Michael is groping. He's not sure what he can do and what he can't. Me, too."

Grady had his hands braced well out from his thighs. His shoulders rode high, his head hung between them. It was an unhappy pose, to say the least.

Teke's instinct was to soothe him. She came out of the chair with that in mind, but thought better of it and approached the dresser. There were a brush and comb on top, a razor and a can of shave cream, the worn wallet that normally sat in the back pocket of his jeans. She touched it, thinking of the way it touched him, then closed her hand and put the fist to her heart to steady its beat. "Where do you shower?" she asked in search of distraction.

"Upstairs."

She looked around for signs of food. "Where do you eat?"

"Upstairs."

"Cornelia doesn't mind?"

"She likes it. She eats what I cook. She says she hasn't eaten so well in years."

"She's a sweetheart," Teke said just as her eye fell on a plastic basket filled with clean laundry. She shook out a towel and folded it neatly, put it on the dresser, reached for another. "So's her son. Leigh is seeing him at the beginning of January. She wants birth control. We talked about it over Thanksgiving, but I kept forgetting to make the call." Forgetting? "It was probably deliberate. The thought of giving her carte blanche to sleep with ion bothers me. She's annoyed at me for that."

"Is that why she's failing in school?"

Teke gave a faintly hysterical laugh. "It may be one of the reasons, but there are so many others, I can't begin to list them. In the last three months, our family has become dysfunctional. That'll ruin grades any day." She reached for a T-shirt.

"It didn't ruin yours."

She shook out the T-shirt, folded it deftly. "Different situation. A dysfunctional family was the norm for me. I didn't know anything else in life. Besides, I wanted to impress you."

Grady made a sound. She looked over her shoulder. He was still on the bed, still with his shoulders hunched. She held a folded shirt to her chest, inhaling its clean scent for a minute, before setting it carefully on top of the towels. Then, impulsively, she approached the bed.

"Why did you come here tonight?" he asked, raising his head.

Her heartbeat sped. "To thank you for taking Michael out and to apologize for what J.D. did."

"Is that all?"

She thought of the agonizing she'd been doing. "I don't know," she confessed quietly. "I'm torn."

"Between what?"

"Wanting to love you and wanting to hate you." She couldn't be more truthful, to him or to herself. "I'm still furious at you for what you did."

"For hitting Michael?"

"Lord, no!" She couldn't believe he would think that. "The accident wasn't *your* fault. What I'm furious about is your showing up after all these years." Then she corrected herself. "What I'm *really* furious about is that you sent me away in the first place. We could have had so much."

"Yeah," he said with a disparaging look around. "A basement."

"There's nothing wrong with this basement," she insisted.

"You wouldn't say that if you had to live here."

"That's not true, Grady. I came from a lot worse than this and you know it. Besides, you said you owned a place with your wife, and even if that weren't so, I'd take living in this basement over living with the turmoil over at my house *any* day."

He looked away. "You don't know what you're saying." "It's what *I* feel." He looked back sharply. "Know what I feel? I feel like grabbing you, pulling you down on this bed, and screwing the living daylights out of you."

Teke felt the stirring of her own deep heat. She thought of the day he had kissed her in the woods. No time might have passed, so strong was the need. She guessed that was part of what had brought her here tonight.

"But that'd complicate things ten times over, wouldn't it?" he went on. His fingers tightened on the edge of the bed. His eyes never left hers. "Damn it, why do you tempt me? You always did, Teke. I shouldn't have taken you when you were fifteen, but I couldn't resist, and I couldn't resist any time I could get my hands on you after that, and then you got so far under my skin that the sight of Homer with his hands on you made me crazy—" He broke off. A weary sigh escaped him. "You're gonna be the death of me yet, so help me, you are."

He rubbed the back of his neck again, but she caught his hand before it could return to the bed. "I'd never let that happen."

He barked out a laugh. "Like you could stop me from going to jail? Like you could stop Michael from suffering brain damage? My *God,* Teke, you're such an innocent at times. You think love can protect people from bad things, but it can't."

She told herself to put his hand down, but in a voice too soft to be heard. His fingers fascinated her; they were long, lean, and strong. She touched the calluses that spoke of his work. They had been there for years, but there were new scars, tiny nicks that a saw or a nail must have caused. Unable to resist, she kissed them, then pressed his hand to her neck and said, "Maybe nothing can protect people from bad things. But maybe love is what makes the bad bearable. You were wrong to send me away and tell me to forget you, Grady. You were wrong to send back my letters and refuse to see me when I went to visit. We had something so good that the wait would have been worth it."

"It's over and done."

She took a shallow breath and hurried on. "That was going to be my line. I was going to tell you that we shouldn't see each other. That I'm okay and Michael's okay and you ought to leave town. There's no way anything can come of this." But her voice lost steam because her eyes fell to his chest, which was spattered with dark hair and looked warm and inviting. She wanted to remind herself that she had three children who needed her, and that, technically at least, she was still married. But the need to touch him was suddenly overpowering. Slipping a hand inside his shirt, she spread it over his chest. Immediately she was transported to a higher place, one she had spent forever dreaming about.

"Teke," he warned.

"Just for a minute," she whispered, as though by whispering she could get away with the illicit. She explored his chest, inching her hand from one side to the other, through a smattering of hair, over one swell of muscles to its mate.

"Teke."

"A minute," she breathed, half dazed. The heat of his body did that to her. It always had.

Bending her head over his so that her mouth touched his ear, she said, "Twenty-two years, and it's still the same." She let her palm idle over his hammering heart, over soft hair, a tight nipple, hard muscle. His heat was inside her now, having moved from her hand, up her arm, into her chest. "One of the things I loved most about you was your strength. You were always my champion. Right from the start. Even when you hit my father."

Grady wrapped his arms around her hips. "I couldn't let him rape you."

Teke shuddered. For years she had refused to think about Homer's threats, but being in Grady's arms, protected, opened a window on the details of that night. Homer had been drunk and ugly. He had been annoyed because she spent so much time with Grady. He had said she owed *him* some of that time. He had grabbed her and torn off her blouse. She had been terrified.

Reliving that terror now, she cried, "You could have let me testify."

But Grady was vehement. "They would have asked for details. They would have taken one look at you and said you had tempted him beyond his control. They would have called you ugly names. I couldn't put you through that."

She remembered her father's rough hands, his leering eyes, his fetid breath—but they were nothing compared to the anguish she had felt when Grady had sworn her to silence. That silence had tormented her for years. Now, she argued, "But it would have gotten you off."

Grady shifted her onto his lap. "There was no physical proof that he wanted to rape you. He didn't get to do it."

"Because you hit him," Teke said against his jaw, "and he fell."

"They would have convicted me anyway."

"But at least I'd have felt I'd done my best to prevent it. I wouldn't have felt so *guilty* all these years. It wasn't fair, Grady. I wanted to help, if not at the trial, then afterward, but you wouldn't let me. It wasn't *fair.*"

He moved his arms over her, supportive and soothing. As she calmed, she felt the rebirth of desire. It was mutual. Grady's voice was thicker. "So, what'll it be? Do we take off our clothes and do it, or do you leave? It has to be one or the other, and soon. I'm pretty close."

Teke could feel the tremor of restraint in his muscles and the hardness of him under her hip. They echoed the race of her pulse, the knot in her belly, the heat between her legs. She wanted him desperately.

But wanting him wasn't enough. She wasn't a teenager anymore. She knew about the complexity of life. She knew about consequences.

Drawing back, she studied his eyes. They were dark and aroused. Wanting to drown there, she moaned, "Oh, Grady, I can't."

Barbara Delinsky

"Because you're married?"

She no longer held any delusions on that score. Her marriage was over. But that wasn't the reason. "Because I'm afraid."

"Of going to bed with me?"

"Of after. You hurt me. I can't live through anything like that again."

He was silent, but only for a minute. "I didn't want to hurt you."

"But you did it."

"I won't ever do it again."

"You said you wouldn't the first time."

"Christ, Teke," he argued, "those were extenuating circumstances. I thought I was doing what was right for you. And I was, really, when you stop to think of it. You've had much more in life than I could ever have given you."

"Like the house, and the car, and the jewelry?" She pushed to her feet. "I would have happily lived without them. How many times do I have to tell you that?"

"And how many times do I have to tell *you* that I didn't *want* you to live without them?"

"You're hung up on money."

"Yeah, because I've never had much."

"Money doesn't matter."

"Like hell it doesn't." He stood and faced her head-on. "III wanted to give you all those things myself, just like we dreamed, only once I was sentenced to prison, I knew I'd never be able to. So I did what I thought was right. You could try to look at it from my side."

"I *do,* but it doesn't make sense. If you had loved me, really loved me, you'd have wanted me to wait for you, no matter what." All those years, that was what had bothered her most, the doubts about the depth of Grady's love.

He glared at her. "I loved you so much I killed a man for you. How can you possibly doubt me, after that?" His eyes narrowed. "I know your problem. Damn right, you're afraid. You're afraid that loving me will upset your cushy life."

Teke stiffened. "I'm afraid that loving you will *destroy* my life, and you can take 'cushy' and shove it."

"Sweet."

"Truthful." She made for the door. "You were right. I shouldn't have come. We're both in bad moods."

"You're afraid!" he repeated, coming after her. "You're afraid of taking a chance on an ex-con."

"Bull *shit*," she exploded, whirling around. "Yes, I'm afraid, but not of that. I'm afraid of being reject-ed again. I trusted you completely once. I believed everything you said about the future we were going to have. Then, with no need whatsoever, you took it all away." She resumed her flight.

"You're impossible!" he shouted after her.

"You're right! So go away! Leave town! Get out of my life! *Again!*" Yanking the door open, she stormed out.

The last thing she heard before sealing herself in her car was Grady's angry, "No way, lady! I've got plans!"

She drove off wondering what in the devil he meant.

For the week prior to Christmas, Annie was up until all hours reading papers, recording exam marks, and calculating term grades. By the time she climbed into the car with Sam and the kids, headed for the ski house, she was exhausted.

Teke had decided not to come. She claimed that it would be counterproductive for Michael to see everyone skiing and not be able to do it himself. Annie could buy that, but she also suspected that the same applied to Teke. Seeing Sam and Annie, and all the other couples they knew there, would be hard for her, given that she was alone.

The Maxwell girls were torn. They had to weigh deserting Michael against skiing with Jon and Zoe, and then J.D. muddied the works by inviting them to join him in Arizona. Jana went. Leigh chose to ski with Jon. So Annie had five people at the chalet. She figured she could handle that, she did, with surprising ease. It helped that Sam rarely let her cook.

"Let's go to the Onion Patch," he said the first night they were there, then, on the second night, Christmas Eve, "I heard Stoney's was great this year," then, when Annie announced she was going to cook a roast beef for Christmas Day, "Save it. I made reservations at the inn."

"Sam," Annie protested, "I haven't cooked dinner once."

"So?"

So it was expensive to eat out all the time. So Sam and the law firm were on the outs. So maybe they should watch their pennies more closely. "Teke always cooked. I should."

"Teke didn't just go through exams. Come on, Annie, I want you to have a real vacation. Beside, if you cook, I have to help, and frankly, *I* need a vacation."

She didn't argue for long. She was no glutton for punishment. Back home she made dinner every night because the kids' schedules precluded eating out, but this wasn't home. School was recessed. She was enjoying the break.

She was also enjoying Sam's attentiveness. Though a better skier than she, he stayed by her side for all but the last runs of the day, when she retreated, half-frozen, to sit in the lodge with a cup of hot chocolate while Sam made his daredevil runs.

It was at one of those times that she unexpectedly spotted Zoe across the lodge, looking out the window forlornly. Clunking in her ski boots around and between sprawled skiers, it took Annie a while before she finally reached her.

"Hi, sweetheart," she said, putting an arm around the girl's shoulders. "How long have you been here?"

Zoe shrugged. "An hour, I guess."

"I thought you were skiing with Leigh and Jon."

"Nah. They wanted to be alone."

"Did they *say* that?" Annie asked. She would tell Jon a thing or two if they had.

"No, but I knew."

"Well, you knew wrong," Annie insisted, then took a different tack. "I saw Susie VanDorn on the slopes a little while ago. They arrived just after noon. You can ski with her tomorrow."

"Uh-huh."

"Want some hot chocolate?"

"Nuh-uh."

Annie sipped hers. "Want to eat somewhere special tonight?"

"Whatever everyone else wants is fine."

Annie settled beside her on the window ledge. Zoe had always been an agreeable child, but what Annie was picking up on now wasn't agreeableness so much as lack of spirit. "What's wrong, sweetheart?"

"Nothing."

"You don't look like you're having much fun."

"I'm tired."

"Do you feel all right?"

"Uh-huh."

"Maybe you're coming down with something."

"I'm just *tired*, Mom."

Okay, Annie thought. Just tired. I'll buy that for

"Well, you knew wrong," Annie insisted, then took a different tack. "I saw Susie VanDorn on the slopes a little while ago. They arrived just after noon. You can ski with her tomorrow."

"Uh-huh."

"Want some hot chocolate?"

"Nuh-uh."

Annie sipped hers. "Want to eat somewhere special tonight?"

"Whatever everyone else wants is fine."

Annie settled beside her on the window ledge. Zoe had always been an agreeable child, but what Annie was picking up on now wasn't agreeableness so much as lack of spirit. "What's wrong, sweetheart?"

"Nothing."

"You don't look like you're having much fun."

"I'm tired."

"Do you feel all right?"

"Uh-huh."

"Maybe you're coming down with something."

"I'm just *tired*, Mom."

Okay, Annie thought. Just tired. I'll buy that for now. "Are you still angry at your dad?" she asked. For the purpose of the trip, an unspoken truce was in effect between Sam and the kids. Annie feared it was a tentative one.

"I'm *tired*," Zoe said, looking annoyed. "Why can't you leave it at that, Mom? Why does there have to be something hidden in everything I say?" She jumped up. "I'm going home. I'll see you there."

Annie let her go, though it took some effort. Given her druthers, she'd have pulled her back, wrapped her arms around her, and coaxed every little torment from the girl's mind. And the torments were there. Sweet Zoe, her pal, had been having a hard time of late. But Zoe was nearly sixteen. Instinct told Annie that she couldn't force herself on her daughter the way she once might have. Everyone needed space. Lord knew Annie did herself, and Zoe was cut from her mold.

So Annie bided her time. Sure enough, Zoe went happily off to the slopes the next morning. Annie guessed that whatever dark cloud had hung over her had simply blown away, and so it was through the rest of the week. During the day the kids went their own way, meeting Sam and Annie at the chalet at night. Such was the plan for New Year's Eve. They were going to relax at the chalet after skiing, then go as a family to dinner and a party at one of the inns near the mountain. When Annie and Sam returned from the slopes at four-thirty, though, Jon and Leigh were alone.

"Wasn't Zoe skiing with you?" Annie asked. "She said you were spending the day on the North Face."

Leigh glanced at Jon nervously. "We did, but she got tired in the middle of the morning and said she was skiing back down to South."

"We assumed she was with you," Jon added.

Annie shook her head. "Maybe with friends. Let's give her a few minutes. She'll be along."

A few minutes passed with no sign of Zoe. Sam, who was at the window watching the front walk, checked his watch. "The slopes have been closed for an hour."

Determined not to be concerned before it was warranted, Annie came to his side. "She must have stopped somewhere on the way home."

"Where?"

She didn't know. It was dark, cold, and icy outside. Families were gathering for the holiday. It wasn't like Zoe not to be with hers.

Curious more than worried, Annie began to call one after another of the friends Zoe might have been skiing with. Each was home. None knew where Zoe was. Several had seen her at lunch, but not since.

With each unproductive phone call, Annie grew more uneasy. Sam was hovering over her by the time she hung up the phone on the last of the possibilities. It was five-thirty. She raised frightened eyes and whispered an urgent, "Something's wrong. I know it, I just know it."

Taking over the phone, he called the management office at the mountain and learned that the base lodge was closed and deserted, but that a sole pair of skis had been left standing against the otherwise empty racks. A description of the skis matched Zoe's.

He called the police.

Annie checked Zoe's bedroom, but it was in the same state of disorder in which she had left it that morning. There was no sign that she had been back during the day. From what Annie could see, nothing was missing.

"Where could she be?" Leigh asked in a frightened voice when Annie returned to Sam's side.

He look agitated as he hung up the phone. "They'll keep an eye out for her, but they won't do anything more until she's been gone longer. They say they have reports of missing children every day of the week, but they always turn up."

"Zoe wouldn't make us worry this way," Leigh said.

Annie didn't think so either. Zoe didn't have a malicious bone in her body. But she had been upset lately. When people were upset, Annie knew, they sometimes did things they wouldn't normally do. "Maybe she wanted to walk around the village."

"How would she get there?" Jon asked logically. "The shuttle bus doesn't go that far."

"A friend might have taken her," Annie offered.

"What friend?" Sam asked. "You've called them all." He pushed a hand through his hair. "There's no note anywhere?"

"Not in her bedroom," Annie said, and went to search the rest of the house. The others joined her. They found nothing. By the time they met back in the living room, it was after six and Annie was beginning to panic. Her imagination was acting up, taking her in directions she didn't want to go. "Where is she, Sam?"

He looked pale, not terribly reassuring, though he wrapped an arm around her shoulders and drew her close. "I don't know."

"Do we just . . . wait?"

"Can't do that." He closed his eyes in a distressed way that furrowed his brows. When he opened them again, his look was urgent. "Did she say anything during the week about wanting to be somewhere other than here? Maybe in Arizona with Jana?"

"She wanted Jana here," Annie said. "She never said she wanted to be there." She looked to Jon and Leigh for confirmation and got a pair of nods.

Sam turned to them, too. "Any hint to either of you? Any passing reference to going somewhere? Any mention of someone new she might have met?"

They shook their heads. "But she's been strange lately," Jon said. "She doesn't talk like she used to."

Annie swallowed back her fear, but the words spilled anyway. "What if a group of college guys lured her to their place?" Zoe might have been flattered and gone, just as Annie been flattered by Jason Faust. But whereas Annie had been in a position to stop things before they gout out of control, Zoe wouldn't be. She was an innocent. And so pretty.

Annie had an even worse thought. "What if some *man* started talking with her on one of the lifts and lured her into his car? What if he said he'd take her into the village and then just keep driving?"

"Jana should have come with us," Leigh cried.

"She and Zoe always watched out for each other."

"Jana *wouldn't* come," Jon reminded her pointedly. "She didn't want to be with my father."

"Let's not get into that," Sam snapped.

"It's true."

"Let's not get *into* it," he repeated sharply.

"I can't just wait here," Annie said, leaving his side. "I'm going out to drive around. She may be walking back from wherever she's been."

Sam reached for the car keys. "You two stay in case she calls," he told Jon and Leigh. "We'll check back every few minutes."

The night was darker, colder, and more icy from the car than it had looked to Annie from the chalet. Cars passed by on their way to New Year's Eve gatherings. Bright lights marked the houses where those gatherings were being held. Between the cars and the bright lights were large, opaque, ominous pockets of woods.

"Oh, God," she whispered, pressing her fist to her mouth as she scoured the shards of landscape that the car's headlights revealed. "We should have kept her skiing with us. But she didn't want to be fussed over. She got angry at me when I did it."

"We'll find her," Sam said grimly, and drove on.

At seven they stopped back at the house. Zoe hadn't called. They left again and drove on, venturing farther this time. They called Jon from the village, but there had been no word from Zoe.

Annie gripped the dashboard, peering out into the darkness as Sam drove. It was after seven-thirty. The situation was more frightening by the minute. Annie didn't understand why Zoe hadn't called or come home. She was terrified. "Zoe, where are you? Where *are* you?"

By eight it had started to snow. Shifting into a lower gear, Sam drove back to the chalet. "I'm calling the police again," he said as they climbed out of the car. "If the local police won't do something, the state police might."

Jon and Leigh were waiting at the door. Their faces fell when they saw that Sam and Annie were alone. Behind them, the phone rang. Annie ran for it, but it was one of the girls she had called earlier, wanting to know if they'd found Zoe. "Not yet," Annie said, shaky and breathless and scared half to death, "but we will." She needed two tries to get the receiver caught on the hook. Her hand was still there when the phone rang again. She snatched it up. "Yes?"

There was a long pause, an eternal five seconds during which Annie fully expected a kidnapper to issue a ransom demand. Then came an unsure, "Annie?"

"Pop? It's me," she said in a quavering voice. "Pop, Zoe's missing. We don't know where she is."

"She's here," Pete said in his sandy voice.

"She's *there?*" Annie cried, putting a hand on her thudding heart. The others crowded around. Sam put his ear by hers so that he could hear what Pete was saying.

"My doorbell rang just before dinner, and she was standing right there, a little cold, but fine."

Annie's knees went weak with relief. She sagged against Sam as Pete went on.

"She said you knew she was coming, but I didn't think you'd send her along without calling me first, and then there was the matter of no satchel. Pretty little Zoe always carries a satchel."

"She's safe," Annie breathed. "Thank God, she's safe."

"It wasn't until I'd fed her a little and asked her about you folks' plans for tonight that she started feeling guilty."

"How did she get there?" Sam asked.

"She hitched a ride."

"Hitched?"

"With someone she knew, one of Jon's friends."

Annie wasn't reassured by that. Some of Jon's friends, particularly his football friends, were pretty high on themselves. She could easily imagine them taking advantage of Zoe. "Is she all right?"

"A little upset."

"Was she hurt?"

"Oh, no. Not that." His voice lowered. "She's upset about other things."

"Let me talk with her."

"Later, maybe."

Sam took the phone from Annie's hand. "I'm coming for her, Pop." Annie sensed that her father was suggesting otherwise, but Sam insisted. "I have to talk with her. It won't wait until morning. Don't tell her I'm coming. She might run off again. I'm leaving now. I'll be down by eleven." He handed the phone back to Annie.

She saw his determination and knew that nothing was changing his mind. To Pete, quietly, she said, "Sam's right. Hold on to her until he gets there, okay?"

For three hours in the car, Sam thought of all he wanted to say to Zoe. When he arrived at Pete's place, though, words weren't necessary. She was curled at the foot of Pete's bed, fast asleep.

After sitting down on the mattress, he lifted her into his arms and cradled her close, as he used to do when she'd been little. As he used to do then, he thought of how special she was, how sweet and gentle, and how much he wanted to give her.

He had failed her. That thought was foremost in his mind when, after a bit, she stirred. She rubbed her face against his sweater and curled closer. Then she went still.

"Daddy?" she whispered.

"It's me, baby."

She said nothing. Sam kissed her forehead. When she turned into him and began to cry, he held her tighter, aching more with each small sob. "It's okay, Zoe, it's okay, baby. Mommy and Daddy love you so much."

She cried on. He shot a helpless look at Pete, who was sitting on his orange crate looking back helplessly, and wondered why a man had to feel so inadequate in situations like these. Women didn't. They were content with the hugging, saw it as a comfort in itself. Sam tried to do the same, but it was tough. His little girl was hurting. That hurt him in turn. He wanted to *do* something.

"You shouldn't have come," she finally managed to say.

"Of course I should have. You're my daughter. I could never have celebrated the new year without you."

"You should be with Mom."

"Mom's okay. You're the one who's unhappy, and since I'm the one who made you unhappy, I'm the one who'll cheer you up."

She started crying again. He wondered what he was doing wrong.

Pete's voice came from across the room. It was like sandpaper, smoothing Sam's fears. "You pulled the cork, Sam. Everything that's been stored up for weeks is flowing."

Sam nodded. He stroked Zoe's hair, rubbed her back and her arm. Fifteen years old—it was hard to believe. He could feel the new shape her body was taking, yet she remained young and fragile. He slipped a hand in hers, remembering the baby who used to curl her fingers around one of his. She didn't do that now. Nor did she pull her hand away.

With his mouth close, he said, "We looked all over for you, Zoe, all over the chalet, all over the mountain. We called everyone we could think of, and all the time I was telling myself that if something happened to you, I'd be to blame. It's been a rough few months, all my fault."

"I want things back the way they were," came her small voice. "I want all of us skiing, not just Leigh."

"That may not happen. Once Michael is well, he and Teke will join us, probably Jana, too. I don't think J.D. will. He's separating himself."

"All because of you and Teke?"

"No. That might have been the catalyst, but there's more to what he's doing. He needs something different in his life."

"If he loved his family, he wouldn't."

"He loves his children very much. That's why he wanted Jana and Leigh in Arizona with him."

"Leigh chose Jon. Jana didn't choose me."

"She chose her father, and maybe she was right. Think about it, Zoe. Jana sees you every day, but not J.D. She knew you'd be spending the holiday with us, but who was J.D. going to spend it with?"

"But I want her back. I mean, I love having Mom to myself—Jana was a pest that way sometimes—but Jana's my best friend."

He stroked her hair. "And she still will be, but that doesn't mean you can't survive without her. Look at Mom. She did Thanksgiving without Teke. She didn't think she could, but she did, and she got a real satisfaction from it."

"But I *liked* things the way they were."

"Me too." He thought about the law firm and the comfortable place he had had there once. The comfort was gone now. He was feeling unsettled. Then again, "But I'm starting to like some things the way they *are*."

"Like what?"

"Like helping your mom. I get my own satisfaction from that. I never got it before, because Teke was always there to help."

"What else?"

"I like being home more. All my professional life I've felt that I had to be working, always working. Hours equal money. But, hell, what good's the money if you don't enjoy it with the people you love? And there's something else."

"What?"

"I like us being together, you and Jon and Mom and me. I may be selfish for saying that, but we haven't had much of it, and it's nice. It'd be even better if you and Jon would give me a chance. I made a mistake with Teke. You can't hold it against me forever." He tucked in his chin so that he could see her face, brushed a tear track from her cheek, and said in a soft voice, "I love you, Zoe. When I think of what I miss most about the way things used to be, one of the biggest things is you. I like the way we used to talk. I like the way we used to do things together."

She was quiet for a while, fiddling with one of the cables of his sweater.

"Whatcha thinkin'?" he whispered.

She whispered back, "I'm thinking I really messed up your New Year's Eve."

"Not necessarily. All's well that ends well. The night is still young."

She bobbed a shoulder against him. "Mom's up there and you're here. What fun is that?"

Sam agreed. "So why don't we pack up Papa Pete and drive back?"

Zoe looked up. Her eyes were watery but bright. "Now?"

"Why not?" he said, grinning. She was the most beautiful child in the world, he was sure of it, and she was his. "First we'll call Mom to let her know

seventeen

LITTLE BY LITTLE MICHAEL WAS INCREASING the range of motion in his joints and gaining strength in his muscles. His movements remained awkward, but he no longer needed leg braces. That fact alone attested to the progress that was often hard to see. For every two good days, there was one bad.

Teke was experiencing the same thing. She met with the lawyer Sam recommended, got a Visa card in her own name, then wrote a check at the supermarket that bounced. She pumped her own gas for the very first time, agreed to chair a committee planning a walkathon to benefit the Constance Land Trust, then had a huge row with Jana.

The row upset her far more than the bounced check. The children were her Achilles' tendon. Where they were concerned, she wallowed in worry and guilt. She was trying to do what was right, but what was right wasn't always popular. Too often she was in a no-win situation.

Such was the case with Jana when it came to the girl's habit of jumping on the T after school and showing up unannounced for dinner with J.D. They had gone back and forth for half an hour and were repeating themselves, with neither willing to back down.

"But he's all alone," Jana insisted in defense of her visits. "That doesn't seem right to me."

"He chooses to be alone," Teke pointed out for what had to be the tenth time. She didn't want to bad-mouth J.D., but this was relevant. He had called to complain more than once, which would crush Jana if she knew. "There are times when he finishes work and stops for supper, *then* arrives home to find you there. Besides, what about *us?* I expect you home at a certain time, and you don't show. I call around in a panic until your father finally calls me. That's not right, Jana. We plan on your being here. We *look forward* to your being here. And you have homework to do."

"I do it there."

"Then your father has to drive you all the way back here. Or is that the point?" Teke asked, knowing that it probably was. "Jana, *he moved out.*" She didn't know how much more emphatically she could say it. "He *chooses* to have his *own place* in Boston. You can have him drive you back here all you want, but it won't make any difference. He doesn't want to live with me."

"I don't blame him," the girl said with a defiant look. "I don't either."

She's upset, Teke told herself, and not for the first time, though the hurt remained. She's having trouble adjusting to the changes in her life. She loves me, whether she knows it or not.

"You don't need me," Jana went on. "You have Michael and Leigh. And Grady." This, accusingly. "You're still married to Dad. What are you doing with Grady?"

Teke's heart skipped a beat. It always did when

Grady's name came up. "Grady is my friend."

Jana snorted in disdain. "He's more than that."

Of course he was, but Teke hadn't let the kids see it. She might have thrown herself at him in private, but when the children were around, she was a model of decorum. "What are you suggesting?"

"Have you been to bed with him yet?"

"That's none of your business," Teke cried, then caught herself. "But you think it is, so I'll tell you. The answer is no," she said conclusively and not without pique. Grady's "plans", the ones he had alluded to on the night they had argued, consisted of tormenting her. He was around more than ever, being helpful and companionable and more appealing than any one man had a right to be, particularly when he had been deemed off-limits by the woman he turned on most.

"Then it's only a matter of time," Jana said. "You embarrass me."

Teke was insulted. She had been the model of decorum, where Grady was concerned. "*Why,* for God's sake?"

"Because you can't stand being in a bed alone. Daddy wasn't here, so you went with Sam—"

"*Not* in a bed!"

"—and now it's Grady. How low will you go?"

Teke bristled. "I should be so *lucky* as to end up with Grady. He's considerate and generous. He shoulders his own weight. He knows about hard knocks. He's paid his dues, and he's survived to become a productive member of society."

"He's a *carpenter,*" Jana sneered.

Furious, Teke raised a shaking finger in the vague direction of Cornelia Hart's home. "I wouldn't turn your nose up at that, young lady, until you've taken a look at what he's done." She tried to keep her voice even but failed. "He's making something beautiful of that carriage house, and it's only the latest of his jobs! You couldn't do what he does, but what he does will be around long after you and I are dead and gone!"

"I'll leave my mark on the world!"

"You do that!"

She watched Jana storm from the room, thinking that things had to get better. After all, Michael was starting to come around. So was Leigh. Two out of three wasn't bad.

Then came the day she took Leigh to see Charlie Hart. "Pills, I would think," she had told him on the phone. Once at the office, Leigh went inside while Teke sat calmly in the waiting room flipping through *Redbook*. Twenty minutes later, when she had begun to grow concerned thinking that in the course of his examination Charlie had found a lump or hint of some other disastrous disease, he appeared at the door and waved her in. Leigh was sitting on a chair looking pale as a ghost.

Sure that one of her imaginings was fact, she asked a frightened, "What's wrong?"

Charlie rocked back on his chair, steepled his fingers, and said with a sigh, "We have a slight problem when it comes to birth control. It's too late. Leigh's pregnant."

Pregnant. Teke's jaw dropped. *Pregnant.*

"From what we can figure, she's probably seven weeks along."

Pregnant? Teke hadn't imagined that one. She didn't know why. She supposed that if her daughter was old enough to have a lump in her breast, she was old enough to have a fertilized egg in her womb. Still, a fertilized egg meant a baby. Leigh was little more than a baby herself. No. That was wrong. She was seventeen. Nearly eighteen. And pregnant. *Oh, God.*

"I told you at Thanksgiving," Leigh said defensively. "I told you *then* that I needed birth control."

"That would have been too late," Charlie pointed out gently. "It probably happened the first or second time you were with Jon. You said that was right around the middle of November."

Pregnant. Teke couldn't believe it.

Leigh was still looking at her. "We held off as long as we could, but it didn't seem fair, finally. Everyone else was doing what *they* wanted."

There it was. Sam again. "It never ends, does it?" Teke asked in a high voice, fighting panic.

"I didn't do it on purpose, Mom."

"Didn't it occur to Jon to use anything?"

"He said we didn't have to worry about AIDS."

"But the *other*."

"He said he'd pull out. He did. Almost."

Teke sought help from the ceiling, but there were no answers written there. "Pregnant," she breathed, feeling suddenly weak.

"Maybe it just looks that way," Leigh told Charlie. "I don't see how I could be pregnant. I mean, I don't *feel* pregnant."

"You will," Charlie said. He was sitting with his forearms on the desk, the counselor now. "There are options," he told Teke. "Leigh and I have been discussing them. She can have the baby and keep it. She can have the baby and give it up for adoption. Or she can terminate the pregnancy. It's still early enough for that."

Teke pushed a swath of hair from her cheek to the top of her head. She couldn't consider options, not when her heart was thudding loudly enough to shake up everything in her head. How could she think of *options* when she couldn't believe Leigh was *pregnant?*

Stunned, she turned to the girl. "Did you know?"

"I don't know *now!* I haven't been sick or anything, I didn't think it could happen so soon, I had
no idea."

Bewildered, Teke sought comfort from Charlie.
"Should I have known? Should I have seen something?"

He shook his head. "There was nothing to see."

"She must have missed a period."

"She says she lost count over the holidays."

"Who's sorry about missing a period?" Leigh
asked, trying to explain it.

Are you now? Teke might have asked if Leigh
wasn't so clearly upset. If Teke was feeling like a
mass of loose bones ready to come apart any
minute, she imagined Leigh was feeling worse. Then
again, maybe not. Leigh didn't understand what having a baby meant. She didn't understand the responsibility, the worry, the time commitment, the
expense. She thought she had partaken of the ultimate in adult freedom by making love with Jon. She
didn't understand that the outcome would take that
freedom right away.

A baby. Leigh's baby. Leigh and Jon's baby.
Teke's grandchild. Sam and Annie's grandchild.
Annie. Teke wondered what *Annie* would say to do.

But Annie wasn't the one in Charlie Hart's office.
Teke tried to remain calm and somehow order her
thoughts. "I think we ought to take this one step at a
time."

They told Jon as soon as he got home from
school. He went every bit as pale as Leigh had been
when she had first learned. To his credit, he was
fast to take her hand and hold it tightly.

"We should have waited," Leigh whispered to
him.

"I should have used something," he whispered
back, "but I thought it'd be okay."

"I still think the doctor's wrong. I don't feel any different than I ever did."

"Leigh," Teke said, sighing, "you just did a home test. The stick turned blue. That's two strikes for pregnant."

Leigh looked up at Jon, and in a voice that was small and frightened, hardly that of a woman needing to make a momentous decision, she asked, "What do you want to do?"

He ran a hand through his hair. As he stared off at nothing, his eyes widened. Teke could practically see the thoughts coming to life in his mind, one after another, all with consequences for his future. "I don't know," he finally said, staring at Leigh's stomach now. He didn't touch it. He looked frightened and as premature a candidate for parenthood as Leigh.

He turned to Teke. "Mom would know. I want to ask her."

Annie, who hadn't even had the advance warning that the two had been making love, was speechless. Her eyes went from Teke to Leigh to Jon, then back to Teke. "Pregnant?" she mouthed.

Teke felt stronger just with Annie knowing. "Seven weeks, Charlie guessed. That means that if she carries to term, the baby will be born in mid-August."

Annie flattened a hand on her head. Her gaze flitted wildly around before landing on Jon. "You promised me you wouldn't!"

He shrugged. "It just happened."

"Leigh, *you* promised."

Leigh looked miserable. Taking pity on her, Teke said, "It's done. There's a baby growing. We have to decide what to do."

"I need Sam," Annie breathed unevenly.

Leigh caught Teke's hand. "Not Dad, though. Don't tell Dad."

Teke didn't see how she could keep something as important from him. No matter that J.D. had left them, he was still Leigh's father. "I have to. In good conscience, I do."

"He'll be furious!" Leigh wailed.

"At me," Teke said anxiously, and sure enough, that was his first reaction.

"God *damn* it, Teke, you were supposed to be on top of things like this. Why didn't you get the girl birth control *before* this happened?"

Teke refused to cower. "By the time I knew it was a problem, the harm was done."

J.D. turned on Jon. "And you couldn't use anything? You didn't have to tell anyone, didn't have to see a doctor, all you had to do was walk into a drugstore and buy a pack of condoms."

"I didn't think—"

"You're right about that!"

"It's a fait accompli," Sam said.

J.D.'s eyes flashed his way. "Uh-huh. One more coup for the Pope men. You set a fine example."

"Come off it, J.D. It's a miracle this didn't happen sooner. We all knew we were playing with fire, what with our families being so close. Hell, it's like they were half-married already."

"Well, they're not married, and she's pregnant. What are you going to do about it?"

They were gathered in the Popes' kitchen. Jana and Zoe were at the Maxwells' with Michael. Teke suspected they knew what was going on—they would have to know at some point—but she couldn't handle Jana just then. Handling J.D. was bad enough.

"*I* can't do anything," Sam was saying. For all his standing up to J.D., he sounded shaken. "It's not my decision to make. It's our decision. In the end, it's Leigh's." He turned to her and gentled his voice in a way that reminded Teke of what a special man he was. "What do you want to do, honey? Have you thought about it?"

"Every minute since I found out," Leigh cried.

So had Teke. She had gone through the options again and again. She had weighed one against the other, had followed each through.

Annie put an arm around Leigh and whispered, "It's scary"—Leigh nodded—"but exciting."

That was what Teke thought.

J.D. leveled a gaze at Sam. "I think she should abort it. I don't see any other way."

"There are other ways," Sam argued.

But J.D. gave the tiny shake of his head that said any greater shake of his head was a waste of effort, his point was so obvious. "She's seventeen years old. She still has to finish high school and then go to college. Sure, she can give the child up for adoption, but that would mean either walking around school through a progressing pregnancy or dropping out. In either case she'd be stigmatized."

"I don't want to give the baby up for adoption," Leigh told Jon. "I don't think I could bear knowing my baby was alive and not with me."

Teke agreed.

Annie nodded. "I agree."

"An abortion is simple and safe at this point," J.D. said. "It would be a quick procedure, Leigh. You would barely know you had it. Your life would go on just the way it would have if Jon hadn't lost his self-control."

"It's not his fault," Leigh said.

"Maybe she doesn't want an abortion," Sam put in.

"Does she want a *baby?*" J.D. retorted. "She's barely eighteen. She doesn't know where she wants to go to college or what she wants to do after."

"I want to marry Jon and have babies," Leigh said.

J.D. scowled at Teke. "Some example *you've* set."

Teke didn't answer. She didn't see the relevancy of it. She agreed with Sam, both that the pregnancy was a fait accompli and that the ultimate decision on what to do about the baby was Leigh's. They could try to guide her if they felt she was making a mistake, but first they had to know her thoughts. "There's nothing wrong with wanting to get married and have babies," Teke told her now.

"Women work in this day and age," J.D. barked. "Look at Annie."

"Don't look at Annie," Annie warned. "She's been thinking lately that she's done lots of things not so well. Teke's right. There's nothing wrong with wanting to get married and have babies. It's a question of the timing. That's all."

J.D. had his hands on his hips, pushing back his suit jacket. "Well, the timing here stinks."

"Not really," Teke told him. "Leigh could finish the school year, graduate in June, have the baby in August, and start college in September if she wanted."

"What do you want?" Sam asked Leigh, again in that gentle voice.

Jon was standing slightly behind Leigh, suddenly taller, Teke thought, and felt a tiny glimmer of hope. "I don't want Leigh to have an abortion," he told J.D., then looked at Sam. "She may have the final say, but it's my baby, too."

"Your baby," J.D. whined. "You're a baby yourself."

"If he were a baby," Sam pointed out, "Leigh wouldn't be pregnant. Go ahead, Jon."

"I want to keep the baby. Okay, so the timing may be wrong, but all we've been talking about for years is getting married. I knew Leigh wanted babies. That was part of the deal. I was going to support her while she raised our children."

"Support her *how?*" J.D. asked. "You don't even have a high school diploma."

"I will in June. I can finish college in three years, and when I'm not in school, I can work.

Teke was thinking that no eighteen-year-old should carry a burden like that, when Sam declared, "You're not working your way through school. We're not poor. We can support you and Leigh *and* a baby, if that's what you want."

For the first time J.D. looked doubtful. He frowned at Leigh. "Is that what you want?"

She nodded.

"Are you *sure?*"

"I want the baby. I want to marry Jon. I can go part-time to college and leave the baby at day care—"

"No, you won't," Teke said, because things had suddenly gelled. "You'll leave the baby with me. I love babies. Taking care of them is what I do best in the world. Once Michael is back at school, what better will I have to do with my time than caring for my own grandchild?"

Annie came to her with tears in her eyes. "Would you do that?"

"In a minute," Teke said, and found herself smiling. "It's really incredible when you think of it. All the times we joked about Leigh and Jon having Popewell kids—well, that time has come. They'll be the most beautiful kids in the world, don't you think?"

Annie hugged her hard and long. After Annie it was Leigh, then Jon. By the time Sam took his turn, they were all grinning, all but J.D. Quietly, while the others were talking, Teke went to his side.

"Be happy for them, J.D. It's what they need most."

"They don't know what they're getting into."

"Do they know any less than we did? And they have us, which is more than we had. If we're there to help, they'll do fine. They love each other. They really do. I'm envious." As she said it, she felt a twinge. She had loved J.D. once. Maybe not enough, but she had loved him. Looking at him now, she felt something still, though she guessed it related to a shared history, shared children, even to a fondness for his strong points, so easy to forget in the anger of parting.

He frowned. "This isn't how I imagined it would be. I wanted everything to be right for our kids."

"Who's to say this is wrong? It may not be happening exactly as we planned it, but if Leigh and Jon are happy, isn't that right?"

He studied her curiously. "You're surprisingly calm. I would have thought you'd be clinging to Annie in a tizzy."

That was what she would have done once, but she had lost the luxury of it the afternoon she'd opened her arms to Sam. "I can't cling to Annie the way I once did. I'm hoping we're friends again, I think we are, but I can't ask her to carry me emotionally the way she always did. I'm on my own more now. Maybe that's good, too."

"Maybe," J.D. said.

"For you, too?"

"Maybe," was all he said before he went to kiss his daughter good-bye.

Sam was sprawled on the den sofa that night, lost in unsettling thoughts, when Jon came to the door. "Where's Mom?"

"Upstairs."

The boy wandered in, looking lost and so young

that Sam felt another of the jolts he'd been feeling for hours. Hard to believe his son was going to be a father. His Jon. Little Jon, now six one and a man.

Jon stuck his hands in the back of his jeans. "Thanks for sticking by me today. You didn't have to." He shrugged. "What with the way I've been treating you and all."

The problems Sam had been brooding about—whether to stay in the firm or leave, and if so, where to go to maintain his family's standard of living with an extra two mouths to feed—fell into the background. Winning Jon back put the mechanics of living into perspective.

Jon darted him an uneasy glance. "I guess I fucked up even more than you did."

"Not my first choice of words, but, yeah, you fucked up. Did you do it to get back at me?" The timing had certainly been right.

"No. Yes. I guess, maybe. But I'd been wanting to be with Leigh for a while."

Sam remembered the endless hard-ons Annie had caused when they had first met. He could sympathize with Jon. "You should have used a condom and protected Leigh better than you did. But we all make mistakes. I'm not sure yours was worse than mine. We're getting a baby out of the deal."

Jon, so huge and invincible on the football field, looked suddenly pale and panicky. "Shit, I don't know anything about taking care of a baby."

"You'll learn."

"What if I can't study when the baby cries?"

"You'll go into another room and shut the door."

"What if the baby gets sick?"

"You'll take it to the doctor."

"What if I'm in the middle of finals and can't?"

"You will. Or Leigh will. Or Teke. Or Mom. Or me."

Jon ran a hand around the back of his neck. "I shake when I think about it."

"Imagine what Leigh's feeling. She's the one who'll be doing the work for the next seven and a half months. It'll be your job to give her moral support."

"How can I do that, if I'm scared to death?"

For a second, studying Jon, Sam wondered if they were making a mistake. He was young, maybe too young to be a father. "You can still reconsider—"

"No, I *want* the baby, it's just scary, that's all."

Sam pushed himself to his feet and put an arm around Jon. "You'll do fine. You love Leigh, and you'll love this baby. You'll grow into the role of father. And you won't be alone. We'll be right there to help you."

"Boy, did I fuck up."

"We all fuck up. What matters is what we do after the fact."

Jon shot him a tentative sideways glance. "Is that why you've been hanging around Mom so much?"

"I'm hanging around Mom because I like hanging around her, and I want her to know it."

"Is everything okay between you two now?"

Sam thought about that. Annie was warm and talking. They were sharing things again, for the most part. There were times when she still seemed wary of him, times when she got out of bed a little too fast after they made love, but they had come a long way. "We're getting there. We still have more to work out, but we're moving in the right direction." He invited teasingly, "You could put in a good word for me."

"Sure thing," Jon said, but he looked troubled.

Sam gave him a squeeze. "Spill it."

"It's dumb," Jon mumbled.

"Nothing's dumb if it worries you."

"I'm really new to this."

"Jon."

"Sex. Can we do it while she's pregnant?"

The squeeze Sam had given him seemed to boomerang right back to his own heart. Poor Jon. He really *was* new to this. "I ought to say you can't. You're only seventeen. But the fact is that there's no physical reason for abstinence, as long as Leigh is comfortable. Any more questions?"

"When do we get married? Where do we live? Will I be there when the baby's being born? What do I *do*—"

Sam stilled the barrage of questions with a bear hug. He smiled. "We'll take it one step at a time, okay?"

It took John Stewart three days to learn of Leigh's pregnancy and then one hour to summon Sam to his office.

"You've done it now," he charged the instant Sam walked in. "You've really done it." He slammed a hand against the window at which he was standing. "First Theodora, now Leigh. For God's sake, Sam, indiscriminate rutting must run in the family."

Sam had been anticipating a negative reaction. That didn't make it any easier to stomach. John Stewart looked uncharacteristically ruffled, but that was small solace for the fact that he was berating Sam and his son. "There was nothing indiscriminate about what Leigh and Jon did. They've loved each other for years."

"Didn't you teach him the facts of life? Didn't he have any idea he could make the girl pregnant?"

"He knew there was that possibility. Like most kids his age, he thought he could beat the odds."

"Well, he didn't," J.S. blustered, "and now we have an even greater embarrassment on our hands than your doing your thing with Theodora."

"I'm not embarrassed about Leigh and Jon," Sam said, raising his chin. "I'm proud."

"You would be. You don't understand the ramifications of these things."

"What ramifications? They'll get married, she'll have a baby, we'll have a grandchild, you'll have a great-grandchild."

"They're not getting married until May. *May.* She'll be blown up like a balloon. It's a disgrace."

"Leigh has always had her heart set on having a real wedding. Real weddings take time to plan."

"She'll look ridiculous."

"You won't even know she's pregnant. Fancy gowns hide a world of sins. She wants a wedding, and that's what we want her to have."

"At my son's expense."

"J.D. agreed to all this. Have you brought him in here and skewered him like you're skewering me?"

"He told me to mind my own business."

"Maybe you should."

"My friends will be sitting at that wedding, talking behind their hands. They'll all know the truth."

"Let them talk. All they are is a bunch of self-righteous hypocrites."

J.S. came away from the window with steel in his eyes. "Those self-righteous hypocrites are my friends and my clients. You've made me look like a fool in front of them. Well, I've had it. My association with you is through. Either you withdraw from this firm, or I will."

It was a new twist on the "I'll vote you out" theme. "Withdraw?" Sam asked cautiously.

"You won when it came to a vote. Each time I called for one, John David either walked out or missed the meeting. He's a coward."

"He's not being put in the middle, that's all."

"He should cast his vote with me, no questions asked. You ruined his marriage."

"No, J.S. I didn't ruin his marriage. Try again."

John Stewart drew himself to his full height. His features were as stiff as the starched collar of his shirt. "Withdraw. Resign from this partnership, or I will, and if I do, I'll take every one of my clients with me. This firm will fold."

"I doubt that," Sam said, but he was shaken. If J.S. meant what he said, a major change was imminent and unavoidable. J.S. claimed the firm would fold; Sam scrambled for counterarguments. "You aren't the only rainmaker around here. We all have our client lists."

"You and Will, maybe. As for Martin and J.D., with few exceptions, their clients originated with me. Those clients will follow me if I ask them to."

Sam didn't think they all would, but enough would to seriously wound the firm. John Stewart's threat wasn't empty by a long shot. "Would you do that to your own son, J.S., whip his practice out from under his feet?"

"If it meant freeing myself from you, I would," J.S. informed him. "Besides, he could always come with me. So could Martin. I suspect both would. That will leave you and Will here with a hefty four-year lease to complete."

Sam's thoughts raced. He knew that the lease would be a killer if the firm was suddenly pared down. Then again, since winning *Dunn* v. *Hanover,* his practice was thriving. But enough? There were no more six-million-dollar fees on the horizon.

Alternatively, he could leave Maxwell, Roper and Dine and open his own firm, but that would require a huge commitment of time, money, and thought. He would be spread more thinly than ever, with less time for Annie and the kids than he'd had before.

In the silence, J.S. grew smug. "I'd start making other plans if I were you. Join another firm. There are some that aren't as principled as we are. You'll find a place. It's either that or stay here and pick up the pieces once I've left."

Goaded by the man's arrogance, Sam shook his head in disgust. "Right now I can't begin to fathom why I ever wanted to be associated with as cold, hard, and heartless a bastard as you." He turned on his heel.

"Let me know your plans," J.S. called pleasantly.

Sam walked out the door without a backward glance. He strode down the hall, around the corner, and down the next hall to his office. Once inside, he went straight to the credenza and pulled out the application Joe Amarino had sent. Of all the possibilities, this was the one that piqued his interest. No matter how often he told himself that he wasn't ready to leave active practice and go on the bench, he couldn't shake the idea of a judgeship. It had its merits. Very definitely. All the more so with J.S.'s latest ultimatum.

He studied the application, then put it back in the credenza, only to take it out again a minute later. A judgeship might be nice. If he could get it. Which he would never know unless he applied.

No one had to know he was applying. Not even Annie. If he didn't pass the first round, no one would be any the wiser. It might be interesting, a judgeship. A new challenge. A chance to make his mark. Fair hours. Good benefits. Security. Respect.

Sinking down at the desk, he uncapped his fountain pen, then drew the application front and center and began writing.

J.D. was reading the newspaper in bed at ten o'clock on Saturday morning when his phone rang.

It was the doorman, announcing Virginia Clinger's presence in the lobby and asking permission to let her in. J.D. hadn't seen Virginia since the day she had popped into his father's office. He was as wary now as then. He had no idea what she wanted, had been rather enjoying lying in bed, being lazy, something new for him. He wasn't sure he wanted an intrusion, least of all one in the form of Virginia. She was an unwelcome reminder of Constance.

But he was curious.

Relaxing his shoulders, he slipped into a robe and opened the front door just as she emerged from the elevator wrapped in a fur parka. She gave him an admiring once-over and a brilliant smile.

"I wasn't sure I'd catch you at home," she purred. "Late night?"

"You could say that." He had rented the first three *Star Trek* movies and watched each one. It was four in the morning before he'd gone to bed.

She presented him with a neatly tied bakery box. "This is perfect, then. I brought goodies, kind of a housewarming gift. Can I come in?"

He stood aside and watched her sashay past. She shrugged out of the fur, revealing a winter white slacks outfit, and eyed him innocently. "Shall I make breakfast?"

"Why were you at my father's office that day?" he asked because it was foremost on his mind.

She didn't blink. "What day?"

"The one after Thanksgiving."

She smiled prettily. "To find out how *my* father was. John Stewart had seen him in Florida. Daddy tells me nothing over the phone. I was in Boston for another meeting, so I thought I'd stop by."

"Without knocking?"

"Mary told me to go right in."

J.D. supposed Mary might have done that, given

that Virginia was a close family friend. And Virginia had presented her story smoothly enough. Granted, she was normally trouble, but he was feeling mellow. He guessed he could take her word on as small a matter as this.

"Breakfast?" she prompted, raising the box.

"Sure." He pointed in the direction of the kitchen and followed her there.

"Great place," she said, looking around. "Are you enjoying it?"

"Uh-huh." More and more, he was. He knew just where everything was now, had mastered the mechanics of the dishwasher and disposal. He had found a maid he liked and a laundry he liked, had found local spots where he could take out great Italian, French, or American, had found plenty of restaurants to eat *in,* at his leisure and at peace. Some were off the beaten track, unusual for John David Maxwell, but refreshing.

Refreshing. It was something new, like being lazy.

Virginia had found a can of coffee and was setting up the coffeemaker. She kept darting him smug little glances. "You didn't think I could do this—don't deny it—I know you didn't. But I can. I'm not a total waste."

"I never said you were."

"People think it. Blondes are supposed to be ditsy. One who has had her nose done is positively hopeless." She finished with the coffee and struggled with the knot holding the pastry box shut.

J.D. came forward, took an easy grasp of the string, and snapped it in two. "Wouldn't want you chipping a nail," he teased, but good-naturedly. Virginia's nails were actually pretty. So were her hands. She added an element of softness to his kitchen. "You're looking good, Gin," he remarked, lounging against the wall with his arms folded on his chest.

"So are you." She took a plate from the cupboard

and opened the pastry box, but she paused to look at him. "You really do look good. I thought you'd be falling apart. But you look calm. Relaxed. I don't think I've ever seen your hair messed before. It's very appealing that way." While he soaked up the compliment, she turned back to the plate and began arranging the Danish. "I thought you'd be in a stew about Leigh. I was coming to console you."

He felt an inkling of unease. This was the Virginia he had expected, the woman who would do almost anything to find grist for the gossip mill.

"What about Leigh?"

"Isn't she pregnant?"

"Where did you hear that?" No one was supposed to know just yet."

"My kids. Leigh confided it to her best friend in the bathroom at school, not realizing that another girl was in a stall. Needless to say, word spread."

"Swell," J.D. grunted.

"It would have come out sooner or later."

"Better later. I don't want my daughter pointed at."

"She won't be," Virginia assured him, "not with Jon anywhere around. He's a school leader. People respect him. Besides, everyone knows they've been going together forever. It's not so bad, J.D."

One part of him wanted to shout at Teke again, or at Jon, or even at Leigh. The other, newer part wasn't sure what shouting would accomplish. He could get on his high horse like John Stewart and blast people for not being as perfect as he was—or he could cool it.

Being perfect wasn't all it was cracked up to be. There was something to be said for watching videos until four in the morning and lazing around in bed the next morning or answering the door in a bathrobe with his hair messed from sleep. There was something to be said for talking back to his father, which he was doing with greater frequency and increasing conviction. Maybe there was something to be said for Leigh and Jon getting married and having their baby.

"Yoo-hoo," Virginia sang, "anybody home?"

J.D. took a breath. "Things change. It takes some getting used to."

She wiped her hands on a napkin. "You really do look good. Better than I can ever remember." She approached him. "*Very* appealing."

"More so than the trainer at the health club?" he asked.

"Definitely." She looped her arms around his neck. "I always had a thing for you. You know that."

He saw the heat in her eyes. "Is that why you came?" He wondered if her underwear was lacy.

"Actually, no. Well, maybe it was in the back of my mind. I miss having you across the street." She planted a small kiss on his cheek.

"Virginia." He wasn't sure he wanted this.

She kissed him again, on the corner of his mouth this time. He was surprised when he felt a small tightening in his groin.

He breathed in her perfume. "You smell nice."

"That's my Obsession," she whispered.

"That bad?"

"Oooh, yes. What are you wearing under this?"

"Shorts." He still wasn't sure if he wanted what she had in mind, but between her scent and her softness, he was weakening. He didn't stop her when she slid her hands down from his neck, opening the robe as she went. When she reached his waist, she pushed the robe aside and looked at his chest, his legs, his shorts.

J.D. felt a deeper tightening. Her appreciation was a turn-on. He decided that what she had in mind might not be so bad after all.

"What would you do," she asked in another whisper, "if I took off my clothes? Would you call me names? Make me put them back on and leave? Have my father cut me off?"

J.D. considered the possibilities, but not for long. He was no eunuch. In a voice that had grown heavier, like his breathing and that part of him covered by his shorts, he said, "I'd do what you want. Good and hard. And I'd let you do it to me." He liked aggressive women.

Virginia stepped out of her shoes. She eased the slacks off her long, long legs and slipped off her sweater and underwear, which was all of one piece and lacy indeed. Before he could ask whether she really had screwed the trainer at the health club, she was naked, raising her arms, tugging a pin from her hair, spreading the thick blond stuff over her shoulders.

He looked his fill. Artificially molded or not, her body was enticing. His breathing grew more harsh. When he grabbed her wrist and gave a little tug, she came to him. He opened his mouth on hers in a hard, wet kiss, then shut his eyes, braced his head against the wall, and enjoyed the sensation of her tongue and teeth on his chest, his middle, his belly. She might have been any woman, but he didn't mind. While she knelt before him, he held handfuls of her hair and moved his hips to the rhythm of her mouth. Seconds before he came, he pushed her to the floor and slammed into her. Her cry of surprise was followed by one of pleasure, but that was all he heard. His own release drowned out all else.

Later, with Virginia dressed and his robe back on, they had coffee and Danish. The coffee was hot and strong, the Danish fresh and sweet. He was working on his second when he realized that she had stopped eating.

"It didn't mean much to you, did it?" she asked quietly.

"It meant the world. This Danish is great. You were sweet to bring a housewarming gift."

Her eyes narrowed. "What we *did* just now, J.D."

He started to take another bite of Danish. Thinking better of it, he set it down. He should have known she would say something. But, damn, he hated that question. It always came from the insecure ones and suggested that clinging would follow, which was all very flattering, but confining. "It was nice, Gin," he said, and sat back, "but do I want you here tonight? No."

Her eyes grew intense. "I could satisfy you again."

"I'm sure you could."

"Then why can't I stay?"

"Because I don't want you here."

"I can come back later."

"You can," he acknowledged indifferently, "but if you're doing it hoping that something permanent will develop, do yourself a favor and stay away."

"Because you're still married? For God's sake, J.D., Teke's been no saint. Look what she did with Sam. Look what she's doing with Grady Piper."

J.D. felt his nonchalance slip. Sam, he could take. He'd gotten used to that. The other bothered him more, on principle if nothing else. "What's she doing with Grady?"

"Three guesses."

He didn't have to take one. "Do you have any proof?"

"She sees him all the time. He 'helps' Michael, that's the excuse. But, look, I really don't care what Teke does. You shouldn't either. You've moved on, J.D. You're more than she'll ever be. And I'll take you married or not."

He scowled. "Don't say that, Gin."

"Why not? I go after what I want, and I want you."

"For the money?"

Her jaw flexed. "For the whole package."

"But the whole package isn't available."

"Then I'll take whatever part of it is."

He scowled. "Where's your pride?"

"It went the way of husband number two," she said, tipping up her chin. "So I don't mince words where something I want is involved, and you're it, J.D. You always have been. You turn me on, on more levels than one. I want you."

"Well, you can't have me," he informed her. "I like the way I'm living, and that means alone."

She looked perturbed. "But you're used to being with people. Don't you get lonely?"

"I see too many people to get lonely."

"Don't you get *horny?*"

"I have women. But I have them when I want, and only then."

"You're a selfish bastard," she muttered with scorn.

J.D. might have paid her displeasure more heed if he hadn't been taken up with self-discovery. "When I was growing up, there was always someone hovering over me. Then I went off to college and met Teke, and for nineteen years she's hovered over me. Now there's no one to hover. I can do what I want when I want. I might get tired of it in a month, but for the time being, I have to say I'm enjoying the freedom."

"I see," Virginia said, and rose from the stool on which she'd been perched. "It's a shame. We could help each other. We're good together."

J.D. thought of what they had done on the floor. Virginia was a good lover, but no better than Teke, and he didn't want Teke. What he wanted, he realized, was to play. His life had always been goal-oriented, its agenda based on order, purpose, and responsibility. Now he wanted to float. He wanted to do things he hadn't done, taste things he hadn't tasted, even break a few rules, just for kicks.

He was searching for his identity, he realized. It wasn't enough to be John Stewart's son or Teke's husband or Sam's friend. He wanted to be John David Maxwell. Strong, independent, self-reliant.

Moving out of the house had been one step in the right direction. Learning to function on his own had been another. There were still other, larger issues to be settled, but he was making progress.

eighteen

FEBRUARY ENVELOPED ANNIE IN THE NEW semester. As with the last, she was teaching three courses. The largest was a continuation of British literature, with mainly freshmen enrolled. The two others were advanced seminars for English majors and graduate students. One was a critical analysis of the works of T. S. Eliot, the other a study of Milton's *Paradise Lost*. She found a poignancy in the last. It seemed that she and everyone else in her immediate world had suffered falls from grace in recent months. Eden was a memory. There was a new, less perfect order to be handled.

Jon had slept with Leigh, largely out of defiance toward Sam, and now had a baby on the way. He was trying to stay calm and do what was right, but he was frightened. Annie suffered for him. He was her firstborn, the baby in whom she had taken such joy. She had wanted him to enjoy a carefree life before responsibility set in, but those years weren't to be. The fact that he loved Leigh was some solace for the fact that they would be parents at eighteen.

Teke had come through in a way that Annie

couldn't have asked of her, but in a way that made sense. Helping Jon and Leigh raise their baby would perhaps be her salvation. It would be the final absolution for what she had done with Sam.

And Sam? He had been changed by what he had done, had become a more thoughtful and sensitive man. Incredibly, Annie's love for him had grown—which was why she worried so that he would stray again.

She believed that he loved her. She believed that he was attracted to her. He told her the first and showed her the second every chance he got. Still, the hurt of what he had done with Teke lingered. Annie had forgiven him on the day she had nearly given herself to Jason, when the humanness of the act had hit home. But the humanness of it was precisely what haunted her. She feared Sam might be tempted again and she would be devastated. She had moments of doubt—and self-doubt—when she was convinced that his attentiveness toward her was solely for the sake of saving the marriage.

He was under pressure at work. A change was in order, but the right opportunity eluded him. She worried that the pressure might get to him, might drive him off in search of external approval.

And she still hadn't told him about Jason. She wanted to—she and Sam used to share everything—but she didn't know how he would react. The not knowing tormented her. Everything boiled down to trust, once so strong, now shakily seeking a foothold in their lives. She was frightened of losing him.

Sam had moments of looking back over the last few months and fearing that he had lost the stability in his life. He had lost J.D. He had lost Michael. He had lost—then found—Zoe and Jon, and as for Annie, he wasn't sure. He was doing everything in his power to show her how much he adored her, but it didn't seem to be enough. By normal standards their relationship was wonderful—but he had been spoiled. Normal standards didn't apply to Annie and him. Their relationship had always been a notch above. It was that last notch he couldn't seem to scale. A small part of her wasn't his yet. Once upon a time, she would lie with him as though nothing in the world were important enough to take her from his side. No more.

He knew that she was disillusioned with him, but he had never claimed to be perfect. And the situation at Maxwell, Roper and Dine was growing worse by the day.

Then he saw a ray of hope. An unexpected phone call sent him home early to wait anxiously, with a bottle of Annie's favorite wine on ice, for her return from school. She was no sooner in than he gave her a hug and popped the cork.

She swirled the wine in the glass, looking wary in an amused sort of way. "Is this a special occasion?"

"Might be," he said. His excitement was growing. He tried to temper it, knowing Annie might think the idea an awful one. "Back before Thanksgiving, one of the superior court judges died, leaving an opening on the bench. I read the obituary at the time, but didn't think anything of it. Several weeks later I started getting calls from Joe Amarino. Do you remember Joe?"

"Sure," she said curiously.

"He's legal counsel in the governor's office now. He suggested I fill out an application for the seat."

Her eyes grew round.

"I didn't hurry to do it," he went on quickly. "Then things got worse with J.S., and I said, What the hell, I have nothing to lose. So I filled out the application and had an interview with the judicial nominating committee, but I didn't expect anything to come of it, so I didn't mention it to you. I didn't want to let you down again." His excitement climbed another notch. "Then my name was one of three submitted to the governor, and still I refused to get my hopes up. But he picked me, Annie. He picked *me*."

Her mouth opened. "He did?"

Sam nodded. Not sure if she was pleased, he said, "It was a long shot. I'm the least political, and the youngest."

"We used to talk about it—"

"Dreaming. We used to think it would be nice if I could go on the bench when I was in my late fifties and ready to slow down. But I'm forty-one, I'm feeling great. Hell, I can't *afford* to be a judge, what with the college tuitions we have coming up and Jon and Leigh's baby, but, damn it, the idea has merit. The superior court is the one to be on. That's where the most exciting cases are tried. It would be a challenge."

She let out a breath. "This is *incredible,* Sam. What an honor!"

She did look pleased. His spirits soared. "Yes, it's an honor, but so are some of the other offers that have come my way." He had already told her about those. "I could go almost anywhere as a full partner, and they'd pay me big bucks. But I'd have to produce for those bucks," he reasoned aloud, "and that would mean long hours in a legal conglomerate. I could go into a smaller firm, but I haven't found one stable enough to take the chance on, so that leaves the possibility of going out on my own, which would be great for freedom. I could make my own hours, keep my overhead low, take home a greater percentage of the profit than I do now. But it would require a huge initial investment, both of time and money. I would need computer systems, telephone systems, furniture, a library. I'd have to use our savings to buy all that, which would put more pressure on me to maintain an adequate cash flow, which means that I'd be working even *longer* hours. I don't want to do that, Annie. I like being around when you are. I've gotten used to it." He paused. She had her hands clasped around her wineglass and was looking as expectant as he felt. "Well? What do you think?"

Her hands came unclasped and went around his neck. He felt the splashing of wine but deemed it unimportant the minute she said, "I think it's an unbelievable opportunity!" She tipped up a face that was alive with excitement. "Such an honor, and it's the perfect solution! You would be leaving the firm to do something new and better."

"Not better in every respect," he cautioned. "My income would go down. That's not so swell right now."

She didn't seem to care. "We have savings."

"What about the kids? More than anyone, you know how much college costs."

"I also know that there are scholarships available, and that our kids could do a whole lot worse than getting their education for free where I work. We could survive, Sam. Easily."

He wasn't as sure as she was, but her confidence made him heady. He hugged her close. "Think so?"

"Definitely. I'm so proud of you. What a *tribute* to you."

"It was the Dunn case that did it."

"It was your whole career that did it."

"But the hoopla surrounding the Dunn case made them take notice." He lowered his voice. "Good thing they only saw the public image."

She held him a moment longer, then drew back and studied her wine. "What you did with Teke has no relevance to whether or not you would make a good judge. You're a fine lawyer. You have the legal acuity and human compassion to be a fine judge." She eyed him cautiously. "Is the governor's choice final?"

"No. My name will be submitted to the governor's council, which then holds a confirmation hearing."

Quietly she asked, "How deeply would they look into your life?"

He understood her unsureness. "Deeply enough to learn if I've ever been picked up for driving drunk, not deeply enough to learn that I made a mistake with my wife's best friend. It shouldn't come out, Annie. I can't be certain, but it shouldn't." He had thought this through carefully. There was always a chance that someone with a grudge would leak the story about Teke and him. Then again, the council might consider it as irrelevant to his qualifications as Annie said it was. "If you're frightened, I'll withdraw my name with no regrets."

"But it's a once-in-a-lifetime opportunity."

"That doesn't mean it's the best thing for us. There's always the chance that ugly rumors will surface. If they do, I'll do what I can to stem them, but you may be hurt. That would defeat the purpose. The major plus of the job is to make our lives better, not worse."

"Sometimes you have to take a risk to make things better," she said. He had a feeling she was about to say more when Zoe came in the door. In a flash the doubt left Annie's face and a smile burst forth. "Guess what? Dad's been nominated for a judgeship! Isn't that *incredible?*"

* * *

John Stewart didn't think it was so incredible. He told J.D. as much in no uncertain terms. "That man lacks the moral temperament to be a judge. He'll never be confirmed."

"I wouldn't be so sure," J.D. said. He was feeling surprisingly calm in his father's presence. Moreover, he was feeling surprisingly pleased for Sam. Their recent differences notwithstanding, Sam had worked his tail off to prove himself a good lawyer. It was nice that he was being recognized. "He'll make a hell of a lot better judge than half the old coots on the bench now."

"Honestly, John David, why must you make comments like that? They only show how ignorant you are. Those 'old coots' are respected men who have served the commonwealth for years."

J.D. grinned. "Give him forty years, and Sam will be one of them."

"Over my dead body. Sam Pope doesn't deserve a judgeship. I can guarantee you I'll be saying that—and why—to everyone I know on the governor's council. I carry clout in this town."

J.D. stopped grinning. His stomach felt sour, and it wasn't the old familiar heebie-jeebies that his father usually caused. It was something different. It tasted like disgust. "What's the point of that? You've already made life unbearable for Sam here. Isn't it enough that you won't have to see him? Don't you realize that he's going to be your great-grandchild's grandfather? Wouldn't it be nice for that child if his grandfather was a judge?"

"It would, if it were anyone but Sam Pope. He could do that child a favor by sinking into oblivion."

J.D. understood John Stewart's dislike of Sam, but the extent of it—the active sabotaging of Sam's career—seemed suddenly overblown. "Why do you hate him so?" he asked.

"He has no sense of morals."

Puzzled, J.D. shook his head. "There has to be something else."

"He has a control over you that I resent. Had it not been for him, you would have married someone far more suitable. But he introduced you to Theodora, so Theodora it was. Listen to you now. You would never be talking back to me if it weren't for Sam's influence."

J.D. couldn't argue with that. "But there's more. You're obsessed with orchestrating his downfall. Was there some argument that you two had that I never knew about? Did he insult you? Did he let down one of your clients or blow a fee or sabotage some crucial negotiation?"

John Stewart actually looked pensive, but only for a minute. He opened a side drawer, withdrew a small framed photograph, and set it on the desk. J.D. had seen it before. An identical copy, right down to the scrolled silver frame, stood among the family pictures in his father's study at home. It was fuzzy and old, a photo of John Stewart as a small child, wearing something that looked like a skirt, holding the hand of a child who was larger and older.

"I idolized my brother," John Stewart declared. "I thought the world revolved around him. I thought it even when he got older and started stealing things from the local five-and-dime. He was spirited. He was clever. He was brave. Did I ever tell you how he died?"

"You said he fell out of a tree."

"That's right. Another boy dared him to climb up high in one tree and jump to another to show just how brave he really was. Henry didn't have a chance. Even if he had reached the other tree, the odds of his catching hold were poor. But he had an audience, and he was a performer, so he took the risk."

J.D. was startled. In the next breath he felt a premonition.

"The first time I met Sam Pope," J.S. said, looking him in the eye without wavering, "I thought of Henry. Sam had the same irreverence, the same dare-the-devil look to him. When I first saw him in court, he was a prosecutor, performing before a jury, taking risks just like Henry would have. He scared the wits out of me."

"Yet you let me bring him into the firm."

"I admired him for that daring, just as I admired Henry. Channeled properly, daring can be a powerful asset. I had been too young to help Henry, but I thought I might be able to help Sam. I thought I might be able to tone him down. I thought that I might keep him in line. Clearly I failed."

J.D. was appalled. "Then you're punishing Sam for being like Henry?"

"No," John Stewart corrected. "I *rewarded* Sam for being like Henry. Now that I've realized my mistake, I'm remedying it."

"But what has Sam done that's so *terrible?* He hasn't destroyed anyone's life."

"He destroyed your marriage."

"Teke and I did that all by ourselves." She had been right about that. "You're using Sam as a scapegoat."

"Your opinion isn't about to sway me, John David. I gave Sam a forum in which to build a private practice. He used it, then abused it, as far as I'm concerned. I will not have him becoming a judge based on a reputation that I was largely responsible in building."

J.D. remembered lashing out at Sam using similar arguments a while back. They had sounded fine to him then. Coming from John Stewart's mouth, they sounded wrong. "Sam built his reputation himself. It was his hard work, his brains, his daring, that won case after case for him."

"No matter. He won't be a judge. You have my word on that."

"Fine," J.D. said, squaring his shoulders and drawing himself up so that the slight difference in height between him and his father suddenly shrank. "You have my word on something, too. If you use your clout to nix Sam's appointment, I'll tell Mother about Mary."

"What about Mary?" John Stewart asked blandly.

J.D. had to give him points for gall. "I think you know," he said, and turned to leave. The silence that accompanied him out of the office gave proof to his words. After forty-one years J.D. had finally found his father's vulnerability.

Teke sat on a stool in the shadows of a narrow building half-hidden in Cornelia Hart's woods. Once the building had been used as a work shed, housing gardening equipment and the like. Now it smelled of wood shavings. Cornelia had loaned it to Grady, who was building a canoe there. Michael, who insisted on wearing Grady's battered baseball hat with the visor shading his nape, was his apprentice.

No other form of physical therapy had interested the boy as this did. From her shadowed corner, Teke could see his concentration. She could also see the improvement in his flexibility as he took each steamed cedar rib from Grady, clamped it to a gunwale, then stretched it over the form to where Grady was waiting. Michael had taken his turn with the sander, the hammer, the band saw that tapered the ribs. He used his hands, arms, and torso. He also used his legs, with crutches at first, then without when they got in his way. With only Grady and Teke to see, he wasn't self-conscious about the awkwardness of his gait. Teke wondered if he realized how less awkward that gait was becoming from one day to the next.

Grady was wonderful with him. He was infinitely patient, infinitely encouraging, infinitely forgiving of mistakes. Watching them together, Teke couldn't help but think that they should have been father and son. Grady had so much to give, Michael was so eager to receive, and vice versa. More than anyone, Grady had helped Michael through his self-pity. With promises to take him into his special "deep nowhere" in the canoe they were building, he had Michael working harder to walk. Grady was the perfect teacher. He didn't believe in giving up. He had been at rock bottom himself but had clawed his way back.

Watching from the shadows, Teke had fallen in love with the man ten times over. Denying it would be foolish. Indeed, as she watched, she had to struggle to recall her anger. The far past was gone; the immediate present was as pleasurable as Teke could want it.

That was why her first reaction was annoyance when J.D. came in from the cold. She resented the intrusion. She didn't want him disturbing the little paradise she and her men had here in the woods.

Her annoyance gave way to wariness. She wondered how he had found them and what he wanted. He looked civil enough. He hadn't come through the door yelling. She took encouragement from that.

Michael, who had been painstakingly hammering a strip of planking to the ribs beneath, looked up in surprise. "Dad! What are you doing here?"

"Looking for you," J.D. said. "Cornelia gave me

directions." He looked formal and out of place in his suit and topcoat. Calmly he walked toward Michael.

Teke envisioned his topcoat—a navy cashmere—covered with sawdust. She nearly warned him away, then held her tongue.

"What are you doing?" he asked Michael.

"We're making a canoe. This is white ash"—the boy touched a gunwale, then a rib—"this is white cedar, and this is red cedar," he finished, pointing to the plank he had been hammering. "When the whole thing's done, we cover it with canvas. Isn't it awesome?"

"Not bad." J.D. found Teke in the shadows. "Is this a new kind of trade school?"

"It's physical therapy," she said. "It supplements what he does at the health club."

"Have we given up on the eighth grade entirely?"

"I go to the tutor after this," Michael said in a way that suggested he heard what Teke did, a criticism beneath the calm.

"I thought you were going to start attending afternoon classes?"

"I still can't do the stairs."

He could do them, Teke knew, but he didn't do them well, and he refused to do them in front of his friends. For that reason his return to school was being delayed.

"So you're building canoes," J.D. said, nodding.

Teke heard his derision. Michael must have, too, given the speed of his response.

"Just one. When it's done, Grady and I are putting it in the water." He stopped suddenly, as though he regretted mentioning it, and sent Grady an uneasy glance.

Grady, who had been hammering on the far side of the canoe when J.D. had walked in, was standing straight and tall with the hammer idle in his hand.

425

J.D. stared at him, but it was to Michael he spoke. "You and Grady have become friends. That's surprising, given that he was the one who ran you down."

"I ran into him," Michael said. "Besides, he's been helping me do things. He's as good as my therapist, without the big bill."

"He does what he does out of guilt," J.D. suggested.

Grady stirred. "Not true. I do what I do because I like the boy."

"You know that he murdered a man," J.D. continued, talking to Michael, looking at Grady.

"I know."

"Do you know who that man was?"

Teke came off her stool. "J.D."

"His name was Homer Peasely," J.D. told Michael, whose eyes widened in surprise. "He was your mother's father. He would have been your grandfather had he lived, but your friend Grady hit him in the head, then kicked him until he was dead."

"Not true," Grady vowed, but J.D. went on.

"He murdered your grandfather, Michael, the grandfather you never had a chance to meet. Then he came to town to see your mother—another man's wife—and he was so wild-eyed and excited about it that he didn't see you running toward the street. He's a murdered and a would-be murderer. That's the kind of man Grady Piper is."

"Homer Peasely?" Michael echoed, facing Teke. "Why didn't you tell me?"

"It wasn't relevant."

"Not relevant?" J.D. barked her way. "He was your father!"

"He wasn't a good man."

"He was a human being. He had a right to live."

"It was an accident," Grady said. "The jury decided that."

"But they sent you away, because they felt you were a danger to society. Well, I say you still are. Look what you've done! First you put my child in the hospital, unable to walk, then you steal my wife out from under my nose. Was that what you had in mind all along? Was that why you came down here from your hole up in Maine?"

Teke didn't know which upset her more, the disparaging of Grady in Michael's eyes or the insult to Grady himself. "You are very, very wrong," Teke told him, leaving the shadows. "Grady came here for no other reason than to make sure I was all right."

"Is that why he stayed? Don't peg me for being blind, Teke. He's in love with you. My guess is he'll snap you up the minute we're divorced."

Michael swayed. Bracing himself on the canoe, he looked uncertainly from one face to the next. Teke started toward him.

"Your father is mistaken," she said. "Grady came here to visit. He stayed when you were hurt. Now he's staying to finish a job."

"And to be with you? Is it true? Are you and Dad getting divorced?"

She put an arm around his shoulder, desperate to keep him close. She had worked so hard, *so hard,* to win back his trust. "We may, but nothing formal has been done."

"She's already seen a lawyer," J.D. said. "She didn't have the guts to tell me. I had to hear it through the grapevine."

Michael pulled away.

"What grapevine?" Teke asked, incensed. She had met with her lawyer in confidence.

Before J.D. could answer, Michael shouted at her, "You didn't tell me about that, or about who Grady killed. What else didn't you tell me?"

"A good deal," J.D. said.

"No," Teke began, but, throwing the old Angels hat to the floor, Michael was on his way to the door at a half walk, half run made more ungainly by his upset.

"Where are you going?" Grady called, rounding the canoe and starting for the door.

"Michael! ..." Teke yelled.

"He's getting away from the two of you," J.D. said, barring the door and their pursuit of Michael. "I should have known not to leave the boy's rehabilitation in my wife's hands. I should have realized how untrustworthy she was after what she did with my best friend. When she needs a man, she picks the closest, easiest one. So now she has my son spending hours"—he spit out the words as if they were dirt—"with an uneducated, unprincipled ex-convict."

Teke, who was terrified that Michael might slip on a patch of ice, begged, "Please, J.D."

Grady was less polite. "Get out of my way," he commanded in a voice that vibrated with anger.

Teke's terror shifted focus. She hadn't heard that tone from Grady since the day he'd said to Homer, "Get your goddamned hands off her."

"It's okay, Grady. Let me handle it." She put a restraining hand on his arm and found the muscles beneath taut with a fury barely contained. "He takes delight in hurting people with words, but they're empty words."

"I mean every one," J.D. said, staring at Grady with a nasty gleam in his eye. "I think you're scum. I have from the start."

"You need someone to blame," Teke began.

"Scum of the worst order."

"Get out of my way," Grady repeated. His face had grown darker.

"Ignore him, Grady," Teke said, and tried to slip

in front of him, between the two men, but Grady wouldn't allow it. Tugging at his arm, fighting panic, she tried with J.D. again. "This is absurd. Why don't we accept that you just don't like the man—"

"I *hate* the man," J.D. said, glaring at Grady. "I want him out of town. He is a bad influence on my son—"

"He's my son, too."

"—and a bad influence on my wife—"

"You *left* me."

"—and an all-around, no-good thug. Got that, Piper?"

Grady's eyes broadcast danger. "Get out of my way," he repeated a third time.

J.D. drew himself to his full height. "Make me."

"He's trying to goad you, Grady," Teke cried.

"Move," Grady said.

"He's trying to get you to hit him," she wailed. "Once, that's all, and he'll charge you with assault." She was horribly aware of the hammer in Grady's hand, the opening and closing of his fingers around its head. "Don't you see? He hasn't been able to get anything else on you. This is his last shot. He's desperate."

The air in the narrow shed seemed suspended for the eternity it took for the truth of Teke's words to gel. Grady took an audibly shaky breath. His hand closed firmly around the hammer's head. Lowering it to his side, he looked at her at last. His eyes said that he knew, that he had learned his lesson, that he wouldn't do anything stupid. They also said that he loved her and would have happily hit J.D. if his goading had taken the form of injury to her.

Slowly, in control, he faced J.D. In a low voice he said, "Michael is out in the cold. He may be in the carriage house or in the car. Or he may be in the woods. He could fall, or freeze. If you don't have the good sense to go after him, just move so I can."

Teke had never loved Grady as much as she did at that moment.

J.D. simply stared at him. After several seconds his stare grew dazed. He frowned, turned around, and stared at the closed door. Finally he opened it.

Michael wasn't in the carriage house. He wasn't in Teke's car, J.D.'s car, or Grady's pickup. As the three stared off into the woods, breathing in rapid white spurts, J.D. groaned. "He could be anywhere in there."

"I know where he is," Grady said, and carrying Michael's jacket. He led them along a narrow path that twisted and turned through the woods until the growth of thick-clad pines and naked birches opened onto a stream that barely trickled through the snow. Michael sat on a tree stump at its edge.

Teke stopped. J.D. stopped behind her. Grady covered the few remaining feet, draped Michael's jacket over his shoulders, and squatted by his side. In the winter stillness of the woods, his words came back crystal clear to Teke.

"If I was wrong in not telling you who I killed, it was only because I didn't want you upset. I didn't think you'd understand. Some people don't. Murder is a terrible crime. I'm the first one to say it. I'm also the first one to say I'd never have raised a finger against the man if I hadn't thought your mom was in danger. Homer was hitting her and threatening to do worse. When he wouldn't let go of her, I hit him. He did let go then. He fell to the floor and banged his head. That was what killed him, coroner said."

Teke remembered the sound of Homer's head hitting the floor. It had been a bloodcurdling *thwack*. She pressed a fist to her mouth.

"Did you kick him?" came Michael's muted voice.

"Yeah. I was angry. I wanted him to get up and

fight me. I'd been holding my temper, warning him to keep his hands off her for so long that I just lost it. But he wouldn't get up. I kept yelling for him to, but he wouldn't. That's when I knew he was gone."

Michael huddled into his jacket.

Grady said, "I worried a whole lot about your mom when I was in prison. I told myself not to, 'cause I didn't have any more claim on her, but I wanted her to be okay. I found out she got married. I found out she had children."

"How?" Michael asked.

"I was working for people who knew other people. There was always someone who could dig up something for me. I came back here in October just to see her and talk with her. I didn't have anything else in mind, so help me. I told you before—if I could've stopped that truck before you ran out, I'd have done it. The last thing I wanted was to hurt a child of Teke's."

Teke fought back tears. For the first time, Grady's pain registered, really registered, and it wasn't the pain of the moment, but the pain he had experienced through all the years they had been apart. It struck her that she'd had the easy end of the deal— just as he had intended. She had been a fool for not seeing it sooner!

The tears came in a slow, steady trickle down her cheeks as Michael asked Grady, "Why are you staying here? Is it guilt?"

"If it was that, I'd have walked away the day you woke up from that coma when I knew you'd be okay. Lord knew no one was rolling out the welcome mat for me here. But your mom was in an awful state, and you were, too, and then I started liking you. You made me feel good, like I was worth something." He hesitated. His voice dropped. "And then there was your mom."

"What about her?"

"Your dad's right. I love her. I've loved her since I was twelve, and I'll love her 'til the day I die, but I wouldn't take her from your dad. Not unless she wanted to go. I don't have much to offer. But I'd protect her and be good to her and love her forever."

Teke caught her breath. She couldn't ask any more from a man. Neither Grady nor she could control fate, and if fate tore them apart again, she might die. But the risk was worth it, just to have his love. Her happiness depended on it.

Running over the snow, she wrapped an arm around each neck, crying first against Grady's cheek, then into Michael's hair. When she could finally speak she whispered, "You both are so special to me. I could have spent the rest of my life sitting back in that shed, watching you work. I need Grady to love me, Michael. I need him to love me in spite of my flaws, and he knows them all. I need you to love me the same way. Will you?"

She held her breath, waiting.

At last, in a voice that was more low than high and beautiful to her in its wry acceptance, he said, "Not exactly the same way, Mom. That'd be pretty gross, don't you think?"

She laughed, hugged him harder, turned her head, and kissed Grady's cheek. Only then, catching a look at the woods over Grady's shoulder, did she realize that J.D. was gone.

J.D. drove aimlessly for a while, first through the streets of Constance, then through Boston. He felt lost and without purpose. When he tried to call on arrogance to lift his spirits, it eluded him. He didn't understand how someone as insignificant as Grady

Piper could have made him feel so humble, but that was what had happened. The man clearly cared for Michael, and he did love Teke. J.D. was irrelevant to their lives.

That bothered him. He didn't want to be irrelevant. To *anyone's* life.

Desperate to ground himself, he headed for the office. His clients needed him even if Teke didn't. His clients looked up to him even if Michael didn't. And his clients paid him. What could be better?

He had barely left the elevator and pushed through the doors of the firm when, for no apparent reason, an image of Virginia Clnger flashed through his brain. It stayed with him all the way down the hall to his office. Not until he had stepped inside, and the image faded, did he understand. Stepping back into the hall, he sniffed. Her perfume was faint but distinct. Either another woman wearing Obsession had walked down that very hall not long before, or Virginia was somewhere in the firm.

He thought of her popping in to see his father unannounced and backing out in embarrassment. He thought of her bringing him a housewarming gift and ending up scorned. He though of four husbands, an appetite for spending, a penchant for gossip, and a nose for trouble.

And he thought about Sam's confirmation hearings and John Stewart's threat.

Without pause he set off down the hall toward his father's office. The door was closed. He threw it open to find John Stewart sitting back in his chair with his hands folded over his middle in a self-satisfied pose and Virginia perched on corner of his desk, her long legs crossed gracefully at the knee.

With the sudden intrusion, John Stewart came forward and Virginia straightened.

"Well, well," J.D. said, "what have we here? A nice family friends visit? Or something more pointed?"

"Haven't you got the good grace to knock?" John Stewart barked.

J.D. hitched his chin toward Virginia. "Did she?"

"Hello, J.D.," Virginia said defiantly. "How have you been?"

"Now that you ask"—he was unable to resist—"I haven't been the same since our little encounter at my place. It wasn't bad. Not bad at all. You're a talented lady." He looked at his father. "Has she given you a taste, or is she just flaunting it in the hope you'll be satisfied just to look?"

"You have a filthy mind," said John Stewart. "Is there something special you want?"

"Yeah," J.D. declared, slipping an arm around Virginia. "Her." He'd be damned if *he'd* be irrelevant. He could play the game, too. "What's happening, Gin?" he asked warmly.

Virginia studied him for a minute before curving her spine to his arm. "Not much," she answered. Her gaze fell to his mouth.

More softly he said, "You never came back. You said you would."

"I didn't think I was wanted."

"I could smell your perfume all the way down the hall just now. It brought back pleasant memories." Even more intimately he said, "I missed you."

Her eyes brightened. "Did you?"

John Stewart cleared his throat. "Should we meet later, Virginia?"

Still looking at J.D., Virginia arched a questioning brow.

J.D. spoke to her in the same intimate tone. "I could go back to my office and wait. Is this something important?"

"We were just talking about Sam."

John Stewart came out of his chair. "It was nothing urgent. We'll talk another time."

"About his nomination?" J.D. asked Virginia, still softly.

She nodded. "We were wondering if the governor's council knows what Sam did to your wife. J.S. was saying—"

"Another time," John Stewart ordered, but she wasn't listening. Her eyes were glued to J.D., whose face was inches above hers.

"J.S. thought that maybe I should make a call. I mean, I'm the one who saw them together that day, and it would be just one phone call."

J.D. had figured as much. His father was dead set on preventing Sam's appointment, but what his father apparently hadn't yet accepted, in spite of J.D.'s earlier threat, was that J.D. had become a force to contend with.

"I thought we had an agreement on that," he said, looking at John Stewart at last.

"*I'm* not making any phone call," John Stewart declared, tapping innocent fingertips to his chest.

"No. You're having Virginia do your dirty work."

"She won't do anything she doesn't want to do."

"You're right about that," J.D. said. His father's days of total control were over. John Stewart wouldn't block Sam's confirmation if J.D. had any say in it. J.D. wasn't irrelevant *at all.* "I doubt she'll want to made a call, once she and I talk." He put a gentle kiss on Virginia's perfect nose. If need be, he would put gentle kisses on every other part of Virginia's perfect body until Sam's confirmation came through, if that would keep her quiet. "Wanna go back to my office?" he asked, letting his eyes roam her face. It wouldn't be such a difficult task. Physically she was easy to take. And he was lonely. And horny. And damned if his father would get away with his bulldozing this time around.

Virginia slipped off the desk. "That's my girl," J.D. said with his most winsome smile. With a wink for John Stewart, he guided Virginia out and away.

nineteen

SAM'S CONFIRMATION HEARING BEFORE THE governor's council was scheduled for four in the afternoon. Annie planned to be in the chamber for the hearing and had arranged to have Jason teach the class she would miss. It wasn't until she stopped for a late lunch in the coffee shop that she realized she hadn't seen him all day. Back in her office, she phoned his apartment, then hung up when the answering machine came on. She wasn't worried. He had never let her down.

Shortly before she was to leave to meet Sam, she received a call from the chairman of the department. "We have something of a crisis on our hands," he said. "Could you come to my office, please?"

She glanced at her watch, calculated she had ten minutes to spare, gathered up her things, and trotted up the stairs to see Charles Honnemann. His office was large and high-ceilinged, with faded Oriental rugs on the floor and cracked oils on the walls. Charles was at his desk, looking grim. On a side chair sat Georgia Nichols.

Annie didn't sit. She couldn't stay long. She wanted to be on her way to meet Sam. The hearing was crucial. She was nervous on his behalf.

Then Charles gave her news that momentarily drove all that from mind. "Jason Faust is in the hospital," he said. "Georgia found him unconscious in his apartment this morning. He's in a coma."

Annie was stunned. "A coma? What *happened?*"

"He took an overdose of drugs."

"Oh, God."

"He's at the Deaconess. The doctors are trying to stabilize him. Did you know about his being unhappy?"

She swallowed. An overdose. There was the issue of money, but he hadn't struck her as being depressed. "I knew there was a problem at home." She wasn't sure how much to say. Jason had confided in her.

"Not at home," Charles said. "Here."

The sharpness of his tone puzzled her. "He was pushing to finish his degree work by June," she offered. "He wanted to be teaching here in the fall." She cast a glance at Georgia, who looked awkward. "Is there something I don't know?"

Charles sighed. "I think you know, but aren't saying."

"I don't follow."

"It appears," he said gravely, "that Jason may have tried to commit suicide because he was in love with you, and the love wasn't returned. Were you aware of his feelings?"

Annie was appalled. She thought back to that day in her office, but it was months ago now. She couldn't *believe* this was related to that. "I was aware that he liked me. He used to tell me so all the time."

"Did you ever tell him back?"

"Of course. I do like him. I respect him. We're friends." To Georgia she said, "Did you speak with the doctors?"

"Just the admitting one," she answered, sounding

as uncomfortable as she looked. "He couldn't tell me much."

"Were you aware of his using drugs?" Annie asked her.

"No."

"Were you?" Charles asked Annie.

"Never." She remembered his offering her pot, but she wasn't telling the chairman that. She had no evidence that he had it or used it.

"Georgia says he talked of having an affair with you."

Annie caught in her breath. "No. Never." She felt justified in the denial. There had been one near consummation, then nothing.

"Why would he talk of it, if it wasn't so?"

"Because that is what cocky young men do sometimes. Charles, I don't understand why you have me here, now, like this." She resented Georgia's presence. If Charles had a bone to pick with her, she felt that her position on the faculty gave her the right to a private meeting.

"Since Georgia is the one making the accusation," Charles said, "I thought she ought to be here to face you."

"Her accusation is unfounded." Annie glanced at her watch. "If you don't mind, I'd like to go to my office, call the hospital, and see if I can get word on Jason, then head to Boston. I have an important meeting there." It occurred to that her class would have to be canceled.

Charles shook his head. To Georgia he said, "Why don't you run along while I talk with Dr. Pope."

Georgia was gone in a flash.

"Charles," Annie warned.

"I'm not happy," he said, staring out at her from under sparse gray brows. "I asked you once before if anything was going on between you and Faust. You said there wasn't."

439

Barbara Delinsky

"There *wasn't.*"

"But it all makes sense. Everyone knows how close you two are. We've seen you head to head in the dining room, in the lounge, in class. The entire department saw you with him at the Christmas party. I tried to warn you then."

"I wasn't *with* him. I was *talking* with him. I like him. He's a friend. And I'm married—happily—to a man who is going to be waiting on the courthouse steps for me if I don't leave here within five minutes. You would be wiser to focus on how Jason is doing than to dream up liaisons between him and me. There was absolutely nothing going on."

"Perhaps you gave him the impression there might be, then let him down."

Annie bristled. "Why are you trying to make something out of nothing?"

"I don't like unexplained suicides."

"He isn't dead yet," Annie said, and let out a breath. She wanted to call the hospital. Then she wanted to be with Sam. "I have to leave," she said, feeling the urgency of it.

Charles scratched the top of his head. "I'm thinking that you ought to consider taking a leave of absence."

Her heart skipped a beat. *"What?"*

"A leave of absence."

She glanced around in bewilderment. It seemed that a tiny germ of rumor had exploded into havoc. "This is *absurd.*"

"I won't have a scandal in my department. God only knows we have trouble enough getting grants nowadays, but a professor-student liaison en route to a suicide will not help the cause. If you very quietly remove yourself from the scene, things may remain quiet."

"Where is this *coming* from?" she cried. "I thought you liked me."

440

"I like this department more."

She stood before him, disappointed and unnerved. She wanted to be on her way but suddenly saw that she couldn't be. Whether there was merit to it or not, a scandal might ruin her career. It might—she nearly died at the thought—hurt Sam's career. She had to hear Charles out. She had to get to the hospital and pray that Jason would wake up and tell the truth.

"May I use your phone?" she asked in a shaky voice. At Charles's nod, she called Sam's office. The instant she heard his voice, she said, "I have a problem here at school. You'd better go on to the hearing without me." She tried to sound calm but failed dismally. She knew it the instant she heard his concern.

"What's wrong?"

"A tough problem."

"Tell me, Annie."

The last thing Sam needed was this, just before his hearing. But she was frightened enough, selfish enough, desperate enough for support, to tell him. "Jason Faust was found unconscious this morning. He's in a coma. They suspect an overdose of drugs."

"Annie, I'm sorry."

"The problem," she hurried on, angry now, too, "is that Charles Honnemann, in whose office I stand as we speak, is suggesting that I'm the cause of Jason's suicide attempt. He suggests that I either had an affair with Jason or led him on to the extent that he was so lovesick that he tried to kill himself."

"That's absurd!" Sam said.

"Charles would like me to take a leave of absence to let whatever happened quietly blow over."

"That's ridiculous!"

His vehemence made her wonder how she had ever doubted his loyalty. Shaking inside, she said,

"That's what I say, but Charles doesn't agree. I have to stay here and work it out with him. My career is at stake. So is yours."

"But he has no proof! This is all speculation and will be so until the boy can speak for himself!"

"I know," she said less calmly, because Sam sounded upset, which was the last thing he needed before his hearing.

"Stay there," he ordered. "I'm coming."

She gasped. "You can't do that. Your hearing is in little more than an hour. You can't possibly get here and back in time."

"I'll postpone it."

"But you can't! It's too important, Sam!"

"This is more important."

"No, no"—-she looked straight at Charles—"it's just a stupid rumor that people with idle minds and inadequate sex lives have bandied about." She was livid. "You can't miss that hearing."

"Is Honnemann there?"

"Uh-huh."

"Put him on."

"Sam—"

"Put him on."

Annie passed the phone to Charles. His expression was stony during the short time Sam talked. When he hung up the phone he said, "Your husband insists on coming here. He says that we are to stay in this building until he arrives. He says that my accusations border on libel and that he will have no qualms in suing me and the college if your career is unnecessarily besmirched."

But the confirmation hearing, Annie thought, and turned away. She went to the farthest corner of the room from Charles's desk and sank onto a chair. It was a straight chair with a high back, baldly uncomfortable, as befitted Annie's mood. She wished Sam weren't coming. They both wanted that judgeship for him. Postponing the hearing, particularly on such late notice, might be a mark against him. His risking that for her made mockery of those last few lingering doubts she'd had.

She sat in humble silence for a while. Then she suddenly came to life and jumped up. She crossed the room, picked up the phone, and called the hospital. Patient information told her nothing. When she tried to connect with a doctor, she was put on hold, where she sat for ten minutes before hanging up the phone.

"I honestly didn't see signs of depression," she said aloud, because that was what she had been brooding about during those ten minutes. She thought herself fairly observant. She had seen signs that Zoe had been unhappy; her running off to Papa Pete had been something Annie might have done herself. Likewise she had seen signs that Jon wanted Leigh, so that Leigh's pregnancy, while untimely, wasn't out of the blue. Jason's attempting suicide, though, made no sense. "There was nothing in his writing. Usually you can tell from that. He's given me original works, short stories and poems, and the themes aren't particularly dark. They run the gamut of emotions. They can't be construed, in any way, as a cry for help."

Returning to her seat, she thought of Sam nearing, thought of the sacrifice he was making and the kind of love that made that possible. Suddenly the story he had given for what had happened with Teke seemed perfectly plausible. It made total sense that he had been wanting Annie so much that he had lost control, thinking of Annie, with Teke. She should have believed his story from the start. She should have trusted him. She felt like a fool.

He came through the door in a whirl of tweed,

looking as close to a knight in shining armor as Annie would ever see. He went to her first, held her tightly for a minute, then approached Charles.

"You've accused my wife of improper behavior involving a student. I'd like to hear the evidence on which you base that accusation."

Charles sat stiffly. "There has been evidence. Your wife and Jason Faust spend an inordinate amount of time together."

"Not inordinate," Annie said, feeling bold now that Sam was here. She stood by his shoulder. "Jason is my leading teaching assistant. He's my right hand around here. In addition, I'm supervising his thesis work. That calls for meetings."

"People have commented."

"What people?" Sam asked.

Charles raised one brow. "Faculty members have spoken to me. I never followed it up because Dr. Pope is well liked by her students. Her classes are among the first filled each term. I assumed there might be some jealousy behind these reports."

Annie hadn't thought of that. She liked to give people the benefit of the doubt, particularly when they were different from her, as so many members of the department were. She was angry now that she wasn't given the same courtesy.

"These reports from faculty members," Sam went on, "are they based on instances where specific improprieties were observed?"

"I never was given specifics, but there were enough suspicions to suggest them."

"Suspicions will never stand up in a court of law," Sam informed him in a voice that Annie could hear coming straight from the bench. He deserved that judgeship. He had to get it. "Suspicions won't even be admitted into evidence. A jury won't be allowed to hear them."

Charles waved a hand. "No one is talking about going to court."

"I am. You've leveled serious charges against my wife. She has certain rights, one of which is that she is innocent until proven guilty."

"No one is saying she's guilty."

"You suggested she take a leave of absence. Wouldn't that be an admission of guilt?"

Charles ran a finger under the collar of his shirt. "No. It would simply give things time to blow over."

"But what is there to blow over?" Sam asked. "So far, all we have is gossip coming from a jealous faculty. What about the girl who was here before?"

"Georgia Nichols," Annie supplied. "I introduced you to her when you were here for lunch once. She's a graduate student. She pals around with Jason."

"Is she in love with Jason?" Sam asked Charles.

"I don't know. But she was the one who found him in his apartment."

"Does she live with him?"

"Not that I know of."

"Then she had a key and let herself in, which means that she has a relationship with the boy beyond that of a passing acquaintance. Perhaps Jason does have a crush on my wife, or simply likes her a lot. Perhaps Georgia is jealous."

"It's possible," Charles acknowledged reluctantly.

"Isn't it therefore possible that her charges are false?"

"She claims Jason *said* that he was in love with your wife."

"Did Jason say it in jest?"

"I don't know. I wasn't there."

"Well, none of us was, Dr. Honnemann, and I would suggest that you squelch any and all rumors until we can talk with Jason himself."

"That may not be possible," Charles said, but his

voice had come a long way from its earlier righteousness. "He's in a coma."

"Then I'd suggest," Sam said without missing a beat, "that we go to the hospital and try to speak with one of his doctors." He slipped a hand around Annie's arm and ushered her from the office.

"Oh, Sam," she cried the minute they hit the fresh air, "I'm so sorry. I didn't mean to screw up everything this way. What will happen with the hearing?"

He sent her an easygoing smile. "Tomorrow. Same time, same place."

She felt a measure of relief. "They didn't give you any trouble?"

"I said it was a family emergency. How could they give me trouble?"

She could imagine dozens of ways. "They may think you have an unstable family or a history of family emergencies that will keep you calling in sick all the time."

"Word is that I'm a workaholic. When I say it's emergency, it's an emergency." He put an arm around her waist and held her close as they walked. "It was no sweat, Annie. Really. You've worked too hard to put up with Honnemann's accusations. The *gall* of him to ask you to take a leave based on gossip."

Annie stopped walking, took his arms, and said, "I have to tell you something, Sam." She hurried the words out before she lost her nerve. The time was right. Instinct—and love of Sam—told her that. "I've been wanting to tell you for months, but I was afraid. There is nothing between Jason and me, there really is nothing, but several weeks after the thing with you and Teke, I'd had a nightmare of a day, topped off by a faculty meeting to which I was late. I was feeling self-conscious and inferior and every negative thing I've ever felt. Jason followed me back to my office, we talked, and one thing led to another. But nothing *happened*," she stressed because Sam had gone pale, "nothing at all! I wanted to feel beautiful and sexy, but I wanted you to be the one making me feel those things. I couldn't do anything with Jason because he wasn't you."

After a minute's silence, during which she died ten deaths, Sam asked a quiet, "How far did it go?"

"There were a few dislodged clothes. That's all. He was upset."

Sam looked more sad than anything else. "Is he in love with you?"

"I don't think so. I talked with him about it afterward. He knows I love you. He knows I can never love him—or *do* anything with him. We really are friends. That's all. He hasn't come on to me once since then. We had, we have a comfortable working relationship. I can't believe he would attempt suicide over me, but there were other things that might have upset him. His dad has just developed serious money problems, so for the first time in his life Jason has to worry about money, and in the midst of all that, he learned that he's diabetic." She remembered his nonchalance. It had to have hid concern. "Could he have committed suicide over that?"

"Or could he be in a diabetic coma?" Sam took her elbow and set off again. "That day you and I ate in the coffee shop, you said he looked peaked."

"That was before he learned the diagnosis. But he hasn't looked well ever since, either." She stopped again, took his arms again. After worrying so long about telling him what had happened with Jason, she refused to be let off the hook by Jason's health. "I'm sorry for all this, Sam. Have I hurt you, doing that with Jason?"

Sadly he said, "How can I be hurt if I was the one on your mind?"

447

"I should have known better."

"We all should at times, but we don't. So, do we love each other, warts and all." He gave her a lop-sided, Sam-gorgeous smile. "I do love you, sunshine, warts and all."

For the first time in months she felt happy. Without a thought to decorum, she wrapped her arms around his neck. "I love you, too, Sam. You're the best thing that ever happened to me." She squeezed him tightly, then whispered, "I've been tormented by this. I thought you'd be angry and turn away. I thought you wouldn't want to look at me. I've been feeling so guilty. I feel so ashamed now."

"Shame is a wasted emotion," he breathed into her hair. "Not productive at all. Come." With an exquisitely gentle kiss to her forehead, he led her on. "Let's go talk with those doctors and see if we can shed a little light on your boy's problems."

The guilt she felt now came from her own light-heartedness. *Sam knew and still loved her.* She might have danced for joy, had it not been for Jason's problems.

They arrived at the hospital fully prepared to find a scene comparable in heartache to the one in which they'd found Michael. They did find Jason's parents, but there was neither fear nor shock. Jason was in bed, and although he didn't look quite up to playing a game of ultimate Frisbee, he was wide awake.

"We were prepared to find you half-dead!" Annie told him after being introduced to his parents. "Honnemann said you were in a coma. Does Georgia know you're okay?"

He nodded. "She called just now." He sounded exhausted.

"What was it?" Annie asked quietly.

"My medicine."

"He didn't tell us that he had been diagnosed," his mother said, "or we'd have brought him home to our own specialist."

"Mother, my doctor here is a specialist, too."

"Well, he did something wrong, didn't he!"

"Ease up, Addie," Jason's father said.

She shifted her body so that she could feel Sam behind her. "Word came back that you had taken an overdose of drugs. Honnemann was in a stir thinking that one of his students had tried to do himself in."

Jason chuckled. He closed his eyes. "The old coot probably imagined I did it for love of you, Annie."

"As a matter of fact," Sam suggested.

Annie was thinking that the discussion would be better saved for another day, when Jason opened his eyes. "He did?"

"'Fraid so," Sam said.

"Christ, Annie, I'm sorry. If I'd thought ahead, I'd have left a note." When Annie rolled her eyes, he asked, "What else did Honnemann say?"

She told him bits and snatches. Now that he was awake, now that Sam knew everything, and with the hearing harmlessly postponed, the situation was actually amusing. She ended by saying, "I imagine the 'old coot' is back in his office, terrified at the thought of being involved in a libel suit." She felt Sam's hand on her back and looked up into his face.

"We ought to let Jason get some rest," he said softly.

She nodded. Pointing to Jason, she said, "Rest. I'll check in with you tomorrow." To his parents she said, "He's a good guy, probably the brightest in the department. I want him well and back in class."

There were thank-yous and good-byes, then Sam was ushering Annie out of the hospital. When he started driving, though, she frowned. "You're going in the wrong direction. We have to head *out* of town. My car's back at school."

"A little later. There's something I want to do first."

The look he gave her was a hint. It was warm and suggestive. It fell from her eyes to her mouth to her chest and might have fallen farther if he hadn't been driving. As it was, he had to swerve to avoid a car barging in on the right.

Annie took his hand. She kissed it and held it to the pulse point at her neck. She didn't speak. Words would have been an intrusion on what was happening between them. She could almost see the tiny ends of the soul-wire that had been severed in October, winding around each other, knotting, connecting in a way that she doubted would ever again come undone. That was how she wanted it.

She never did tell Sam. Not with words. Rather, after he left the car with the doorman at the Ritz-Carleton, hustled her inside, and booked a room high up, with a view of the Public Garden that they barely saw, she showed him by loving him with her body.

He showed her back in spades.

J.D. arranged to take his children to dinner. He wanted to talk with them. He hadn't been much good at that in the past, but he hadn't been much good at taking care of himself until he had actually had to do it. He was hoping it would be the same with the kids.

After picking them up in Constance, he drove west to a landmark country inn. It had been there for years and reeked of history and stability. Since what he wanted to discuss with the kids involved change, he thought the ambiance might comfort them. At least he hoped that. He wasn't sure it would work. He was new at psyching kids out.

Leigh looked well, not pregnant at all. Jana, who loved being with him, was in her glory. Michael swung along on his crutches, appearing to the unknowing bystander like a boy recovering from a broken leg.

They started with chowder. J.D. decided not to bring up what he wanted to discuss then, lest something go wrong and the rest of the meal be spoiled. The same reasoning applied during the salad course, even during the in-between time when they were working on a second basket of cornbread. He considered speaking when the entrées arrived, but everyone was so amiable that he didn't have the heart.

Leigh talked about exactly what her baby looked like at that very moment. Jana talked, in gory detail, about the thriller she had seen the night before. Michael talked about his canoe.

J.D. knew he was testing him, and though the subject matter bothered him, he didn't say a word. He had thought a lot about that afternoon at Grady's. He hated the man. But it was an irrational hate. And J.D. prided himself on being a rational man. The rational part of him said that Grady had aided in Michael's recovery. It also said—though he would never admit it to Sam or Teke—that Grady wasn't dangerous. It *also* said that with Michael still angry at Sam, he could use a male role model now and again. J.D. wasn't thrilled about Grady being it. But it was okay. J.D. would see his kids, too. He had a lure.

By the time dessert arrived, he was wondering just how to broach the topic. Jana solved the problem by asking, "So, what's doing with you and

451

Mom? That was what you wanted to talk about, wasn't it?"

"Smart girl," he said, and took the coward's way out. "What do you think is doing?"

"I think you're filing for divorce."

"How would you feel if I did?"

"She deserves it."

"That's not fair," Leigh said.

Michael agreed. "There are two sides to every story."

"Where'd you learn that?" Jana asked him.

The uneasy look he sent J.D. said that Grady had told him. J.D. was about to say something derogatory about pithy little maxims when he stopped himself. Sam might have said that, just as well as Grady, and he respected Sam. There *were* two sides to every story.

"We haven't sat down and discussed details," he told them, "but I do think a divorce is in the cards." There was a silence. He looked from one face to the next. "Well?"

"You don't look unhappy," Leigh said.

"Intellectually, I am. The dissolution of any marriage is unfortunate. Emotionally, though, I feel relieved."

"Relieved to be done with us?" Michael asked.

"God, no. If anything, I'm just starting." He'd be damned if he'd be irrelevant to the lives of his children. "A year ago I wouldn't have taken you guys out like this, not without your mom. It's not bad, is it?" He found a personal satisfaction in knowing he could handle it.

No one answered.

"It's bad?"

"It's weird," Leigh said.

Jana shrugged. "I think it's just fine. Mom can be a pill sometimes."

"Are you still angry at her for what she did?" J.D. asked.

"Aren't *you?* It was *awful*."

"Yeah. I wouldn't recommend any of you doing it to your spouses. But I think"—he hesitated—"I think it may come out okay."

"Are you seeing someone new?" Leigh asked nervously.

"No."

Michael looked skeptical. "Will Clinger said his mom goes to your place, and that she calls you all the time."

"Will Clinger is as much of a gossip as his mother. Yes, she's been to my place. She brought breakfast once not too long after I moved in." He saw no point in saying what they had done on that occasion or subsequent ones. "We go back a long time, Ginny and I. We're good friends."

"Are you gonna be husband number five?"

"No way. Remarriage isn't in my immediate plans."

"What is?" Jana asked.

"Actually, a move to Palm Beach."

"Florida?"

"All the way *there?*"

"Are you *kidding?*"

Jana rose above the barrage to ask, "Are you opening a new branch of the firm, like Grandpa always talks of doing?"

"No. I'm joining a different firm." That was the whole point, to be where his father wanted to be but beat him to it. "This firm already has an office there."

"In Boston, too?" Michael asked.

J.D. thought he looked the most frightened of the three. It was understandable, since he was the youngest. It was also flattering. He liked the idea

453

that he would be missed. Irrelevant people weren't missed. "In Boston, too. But I'll be working in Palm Beach."

"Why?"

"It's so far!"

"Was Grandpa mad?"

"I haven't told Grandpa yet. I wanted you three to know first. No one else knows, not even my partners-to-be. If you all think it's okay, I'll call them tomorrow."

No one spoke.

J.D. felt a flicker of annoyance. In the past he would have *told* them his decision. He was trying to understand that they would be feeling unsettled. He was trying to give them a say in his future. He was trying to do what he thought *Sam* would have done. The least they could do was try to please *him*.

"Well?" he asked.

"What would you do if we said no?" Jana asked right back.

I'd go anyway, he said silently. He had made his decision. He had to be out of Boston, away from Teke and Grady and away from John Stewart. "If you said no, I'd try to explain to you that I need this change. I've been working under your grandfather's thumb for too long. I have to go out on my own. Besides, I have friends in Palm Beach. I like them, and they like me." Enough to bring their estate work to him, which would drive John Stewart *nuts*. "I'll have plenty of work to do, I want to take up golf, and the weather is warm. I'll get a great place with extra bedrooms for you guys, and a pool. Just think of the vacations you'll have."

"What about Sutters Island?" Michael asked.

"Ahhh, Michael," he said sadly, "the kinds of vacations we had at Sutters Island are things of the past for me. You kids will still go. Same with the ski place. And there may be times when I join you there, but I have to do something new now."

Leigh was wary. "Don't you want to be around when my baby is born?"

"I'll fly back the minute you need me."

"But it'll be born by the time you get here."

"Then I'll see it in the nursery. I'll *be* here, Leigh. I'm not abandoning you."

"Sure sounds it," Jana grumbled.

"No. There are telephones. We can talk whenever we want."

"You always yell when the phone bill's too high."

"I won't now. I promise. Besides, look at it this way, Jana. You have two more years of being at home, then you're going off to college. You'll probably see me as much down there then as you would if I were up here."

"You're leaving us alone with Mom."

"Is that so awful? Does she beat you?"

"No."

"Starve you?"

"God, no. She practically force-feeds us."

"You don't look to be suffering," J.D. said with a cursory glance at Jana's slender frame.

"She nags."

"About what? School? Talking on the phone too much?" J.D. couldn't find fault with that. "Spending more time with Zoe. You really should, Jana. Zoe's gone through a hard time, too."

"I know," Jana admitted, "but she is so *sweet.*"

"What's wrong with that?"

"She's too good. She isn't enough fun. She won't go drinking with us back behind the town dump."

"With who?" J.D. demanded. "Who's drinking behind the dump?" Only after he had reverted to form did Jana's mouth quirk. "You're kidding me.

Don't do that, Jana. I don't like drinking, and I don't like the town dump."

"Did you buy a place in Florida yet?" Michael asked.

He took a steadying breath and turned to the boy. "No. I was waiting until the decision was final." He looked from one to the other. "So? What do you think? Should I do it?"

"Grandpa will hit the roof," Jana warned. "How would you like it if I did that to you?"

God save me from smart-mouthed daughters, J.D. thought. "I'd hit the roof, too," he said. "But maybe it would be different if it was you and me. Grandpa and I may be partners in the firm, but he's always been my boss. I don't think that's right. I wouldn't do it to you. If you wanted to come work in my firm, I'd keep my nose out of your business." Or try, at least, he prayed in another Sam-like move.

"Could I come to work in your firm?"

"I don't see why not, assuming you did well in law school."

"Even with all those other partners?"

"By then I'd have as much clout as any of them. If they didn't want you, you and I would take our business elsewhere."

She brightened at that. "Really?"

"Sure." He was ambivalent about women lawyers, but he was sure Jana would be the best of the bunch. He broadened the invitation. "The same holds for either of you two. I'm not averse to having a family firm."

"Don't count on me," Leigh said. "I want six kids."

"And I want adventure," Michael said with a spirit J.D. hadn't heard from him since that long-ago Labor Day afternoon on Sutters Island. "It's just as well you're breaking up with Grandpa, because now I don't have to feel so bad about not being a lawyer.

I want to build boats, then take them exciting places." His eyes lit. "I could cruise through the Everglades. That'd be near you."

"In a canoe?" Jana asked doubtfully.

"Not in a canoe," Michael answered. "In a hydro-foil. I'd be doing a documentary on the effects of global warming on the alligator population. Maybe I'd bring you a baby one to raise as a pet."

"Do that," Jana said with a lopsided smile, "and you'll find it right back in your bed, way down so you wouldn't know it was there until you stretched out your legs and touched the scales with your toes."

Leigh made a face. "That's disgusting."

"What I really want," Michael said, "is a dog. I've always wanted one."

"Dad hates animals," Jana reminded him.

"But Dad's moving to Florida. Wouldn't it be great if he gave us a dog as a going-away gift?"

"We're not going away," Leigh said "He is."

"Then a leaving-us gift."

Three pairs of eyes turned to J.D. "Why do I feel like I'm being manipulated?" he asked. No one answered. And he didn't even care. He had good kids. If they wanted a dog, he'd get them a dog. As long as they left it with Teke when they came to visit him, they'd do just fine.

Teke was wearing the silk wrap J.D. had given her the Christmas before last, the one that was extraordinarily conventional. If she were ambitious, she would splash it with paint, dot it with rhinestones, or appliqué something bright and clashing onto the lapel. But it was comfortable—and the more she wore it, the more she had it dry-cleaned, the more comfortable it became. The robe held memories of

Sunday morning brunches in the kitchen and late night tête-à-têtes with the kids. It was the one she had opened when she had given herself to Sam, the one she had run after Michael in, the one she had worn to the hospital that awful day.

The robe held a mixed bag of memories, but she needed them all. She realized that now, sitting on a corner of the sofa, nursing a cup of coffee. A person couldn't wipe out the memories that shaped her being. She was a blend of past, present, and future.

At the moment Teke was thinking mostly of the future. The kids were with J.D. The house was silent. Habit would have had her in the kitchen, making goodies for them to eat the next day. But she had consciously kept herself from baking. The kids had plenty of goodies, they didn't need more, and she didn't *have* to be busy all the time. She had taken a long bath and enjoyed that. Now she was relaxing, thinking about the kids getting older, thinking about taking care of a grandchild. Inevitably she was thinking about Grady, wondering what his role would be in the memories waiting to form.

The doorbell rang. She knew it was Grady well before she opened the door, could feel him in the air, in the way her heart beat that little bit faster and her cheeks warmed. The intense look on his face accelerated her response.

"Are you alone?" he asked in a low voice.

She nodded. "The kids are with J.D. I don't expect them back until ten." It was eight.

He came in and closed the door. Silently he took her hand, studying the ringless fingers for a minute. Then, while her heart beat faster, he led her up the stairs. He went all the way down the hall to her bedroom and once there, drew the covers back from the bed.

Pushing his fingers into her hair, he held her face

for a devouring kiss. Hunger was heavy on his tongue, and arousing. Teke never considered resistance. Her anger was long gone, and as for her fear, she figured it was absurd. He wouldn't leave her. He hadn't left her in the first place. He had been *taken from* her. There was a difference. But none of that was relevant to the moment. She had been wanting him for months, needing him for years. Grady was part of who she was. He was her completion.

He kept his mouth on her—on her lips, her ear, her neck—while he removed his clothes. He tossed one piece after another aside, each in a different direction in a claiming of turf with which Teke found no fault. J.D. had shared this bedroom with her for nineteen years, but his stay was done. Teke couldn't think of a more appropriate place for Grady and her to make love.

After sending her robe puddling at her feet, he brought her body hard to his. She cried out at the pleasure, which was strong and stunning and such an incredible relief that she cried out again, this time into his mouth, which had captured hers again. Stretching, she twined her arms around his neck, sliding her bare skin against him in an effort to feel as much as she could. He was home, he was haven, he was heaven.

Heaven was the last conscious thought she had, because sensation took over then. She sensed the cool of the sheets against her back, the heat of Grady's body against her front, the texture of his torso and limbs against her smoothness, the hugeness of him between her legs. Sounds came from her throat, but all she heard was desperation, and it was without shame. She loved Grady. She adored Grady. She *worshiped* Grady. Since she was ten. Never changed.

Grady inside her was like no other experience in

her life. It was shattering and resurrecting, stroking and burning, building to the kind of climax some women killed for. She would have happily died herself, just then, if only to keep him inside forever.

It wasn't physically possible, of course. After releases that brought simultaneous cries and near endless spasms, he sank down over her, let his breathing slow, then slipped to the side.

With a hand that trembled, he smoothed her hair back from the dampness of her face. "My Teke," he whispered.

She smiled, caught his hand, pressed it to her mouth.

Still whispering, he said, "You're in my blood. Have been since you were ten and standing there with a bandage 'round your leg looking scared. I need to take care of you. I think I was born for that."

After taking care of others for so many years, she felt a new burst of warmth inside. She rolled to face him and used her fingertip to trace his nose, his mouth, his collarbone. His body entranced her. It had been through so much in the years since she had seen it last. Still, it was strong and dignified. And virile enough to put all other men to shame.

"I want you, Teke."

She grinned. "You have me."

"More. I want you more. Are you still afraid?"

She shook her head. "How can I be afraid, when this is so nice?"

"Still angry I sent you from Gullen?"

"That was then. This is now."

"How do you know I won't leave you again?"

"Because you didn't leave when Michael was sick. And you didn't leave when J.D. stayed on your back. Besides," she added with a smile, feeling smugly a woman and stronger than ever before, "I wouldn't let you go this time. I'd fight back."

A grin played with the corner of his mouth. "You would, huh?"

"You bet."

"Will you marry me?"

Happiness bloomed. "You bet. But where'll we live?"

"Here in Constance. There's plenty of work for me here."

"I'm asking J.D. for the house. Would you live in it?"

"Maybe."

"In *my* house?" she teased.

"I just made it mine," he said with an arrogance that reminded her of J.D., only, so, so much nicer.

"What about kids?" she asked.

"I want yours."

"I want yours."

"Shelley?"

"And ours."

There was an audible catch in his breath, then a soft, "Can we?"

"Lord, I hope so."

"You wouldn't mind?"

"It's what *I* was made for." She ran a hand down his body, drew it back up his thigh and inward. He wanted her again. She wouldn't have trouble conceiving. There was an open spot in her just waiting for Grady. And his child. And hers. And theirs. Such a rich, rich life. She was blessed.

twenty

SAM'S APPOINTMENT CAME THROUGH AT THE beginning of March. After phoning Annie with the news, he strode down the hall of the firm as he had done five months before to share exciting news with his best friend. He still considered J.D. that. Twenty-two years of a relationship couldn't be wiped out in a few careless minutes. With J.D. heading for Florida and Sam for the courthouse, they would never be as close as they had once been. But J.D. was part of who Sam was. He liked to think the reverse was true.

J.D. shook his hand when Sam gave him the news. "It's what you want," he said. "Congratulations."

"I couldn't have done it without you."

"Maybe not," J.D. said with an arrogant smile. "I just hope you won't be bored."

Sam hoped not, too. He was used to working a courtroom, not sitting back and watching it be worked by others. A judge's job was more passive than what he was used to. Now that the appointment was a reality, he hoped it was the right thing. "I have the option to stay for life, but there's no requirement that I do. If I start going bonkers, I'll resign."

"John Stewart will not be pleased that you got the appointment," J.D. said. His smile had become a mischievous grin not unlike the one he had produced twenty-some years earlier when Sam had convinced him to miss a week's worth of classes for the sake of experiencing Mardi Gras in New Orleans.

Sam grinned back. "I don't figure he will be. Thanks for keeping him in line." He didn't know how J.D. had done it and wouldn't put him on the spot by asking, but it was the only thing that made sense. John Stewart had been determined that Sam not get the job, and he was a tough man to thwart. J.D. had thwarted him all right. Sam was not only grateful, but proud of his friend. "Now, if you could do something about Michael . . ."

"Ahh, Michael. Michael has a mind of his own."

"Does he talk to you about me?"

J.D. shook his head.

Sam sighed. "Maybe he'll be impressed enough with the 'Your Honor' business to lay down the hatchet. I really miss him. I'd like to keep an eye on him once you move south. When will that be?"

"April fifteenth, give or take. I bought a great place with a private patio and swimming pool. The kids will love it."

"I bet," Sam said. Zoe had already told him about the pool. Jana wanted her down as soon as J.D. moved in. Poor Zoe was convinced that the invitation came only because Jana didn't dare inflict J.D. on any other of her friends, and Sam couldn't deny the possibility of that. But he suspected more was at work. Zoe and Jana had a history, just like Sam and J.D. "My swearing-in is in a couple of weeks," Sam said. "Will you come?"

"If I can. Let me know when they set the date."

Sam promised he would. He left J.D. and went

home to celebrate with Annie and the kids. The following evening he walked through the woods to the Maxwells' house. He carried a large package for Michael, who was doing homework in the sunroom when he arrived. "What subject?" he asked, looking over the boy's shoulder.

Once, Michael would have put his homework aside the instant Sam walked in. Now he said, "Math," and went on with his work.

Sam noted that his handwriting had improved. "How's it coming?"

"Fine."

"How're you feeling?"

"Okay."

"When do you think you'll go back to school?"

"I don't know."

"The thought of it must be a little scary."

"A little."

"Anything is, at first, when you've been away from it for a while. You dread it for days. When you finally do it, you find it isn't half as bad as you thought it'd be."

Michael shot him a dry look.

"Sorry." Sam hated to sermonize. "But you have to be back at school if you want to play baseball. Tryouts will be starting in another month."

Michael was horrified by the suggestion. "I can't play."

"Sure you can. There's nothing wrong with your eye or your instinct, and those are the two most important things."

"I can't *run*."

"From what I hear, you do pretty well when you want to. Besides, a pinch runner can round the bases for you until your legs are back in shape. That's what they do in the majors when a slugger can't run."

464

Michael returned to his math. "Who says I can still hit?"

Sam gave the boy a once-over. "You may be rusty, but it'll come back. My guess is that with all the therapy you've been doing, it'll come back better than ever. While the rest of the guys have been running up and down a basketball court, you've been lifting weights."

"It's physical therapy."

"It's pumping iron. You're taller than you were last season. You're broader in the shoulders. I'll take you out hitting any time you want." He held his breath.

"No thanks."

"You won't know until you try."

"I'll wait."

Sam released the breath. He wasn't sure how to reach the boy, but it wasn't for lack of trying. With a thunk, he set the package he carried on top of Michael's homework.

Michael sat back. "What's this?"

"Open it and see."

After a short pause, Michael tore at the brown paper wrapping. He had little more than a swath of it off when his face came alive with an excitement that made Sam's efforts well worth while. The rest of the paper came off to reveal the editing deck and controller that Michael had been wanting.

"It's nice," the boy said without looking up. "Is it a bribe?"

"Yes," Sam said without a qualm. "I want you to do the video for my swearing-in and the reception afterward. How 'bout it?"

Michael moved his hand reverently along the outside of the box. "I can't handle a camcorder and crutches, too."

"Then leave the crutches at home."

"I need them."

"Do you?" Sam asked. He knew Michael didn't. His tone of voice said that. "I can help you set this up, if you want. My parents would love to have a tape to bring back home with them. Same with Annie's dad. So. What do you say? Will you come?"

"I don't think so."

"I'd really like you to." He draped an arm around Michael's shoulders and gave him an affectionate shake. "Come on, Mike. You can't stay mad at me forever. I miss the time we used to spend together. Your dad's going to Florida, Jon's getting married, who am I gonna play ball with if not you?"

"You'll find someone."

"I want *you.*"

When Michael didn't respond, Sam took a deep breath and straightened. "Okay. I'll give you a little more time, but only until my swearing-in. I want you there, Michael. It's a big day in my life. I want everyone I love to be there."

"My mom will be there."

Sam ignored the hint of something untoward existing between them. "Yup, your mom and your sisters, and my kids, and my wife, and my parents, and Papa Pete, and all our friends. But I want you there, Michael. Try?" Giving his shoulder a final squeeze and a pat, he left the boy to his thoughts.

Teke did everything she could to convince Michael to attend the swearing-in. She saw it as a milestone, the start of something new for them all. She knew that in twenty years he wouldn't remember whether he had gone back to school in March or April, but he would remember whether he had gone to Sam's swearing-in. She didn't want him staying away and regretting it later.

But he wouldn't listen to reason. She tried every argument. She had Grady try, thinking for sure that would help. Michael looked up to Grady much the way he had to Sam. In the end she realized that was part of the problem. As far as Michael was concerned, since he had Grady he didn't need Sam.

Finally she appealed to J.D. "He'll listen to you. Talk with him. He's being stubborn."

"I'm not good at talking to the kids."

"But you're the only one who can feel what he is. You were just as hurt by everything that happened as Michael was."

He shrugged. "I've come out ahead."

Teke knew that J.D.'s pride wouldn't let him admit he had been hurt, and yes, he had come out ahead in terms of standing on his own two feet. But she needed his help. It struck her that with regard to emotions, it was one of the few times she ever had.

"Sam betrayed you, just like he betrayed Michael," she said. "In that sense, what you say carries more weight than what I say."

J.D. took his time considering her plea. He looked legitimately contemplative, which was something new on the home front. Without Teke to mother him, or Sam to calm him, or Annie to buffer whatever emotions raged, he seemed to be taking responsibility for himself. It was good, she thought. The part of her that wanted to remain J.D.'s friend was pleased.

J.D. agreed to talk with Michael, not so much to get him to attend the swearing-in as to prove to himself that he could rise above what his father was. John Stewart believed that when a person wronged you, you punished him by withdrawing your favors and writing him out of your life. That was what he'd done to Sam. But J.D. believed that vindictiveness could be carried to extremes. Barring one instance, Sam had been a loyal friend. His good points were better than good. They were fine and admirable, not the least of them relating to his affection for Michael.

He found the boy in his bedroom, which was upstairs again, now that climbing the stairs had been deemed crucial therapy. The place was a mess—thank you, Teke, J.D. thought dryly. After stepping over a towel damp from the shower, he positioned himself between the television set and his son. "We have to talk."

"Now?" Michael asked in dismay. "This is my favorite program."

J.D. shot a look over his shoulder at a pair of teenage boys with sideburns the likes of which he hadn't seen since he'd been a teenager himself. "Now. I can't stay long. Just turn it down," he said as a concession. When the voices lowered, he slipped his hands into his pockets. "Your mother tells me you won't go to Sam's swearing-in. I think you should."

"Why?"

"Because Sam's been a friend of the family since you were born. He helped raise you. He taught you to play ball. He loves you."

"He caused you and Mom to break up."

"No. We'd have done it anyway." It wasn't necessarily true. If nothing had rocked the boat, he and Teke might have gone on forever, with Sam and Annie's assistance. Unless something *else* had rocked the boat. Like one of J.D.'s affairs. So Teke had been caught instead of him. He had been lucky.

"Why would you have broken up anyway?" Michael asked.

468

"We weren't making each other happy."

"You looked happy enough to me."

"You weren't aware of what we were feeling inside."

"What were you feeling?"

J.D. had let himself in for the question. But what could he say? *Your mother wasn't exciting me anymore. I like being with different women. My life was as structured as my father's life, and it was depressing me.* Any of those might reflect badly on him, so he said, "We were feeling that we were missing something in life."

"Is that why Mom was with Sam?"

"No. I think she was with Sam because he happened to come to the house at a time when she was feeling low."

"She could have said no. *He* could have said no."

"There were other things on his mind. He wasn't thinking as clearly as you and I are now. That's the key, Michael. You have to be rational. You have to ask yourself why you are doing what you are." That was Annie's approach, actually. J.D. was trying to follow it. "You have to look ahead and consider the consequences of your actions. You're not doing that, when it comes to Sam."

"Grandpa kicked him out of the firm."

"So Sam ended up with something even better. *Don't* compare yourself to your grandfather. He let his anger get the best of him. He has cut himself off from Sam completely. But he'll be the one to suffer without Sam. Do you want to suffer, too? When do you stop punishing yourself?"

"I'm not punishing myself."

"Looks it to me," J.D. said. "You could use Sam's help."

"So could you, but you're going off to Florida."

"That's because I've taken Sam's help for so long

that it's finally time to stand on my own. He's been a crutch. I have to start walking without him."

"Well, so do I."

J.D. shook his head. "You're only thirteen. There's still a lot you can learn from Sam. You've been lucky to have a friend like him. So have I."

"Then why are you *leaving?*" Michael cried.

He sat down on the bed, arm to arm, beside Michael. "I have a chance to do something new. You kids are old enough to fly down and spend time with me. Sam and Annie will, too. Sam made a mistake, but he's a good man. I won't throw him away as my father has. I'm not that dumb."

Michael fiddled with the remote control. "You think I'm being dumb?"

"I think you're being shortsighted."

There was a pause, then an unsure, "You think I'll be sorry if I don't go?"

"Yes. I do think that."

"But I still *walk* funny."

"Ah, for God's sake, you don't," J.D. said impatiently. "You walk *different* from before, but not funny. I've seen pigeon-toed people who walk funny—*you* don't walk funny. Sometimes you have to accept things, Michael. This experience has changed you in lots of ways, but you have to use it to get you ahead. That's what I'm trying to do."

Michael looked up. "You are?"

J.D. nodded.

"Are you going to the swearing-in?"

"I wouldn't miss it. Sam will be a big man up there on the bench. I want people to know that I helped get him there." He cracked a cocky smile. "So. Are you going or not?"

"I don't know."

"You'd better decide soon," J.D. advised, rolling to his feet on his way to the door. "You'll need a pressed shirt and a blazer and dress pants that fit. That *fit,* Michael. At the rate you've been growing, you're probably out of your old ones. I'm telling your mother to get new ones. I want you looking like my son."

He went down the stairs to tell that to Teke.

Annie took charge of the reception. It was being held at the Four Seasons, an easy walk across the Boston Common from the governor's office, where Sam would be sworn in. She wanted it to be lavishly dignified, which meant a buffet with plenty of food, beautifully cooked and presented. She also wanted a pianist. And fresh flower arrangements. And invitations that were just a little different from the norm, dignified but individual. That was how Teke would have done it, had Annie allowed her to take over as party planner. But Annie had a point to prove to herself and those around her. She wanted everyone to know that her skills weren't limited to the classroom. The reception for Sam's swearing-in was her debut, a time for her to shine as Sam's wife. She bought a stunning new dress. She added tiny little touches to her makeup. She wanted everything to be perfect, and as the day approached it looked as though it would be. Invitations went out, and acceptances came in. One hundred and fifty friends and colleagues would be joining family for the occasion.

Among them were several of Annie's faculty friends, plus Jason Faust, plus Charles Honnemann. She had invited Charles strictly as a courtesy. He had given her a wide berth since the mystery of Jason's overdose had been solved, so she was surprised when he accepted the invitation.

But people loved being with a winner, and Sam

was that. She was proud of him for it. She felt good knowing he was hers.

The big question, as the day approached, was whether Michael would come. Sam wanted it desperately. Michael's presence had become symbolic to him of the end of an ordeal. But Michael wasn't committing himself. No one seemed able to make him budge.

The swearing-in was called for five in the afternoon. After installing his parents in a suite at the Four Seasons, Sam returned to Constance to change clothes. Annie was waiting when he stepped out of the shower.

She stood on tiptoe and coiled her arms around his neck. He smelled of soap and Sam, her favorite combination. "How do you feel?"

"Nervous. Why did we invite so many people?"

"We invited them because they're our friends and want to share this with us. And because I am so proud of you." She kissed him once, then nipped at his mustache. "I want everyone to know what you've achieved. I want everyone to know you're my man."

He caught her mouth, kissed her, framed her head with his hands, and ran his eyes over every inch of her face. She felt the tenderness of it and was deeply moved. "You're beautiful," he whispered.

"Wait till I shower and put makeup on."

"I like you this way. It reminds me of the waif of a girl I met when I was nineteen and fell in love with on the spot. You haven't changed, sunshine."

"Yes, I have. I have cellulite."

"Where?"

She touched her backside.

He swung her around and kissed the body part in question. "Smooth as a baby's," he said, and took her back in his arms. "Thank you for planning all this. It'll be great."

"I hope so." She caught the flicker of a frown creasing his brow. Michael was never long gone from his mind. "Do you think he'll come?"

"Don't know."

"If he doesn't, Sam, it'll only be because he's young. We can't expect him to be mature at thirteen. I certainly wasn't."

"But he knows how much it means to me. Maybe that's the trouble. Maybe I shouldn't have told him. I gave him the tool to hurt me."

Annie hurt on Sam's behalf. "One part of me wants to run over there and shake some sense into the kid. Only he's bigger than I am, now."

"Anyway," Sam said, "you can't force something like that. If he comes, it has to be of his own free will."

As Annie let him go and stepped into the shower, she prayed it would be. She had done her best to convince Michael herself. She couldn't do more.

By the time she was done with her shower, other thoughts took over. She had painstakingly shopped with Zoe for a dress and now helped her into it. She wanted the girl to feel beautiful in the ways Annie hadn't when she had been her age. By the time Annie was done, Zoe's hair was like waving gold silk, her cheeks were faintly blushed, her earlobes delicate with tiny diamond studs. Sam whistled when he saw her, and her blush deepened.

Sam whistled at Annie, too, when she stood only in a lacy slip. He whistled again seconds after he zipped her dress, then again when she came down the stairs ready to go.

Jon raced in seconds later, after stopping at the Maxwells to give encouragement to Leigh, who had been through a frenzy of clothes hunting that afternoon when the outfit she had chosen to wear was suddenly too tight in the middle. She was too thin to look pregnant and too bloated at the waist to feel thin. Annie remembered that stage and how quickly it passed.

"Any sign of Michael?" Sam asked Jon.

"He was there."

"Is he coming?"

"I don't know. He hadn't gotten dressed yet."

Annie put a reassuring hand on Sam's arm. "He's fighting it. Give him time."

"There isn't much left," Sam said sadly, and led the way to the car. To Annie's relief, he seemed to push the sadness from mind during the drive from Constance to Boston. She had the kids to thank for that. With the reality of Sam's new job finally sinking in, they had a steady list of questions for him.

"What do my friends call you?" Zoe asked.

"Zoe's father."

"I'm serious. The Honorable Judge of the Superior Court of the Commonwealth of Massachusetts Samuel F. Pope?"

"Judge Pope will be fine," Sam said.

"Will that scare them away?"

Jon answered. "Nah. My friends are psyched. They're already planning to get their speeding tickets fixed."

"Forget it," Sam advised.

"My words exactly," Jon assured him.

"What is Mom called?" Zoe asked.

Sam said, "Dr. Pope."

"Judge and Dr. Pope?"

"Are we talking about a formal introduction here? That would be the Honorable and Mrs. Samuel F. Pope." He glanced at Annie. "The Honorable and Dr. Samuel F. Pope? That's not right. The Honorable Samuel F. Pope and Dr. Anne H. Pope."

"The Honorable and Mrs. is fine," she said.

"How many robes do you have?" Zoe asked Sam.

"Three. One to wash, one to wear, one to keep my closet in line."

"Did Joy mind leaving the law firm?"

"Nope. She's getting more money for working shorter hours."

"Does the court adjorn for the summer?"

"No."

"Then when do you take your vacation?"

"Whenever I want. I let them know."

"Will you find lawyers in contempt of court?"

"Sooner or later, I assume."

"Like on TV?"

Jon groaned.

And so it went. Smiling, Annie might have liked to freeze the moment in time. These three, so precious to her, were in synch with each other. There was a feeling of excitement and hope.

The excitement grew the closer they came to Boston. Before Annie was quite ready for the intimacy to end, she was being ushered into the State House and up to the second-floor corner office where the governor and an official photographer waited. There were pictures. The room filled with people, none of whom was Michael. There was a brief introduction by the governor, then all sixty seconds of the actual swearing-in, then hand shaking, congratulations, and more pictures. It was an emotional time for Annie, whose throat grew tight whenever she heard the words *Your Honor* directed at Sam.

When almost everyone else had set off across the common, they followed suit. Sam was flanked by several other judges, who talked as they walked. From time to time Annie saw him anxiously scan the people walking ahead of them. He caught her eye. She shrugged. She hadn't seen Michael, or J.D., either. Her heart broke for Sam, who had so badly wanted them there.

Fortunately the room where they were holding the reception was packed, and the air festive, by the time they arrived. The tablecloths were a pale gray, the flowers a rich burgundy. Soft music wafted from a grand piano in the corner. Wine flowed. Smiles abounded.

Teke was with Sam's parents, who knew as few people there as Grady did, which made Grady feel better, Annie guessed, though she also guessed he would have preferred to be somewhere alone with Teke. He didn't take his eyes from her long. The fascination seemed mutual. Grady, in a new suit, put most other men in the room to shame. Annie was pleased for Teke.

She and Sam moved through the crowd, shaking hands and hugging friends, laughing, enjoying themselves in spite of the tiny twist of sadness they both felt. Annie kept glancing at the spot where the children were gathered, hoping to see Michael there.

Then J.D. appeared at the door. He was alone. She found Sam's eyes. They were filled with defeat.

She was about to go to him when his face suddenly brightened. Glancing toward J.D., she saw Michael come up from behind. He was wearing a new blazer and slacks, looking adorable and terribly grown-up.

Annie felt a great swelling fullness inside as Sam excused himself and strode across the room. He stopped several yards from Michael and waited. Annie stopped, too, with her heart in her throat.

Michael didn't once take his eyes from Sam. He blinked and swallowed. In a flash of Annie's memory, he was a scared little boy on his first bicycle, with Sam calling, "You can do it, Mike. Give a push off, then pedal. That's it. Good boy. Keep going. You've got it." With the videocam in one hand and his eyes filled with sudden determination, he walked forward.

That was all Sam needed. He met the boy halfway in a hearty hug. "I'd just about given up hope."

Annie arrived just as Michael said, "By the time I decided to come, I couldn't find a belt that fit. Mom had already gone, and Dad didn't have the key to your place, so we had to stop at a store and buy one."

Sam was grinning from ear to ear. "Better late than never. Now we can *celebrate.*" His eyes took on a gleam. He raised his head.

Michael stopped him. In a voice that was more man than boy and playfully stern, he said, "Don't you dare do it, Sam."

"Do what?" Sam asked innocently.

"Make a big announcement that I'm here and that you want to toast my recovery." Annie agreed that it would have been a typically Sam thing to do. "Don't do it," Michael warned. "I'll die."

Sam chuckled. "Okay. I won't. I suppose this is my day after all. But you've made it for me, Mike." With a final hug that should have embarrassed Michael, too, but seemed heartily welcomed, Sam released him, collared Annie with one arm and J.D. with another, and grinned a silly grin. "Okay. We're ready. Start filming."

Annie wasn't sure his behavior was particularly judicial, but somehow that didn't seem to matter. While she basked happily beneath the warmth of Sam's touch, Michael stepped back and put the videocam to his eye. From behind it came his deepening voice. "The twelfth of March, 1993. Four Seasons Hotel, Boston, Massachusetts. The occasion is Sam Pope's installation as a judge on the superior court of the commonwealth of Massachusetts. That's his best friend, J. D. Maxwell, on his left, and his wife, Annie Pope, on his right. And here come the rest crowding in. There's Zoe and Jon and Leigh and Jana and Teke and Grady and Papa Pete and Mr. and Mrs. Pope from Oregon and half of Constance. Hey, what's on the tray that the guy with white gloves is carrying? Are those chocolate-covered strawberries? *Awesome. . . .*"

epilogue

MICHAEL WAS STILL FILMING. HE HAD ALREADY used up two cartridges recording the nervousness in the waiting room and was working on the third. Things were getting monotonous. But he kept filming. It was either that or fall asleep, and he refused to fall asleep. He didn't care if it *was* four in the morning, he wasn't missing the birth of Leigh's baby. Of course, it might have been nice if they'd let him into the delivery room with Leigh and Jon. Videographers did that all the time. Okay, so he had a cold. Wasn't that what dentist's masks were for?

So he was relegated to the waiting room. For the umpteenth time, he backed himself to the wall and panned the gathering. It occurred to him that he could splice and edit and juxtapose this shot with the earlier ones to produce a hilarious statement about fatigue. With each panning, the bodies sank lower against each other and the backs of their seats.

On the far left, scrunched together on a vinyl sofa that was a gross shade of green, were Sam, Annie, Zoe, and Jana. Fresh from the airport, J.D. was slouched on a single chair beside Jana. Papa Pete

479

was asleep on another single chair, and on a smaller sofa to his right were Teke and Grady.

"What's taking so long?" Jana complained sleepily.

Zoe was only slightly more awake. "Do you think something's wrong?"

Annie squeezed her hand. "First deliveries always take longer. They'll be fine."

She and Sam shared small, excited smiles. He took a breath and looked around. "So. Is it a boy or a girl? Let's have the latest count."

Michael would be furious if it wasn't a boy. He wanted someone to play with. He was tired of being in the minority.

From the others came a tired outcry of votes, the sudden sound of which brought Papa Pete awake with a start, all of which Michael captured in the lens of his camera. He also captured the anxious look Teke gave Grady and the reassuring way he touched her hand.

With the exception of the few short minutes when he'd first learned whom Grady had killed, Michael had liked Grady. He wasn't a big talker, but when he spoke he had something to say. He treated Michael like an adult. And he was good to Teke. Much as there were times when Michael missed his father and wished his parents would get back together, the grown-up part of him could see that his mother was happier than she had been in a long time. Not that she had ever seemed *un*happy. Just that now she seemed better.

He swung his lens to the left, over Papa Pete, to J.D. Florida was agreeing with him, and Michael could understand why. The place he had bought there was awesome. Michael had been to visit twice and was going again once the weather got cooler. J.D. liked the people there. He liked his law firm, and he liked playing golf. Michael guessed he was dating, though J.D. didn't talk much about that, and Michael didn't ask. He wasn't ready to know. He was used to seeing his mom with Grady—it was as if they were made for each other—but seeing his dad with someone other than his mom would be weird. He supposed he'd get used to it in time. He was just glad the thing with Virginia Clinger had cooled. She was bad news.

"Maybe the baby is upside down and backside to," Jana said. "That would slow things down."

"They would have know that before," Zoe reasoned, and looked up at Annie. "Wouldn't they?"

Annie nodded. "The baby's fine. I'm sure."

Michael swung the videocam to Teke, who didn't look sure at all. She looked terrified. Grady took her hand and held it.

Papa Pete's head lolled before returning to his shoulder. It came erect in the next instant, though, because Jon swung through the double doors looking as if he'd been sacked ten times in a row but wearing a smile a mile wide.

"It's a girl!" he cried, and stood there, not quite knowing what to do, until the others crowded around him, hugging him, hugging each other, laughing, crying, asking questions.

A girl. Michael should have known.

"How big is she?"

"Who does she look like?"

"How's Leigh?"

"When can we see them?"

The babbling continued nonstop until, shortly thereafter, Jon was allowed to carry his daughter into the hall just outside the delivery room, where the Popewells waited excitedly.

"Look at her!"

"She's beautiful!"

"That's your mouth, Jon!"

"And Leigh's nose!"

Michael stood back, filming. After a minute, though, he let the videocam fall to his side. It struck him that there was something about what he was watching that could never be picked up on film. The Popewells were together. They were happy. They were enlarged now by two, if Grady was counted, and given the way he was part of the festivities, it looked like he was.

It was a miracle.

Michael thought back to all that had happened in the last year. He remembered the dark days when he had thought life was going straight downhill and nothing would ever be the same. He had been right about the last; some things would never be the same. Changes had taken place. But they weren't so awful. Actually they were pretty good.

Sam snapped his fingers and crooked a finger his way. "Get over here, Michael. This is *your niece.*"

Michael joined the group. His gait was slightly unsteady, though not because of any lingering effects of the accident. Those were pretty much gone. He intended to be point guard this year, and he intended to be a starter. No, the shakiness had to do with the sense of witnessing awesome things in the here and now.

Without a thought to the camcorder, he stared down at the baby. He had never seen anything so small in his life.

"Isn't she incredible?" J.D. asked with an arm around Jon.

Annie and Teke were hugging, Sam and Grady were slapping each other's backs, Jana and Zoe were shoulder to shoulder cooing at the baby.

The baby had one eye open. As Michael watched, she opened the other. He could have sworn she looked straight at him, and he knew just why she would. He was the one who was closest to her age, the one who would be around when she was little, the one who would protect her. Second to Leigh and Jon, she was his.

Maybe a girl wasn't so bad after all.

He looked up at the others with a grin.

It was a miracle.

You have been reading a novel published by Piatkus Books. We hope you have enjoyed it and that you would like to read more of our titles. Please ask for them in your local library or bookshop.

If you would like to be put on our mailing list to receive details of new publications, please send a large stamped addressed envelope (UK only) to:

Piatkus Books: 5 Windmill Street
London W1P 1HF

PIATKUS

The sign of a good book